The
SPARE
BEDROOM

THE
SPARE
BEDROOM

Elizabeth Neep

bookouture

Published by Bookouture in 2020

An imprint of Storyfire Ltd.
Carmelite House
50 Victoria Embankment
London EC4Y 0DZ

www.bookouture.com

ISBN: 978-1-83888-639-4
eBook ISBN: 978-1-83888-638-7

To Mum, Dad, Thomas and Rachel – for all adding
so much to my story.

PART ONE

Chapter One

Hair soaked, mascara-stained, broken umbrella clutched in my hand – this was Sydney. *Sydney.* It wasn't supposed to rain. Where was my golden tan? Where was my I'm-not-a-tourist-I-actually-live-here glow? Where was my boundless energy and newfound talent for volleyball? I'd been holding it together, pinning on a smile, but it was time to call a spade a flipping spade. So far, Sydney was crap.

Since the second I had hopped off the plane it had been non-stop rain, relentless rudeness and now this. Kicked out of my 'you can stay for three months until you get settled' accommodation onto the rainy streets of Coogee with nothing but my two-tonne rucksack, a broken umbrella and a deep suspicion that I was still saying Coogee wrong. Coo-geeeee? Cudgey? Cude-I care any less?

Trudging round Woolworths (a bog-standard supermarket in Sydney, not a pick-and-mix or tiny Coke can in sight), I left puddles behind me as I went. I didn't even need anything. I was just trying to get dry. In fact, I did need something. I needed a lot of things. I needed sunshine, a job, rent money and somewhere to stay until I could get the above figured out. I turned down the next aisle. No, no rent-free accommodation down this one. Did I really leave my steady life in England for this? This was meant to be my do-over. My chance to rewrite a happily ever after that had somehow gone so wrong – one that everyone else seemed to be getting right. Even my forever-young best friend had drifted into adulthood, buying a two-bedroom house with her partner. Zoe would have a fit if she knew my 'sure thing' accommodation was about as sure as everything else in my life right now. I turned down the next aisle. Wine. Well, it couldn't hurt, right? I grabbed the first bottle of red I saw, then realised it was twenty-six dollars and went to put it back quicker than you could say—

'Jess?'

I froze, hand refusing to release the red. It couldn't be. No one knew me here. That was the point in coming, after all. A fresh start, a fresh chance to salvage my twenties - before they slid into a decade demanding more milestones than I'd manage to reach.

'Jess? Is that you?'

It just couldn't be. There was no way. But then, Zoe had made me delete him, unfollow him, block him, *erase* him years ago, severing the ties of our 'connection' even though by then we hadn't spoken in weeks. I had put up a fight at first, hooked to my digital self-harm, reminding every inch of me what we used to be. Then I had surrendered, bruised by her final blow: *no amount of watching his stories is going to change yours…*

'Jess?' the all-too familiar voice rang out again. It wasn't. It *couldn't* be. But in my down and out state, I could have sworn the voice sounded suspiciously like my…

Ever so slowly I unclutched the bottle. Even more slowly I turned. And finally came face to face with someone I had spent the last three years trying to forget. Sam. My ex-boyfriend.

'Jess? What the…' The words spilled from his stubble-framed mouth, rough hands reaching to rub his disbelieving eyes. I stared on, frozen to the spot. I had been ready to give someone – anyone – a mouthful but had all of a sudden lost the ability to speak. Against a backdrop of white wine, Sam's tanned figure looked like a mirage.

'What are you…' His second sentence trailed off like his first. I shook my head, still and silent, my heart making enough noise for both of us. His wide eyes met mine as he began to shake his head too, no doubt hoping he'd wake up soon. If there were other people around, I didn't notice them. Sam demanded my full attention. I watched his face spread into a smile as he looked me up and down – and not in a good way, not like the first time all those years ago. Heart beating, hands sweating, I said nothing. I held my breath. Maybe if I held it for long enough I'd die right here, right now. Why was he here? In Sydney? On the other side of the world? And why was I here – mascara-stained with the remains of a crappy umbrella that looked like a flipping stick?

'Jess, you're here.' He reached a hand further towards me, as if wanting to touch me to see that I was real. I flinched, torn between wanting to run and hide or shelter in the warmth of his arms. It was Sam. *Sam.*

'I am,' I confirmed, not knowing whether I was convincing him or me. It wouldn't be the first time I'd dreamt of such a run-in, but never once here, never once like this. Of all the places I'd imagined him being, all the rooms I'd scanned hoping, dreading, that he'd be in them, all the times I almost risked finding him again, *friending* him again, I could never have imagined this, here, *now.* My eyes darted to his basket – avocados, chia seeds, blueberries: the ingredients of a grown-up – to the shelves, stacked with unfamiliar brands, trying to make sense of our surroundings. Sam cleared his throat and asked the one question I'd been trying not to ask myself ever since I'd arrived in Australia: 'Why?'

For a fresh start, for a chance to…

For me? his eyes seemed to ask. No, Sam, not for you. It's not all about *you.*

He hadn't changed a bit, not really. Older, more refined, getting better with age. And lighter somehow – whilst I felt the weight of my rucksack rest heavy on my back.

'For work?' he asked with momentary confusion as he looked from my rucksack to my sopping hair and down to my lips, lingering on the latter just a little too long.

No, I thought as my eyes started to well with tears. Stop it, eyes, *stop it.* I had to keep it together. I could just tell him the truth. That I'd come to Sydney to escape the nothingness and noise of London only to find Australia was the same. Just this time with tans and accents.

His free hand reached towards me for a second time, still wanting to hold me together after all these years. He looked so composed, sorted. For once, it would be nice for him to see me the same. In just a moment we'd both move on again and Sam would never need to know I needed a job, rent money…

'You look like you need a drink,' he said before I could say anything. Did I? *Did I really?* What gave him that bloody impression? The fact I had just been clutching a bottle of red for dear life? Or that I had near enough cried when I saw the price? Perhaps it was the way my pasty white legs were caving under the strain of a backpack bigger than both of us put together. I looked like I needed a drink? This one was a genius.

'Hmmm,' I said as my mind berated me for even considering it. This was my blank slate, *my* do-over. But at the risk of coming across like a crazy ex-girlfriend totally 'not cool' with bumping into her drop-dead ex for the first time in forever in the last place either one of us would expect…

I forced a smile and said, 'That would be nice.' For a moment Sam looked stunned; was he just asking to be polite? Like that's just what grown-up ex-boyfriends should do. If only I knew how grown-up ex-girlfriends should act in return. I studied his face as he smiled again. I guess he was just thrown by this whole scenario, though judging from his smile, it didn't seem like a totally unwelcome surprise.

'Have you got time?' Sam asked generously. We both knew I had nowhere to go. 'There's a nice place a few doors down—' Sam started to say before stopping himself. I was in no state for nice. 'Or…' His sentence trailed off, as if trying to put the brakes on for a moment, gauging how I might respond. He looked around the supermarket again as I tried to convince myself he wasn't embarrassed to be seen with me. Or what, Sam? Just say it, *say it*. 'Or… we could head to mine?' He let the words hang between us, a twinkle in his eye. He shrugged, as if trying to pass the invitation off as no big deal. Like this whole random run-in wasn't a bloody great, monumentally big deal. 'It's just round the corner.' He shrugged again and without waiting for my response, reached a hand out towards my face as I gasped, heart racing faster – before his arm seamlessly passed me and reached for the bottle I had just put down. 'Your favourite, right?' He grinned again.

I shrugged, not giving him the pleasure. I would never give him the pleasure again. Stop it, brain, stop it, stop it, *stop* it.

Smiling and shaking his head in disbelief once more, he turned towards the checkout. My mind objected whilst my legs followed. Of course, they did. I'd followed him all the way to Australia – unbeknownst to me, but still. He looked over his shoulder to check I was still there. I desperately wished I wasn't – not looking or feeling like this.

'Yeah, so we'll head back to mine,' Sam repeated as if trying to convince himself it was a good idea. 'Then you can get dry. I assume you have a change of clothes in there?' He raised a mocking eyebrow at my supersized rucksack, trying to make light of the situation.

'Nope. Just the body of the last guy who mocked my backpack.' I smiled sweetly, trying to quip back the control I could feel quickly tumbling away. Sam laughed out loud and with one hand pulled the rucksack off my back and slung it over a single shoulder, disposing of my umbrella-stick at the same time.

'Sound good?' he asked again, my mouth still closed, my mind working on overdrive to make sense of the scenes playing before me. 'It's about a ten-minute walk away?'

'Oh, I…' I began, remembering for a moment that this wasn't a dream. It was too weird. Why was he here? And why did he want me to come back to his? Back to Sam's usually ended one way. And, as much as that familiar thought still sent shivers down my rain-soaked legs, did I really want to fall back into bed with the one man I knew for a fact could break my heart? Well, yes. I did. But I wouldn't. I *couldn't.* I had come to Sydney for a new life, not my old one. But here it was, staring me in the face, randomly finding me one unbought bottle away from a breakdown. It was impossible, yet undeniable. Yes, I had promised Zoe this trip was about me moving forwards, moving on, just like when she'd helped me block him post break-up. But she'd also made her promises in return. *I promise you, Jess*; her words circled around my mind as I studied Sam's expression mere inches before me. *If you and Sam are meant to be together, you'll find a way back to each other – and it won't be through ruddy fucking Facebook.* Well, she was right about that. And here he was. Surely, that had to mean something?

'Are you sure you don't mind?' I couldn't help but ask. This is your chance, Sam. Your opportunity to steer us both back in the right direction, because I sure as hell don't know which way that is. 'We could raincheck…' I tried to give him, give us, an out, not meaning to make him laugh in the process. He always did find me funny. 'If you already have plans, we could just…'

'Jess. It's you.' Sam smiled, saying the words I had so longed to hear. 'Here, now,' he continued, laughing at the hilarity of it all. 'I'd cancel my plans if I had any.'

'In that case…' I smiled, ready to surrender, but he had already started to lead the way. I followed, my heart thudding and mind tumbling with memories I had tried my best to lock away.

*

9 September 2012 – Nottingham, England

Three thuds shocked me from sleep; three more saw me struggle to my feet. I skirted around the pint of water I had placed strategically by my bed, stumbling into the pile of papers yet to find their place in my room. *Shit.* My head throbbed like the bassline in the club we had been in only hours ago as I staggered to the light switch on the other side of the room – and here I was thinking our student fees would stretch to a bedside lamp. The mirror threatened me with my reflection: last night's make-up scrawled across my off-white face. *Thud, thud, thud.* There was no time to rectify it now. At least I had come home earlier than the rest of them, muttering every excuse other than the truth: *I can't wait to get to the studio again.* I swung open the door to see clenched knuckles raised, preparing for the next knock.

My eyes narrowed as the harsh fluorescent light from the corridor flooded into my room, the fist lowering as the face behind it emerged: stubbled and strong, the angles of his jawline mirrored in the contours of his wedged shoulders, pulling his top taut. Blinking slowly, I searched his green eyes for answers, but they were too busy scanning my oversized T-shirt, emblazoned with whatever beer they were pushing to freshers, as I pulled it further over my bare legs.

'Tell me you're Jess.' His forehead crinkled, his expression caught between cross and concerned.

'I'm Jess.' I nodded. I'd crack quickly under torture – especially if the perpetrator looked like him. I spared one hand from my hemline to salvage my hair.

'Thank fuck,' he sighed, somewhere between exuberance and exacerbation. Even his appearance seemed in conflict – his floppy fringe frivolous, rich-boy boat shoes tied tight. He turned to leave, my body knowing to follow. Seconds later he pointed to a pile of sequins, hair and impossibly long legs, concertinaed into a ball against the wall.

'I think she belongs to you.'

I looked at the figure. I couldn't see her face but it was impossible not to recognise that dress. It was the one she had tried to get me to wear as she'd invited herself to get ready in my room – the one she'd taken her scissors to just to shorten the hemline. I'd told her it made me look like a prostitute. She'd told me I looked like a call girl. Two very different things, apparently. I looked from him to her as I forced my shirt further down my legs. *Right now, I look like a prostitute.* The tramp, the princess and the boat-boy. It wasn't quite the tangle I had expected for my first night at uni.

'You *are* Jess, right?' he pressed on, his broad stature making him look older than the drink-stains on his T-shirt betrayed him to be.

'I am.' I nodded again. 'And you are?'

'Good.' He dismissed my question, looking back to our bundle. 'She stumbled into my room' – he pointed a few doors down – 'looking for you. Claims she's drunk.' He raised his eyebrows at her slumped figure. I couldn't help but laugh. *I think she might be on to something.*

'She said that you'll look after her… that you're her best friend.'

I looked down at her, pretty and passed-out. We'd known each other for a minute. But she was cool and intelligent and messy and feisty. I could think of worse friends to have.

'Do you even know her? Or is she just some crazy girl off her tits?'

'Yes.' I smiled again. 'And yes.' Then, rolling my eyes, 'Her name is Zoe.'

He laughed, softening a little now his mission was complete. Well, almost. 'Need help getting her inside?' He grinned, arms folded as he watched me try to navigate her limbs whilst trying not to expose either of us in the process. Reaching his arms underneath her legs, he lifted, as she folded against him. I held my breath as he entered my room – messy and unfinished but awash with colour, my paintings and sketches stuck to the bare white walls. Charcoal ladies danced across parchment in lines and motion, early sketches of rolling sand dunes and swirling waves sending us somewhere sunny.

'Woah.' His eyes scanned the walls, fixing on the yellows and blues of a landscape not yet formed, as I kicked a rogue pair of knickers under the bed. 'You picked these?' He looked to me, seemingly unaware of the woman still in his arms.

'I made them,' I said, as his smile sent his dimples deeper. Bending slowly, he placed Zoe across the blankets I had gathered on the floor as she murmured, 'I want to go back to the party.' *Shit.* She knocked over the pint glass, sending water over the stack of papers I had left loose. He moved to save them, gathering the sheets on bended knees as I soothed Zoe back into her drunken doze. 'You *are* the party, Zoe.' The man laughed, more awake and yet less on edge, apparently no longer so anxious to get back to bed. He wiped down the last of the papers with his shirt, handing them back to me.

'What's that?' He nodded to a black and white flyer, its bold, boxy designs demanding attention from the top of the pile.

'Oh.' I looked at him, a little sheepish. 'It's an application form.' I shrugged.

'For?' He smiled, encouraging me on, all of a sudden.

'An art competition – *Art Today's Voices of Tomorrow*,' I explained, the paper in my hands now hidden from view, as his eyes found their way back to my face.

'Never heard of it.' The guy shrugged. I didn't expect him to. I guess it was pretty niche if you weren't into that kind of thing. 'But for what it's worth' – he fixed his eyes back on mine – 'I think you should apply.'

'Thanks.' I smiled, looking down at the paper. 'But I don't take advice from strangers.' I looked at him again, a playful grin matching the look in his eyes.

'I'm Sam,' he said, pushing himself to standing, offering me a hand to pull me up. *Sam.* 'Hope to see you around, Jess.' He looked again from my paintings to me, turning to leave.

'I think he likes you,' Zoe whispered, forcing her heavy eyes ajar. I looked up to see the door close, but could have sworn I heard him laughing from the other side.

Chapter Two

1 August 2020 – Sydney, Australia

Sam and my backpack walked half a step in front of me, as I felt my brain fall further and further behind. At the next bend he turned, smiled and asked, 'You okay?' No, I wasn't okay – shocked, scared, excited, but miles away from the humdrum of okay. What the hell was happening?

I silenced the thought, pressing onwards through the now relenting rain, cursing even the weather for calming at Sam's cue. He made everything better.

Together we followed the pavement tracing a deserted Coogee Beach, winding up the ever-ascending roads until my heartbeat was racing once again. I'd been up and down this hill far more times than I'd liked over the past few weeks, walking the way from the six-person house share that turned out to have only one bedroom and two beds – "at least they are doubles" – to whatever nondescript bar or coffee shop I could hand my CV into. My bedmate's wandering hands this morning were the final straw. At least at the Coogee Backpacker I'd have my own bunk – for a night or two at least. I knew Sydney was expensive but *that much* to be nestled into a room with drunken travellers all about a decade younger than me? All about the same age I was around the time I met Sam. I tried my best to ignore the threat of dorm rooms: Sam was here, *we* were here, heading back to his. Sam didn't say much as we went, and I was glad – partly because my brain was struggling to master coherent thoughts, never mind sentences. Mostly because this bloody mountain was killing me and all my effort was going into pretending I wasn't already out of breath. Finally, almost at the top of the hill, he turned left onto Oberon Street. I'd passed the big cream house he gestured to a number of times that week, dreaming of earning enough to afford my own room, never mind my own place. Never for one millisecond did I imagine Sam would be inside.

'Here it is.' He smiled, walking down a handful of stone steps and along the path to a big blue door. I tried desperately to calm my heartrate as I watched him walk away. He hadn't changed a bit: strong shoulders, slim legs and an effortless T-shirt-meets-jeans style that I knew for a fact took less than three minutes to curate.

'Three-four-one O-ber-on,' I read the brass door numbers aloud, trying to say anything other than the thousand thoughts flooding my mind. 'Hey, that kind of rhymes.'

Sam looked at me with his best puppy-trying-to-do-algebra expression – a face I'd seen countless times before, as I made an equally familiar mental note to: *shut up.* 'Erm… yeah, sure, if you like.' Puzzlement was soon replaced by joyful disbelief as he took me in again. 'I can't believe you're actually here.' His laugh was full and unreserved, and I cursed every hair on my arms for standing on end. 'What are the odds?' He looked from me to the ocean stretching out behind us. All my energy was going into not asking that question, my mind refusing to entertain the thoughts filling my heart: *It's Sam. He's here. It's finally happening. Again.*

Turning the key in the door, Sam beckoned me into a large stone-floored entrance hall. He ditched my rucksack unceremoniously and led me into an open plan kitchen-living room, all clean, white and bright – nothing like the university halls we had pretty much co-existed in during our time in Nottingham. He gestured towards a spot on a beautiful grey L-shaped sofa and I sat down, still shell-shocked, still skin-soaked, my reservations reminiscent of the first time Sam had taken me back to his. My mind wandered to scenes of two lust-drunk teenagers. I forced myself to focus on the ornately hung abstract artwork that added colour to the walls. Sam had never had an eye for design but it looked like late-onset taste had finally kicked in. He was clearly doing well for himself. I groaned inwardly at my unflattering comparison. Before I had worked out how to not drench the couch, Sam was handing me a large glass of Malbec and suddenly I didn't care. I let the corner seat engulf me whilst I took my first tentative sips of wine.

'So, J,' he began, taking a seat next to me. 'And I say this with love.' His eyes twinkled, his brown skin wrinkling at the cheeks, my mind clinging to the word. How could he be so calm, act so normal after all this time? 'What the hell, may I ask,' he said, 'are you doing here?'

I could have asked him the same thing.

'It's a long story.' I slumped further into the sofa, taking a massive gulp of wine. An unflattering one, one that would tell us what we both already knew: *you won.* I looked around the room, from the pristine kitchenette to the perfectly curated cushions placed on the other chairs around the living space. It was a big place for one person. Did he live here alone? If yes, he was doing better than I thought he was, which kind of made me feel worse. If no, well – who the hell was he living with? My pulse picked up pace at the thought.

'Okay.' Sam shrugged nonchalantly, mimicking my actions to a T. For a moment, forgetting so much time had passed, I leaned over to thump his arm, careful not to spill any wine. He feigned shock, but after all this time we were still predictable. The place where our skin had touched still tingled; I wondered if he could feel it too.

'No, Sam,' I said, as he smiled at the familiarity of my scold. 'Your line is "well, we've got nothing but time."' I rolled my eyes mockingly.

'Oh man.' He threw a playful hand to his forehead. 'I never did remember my lines.' He smiled again, winking in a way only few people could pull off. 'Okay, J, take two.' He puffed up his chest and cleared his throat. 'Well' – dramatic pause – 'we've got' – eyes widening – '*nothing*' – emphasis added – 'but time.' He grinned, revealing a set of bright white teeth, his canines still a little too pointy. 'Better?' he asked eagerly, his demeanour now not dissimilar from a puppy having *cracked* algebra.

'Much.' I nodded, taking another gulp of wine. Sam was here, on the other side of the world. The thought rolled round and round my mind. I studied the apartment, gorgeous and grown-up. I looked at Sam, exactly the same. What was *he* doing here? Maybe if I could just sound it out, find out how long he'd been here, how long he planned to stay, I could play my cards accordingly. Not that I had much in my hand to play. I scanned the room for evidence of housemates but could already tell from the way Sam's arm reached its way along the back of the sofa, that we were alone. 'I'll tell you everything,' I deflected with the best of intentions. 'But you have to tell me what the hell *you're* doing here first.' I laughed, taking another sip of wine, willing it to settle my heartrate.

'You always did get your own way.' Sam laughed warmly, flirtatiously. That wasn't true. If it was, we never would have gone our separate ways in the first place. 'Shoot.' He grinned.

'Why are you in Sydney?' I asked, starting simple but knowing that with us, nothing ever was.

'I got offered a job here,' Sam began, not one for using more words than necessary. 'Soon after we…' He looked serious for a moment, like he couldn't quite bring himself to say it. 'It was good money…' Clearly. '…and I was only going to stay for a year, but then I met some amazing people…' He broke off for a moment, casting an eye to a wood-framed photo of two torso-baring surfers, each with one arm slung around each other, the other cradling their boards. I should have bloody known he'd find his way back to a beach. This was a step up from his hometown of Brighton, I guess – though Sam would never admit it. I studied the photo more closely, as subtly as I could, Sam's sentences fading into the background. One face was his, beaming from ear to ear. The other was darker, both his skin and his hair, which flopped wet and wild onto his well-proportioned face. '…one thing led to another and I'm still here,' he finished, drawing my attention back to him. I could see that, but I needed to hear him say it to remind me it was real. 'For now, at least,' he added, a little noncommittal, as if leaving the conversation open for wherever it might go next. 'Can I get you any more wine?' He looked down at my empty glass, playing the perfect host. Except, it didn't feel like he was playing, any more. It felt like he'd arrived. Meanwhile I'd felt anything but since I'd stepped foot on Sydney soil. His hand grazed mine as he passed my glass back to me.

'Your turn.' Sam reclined further, laying his wine-free hand along the back of the sofa again, his toned arm another testament to his surfing addiction. I took another sip. 'So, you're here for work too?' he prompted, choosing to put the improbability of our situation to one side. My eyes traced his lips as he framed the question, studying each word for ways to evade the truth. I could just tell him. Tell him how my job at an all too niche magazine in London had finally 'reached a natural end' (aka, I'd been made redundant without the hefty pay-out – *thank you*, digital revolution). How my houseshare had also 'reached a natural end' (one boy, one girl, one bottle of tequila and the rest is history). How Zoe had suggested we move to Sydney together, before deciding to buy a two-bedroom house in Colchester instead. How on one last night out with the *Art Today* girls I was introduced to a friend of a friend who knew a friend who had a friend with a spare room in Sydney. A spare room that I could stay in 'for three months until you get settled'. A spare room that turned out to be a spare corner of a bed. And then, when I had come to Sydney, it had all gone tits up and I had ended up in Woolies without a pick-and-mix, an effing clue *or...*

My eyes darted from Sam, tanned and toned, to his apartment, an actual home. Then to my rucksack on the floor full of my clothes, messy and worn. Sam had been training to be a doctor when we were together, and I had loved and hated it in equal measure. On the one hand, there was the 'my boyfriend is a doctor' prestige;

on the other hand there were changing rotas, nightshifts and the fact that your worst day as a humble fine art student could never ever trump the shift in A&E dealing with a four-car crash on the motorway. Clearly, Sam had never painted in oils. He would have qualified by now, qualified into adulthood. It sometimes felt like everyone was growing up and I was just getting old. Just once I wanted someone to think I was doing better than I was and who better than my ex in a fleeting moment in a foreign country? I'd have a job soon enough anyway, not that he'd even be around by then to care. So it wouldn't technically be a lie, just a little truth in advance.

'Yeah, for work.' I nodded, unable to meet his eyes. He could read me like a book; at least he used to. A silence stretched on as my mind struggled to keep up with my mouth: *why did I say that? I don't have a job. I don't have anything here.*

'My job at *Art Today* ended.' Well that part was true at least. Sam's brow crinkled in concern as he reached his arm a little further in my direction, still instinctively protective of me. I studied it, unsure of what move to make next.

'Oh, Jess, I'm so sorry.' He stroked the top of my arm for a moment before pulling away. I guess neither of us knew how to sit alongside each other without a magnetic pull drawing us together. 'That sounds tough,' he said, pity scrawled across his face. I'd dreamt about the next time I'd see him a thousand nights over, nestled in the corner of my too-big double bed back home. Pity was never part of the plan.

'Let me *finish*, Sam,' I joked, giving him a playful push against his strong chest. Sam's laugh filled the room again, turning my words from innocent to innuendo in one lift of his eyebrow. 'My job at *Art Today UK* ended…' Okay, so my words weren't entirely innocent. Where was I going with this? This was honestly going to be okay. The chances of him ever following up anything I said were minimal. About as minimal as me accidentally following him to Australia. '…because they transferred me here to the Australian edition.'

The lie hung between us; like toothpaste out of the tube, there was no getting it back in now. I watched Sam register that I actually had a job here, his free hand playing with his facial hair for a moment before a smile spread across his face. He reached his hand out to stroke my shoulder again, closer with every fib, closer to all he'd hoped; he'd always thought art journalism was a good fit for me.

'Jess, that's amazing!' He pulled me into a hug, his scent filling my senses for the first time in years. 'You have a job in Sydney.' He laughed again, breaking away. 'I actually can't believe it.' He shook his head. That made two of us. 'When do you start?'

Good question. I searched my mind for a good answer. I could just say Monday and pray I'd never see him again; there was a first time for everything.

'I'll have to drop by and say hey,' Sam continued. Shit, shit, *shit*. I could just come clean now, tell him I was joking. Or tell him that I was applying for a job there but it hadn't quite come through.

'Sam I…' I began, somewhere between guilty and dumbfounded. Sam's body lingered a little closer, his eyes darting to my mouth, watching for what it might say – or do – next, caught between delight and disbelief. 'In two weeks.' The words spilled out as Sam softened again. 'I start in two weeks.'

Oh crap. You've done it now, Jess.

'So you have a bit of time before then?' Sam asked eagerly. Why, what did he have in mind? I imagined anything but the truth: I had a hell of a lot longer than *a bit of time.*

'Yeah, a little,' I lied; it was too late to go back now. 'I wanted to see a bit of Sydney first.'

'Alone?' Sam said, a little too hurriedly. Did he want me to be alone? I studied his expression, questioning his motive for bringing me back here for the hundredth time since I'd arrived. My heart started to gallop, everything opening to him again. For a moment, I stalled. I could lie about this too. Just a hint of someone special, a brief flash on his face of excitement morphing into envy; isn't that what every ex wanted? But I wanted one thing more. And looking at Sam, awaiting my response, his arm on the sofa, inching closer still, it seemed like we finally wanted the same thing, all over again.

'Alone.' I nodded as Sam smiled broadly and my heart leapt in my chest. 'And you? Do you live here alone?' Sam cast a quick look to the photo of him and his surfer bud propped up on the side table as I took in the size of the space once again. He hesitated for a moment, forcing his gaze away from the picture and back to me. 'A lot of the time,' he said, still a little nervous. I guess we both were. It had been so long. 'But technically there's the two of us here. Hey, where are you living?' Sam drew my attention away from his hot housemate. I gave a shifty look to my abandoned rucksack, praying it wasn't obvious. I wouldn't take a job on the other side of the world without having somewhere to live. That would be silly – the irony of the thought caught in my mind, stalling my response. And I sure as hell couldn't tell him I was struggling to afford a hostel. No, he was a grown-up, and he thought I was a grown-up. A grown-up wouldn't lie. A grown-up would have an…

'I have an apartment.' My voice and brain became further detached. Shit, shit, *shit*. 'In Randwick,' I added for good measure. At least this lie was confined to a slightly cheaper part of town; it's where I was hoping to be before all this happened anyway, before I realised I hadn't a hope of affording a place until I got myself a job. Sam was just speeding up my timeline. I'd make it all happen before he even had a chance to realise it was ever in doubt.

Sam smiled before looking down at my rucksack, back up to my smudged cheeks. I looked like a homeless person, because in actual fact I *was* a homeless person. 'It was meant to be ready today but the landlord decided to do some last-minute renovations.' I knew my answer wasn't enough but that I'd already said too much. I forced a smile, hoping it would move the conversation forward. Sam exhaled deeply, trying to keep up with my job, my being here; I always did exhaust him – and not in a good way, not like the first time all those years ag— stop it, brain, *stop* it. His hand inched ever closer along the back of the sofa. Part of me longed for it to curl around me, to draw me in, for him to lean in and kiss me, to stop any more stupid sentences falling from my stupid mouth.

'So, you're not allowed in your apartment yet?'

I nodded, every inch of me wanting to retreat, wanting to start again.

'And you've got two weeks before you start your new job?'

I nodded, nervously. He knew; I could tell he knew. I should have known better than to lie to the one person who knew me better than I knew myself. *Had* known.

'So, what are you going to do until you're settled?'

Settled. That sodding word. The word that made anyone single, unmarried, mortgage-less or childless feel like they were in a perpetual state of flux, like they were invited to a fancy dinner party but didn't know the right way in.

'I'll probably just put myself up in a hotel or something,' I said, as if putting myself up in hotels was an everyday occurrence in the life of young professional Jess.

'Will your work cover it?' Sam pressed me further. Highly, highly unlikely, Sam, seeing as *Art Today Australia* don't even know I work for them. I shook my head, as his eyes searched the room around us. I knew that face. Problem-solving Sam. Dissecting my decision, finding a better cure. 'We could put you up in our spare bedroom for a bit?' Sam said, a glimmer of hope in his eyes.

They had a *spare* bedroom? I'd spent the last few weeks on a third of a double bed and Sam and his surfer had three bedrooms? For just a moment I felt vindicated. Sam could never know the truth about me or my life since he stopped being a part of it. 'We really wouldn't mind.' He smiled his gorgeous smile. It hit me in my stomach. Why was he being so nice? The last time we saw each other definitely wasn't nice. But I guess that was a long time ago; maybe now things could be different. Sam's arm reached out to touch me again, sending tingles down my arm and up my legs. My body softened to his, every inch of mine remembering his so well.

'No, I couldn't.'

Finally, something truthful fell from my mouth.

I couldn't. Move in with my ex? It would drive me insane. *More* insane. Sam had broken me, broken everything. I couldn't let him do that again. I looked at him, his face displaying the kind of smile you reserved for best, his eyes alight with promise as if to say: *I can fix this, let me fix this.* I had waited so long for him to fix it, even longer to be over him. How was living in the next room going to help? Unless, maybe he didn't want me to get over him, perhaps he'd prefer me under...

'Sure, you can, we wouldn't mind a bit,' Sam repeated, his eyes darting again to the photo. 'Jamie's a doctor too. We'll be on shift all the time; the house will be pretty much empty. You can just spend a few days here using our Internet, preparing for your job.'

Was I a love interest or a charity case? I still couldn't tell. I stood up and caught a glimpse of myself in the mirror. I looked like the latter. In any case, was I really in a position to argue? Where else would I go? I had a couple of weeks, tops, to get a job and save enough rent to get my own place. How was living out of a rucksack in an overpriced hostel dorm-room going to help me achieve either of those things? And I couldn't call my parents and ask them for money and have them think my plan had failed, again. Wasn't it better to stay in the artisan apartment of two young professionals? Maybe some of their 'settled' would rub off on me. And anyway, what was the worst that could happen?

Actually, I knew the worst that could happen. I'd either get drunk and try to make Sam jealous by coming on to his hot doctor housemate who'd then politely ask Sam to kick the crazy girl out. Or there was the teeny tiny chance I'd fall even more madly, obsessively, unworkably in love with my ex-boyfriend. Unless, perhaps, we wouldn't be so impossible on the other side of the world? We were different now, both older; *he* was wiser. But no, this was my fresh start, and I'd already made an absolute cock-up of that. Not that Sam knew. And I had every intention of keeping it that way.

'Sam, I can't,' I objected.

'Of course you can, Jess,' Sam said. 'Remember how much fun we used to have?' *Remember?* I'd spent the last three years trying to forget.

'Wouldn't that be a bit, well, strange?' I tried my best to argue but could feel my resolve sliding away.

'Not as strange as bumping into you on the other side of the world.' He laughed. He was right. Maybe the strangest thing was to let this moment slip away to nothing?

'Just for a couple of days,' I said, hope and trepidation wrestling in my stomach as I allowed myself to sink back into the sofa.

'I'll give you a week, J – tops.' He winked again, confident, infectious. For a moment I could feel excitement flooding out my nightmare of bed-shares and bunkbeds. Now I'd be dreaming just a door away from his. For now at least. My heart hammered at the thought. And I could save some money, just while I found a job. A real job.

'Only if you're sure,' I added.

'I'm sure.'

'Thank you so much.' I couldn't help but throw my arms around him, his body melting into mine as the disappointments of the last few weeks started to fade away. 'Just a week,' I confirmed into Sam's shoulder. One week. One week to fulfil every lie covering my not-so-successful Sydney life before Sam could find out what a false start my twenties were proving to be. But for now, wrapped in the warmth of his embrace, things were finally starting to look up.

*

12 September 2012 – Nottingham, England

'Look, Jess. Oh *shit*, he's coming over.' Zoe looked up from her glass of wine to the broad torso of a man walking across the bar towards us. She smoothed down her black, long-sleeved silk top with a plunging neckline that left little to the imagination.

'And what am I supposed to do? Just sit here and make small talk with the best friend?' I looked up from picking the final bits of paint out from underneath my chipped nail polish. It was midnight and I was hungover and halfway through fleshing out the rolling pencil lines that had mapped out my latest landscape.

'Just five minutes.' Zoe's eyes pleaded with me, looking from me to the man approaching, brimming with possibilities.

'Can we join you?' The man looked down at our table, very much at Zoe, very much alone. Zoe shrugged. In reality, she'd clocked him the second we'd walked into the bar: the only face looking our way against a backdrop of broad swim-team members drinking and laughing in the opposite direction.

'We?' Zoe asked, looking her poor victim up and down as he slid into the booth beside me. Great, now I was trapped. Zoe's made-up eyes darted to mine: *five minutes, I swear.*

'Yes, we.' The guy spoke in an unmistakable American drawl adding colour to his tone. 'I'm Austin.' He smiled, as if his accent wasn't enough to place him. 'And this is…' He looked up towards the figure approaching.

'Sam.' I couldn't help but smile as he slid into the space next to Zoe.

'Jess!' He grinned across at me, pushing a hand through his thick, brown hair.

'Zoe.' She threw her own name into the mix, while I tried to warn her with my eyes: *you already know him. He lives down the hall. He's carried you home. He's seen your pants.*

Sam laughed, sending me a mischievous look: our first private joke.

'You know each other?' Zoe looked from Sam to me, trying and failing to make sense of us.

'Just a little.' Sam replied. 'I'm living at Holymoor Halls too.'

'Amazing, and Austin are you—'

'Have you sent it off yet?' Sam spoke across the table, our conversation criss-crossing Zoe and Austin's before they made their way to the bar and Sam came to sit next to me. *Five more minutes* – Zoe motioned across the room with her free hand, her other now laced in Austin's. I shrugged and smiled, looking back at Sam, now off the clock.

'Not yet. It's very competitive, though,' I said, looking to his earnest eyes, his encouragement making it harder to find reasons to not send off my application, to not throw my hat into the ring.

'That's what people said about medicine, but they still let me in to study it,' Sam joked. He had a way of making competition and decisions and, well, *life*, look easy. No doubt a symptom of privilege, but one I was pretty sure I wouldn't mind infecting me.

'You'll make a good doctor.' I couldn't help but look down at his hands, big and strong.

He looked down at his beer, studying its froth. 'It was the only option really.'

I searched his smile, not sure why his options were so limited. Unshakable pressure? Undeniable calling?

'Not as cool as art, though.' He lifted his pint to his lips, taking another swig. I did the same, feeling the rush of intoxication soothe the places where my hangover still lingered.

'Oh, I don't know.' I put my hand down by my side, accidentally touching his, electricity amalgamating with the alcohol. 'I know which of us would be more helpful in a crisis. Quick! Is there an artist in the house?'

'Art therapy can save lives, you know!' He laughed, putting his hand on top of mine, nothing accidental about it. I looked from Zoe and Austin, now entwined at the bar, to my and Sam's hands interlaced on the table, not knowing why our connection felt more intimate. Perhaps the promise of something longer than *five more minutes.* 'Maybe you can teach me how to draw sometime?' He turned his face towards me, inches from mine.

'Maybe, if you buy me a drink.' I scanned his face, from his eyes to his nose and down to his neck, not knowing why or how he was making me feel so sure.

'*Deal.*' He grinned, letting go of my hand, now bonded by the possibility of more.

Chapter Three

'Deal?' Sam asked, as I sat motionless, torn between not knowing if I should stay and definitely not wanting to go. 'Stay in our spare bedroom for a couple of nights, a week, tops?' He had a way of making it sound like the most natural thing in the world.

'And you're *sure* your housemate won't mind?' I asked again, not knowing which answer I'd prefer, whether he was a step away from or towards where I was meant to be. But we were *here*, now – that had to count for something. Sam hesitated for a moment. I knew he hadn't asked him; he hadn't broken away for a second to look at his phone.

'Jamie loves having guests.' He nodded, as if convincing himself that this would all be okay. I saw his steady shoulders jump for a second at the sound of a key turning in the door. 'Ah, now you can ask Jamie yourself!' He recovered his smile, forcing it from ear to ear. I sat back down on the sofa, grabbing one of the large cushions to hide my atrocious attire; if only I could find a blanket to cover my face. Sam's friends were always fit. Gorgeous doctors tended to attract gorgeous doctors; it was an epidemic. Looking towards the archway into the room, the surfer guy from the photo materialised before me. Six foot something, his height only magnified by his skinny black jeans. My eyes followed his legs upwards to a torso you could tell was toned even through his T-shirt, past his tanned arms and further still to a bearded face, thicker than Sam's own shadowy jaw, perfectly framed by a floppy wet fringe.

'Dude, the surf was great,' Jamie began in a thick Australian accent, cradling a damp wetsuit in his hands, before noticing me on the sofa. 'Oh.' He stopped, affronted. I looked down at my clothes and held the cushion more tightly.

'You must be Jamie,' I said. Sam was now standing, his head turned away. Jamie stood still for a moment, wetsuit still in hands, a curious expression on his face. For a moment, the intensity of his dark stare stole what was left of my sanity before his warm laugh shocked me back into the room. I felt my cheeks flush pink; what had I said?

'Man, I'm flattered.' He laughed again, casting a confused look at Sam. What was going on? 'Sorry to disappoint you…' His face creased into a smile, whiter against his tanned skin. '…but Jamie is far more exciting than me.' He shook his head, glancing back at a silent Sam. Were they going to let me in on the joke? 'And you are?' He looked from me to Sam again, neither of us quite sure why he wasn't saying more. Clearly, we all had questions. So, there were three of them here? Please tell me this 'spare' bedroom wasn't another bloody bedshare. Unless maybe… I looked at Sam. Was that why he looked so sheepish all of a sudden? He was hoping for a bit longer, alone together, for the sleeping arrangements to kind of just work themselves out?

'I'm Jess,' I stuttered, as not-Jamie's eyes widened in something like recognition as he began spreading his wetsuit taut across the kitchen table.

'Joshua.' He came across to offer me his hand. 'Sorry, it's still a little wet.'

'So am I…' I looked down at my outfit before I rushed to add, '…from the rain.' Joshua started to laugh again, as we heard another key turn in the front door.

'Sounds like Jamie's back too.' Joshua moved back across the room, leaving me to try and hide my shabbiness from suitor number three. I followed their gaze towards the doorway just as a five-foot eight, perfectly tanned, impeccably toned, Lycra-cladded blonde swanned effortlessly into the space between us. The real Jamie looked from me to Sam and back again, perfect smile not once fading from *her* flawless face. 'Hey, Bub.' She said to Sam, who was now standing in the little kitchenette with Joshua, physically and metaphorically distancing himself from me. I tried to catch his eye again but all of his attention was on her. Who was she? Joshua's girlfriend? Was that how she and Sam had met? The Malbec in my hand began to feel less inviting, along with Sam's earlier invitation. I looked at him, willing him to make the necessary – *so very* necessary – introductions for the second time that afternoon.

'Hey, Bubby,' Sam replied, casting a guilty look in my direction. What was happening?

Bub? Bubby? My eyes darted between them. Maybe it was an Australian thing?

'Hey, Bub.' I tried to smile sweetly at Jamie, before hearing Joshua stifle a laugh. At least one person was finding this situation funny. I fixed my eyes on Sam, willing him to explain.

'Jamie, this is Jess,' Sam explained to the Victoria's Secret model before us, her eyes narrowing for a split second before becoming large and sparkly again. I fixed my eyes on Sam, still willing him to explain, but this time to *me*. 'Jess and I were…' Sam turned to me, his eyes suddenly struggling to meet mine. I prepared myself for what he might say, doubtful that he'd settle on a clear-cut status given that so much was still left unsaid. '…we were good friends at university, and I just bumped into her at the shops, can you believe it?' Sam said with a well-meaning enthusiasm, one that hadn't seemed strained before. Good friends. Good *friends*? Of all the ways I thought he'd buy us some time to work out where we were at now – over twenty-thousand hours and twenty-thousand miles since we'd left things – I didn't think *good friends* would be it. But what were he and Jamie? Were they *good friends* too?

'Oh well, honey,' Jamie began in an accent that *sounded* like honey. 'You must stay for dinner!' She beamed her pearly whites at me as I wished I could shield my eyes.

Dinner? I'd just agreed to stay for a week. Sam had said this would be okay. Why wasn't he making things feel okay now?

'Joshua, can you stay too?' Real Jamie tuned to Fake Jamie as I tried to make sense of their dynamic, of Sam's new friends, a new life unfolding before me. Joshua smiled back at her, eyes full of admiration, a flirtation I all of a sudden wanted to fan into flames. They were together, right? That was the most likely explanation?

'No, sorry. Gotta dash actually,' Joshua replied, turning towards the door as my heart beat faster. *Kiss her, just kiss her.* I willed the two of them together. Instead, Joshua swivelled to face me again, locking eyes with mine – a glimmer of intrigue filling them as I forced myself not to look away. I studied their colour – a blue made all the brighter against his burnt olive skin.

'Nice to meet you, Jess. I told you she was more exciting than me,' he said and winked. *Yes, but no one told me she was a woman. No one is telling me what she's doing here now.* I offered him a weak smile in return, which I willed to become stronger, sure that Joshua had just seen something like fear in my eyes.

'Hopefully, I'll see a little bit more of you…' Joshua said, smiling again and making his way towards the door into the kitchenette, '…around,' he added before turning to disappear out of it.

'Dinner?' Real Jamie, still here, one hand on her skinny hip, repeated her offer.

'Well actually, Bub,' Sam interjected, an unusual stutter in his voice. 'Jess has just had her accommodation fall through, I was thinking she could stay in the—'

'Box room. Absolutely, we'll sort it, no problem.' Jamie grinned. 'Sam's probably told you I love pretending to be the hostess with the mostest.' She laughed, opening her arms and beckoning me to stand up for an embrace. I hesitated, noticing a squiggly emblem on her thin Lycra top that no doubt indicated it was designer. Jamie duly ignored my hesitation and flung her arms around me. *Yes he did mention that*, I thought into her shoulder, *but he also forgot to mention so many other things about you.*

'So, you'll stay with us for a few days, yes?'

I looked at her, struggling to hide my confusion. She asked so eagerly I felt like saying no would break her heart. I'd heard Australians were hospitable, but surely this was taking the piss. Something told me she'd never have to pretend to be the perfect host, never have to *pretend* to be anything. Unlike me. I turned to Sam, shifting from foot to foot, unable to stand still. He was practically begging me to say yes only moments ago. So why did I feel like he was regretting it now? This was okay, right, Sam? Explain everything and make it all okay.

'Only if you're sure?' I asked again, inches from her face.

'Any friend of Sam's is a friend of mine, right, mate?' She turned to look at Sam, who, try as he might, couldn't hide his smile. Mate? Oh, they were just housemates. That made sense. I had always thought Sam was gorgeous but this woman was way out of his league, not to mention completely not his type. Maybe this would all be okay. Jamie and I would become friends and she'd take me out around town, and we'd joke about Sam's annoying little habits and I could find out if he was seeing anyone and…

'I'll get the box room ready, then, shall I?' Jamie asked Sam rhetorically as she glided towards the kitchen. The box room? Sam had called it the spare bedroom – and he'd made it sound like it was ready? He'd made it sound like a lot of things.

'Thanks, baby,' he said. 'That would be wonderful.'

Baby. I knew baby; *I* was baby. Or at least, used to be. Sure enough, Jamie leaned in, pressing her hands on the dining table in the centre of the kitchen, poking her pert bottom just a little further in my direction, before kissing my ex-boyfriend full on the mouth. He tried to hold back – for my benefit, not his own – but softened at her kiss, powerless against it, reaching a hand up to her hair before stopping himself.

'No worries.' She smiled from Sam to me, a brief look of confusion darting across her face. I forced myself to look thankful, before watching her bound out of the kitchen.

Sam looked over to me, eyes wide with embarrassment.

'Jess, I…' he began, making tentative steps towards me, trying to explain now that we were finally alone. What was going on? Why had he invited me here? Why had he not told me about Jamie when he'd had the chance? He came to stand before me as I felt tears of confusion threatening to rise to the surface. 'I can explain…' Sam's sentences faded into nothingness as Jamie came back into the room, halting for a second on seeing Sam standing so close to his *good friend from university*. He took a step back.

'Jess, come with me.' Jamie looped an arm into mine, steering me away from Sam. 'You can have the first shower.' As if she needed one; her gym-bunny outfit didn't look like it had seen even one drop of sweat.

'Only if you're sure?' I asked, automated, stuck on repeat. I wasn't sure of anything now.

'Absolutely.' She grinned, leading me further away from Sam and any more of those half-sentences he was about to try and fail to say. 'No worries.'

No worries, Jamie? I'll give you no fucking worries. My heart hammered as she steered me further away from Sam. Not only was I now tan-less, jobless, *home*less, I was about to spend the next week trying to solve my mess of a life in my heartbreakingly gorgeous ex-boyfriend's spare bedroom, whilst trying to work out just what exactly Jamie was to him. I guess I could now add *clueless* to my less-than list.

Chapter Four

No one wants to like their ex-boyfriend's new… well, whatever she was. And yet, hating Jamie was proving trickier than I'd thought.

'I've put fresh sheets on the bed.' She halted her blur of activity to rest a hand on the doorframe into the spare room. Inside was a double bed almost as big as the room itself, disguised with a dozen unique print-design cushions, a little like the ones that lined the living room. So, *she* was the design-eye. I should have known Sam hadn't finally fallen for da Vinci; he'd thought *Homes and Gardens* was a renovation show. I glanced from Jamie back to the colour-pop cushions. I dreaded to think how much each of them would cost. My guess was if I sold them I'd have enough to pay the deposit and first month's rent for a place of my own. I was pretty sure 'thou shalt not steal thy host's things' was printed in bold in the House-Guest Bible. I guess Sam now belonged to her too. But if he did, why the hell wouldn't he tell me? Why the hell was I here to begin with?

Jamie went further down the corridor, turning into what I assumed was the master bedroom – not that my assumptions were serving me all that well since arriving in Sydney. I didn't follow, not risking the sight of Sam's things intermingled with hers. So it was just the two of them. And me. The spare girlfriend in the spare bedroom? Jamie reappeared, thrusting a pair of silk pyjamas into my hands and steered me in the direction of the bathroom – probably not wanting me to get whatever flea-ridden rags I had in my rucksack all over her sheets. If she knew who I really was I imagined she'd be steering me towards the door. But I guess if I knew who I really was I might not have found myself here in the first place.

'Sorry we can't offer you a bath,' Jamie apologised. I got the sense that she did this tour a lot. But never to an ex-girlfriend. Not that she knew that's what I was. I, for one, was planning to keep it that way.

I padded into the exposed sandstone room and looked up at their fresh-water shower. 'I think I'll be okay.' I smiled weakly, wanting desperately to believe that was true.

'Help yourself to anything in there,' I heard her shout as I closed the door, tears rising, breakdown imminent. I croaked my thanks, rushing to the shower, turning on the taps and in the shelter of the rushing water letting my tears fall. *How the hell did I end up here?* It was a question I had asked myself countless times before but never once in my ex-boyfriend's apartment, never once overusing his new girlfriend's expensive Clinique bodywash. Surely, that's what Jamie was – the real Jamie. They lived together; they called each other baby; they kissed on the mouth. I couldn't stay here. I just couldn't. I had to get out.

Wrapping a towel around myself – all assurances that my travel towel was as good as any shot to hell with the feel of its fabric – I rushed to retrieve my mobile from on top of the toilet lid. I scrolled through my contacts in search of a saviour. Mum, Dad. It had taken all my strength not to call them when my first few days hadn't gone to plan, when I'd got kicked out of my accommodation for rejecting Handsy, when all I could see was rain. I was a twenty-seven-year-old woman; I couldn't keep running back to them. They'd been unconvinced about me coming anyway, nervous about what I'd find here. I'm sure Sam hadn't even crossed their minds. I flicked to Zoe, the only person I really wanted to talk to. But I couldn't. She'd encouraged me to come here, said a fresh start would do me good. What would she say when she found out I'd landed myself just a corridor away from the very stumbling block that had kept me stuck in a moment that everyone had managed to move past? I really didn't have the energy to find out. I'd just stay for one night. Grin and bear it. Tomorrow I'd start again.

Emerging into the living space twenty minutes later, I found Jamie putting the first load of my washing into the machine. I pondered afresh whether she was really that nice or if her pass-agg was simply off balance. Sam had barely moved an inch in the whole time Jamie had been sorting me out, his face still showing the same expression of apology (for me) and admiration (for her). Each time it looked like Jamie was about to leave us in the same room together, Sam's goldfish impression had started afresh, like he was about to say something, about to explain – and then she'd come back in again. But what could he possibly say to explain this one away?

'Can I help with anything, J?' he offered.

'No,' both Jamie and I said in unison, before I remembered I was no longer his J.

'Oh… I…' Sam began, never brilliant at resolving tension.

'No, I think we're almost there, baby.' Jamie was clearly more adept at addressing the awkwardness and chimed in, moving across to open the fridge. 'Sam, these aren't organic?' She held her smile, her cheery tone, but gritted her teeth slightly at the vegetables in her hands, teetering on the edge of annoyance.

'Is that a question or a statement?' Sam asked, with a hint of apology.

'Just answer the question,' she said and forced a little laugh.

Definitely a question then, and definitely a passive-aggressive one at that.

'Does it matter?' Sam asked.

'It matters to me,' she replied, retaining the lightness in her voice. 'But no bother.' She turned to me with a massive grin. 'Jess is a good excuse to eat out anyway. I want to hear everything.' Would she, Sam? Would she want to hear *everything?* Sam looked more uncomfortable by the second. I wasn't going to rescue him.

'Did you want to eat out, Jess? We know some really nice places, our treat.' Jamie smiled in my direction. Did she really need to look like that? I looked down at my borrowed silk pyjamas, pushing my towel-dry hair from my make-up-less face. As much as I would *love* to be taken out to dinner with my ex-boyfriend and his nice-as-pie girlfriend, I really couldn't stomach it – the company, not the food; I could stomach the food, I was *starving.* I looked down at my phone. It was half past seven. Somewhere between Woolies and our walk, a part of me had begun to hope I'd be too distracted by Sam by now to be hungry for anything but him. And yet here I was being invited to dine across from Jamie, so he could really see the 'before' and 'after' of girlfriends past and present. Swallowing my stupidity, I looked towards their eager expressions, the fridge now closed and non-organic produce and their domestic bickering safely locked away. Was it too early to call it a night?

'I think, actually,' I said, 'as long as it's okay with you, I might just go to bed. It's been… quite the day.'

Quite the day? What twenty-seven-year-old in their right mind says, 'Quite the day?'

'Absolutely,' said Sam, a little too quickly.

'No worries. Now, you take this,' she said, extending a small silver key in my direction. 'Come and go as you please. The Wi-Fi code is stuck on the fridge and the Mac doesn't have a password. Help yourself to anything in the cupboards. We'll probably be up for a little longer.' She looked at her chunky designer watch. 'Yeah – we'll defo be up for a bit.' She smiled, her big display of hospitality somehow making me feel even smaller. 'But here's my number, just drop us a message if we're being too loud.' My mind instantly wandered to the many ways they could keep me up at night, none of them good – for me at least. 'Or if you change your mind, feel free to join us.' Cue even more outrageous images.

'That's okay,' I replied quickly. 'I'll be out like a light the second my head hits the pillow.' I yawned at the thought. 'Thanks again for having me.' I looked from Jamie to Sam and back again, trying not to vomit or cry. 'I really appreciate it.'

'Oh, stop.' Jamie raised a manicured hand in my direction. 'Like I said. Any friend of Sam's is a friend of mine.' Sam tried to catch my eye, but I looked away.

If only she knew, I thought, heading into the spare bedroom. *If only she knew.*

*

The room was every bit as gorgeous as the rest of the apartment. White, light and bright – just like the living room, with a large surf-blue bedspread and shabby-chic wooden tables on either side of the bed, piled high with Sam's magazines. A used surfboard hung on the wall, a single crack running from end to end. I reached up to run my fingers from one side to the other, letting my nails move into the etched 'S' on the board's tail. Sam looked great on a surfboard. A bolt of longing shot across my chest. This was ridiculous. I rallied all the perspective I could muster. Sam wasn't mine. He hadn't been mine for years. And I'd had relationships since ours, some more serious than others (tequila-housemate nights falling very much under 'others') but I had always kind of thought – always kind of hoped – that our paths would somehow forge back together. It had never felt like the end. And here I was. In *their* home. Sam was not mine. He would never be again. Sitting on the edge of the bed, looking up at the surfboard, I bit back the tears. I wouldn't cry again, not here, not with the two of them on the other side of the door doing God knows what – shut up, brain, *shut up*.

Flinging my body back to lie on the bed, I let Jamie's Egyptian cotton sheets please and patronise me in equal measure. My stomach groaned, and I longed for more than Sam. My head now sinking into a foot of goose feathers, I rolled onto one side to be confronted with a picture of the two of them that Jamie hadn't thought to take down – why would she? She thought we were just friends. We were just friends – the kind who had seen each other naked and yet hadn't seen each other for years. The kind who had planned a future that only one of us had managed to make. Together they stared out of the frame, Sam's hand extended to the back of the camera while his other clutched Jamie around her tiny waist. If only this one had been in the living room, I might have known not to stay, but then Sam had insisted; why on earth would he want me here? Unless he really did just think of me as a friend now. I looked at the photo again. Just like in the one of Sam and Joshua, they were both wearing wetsuits, pulled down to their middles, the sand and sea caught in the background. *That* was Sydney. It just wasn't my Sydney, I thought, switching the light to black, my mind sifting through all the next moves I could make to rectify my second start all over again. As I turned onto the cold side of the bed I berated the tiny bit of my heart hoping that second start could still be *ours*.

*

18 September 2012 – Nottingham, England

'Can you paint me like one of DiCaprio's French girls?' Sam lay on his side across the length of my bed, his slim-cut jeans straining to bend, his strong legs visible within them.

'I guess, but *my* French girls stay *still*.' My eyes, like my tone, told him to stop moving for the umpteenth time. I looked down at the sketchpad in my hands, not sure how me teaching him to draw had turned into me studying his profile, but not entirely unhappy about it. I used the length of my pencil to measure the gap between his eyes, the length of his light laughter lines down to his lips, the symmetry of his mouth – a mouth that for all of our drunken moments was yet to be on mine. I pushed my pencil into the page lightly, then harder, darker, building depth with every sketch, trying to capture something of him.

'So, I'm not allowed to talk at all?' Sam mumbled out of the corner of his mouth. 'Not even to ask you what the hell happened with Zoe and Austin the other night?'

I narrowed my eyes, trying to be quiet, *zen*, but powerless not to take the bait.

'I think everyone in the bar knew what happened that night.' I laughed, recalling images of the two of them, bound together, as I'd looked at Sam and hoped for the same. *Maybe we are in the friend zone?* I wondered for a moment, but the look caught by my pencil told me that wasn't the case.

'So, what now?' Sam mumbled again, a cute ventriloquist – for my entertainment only.

'Nothing,' I said, lifting my head intermittently to capture the contours of his face, forcing my eyes to remain above his neck. 'Zoe doesn't do relationships.' I looked at him, as Sam rolled his eyes: *why does that not surprise me?* 'Not like that, she just doesn't want to settle down, she has her… reasons.' My look dared him to challenge me. We'd only known each other for a few days, but Zoe's secrets were safe with me. People had told me so much about university, exactly what to expect. But they'd never told me of bonds born so quickly and yet built to last, of the intensity of spending every waking moment together: sharing your breakfast with the people who shared your night.

'And how about you, Leo?' Sam fixed his eyes on mine, trying to hold my stare, which was torn between his real face and my imitation of him. 'Are free-spirited artists the relationship type?'

'Maybe.' I shot him a look as he craned to see my sketch. I wanted to keep him guessing.

'Right, your turn.' I jumped to my feet and pulled Sam up to stand, enjoying our contact.

'Okay, okay.' He surrendered, holding my hands in his for just a second too long before picking the sketchpad up from the chair. 'Jess, this is *insane*.' He beamed across at me.

'Well, it's your face,' I quipped.

'Yes, I know my face isn't normal,' he laughed, 'but nor is *this*.' He gestured to my drawing as I felt a warm glow fill my stomach. It was all I was good at, all I wanted to do. 'I can see why they shortlisted you.' I had just got the email this morning, the excitement feeling like it might never wear off. Winning was such a long shot but one of the judges had said I was 'going places', and even recommended me to a personal contact who ran an evening class in London that would help 'develop my skills'.

'I'm not following that.' Sam got to his feet, coming to sit on the bed beside me.

'You have no choice.' I laughed, pointing back to the chair. 'You got yours.' I framed my face with my hands, beaming broadly.

'There's no point,' he said, a hint of seriousness laced in his voice. 'It'll be shit.'

'Define "shit"?' I probed, knowing that when it came to art he'd not know how to.

'Not this.' He gestured around the room, his hand finding its way to mine as he rested them back down.

'Well, beauty is in the eye and all that…' I laughed again, squeezing his hand tighter.

'That's what scares me.' Sam grinned, turning to look at me. 'It's so subjective. I'm a medic. We like science, solutions, security…'

'Alliteration?'

'I'm sssssssserious…' Sam joked, pulling me a little closer still.

'Come on.' I poked his side, playful, flirtatious. 'Not everything in life needs to be *perfect*, Doctor,' I mocked, as he grabbed hold of my hands, pinning me to the bed, pressing his weight on top of me, and then his lips on top of mine, kissing me lightly at first, then with more pressure. He pulled away, my breath caught, my mind nowhere but him.

'Well' – he grinned down at me – 'can't blame a man for trying.'

Chapter Five

2 August 2020 – Sydney, Australia

I woke with a start. Where was I? I reached for the light, the faces of Sam and Jamie staring back at me from the photo frame. *Shit*, that's where I was. Sam's sodding apartment. But not just Sam's – Sam and Jamie's apartment. *Their* apartment. That they shared together. Because they were together. I felt sick. I checked my phone and a notification from Zoe flashed up. My stomach flipped. I couldn't tell her where I was, not when she'd sent me off to get my shit together. Not when she had it all sorted. I swiped away the notifications before clocking the time; it was only quarter to three. Now my stomach groaned; I hadn't eaten since breakfast yesterday. And a liquid dinner didn't count. I needed food. 'Help yourself to anything in the cupboard,' Jamie had said. 'Come and go as you please,' she had said. Well, if she insisted.

Savouring the touch of the sheets, I slunk out of bed and towards the door. Pulling it open, I braced myself to hear moans of pleasure rising from the master bedroom, or worse – the L-shaped sofa where I had left them hours before. I remembered the way Sam used to touch, used to taste. When would my brain just learn to *shut up*?!

Greeted with silence, I proceeded to push the door open, tiptoeing across the corridor and out to the kitchen-living room. Made it. Now, food. I just needed something quick and easy. Opening a cupboard, I prayed for Pringles. Instead, I was greeted with an array of ingredients. Damn. I remembered Sam's basket from the day before and Jamie's horror that he'd not bought organic, when the Sam I knew literally didn't look at the price before purchasing something, never mind the origin of the products. I bet she could cook. I mean, who has a sculpted body like hers from eating Pringles? Moving like a mime, hands searching my way around the unfamiliar space, I found my way to the fridge. As I opened the door, light cascaded into the darkened room.

'Jess?'

Slowly and without turning round, I closed the fridge door and, half asleep, I got down onto all fours and crawled underneath the kitchen table. Shit, shit, shit. I thought they had gone to sleep. But no, I should have known. After watching a romantic movie (okay, well, some action film with a couple of love scenes – this was Sam after all), they would have cosied up, laughing fondly about how lovely it was to be able to give back to the community by taking in the riffraff. He would have looked into her eyes and said, 'You know how beautiful you are, J?' and she would have forgiven every annoying thing he had done that day and let him take her in his arms and kiss her, kiss her harder, and then her neck and then her collarbone and then… stop it, stop it, *stop it*. And now they were there, entwined on the sofa, naked bodies pressed together. And I was here, on my hands and knees underneath their table having just tried to rob them of their leftovers in broad fridge-light. I had to get out of here. I could just see the archway leading to the hall; if I was quick I could make it back to the box room and deny being awake in the night at all costs. Slowly, on my hands and knees, I began to crawl in the direction of the arch. Suddenly the room filled with light and I stopped still, looking up into the face of my puzzled ex-boyfriend once again.

'Jess?' Sam gazed down at me in his girlfriend's slinky pyjamas. Kill me, kill me right now. 'What are you doing?' he asked, rubbing a hand to his sleepy disbelieving eyes.

'I, erm… got hungry.'

'So, you decided to lick the floor?'

Slowly I unfolded myself to stand, dreading having to face Jamie in her own slinky pyjamas or worse, even less. I looked over to the sofa; there was no one there, only a messy set of sheets and a single set of pillows. 'No I… I didn't think you'd be in here,' I said. 'Where's Jamie?'

'She's in her room,' Sam responded, his voice in a whisper, his hair all fluffy and cute.

'Her room?' I asked.

'Jess, I— about earlier…' he said, still in a whisper, eyes darting to the archway into the room to double-check Jamie wasn't about to appear. Was he finally about to explain what he couldn't bring himself to say when he had first brought me back here? *Why* he brought me back here? I looked again at Sam's single set of sheets. Now I wanted this explanation even more.

'Jess, yesterday when I saw you…' Sam followed my distracted gaze to the sheets and then looked back at me, allowing his sleepy eyes to drift down to where Jamie's silk cami was slightly puckering over my chest, his cheeks pinkening as he took another step towards me, like a sleep-drunk moth dreaming towards a flame.

'Jess, you look…' A smile circled the corner of Sam's mouth as all talk of yesterday, and explanations and Jamie melted away, his gaze on mine. But I didn't want to melt, not now. I wanted to know why Jamie wasn't nestled up right next to him.

'Isn't her room your room?' I asked in confusion, smoothing down my pyjamas, forcing Sam's heavy eyes back to my face and breaking the spell of whatever lingered between us.

'It's a long story,' Sam replied, now moving past me and towards the kitchen cupboards. I looked again at the sofa where Sam had been sleeping alone, confusion rising along with a glimmer of hope. Maybe I had got this all wrong after all?

'Well,' I said with a dramatic pause. 'We've got *nothing* but time.'

'Jess, it's three o'clock in the morning,' Sam sighed, eyes lingering on the lace of my top once more before shaking his head. 'Go to bed.' He turned around to thrust a tube of original Pringles into my hand. Finally, a result I was after. 'I'll explain in the morning.'

*

9 December 2017 – London, England

'… over and over and expecting a different result…' Zoe shouted the definition of insanity across the table before trudging the sticky venue floor to slide into the equally sticky booth beside me. It was kind of ironic, given that I was also stuck – not to mention a little bit insane. I looked up from my phone, barely registering my best friend trying to shake me free.

'He's there with someone. I know he is, if I can just…' My sentence evaporated at the intensity of her stare. I held up my screen displaying a photo of Sam and Austin, suited and booted with berry-red flowers in their buttonholes. Thankfully, his caption made clear it wasn't his shotgun wedding. That and the traditional church pews behind him. Sam had never wanted to get married in a church. He'd told me, around the time he told me that he wanted to get married to me. What the post didn't make clear was who owned the cut-off arms slung around Sam and Austin's shoulders from either side, cropped for the very tiny square that seemed like such a bloody great big deal to me.

'Jess, you need to stop this now.' Zoe held my gaze, eyes wide with empathy. I knew she wanted her friend back, but all I wanted was Sam. My best friend, my future. Zoe placed a steady hand on my shaking arm. 'Everyone else has moved on.' She looked down at the two faces we had once spent every moment with. 'Can't you see that no amount of watching his stories is going to change yours?' I hated to admit it, but I knew she had a point.

'It's just so hard though,' I argued, as I surrendered my phone to Zoe, desperately in need of a detox. I took another sip of my vodka and Coke.

'No one said break-ups were easy.' Zoe held my arm a little tighter.

'Sam seems to be doing okay.' I nodded to the phone in her hands, not letting myself think the worst thought of all: *this could be the last time I see him.*

'Yeah, on Instagram,' Zoe scoffed, always knowing how to make me feel better. 'Trust me, Jess, there's no one way of handling a break-up. I think we all just muddle our way through.' Easy for her to say; she'd never been in love. She didn't even want to be.

'But what if he's with someone else?'

'He might be for a time, and then he might not.' She shrugged, casting one last look down at Austin and Sam, both friends of hers she used to know so well. 'Some relationships are just meant for a moment, others are meant to be for forever.' She smiled. 'And somehow, some way, those ones find their way back together again.'

Chapter Six

2 August 2020 – Sydney, Australia

Pots and pans clashed and the smell of pancakes wafted in as I roused myself from sleep. Sam's pancakes. Sam's explanation. I'd had about two hours' sleep but felt wired, my mind oscillating through the various explanations Sam and Jamie could have for not sleeping in the same room. They were having a fight, one of them was sick, they weren't really a couple – just really close friends who kissed on the mouth. Stranger things had happened. My being here, Exhibit A.

I rolled over to face the empty pillow beside me. Or they're breaking up – it made more sense after yesterday. What kind of man bumps into his ex-girlfriend and invites her to stay with him and his current girlfriend unless he wants to put the final nail in the coffin? Or nail something else completely. All that 'Bub' and 'Bubby' bullshit, the overenthusiastic way she welcomed me, the photo of the two of them territorially displayed on the bedside. Is that why Sam didn't tell me? Why he couldn't possibly explain with her in the same room? It would make sense of the awkwardness, the momentary tensions, Jamie's attempts to be so kind – to both of us – as they sorted out the logistics they needed to finally move out, move on.

I reached out to the frame sitting on the table and tilted the happy couple face down. *But why should I care?* I felt Zoe's presence reverberate from her unread messages side-swiped on my phone. Why should I care whether Sam was single, after all this time? I shouldn't. *Everyone else has moved on*; I remembered Zoe's words from the last time we had looked at his social media together then blocked him together – back when the two of us used to do everything together. Everyone else had moved on. I had come to Sydney to do the same. I was moving on, I *would* move on. I wouldn't hang around long enough for Sam to reject me; not this time.

Slinking out of bed for the second time that morning, I stepped over to gaze in the full-length mirror. Still pale as snow, but traipsing around Coogee's undulating streets for weeks had done wonders to my legs. I smoothed down my bed-hair, straight and brown, nothing like Jamie's sun-kissed locks. Mascara stains removed, skin Clinique-d, my unmade face showed no trace of the shitter-than-shit day I'd had yesterday. Taking a deep breath, I pushed open the door and followed the smell of pancakes all the way to the kitchenette.

'Morning,' I said, a little too seductively as I turned the corner, part of me still longing to create final memories more flattering than the ones Sam and I currently shared. Not one but two flawless females looked up at me with surprise, caught in the middle of a conversation they clearly didn't want me to hear. The stranger narrowed her striking blue eyes for a moment before smiling. Pushing brown waves from her perfectly proportioned features, she turned towards Jamie, whose own fresh face made mine feel weathered in comparison.

'Morning, Jess!' Jamie stood on ceremony, more than a little on edge. 'This is Alice.' She gestured towards her friend, now leaning her slender elbows on the table I had hidden under only hours before. 'She's a doctor too,' Jamie added, as if I wasn't intimidated enough. Alice held her smile: a severe case of the gorgeous-doctor epidemic. 'Did you sleep well?' Jamie asked, a smirk dancing around her bee-stung pout as she shot a look to Alice.

'Yes thanks, I was… very, silky.' I hesitated, unable to gauge the room.

'And hungry?' She stifled a laugh, as her friend did the same and I tried not to blush, shame filling my stomach. 'Sam told me he caught you heading for a little snack.'

'Yeah, he—' I began, all of a sudden confused. Confused about their sleeping arrangements and that she didn't mind me knowing. Surely, whatever reason they had for that was private. Unless she was getting over it now? Ready to finally move on herself?

'I'm so sorry we didn't get a chance to give you a proper meal before you went to bed.'

'Oh no, don't worry. I was so tired,' I said, trying to read Jamie's expression. What had she and this Alice girl just been saying about me? About Sam? About both of us?

'Yeah, I figured. That's why I let you sleep this morning. We went for a quick run, but I thought you'd rather the lie-in. Maybe tomorrow?' she asked, looking me up and down as I tried to subtly hold in my stomach; something told me I wasn't up to scratch.

'Yeah, maybe.' *Maybe when Elle Macpherson wants to lend me 'The Body'.*

Alice nodded in my direction, entirely unfussed, as I tried not to clock how different I'd look post-run. They were dressed head to toe in Lycra, not a single drop of sweat between them – just like Jamie had arrived home yesterday, back when I thought I was the only ex-girlfriend in the room. Would she tell me what was going on with her and Sam if I asked? I had so few answers, so many questions.

'Pancakes?' Jamie asked me, sliding a perfectly circular one onto a plate to complete the stack.

'Is the Pope a Catholic?' I smiled, taking a seat and searching the room for sight of Sam. Jamie must have caught me looking as she smiled, handed me the short stack, answering my unspoken question, a brief moment of sadness flashing across her face before she recovered her smile once again. 'He's already gone to the surgery.'

'The surgery?' I looked from the pancakes to her.

'You know, for work,' Jamie replied, smile still pinned to her annoyingly attractive face.

'No, it's just, Sam said he'd rather die on the hospital floor' – bad choice of words – 'than work in general practice.' He had loved the pace, the prestige and the drive of working in a hospital – mostly because it made him feel like House.

'Things change.' Jamie shrugged. Yes, things did change – but to what? My mouth hung open, wanting to ask but knowing that all my questions were meant for Sam. He'd brought me back here for a reason and my guess was that these 'changes' had something to do with it. After all, *things* changed but people didn't. And I was still the same girl he fell in love with.

'Anyway, he finishes at six and then we thought we'd go out for dinner.' Dinner? If they were on the rocks they were handling it better than Sam and I ever did. But I couldn't do dinner with the two of them – not yesterday, not today – not until I worked out what the hell was going on – in their lives and in mine.

'So, you're not at work today?' I asked, looking from Jamie to Alice, hoping they'd be disappearing soon. I needed to find a job, *any* job, and get myself some accommodation without them finding out I'd lied. An improbable task made all the more impossible by Jamie lounging around.

'She's not, but I am.' Alice pushed back her empty plate and stood to go, her legs all Bambi in width, Amazonian in length.

'Dinner later?' Jamie asked Alice, sitting down across from me, a stack of pancakes piled high – surely she wasn't going to eat that. So this dinner was a group vibe, a doctor vibe? Maybe Joshua would be there too? Not that anyone had said he was a doctor. I just assumed. I guess I had assumed a lot of things.

'Sorry, plans.' Alice didn't sound sorry at all, reaching for her gym bag before heading towards the door, managing to exude coolness without lacking warmth.

'No worries, I'll invite someone else,' Jamie said, taking another bite. Alice rolled her eyes before locking them on me.

'Seriously, Jess, don't let her set you up with anyone. This girl needs to learn that singleness isn't an illness to be cured,' she said to me, every word meant for Jamie, their playful openness laced with a hint of sincerity. Was Alice the break-up support that Zoe had been to me? Before I used up my credit. I gulped like the gooseberry they so clearly thought I was as Alice turned to exit the room and Jamie's phone buzzed to life.

'Sorry.' She mouthed an apology my way as she picked up the call. From the other side of the room I could hear clipped parts of her one-sided conversation.

'Calm down… it will be okay… I'm off work today… we could grab a coffee… take a breather.'

I took another bite. Who was she talking to? Was this her *new* boyfriend? My stomach tumbled with something like hope. Hanging up the call, she said, 'Sorry about that. That's our friend Tim. He's a curator, puts on exhibitions in galleries…' Yes, I know what a curator is, Jamie. 'He's putting on an exhibition at CreateSpace, they kind of host travelling exhibitions and pop-ups and stuff…' *Yes*, I know what CreateSpace is, Jamie. I smiled through gritted teeth. After years of sifting through the archives of *Art Today*, booking in the editor-in-chief's Skype calls so she could hobnob and leech off the other editors around the world, even the Sydney galleries were on my radar. And to be fair, CreateSpace managed to punch above its weight. It was such a cool space, all red-brick and high ceilings and known for hosting some of the best up-and-coming talent – up-and-coming talent our editor-in-chief would get wind of, feature first and pass off as her own. And why would anyone argue with her? As far as art scenes go, London was notorious and Sydney couldn't help but feel a little out of the loop. Back when I was painting, the only scene I cared about was the one in front of me. Sadly, the industry didn't feel the same.

'But he's struggling, you know?'

I nodded, even though I didn't know. After months and months of not being listened to at work, I'd elected to let the details wash over me. It was hard to be in the loop when it was clear people didn't want you in it.

'He and his partner – professional *and* personal – they broke up,' Jamie went on, as I searched her face for any flinches at the b-word. 'And now he's grappling to make the exhibition work alone,' she looked genuinely worried for her friend. Her kindness prompted the same sinking feeling: *man, I'm such a bitch.* The woman was living with a maybe-ex or almost-ex and she still seemed more concerned about her friend's break-up. Clearly, she was a saint.

'Can't he just advertise for an assistant?' I asked, looking far too interested in my pancakes.

'He did.' Jamie sighed, taking a bite of her own. 'Put an ad out for one ages ago but it's just a bad time of year for it, I guess?'

I looked up from my breakfast to catch Jamie shrug and took another bite in attempt to bite my tongue. It wasn't like I could apply. As far as Jamie was concerned I already had a job. Not that I would be qualified, anyway. Working for an art magazine had ironically meant I hadn't set foot in an actual gallery in years.

'He'll be fine. He's just stressed.' She changed tack, returning the topic to me. 'Anyway, tell me about *Art Today Australia*,' Jamie encouraged. There really wasn't much to say. Nothing in fact – not as far as my working there went. I put down my fork, suddenly less hungry. 'You're a painter, aren't you?'

'Used to be,' I corrected a little too quickly.

'We have your painting in our room,' she continued. *Your* room, I thought; Sam called it *your* room. 'It's a pity you have a job lined up; you'd be perfect for this CreateSpace role.'

If I didn't know any better I'd think she was mocking me.

'Yeah, it's a shame,' I said, all appetite now evaporated in the awkwardness. I didn't want to work there, but it was a job. And that was more than I had right now. I really needed a job.

'Sam mentioned you have two weeks before you start.' Jamie's eyes searched my face. It was her turn to look a little awkward. So Sam had managed to fill her in but I was still none the wiser? I wonder what else he had said about me. 'You don't think you could just…' Her sentence trailed off as I filled in the blanks. Jamie was asking for my help.

But I couldn't, could I? I had a job at *Art Today Australia*, apparently. Wouldn't working at CreateSpace be a little too close to home? I looked into Jamie's desperate eyes and tasted the irony. This was all a little close to home.

'Never mind.' Jamie shook her head, thinking she was asking too much which, given that I was currently sleeping in her spare room, seemed a little rich. But what else could I do? I had told them I had a job and it wasn't like I'd be any help to this Tim guy, either. 'I'm sure you could do with a bit of space before starting at *Art Today*.' She beamed. A little space seemed exactly what we all needed. Not that any of us were going to get that here. I needed to get a job, a proper job, a permanent job, to actually start living my lie.

'Yeah, I'd best get over to the office actually,' I said, placing my knife and fork together and thanking Jamie for the food. I needed to get out of here. The sooner I could get a job, gather a deposit and be on my way, the better. Sam and Jamie's break-up was none of my concern, I tried to convince myself again and again.

'But I thought you didn't start for two weeks?' Jamie asked.

Oh shit, that's right. That's what I had said, what Sam had said. What *she* had just said.

'That's right,' I said, thinking on my feet. 'I just need to pop down this morning to iron out the details.'

Details such as the fact that I wouldn't be working there at all.

'Well, when you're done you can join Tim and me for coffee.' Jamie looked hopeful and for a moment I felt even worse; she was trying to be my friend. 'He just needs a bit of support, you know how hard break-ups can be.' A sadness caught in Jamie's smile. 'Plus, I try to get by with the art chat but he'll love being around the real deal.' She smiled again as I gave her my excuses and shame filled my stomach; right now, it felt like there was nothing real about me.

*

6 November 2018 – London, England

Gazing blindly at my photocopies, I tried to ignore the loud heckles echoing from the other side of the office. A gaggle of women had started to gather around my colleague's monitor, each one pristine in Prada and with more money than sense. I knew better than to go over there. There was only so many times you could be told 'for editorial eyes only' without punching someone in their editorial eye.

'Oh my *God*,' I heard one of them cackle over her computer.

Whether it was a press release about a new sale, images of the Tate's latest curation or a 'there's celery *and* dips in the communal area to celebrate my big five-oh' email, I knew it wasn't anything my simple PA brain could handle. This time I had a horrible feeling they were laughing at an email from me. Once again I had passed on some suggestions for strengthening this month's issue and once again I had been ignored. Seeing them all gathered round and sniggering at the screen made me nostalgic for their silence. Maybe now was the time to stop trying to be heard. I plugged my headphones in to drown out their noise.

I checked the time – quarter to twelve – before returning the Post-it covering my computer clock. It was meant to make the day go quicker. How was it not lunchtime yet? Screw it. I reached into my bag and grasped the Tupperware, cursing the fact that I was now the kind of girl that owned Tupperware. I unclicked the lid: celery *and* dips. Well, if you can't beat them… I crunched down on the tasteless stalk. Kill me now. It was Zoe who suggested I start to eat better. Zoe, who I'd watched eat three Happy Meals back-to-back on more than one occasion. She'd read that a clean diet could improve your mood. And, well, mine had been sporadic at best since the break-up, maybe even since moving to London. I looked across at them, still laughing and joking, covering their sniggering mouths with hands heavy with diamond wedding bands. I looked down at my own bare, celery-clutching hand before I saw an email from Devon Atwood, *Lady* Devon Atwood, editor-in-chief of *Art Today* ping into my inbox. I had emailed her my comments on the latest issue too, suggesting an unknown artist for our 'ones to watch' slot.

I clicked open the email.

Editors. Now.

Why she couldn't just email them directly was beyond me. But that was Devon – once an inspiration but after years in the industry, now just an imitation. I knew better than to think she'd give my suggestion a look-in; the layered abstract brushstrokes were far too original, the artist far too anonymous to warrant occupying the pages of her magazine. I took one last wistful look at the print-out pinned beside my monitor, savouring the artist's blue – a hue so deep and unique that I'd never seen it before and doubted I'd see again. Certainly not in the pages of Devon's magazine, anyway. And here I was, thinking *Art Today* would actually care about art. Striding across the room to gather her editors, I said, 'Devon needs you in the—'

'Midday meeting. Same as every Tuesday. We know.' Mary-Anne, features editor and leader of the tribe closed down the window before I could see. Well, if they knew, why did I have to bloody come and get them every time? Reluctant to follow any instructions, never mind mine, the ladies dragged their heels as they followed me across the office.

'Sit,' Devon demanded. Her editors obeyed as I followed suit, parking myself a little behind, poised to take the minutes. 'I want to look at the February issue again. Something's not quite right.' I didn't need to write that down; it was the same as always.

'But we've already sent the magazine to print,' Mary-Anne rebutted. More fool her – but she had a point. Devon returned her best Hitler impression. No 'tache though – I should know; I booked her hair removal appointment last week. 'But we can call them up and halt the print run,' she recovered. 'Can you put your finger on what's troubling you? Which section?'

The Modigliani feature needed more personal reflection. The main editorial wanted more text-free images. Oh and, the '5 minutes with Maria Le Fenora' was trying too hard to be witty – she just wasn't funny. I looked at Devon, willing her to recall my email, though I was sure she hadn't even opened it. Devon watched as one of her minions flicked through the mocked-up pages of the issue, print-outs from our competitors splayed across her desk. There was once a time, years ago, when Devon had had a vision of her own but decades of criticism and comparison had undoubtedly taken their toll. The rest of us watched her expression with bated breath. The spreads pressed on. Good, good, good – Modigliani feature. Right on cue, Devon held out a hand to halt the turning pages. The silence thickened as she moved her face further forward and fingered the print-out, comparing the copy to a similar feature from the art pages of *Vogue Australia*.

'More images?' the art director questioned even though the gallery stock photographs dominated the page. Devon didn't even bother to shake her head.

'The piece could do with more history, explanation of the rich heritage the artist—'

Devon raised a hand and I shuddered. Personal reflection; the piece needed more personal reflection. We didn't pay that journalist to regurgitate Wikipedia, for Christ's sake.

'What does he think?' Devon asked, eyes darting again to the other examples around her.

'He likes it,' Mary-Anne said, a hopeful smile pinned to her pretty face. She had more chance of convincing me that celery and dips were a treat.

'Where does he say that? There's no opinion. No reflection.' Devon picked up the sheets to thrust them in her face. Hate to say I told you so.

'This is why I have to call these meetings,' Devon continued, now in full flow. 'I can't trust any of you to spot such simple things.'

I could. I can. Just check your inbox, it's all there.

'I did.' The words were out of my mouth before I could stop them. Instantly, everyone at the table turned around. Steely eyes looked me up and down. For a split second, I missed being invisible.

'Jessica.' Devon said my name like a threat. 'Please don't interrupt.' She scribbled the notes I had noticed onto the page and sighed. 'Next.'

I stared on, silencing my anger, my mind drifting back to Freshers' Week where we had all arrived, young and ambitious, knowing we were going to do something great, were going to *be* something great.

'Next.' Devon waved a hand again. The sheets before us moved on, displaying something new as I desperately longed for something new myself.

Chapter Seven

2 August 2020 – Sydney, Australia

I could do this. I could *do* this. I looked up at the iconic *Art Today* plaque above the doorbell, the same one that had stared down at me as I cleared all my things from the UK office. I never thought I'd come face to face with it only weeks later, thousands of miles away.

Though I guess it wasn't the most unlikely face-off I'd had over the last twenty-four hours. It hadn't taken me long after talking with Jamie to decide that I was actually going to head to their offices and ask if there were any jobs going – after all, it wasn't like I got fired from my last one. I might actually be able to make this lie come true before anyone realised it was a lie in the first place. And for once, I wanted to do what I said I was going to do.

So what if I didn't *love* my job at *Art Today*? Things could be different here. I needed things to be different here. I reached my hand to the doorbell and buzzed. A muffled voice crackled through the intercom, 'Yes?' The clipped and uninterested tone must be mandatory across the globe.

'I'm here for Hannah Sommers,' I said, before I could fully register the insanity of what I was saying. Hannah Sommers, editor-in-chief of the magazine, was notorious – if Devon hadn't spent so long obsessing over what she was doing and turned her attention to our own financial situation I might still have my job. There was no way she was going to have time for me, but I had to try. I had told Sam and Jamie I had a job here.

'Do you have an appointment?' The voice on the end of the line crackled.

'No, I was… hoping I could have a quick word with her?' I asked, knowing my hope was as slim as I imagined this receptionist to be.

'You and everyone else, honey,' the voice quipped before the line went dead. *Crap.* I turned to walk away from the imposing doors, knowing there was no second chance, knowing that I'd have to spend my afternoon looking for whatever menial labour this city had to offer. I sat on the nearest bench and rested my head in my hands. Maybe it was time to go home? Finally face the onslaught of questions as to why my Sydney dream had stalled? I took out my phone, clutching it in my hands, the messages from Zoe still demanding a reply. *Not yet, not until I've sorted this mess out.* Reaching into my bag, I pulled out my folded CV and studied its scanty lines. There was once a time when everyone's CV boasted the same – the only difference being what GSCEs or A-levels we had anguished over. I dreaded to think how mine would compare to some of my classmates' now. As I looked out into the swarms of strangers walking by, their figures blurred into a colourful hue of activity until my eyes locked on a figure more familiar than most. It was Sam's friend, the one I'd thought was his housemate, the one I'd thought I would drunkenly hit on before I realised his real housemate wasn't quite my type. I couldn't help but take one last look at his ripped jeans, oversized T-shirt and the slight dimples etched in his cheeks, before looking away. But before I could, my eyes caught his and I knew it was too late. He was coming over.

'Jess?' He tilted his head, walking closer still. 'It's Jess, isn't it?' he asked again. I nodded as he came to sit down on the bench beside me. 'It's Joshua.' He smiled to reveal a set of straight, white teeth. I knew who he was; I just didn't imagine he'd remember me. I hoped to God I looked different from when he had first seen me at Sam's – *correction, Sam and Jamie's.* I looked down at the papers in my hand and wondered how to stash my CV away before Joshua could see it; too late again.

'Job hunt?'

Yes, for a job I told your friends I had.

'Just firming up some things with my new boss,' I said, even though his kind eyes made me want to spill my whole sorry story. Joshua looked down at the papers before locking his gaze back on me, brow furrowed as he tried to make sense of why my employer would want to see my CV after already offering me a job. Now it was his turn to shake his head. I could tell he didn't believe me but couldn't help but smile all the same.

'Yeah, Sam mentioned that you were starting in a couple of weeks.' He grinned, making his dimples even deeper. Who had Sam not told about that? The fact he was telling so many people about me had to mean something. My eyes darted from Joshua's unwavering smile to his brown collarbone as I wondered what else Sam had shared about me.

'Firming or firmed?'

'Huh?' I tried to hide my startled expression, tired of being caught in the act.

'As in, are you going or have you been?' he continued. 'To see your boss?' Oh right, yeah.

'Been,' I assured him, smoothing down my crisp white shirt, all of a sudden overdressed against Joshua's laid-back Sydney attire. He looked every bit as cool as his photo, that *damn* misleading photo.

'Sweet.' Joshua smiled again; it really was a lovely smile. I tucked my CV away, attempting to strike the balance between protecting its edges and my feigned nonchalance.

'Just chilling this afternoon?' Joshua pressed on, in no rush to get anywhere. I looked out across the magnitude of people, all with somewhere to be, and nodded.

'Just chilling.' I smiled, wondering how far I'd have to commute for a barista job that was nowhere near anyone I needed to remember to lie to.

'So, you can come to lunch?' Joshua said, rising to his feet. It wasn't like I could say I had plans after just telling him I didn't.

'With you?' I gazed up at him, dumbfounded. Why would he want to go to lunch with me?

'No, with Barack Obama.' Joshua laughed. So Australians could do sarcasm, too. 'Yes, with me.' He smiled again. 'Unless you'd still rather I was Jamie?' He laughed at the memory, at the crazy English girl mistaking him for a cold hard stunner. Yes, I wished he was Jamie. Things would be so much simpler if he was Jamie. And Sam was just Sam.

'And Sam,' Joshua added, as if he had just read my mind. I looked into his piercing blue eyes again, scared by how much they seemed to see. 'I'm heading over to meet him in Woolloomooloo now,' he continued. Sam never used to get lunch, he never used to have the time. But then again, he never used to work in a surgery. He never used to live in Sydney. Jamie was right; things did change, some things at least.

'Woolloo-what?' I spluttered before I could stop myself. Joshua laughed loudly, placing a sun-kissed hand to his forehead in feigned despair.

'It's across town.' Joshua smiled again, his eyes brighter in the midday light; the rest of Sydney remained grey.

'Won't he be a bit surprised I'm there?' I asked. How the hell was I going to get a job by sitting around eating pancakes and going out for lunch all the time?

'Not as surprised as yesterday.' Joshua said, eyebrows raised. 'In a good way, obviously,' he added.

Joshua beckoned to me to follow, back towards Sam. Maybe it was more obvious than I dared let myself think.

Chapter Eight

'Jess.' Sam's eyes widened in surprise. 'What the—' he began, looking from Joshua to me with something like suspicion as we approached the tiny café they had chosen for lunch. The light grey awning highlighted the casual suit Sam had chosen to wear for work. He wore his shirt collar open and looked better here, more chilled, at ease.

'Look who I found loitering around *Art*—' Joshua seemed to stop himself upon seeing my stare, desperate for him not to paint me on the wrong side of their offices. I held his gaze, not sure how he could possibly know the truth about me, but sure he could see it, somehow.

'And I thought Jess could join us for lunch, give you guys some time to catch up.' Joshua explained as I looked across at Sam's baffled expression, trying to work out what he was thinking. We already had time to catch up. Ample. I was staying at his. Unless he meant without Jamie? There had been so much he wanted to tell me. I looked from Sam to Joshua, unsure as to whether Sam was going to tell me here.

'Perfect,' Sam said, forcing a smile. Clearly, now wasn't the time. He began to lead the way to our table, pulling out a chair for me as I tried not to look confused by his chivalry. He was either overcompensating for the situation or trying to impress me all over again. Joshua sat beside me. I looked around the intimate space, the bright flowers blooming against its exposed brick backdrop, a beauty in the brokenness I couldn't even hope to achieve.

'How's your morning been, mate?' Joshua beamed at Sam. I looked between them, Sam in his suit, Joshua in his worn T-shirt. It was as if the two sides of Sam had finally stopped wrestling, taking up residence in two separate bodies.

'Yeah, good.' Sam pretty much dismissed the comment, turning his attention to me.

'How's your morning been? Jamie said you'd headed over to the magazine?'

They couldn't stomach sleeping in the same room but maintained a constant stream of messages? I cast aside the thought. Sam would tell me everything, I was sure of it – just as soon as he had the chance.

'Yeah, good.' I matched Sam's short replies, neither one of us wanting to give much away. 'I'd say Joshua's had the best morning of all.' I looked down at his casual attire with a playful smile. Clearly, he wasn't stuck in a surgery or an office. 'What is it you do again?'

'I'm a youth worker,' he replied, his giddy smile clearly indicating that he thought it was the best job in the world. Before he could tell me more, the waiter interrupted. 'Flat white and a club sandwich for me, please,' Joshua said, as I picked up the menu I hadn't managed to look at yet.

'A youth worker?' I asked, Joshua clearly impressed by my interest.

'Another flat white please and can I have the quinoa salad?' Sam ordered, his sentence cutting through Joshua's attempt to reply. In all the years I'd known him he'd never ordered a salad. I forced my attention back to my menu.

'Iced latte and a bacon and avocado sub,' Sam said to the waiter, smiling at me. 'That's what you want, right?' he checked, already knowing the answer.

'Yes,' I said, not sure why Sam looked so proud. 'So, Joshua.' I redirected my attention, still not knowing if Sam was on the menu. 'What does a youth worker do?'

'A youth worker? Well, we work with youth,' he replied, grin unwavering. I laughed out loud, taking a sip of the iced water on the table in front of me.

'No, but seriously,' I said, laughing into my glass. Out of the corner of my eye, I could sense Sam's eyes on me. 'Like, what does a normal day look like for you?'

'Usually a lot of milkshakes with young people who are struggling with school or life outside of it,' he went on, proud but not boastful.

'Like mentoring?' I asked, not wanting to sound so dumb but distracted somehow by Sam's awkward body language, shuffling and stiffening across from me.

'Exactly like mentoring…' He laughed and I couldn't help but be invited in.

'How's Zoe?' Sam's voice cut through our conversation.

'Oh, erm,' I stuttered, not quite sure where the question had come from. Joshua looked down at his lunch, seemingly shrugging off the conversation's change in direction; something told me he wasn't easily ruffled. I took a bite of my sandwich as I studied Sam's expression.

'She's great,' I replied, unsure as to why Sam wanted to steer the conversation away from Sydney and back to our past. If I didn't know any better, I'd say he was jealous. 'Great,' I repeated. At least I thought she was; we hadn't talked since last week and even then, I had painted her a picture much prettier than my current reality.

'Still partying her way across London?' Sam joked.

'No, actually. She's all settled down with Ben, bought a house just outside the city.' I smiled, willing my own envy not to escape through the words.

'You're kidding?' Sam laughed, Joshua's attention fully on his own lunch now that Sam had eaten into our conversation.

'Nope.' Although a small part of me wished I was. I was happy for her, obviously. I just kind of wished she was happy here with me, still making memories, out on some misadventure. Like we always said we would before she started to change and I remained the same.

'Wow,' Sam said. 'I always knew she'd get there.' His eyes caught mine. *We thought we'd get there too. Now I don't even have a map.* 'Remember when she always talked about travelling here?' Sam continued. I did. A little too vividly. 'I actually thought I saw her last August but knew it wasn't the right time.'

'Right time?' I asked, unsure as to what that would be but somehow knowing my own arrival had missed it.

'The Brit window,' Joshua interjected, re-joining the conversation. I remained distinctly none the wiser.

'The travellers tend to turn up around November time,' Sam said, 'in the lead-up to summer.'

'That's when all the jobs are around,' Joshua chipped in, looking at me in earnest.

'You'll see the odd one wandering round with a rucksack in August,' Sam said, his tone playful, eyebrow raised. 'But all the bars and restaurants will be on shut-down waiting for work to pick back up.' I took another bite of my sandwich, the chances of me getting work the only thing getting slimmer. 'No one even tries looking,' he continued, my mind recalling Jamie's phone conversation with Tim and his position still unfilled. 'Thank God you had a proper job to come to.' The final kick.

'Jamie!' Joshua exclaimed before I could think of a suitable response. *No, I'm Jess*, my mind couldn't help but object after all the mistaken identities of the last twenty-four hours, before I saw Jamie across the café, coming over to meet us. Out of the corner of my eye, I studied Sam's expression, trying to work out if he was happy, sad or indifferent to see her. Whether his eyes lit up the way they had when he saw me. Joshua's reaction was easier to gauge as he rose to kiss her on both cheeks. Gone were her leggings and in their place a pair of spray-on blue jeans leaving little to the imagination, her light grey shirt matching Sam's suit to a T. My eyes flicked between them, my mind trying to put two and two together and still coming up short. Sam looked uncomfortable, just like he had when she had arrived home yesterday.

'Sit down, Jamie.' Joshua's face lit up as he pulled out the empty seat at our table. If they were breaking up, she was handling it all far better than I would.

'She can't,' Sam said, almost defensively. Jamie looked stung by his response. For a moment, I was almost sure he wanted me to himself.

'I can't,' Jamie repeated, not even looking at Sam as she shook her pretty head, her loose ponytail bouncing behind her. I could only imagine how hard it must be to live with someone you used to love. 'I'm just on my way to meet Tim at CreateSpace. Couldn't not say hey when you're just next door, could I?' she added. Well, she could. I shuffled in my seat, looking down at my fork. I'd told her I was busy. I'd told her I couldn't make it. I looked up again to Sam, catching his eye, unable to read his expression.

'How is he?' Sam asked, concerned.

'Been better.' She shrugged. 'But you know what he's like.' She smiled back at him, sadness emanating through her words as I remembered Zoe saying: *no one said break-ups were easy. I think we all just muddle our way through.*

'But he's screwed without Carlo, right?' Sam asked, as Jamie shook away his insensitivity.

'He's not *screwed*,' Jamie objected. 'He's just, you know, hurting a little…' I looked between them and wondered whether Jamie was feeling the same. 'I'm just going to give him some free therapy now actually; CreateSpace is proving *hard*.' That job. That stupid job. Seemingly the only one going this side of summer. 'He just needs a spare pair of hands to help him out while he gets through the worst of the break-up,' Jamie continued pointedly. Sam looked saddened by her words. I couldn't help but feel the same, feeling awful for Tim, feeling awful for her.

'Do I know him?' Joshua looked from Sam to Jamie in confusion.

'No, but you can join us if you like?' Jamie's answer was filled with affection, Joshua clinging to her every word.

'No, no,' Joshua said. 'I've got to dash after this, maybe some other time?'

Jamie rolled her eyes playfully before checking her phone and gathering up her things.

'Jess, maybe you could…' Sam fixed his eyes on me before thinking better of it.

'What?' I asked, even though I knew what he was about to say.

'You couldn't just help Tim out for a bit, could you?'

'I'm not sure I'd be that much help.' I looked between their three imploring faces.

'Are you kidding me?' Sam laughed. 'You'd be brilliant.' And despite my trepidation, I couldn't help but glow at Sam's public vote of confidence. But I thought he'd said he wanted to spend a bit of time together before I started my job?

'Plus, it's so near my work, we can…' His sentence trailed off again as if he'd only just remembered Jamie was still in the room. I looked between them now, stuck between a rock and a hard place. I didn't want to work in a gallery, not any more. But it would buy me some time and all I needed was a bit more time. Plus, it wouldn't hurt to do Jamie a favour after she'd been so kind to me. And then there was the fact that I'd be spending the next two weeks working just across from Sam.

'Jamie,' I said, 'can I still come with you?'

Chapter Nine

Jamie and I navigated the two busy streets between the café and CreateSpace, until the crowds started to peter out. Several onlookers openly stared as Jamie sauntered past. She didn't seem to notice, too intent on asking me how my morning had been, what I thought of Sydney, what I thought of bumping into Joshua before lunch. As if that was the most shocking run-in I'd had all year. My answers ranged between one word and two, not wanting to tie myself in more knots than I already had. Still, she persisted. She was either the nicest woman I had ever met, or the most strategic cold-hearted bitch to ever walk the planet. It was too soon to tell. A small part of me hoped she wouldn't be around long enough for me to find out, a part of me that with every passing nicety made me feel like there was definitely one cold-hearted bitch between us. Despite being the one thing we had in common, any talk of Sam was minimal. And I couldn't blame her. I wouldn't want to talk about the fact that my soon-to-be ex-boyfriend was sleeping on the sofa either. Jamie talked on and on, slowing to a halt only to look up at the red-brick building before us.

I had seen photos of CreateSpace in *Art Today* from time to time, but the reality of it before me was breathtaking: an empty shell of enormous rooms waiting to be hired out by curators. True to its name, the space itself was a blank canvas to be drawn upon, but perhaps due to its cool urban structure, the art held within it was almost *always* contemporary. It seemed to have none of the ponce of the art world I had known, its walls brimming with artists who cared more about the impact of their work than their fame.

'You'll love it here,' Jamie said, taking off her sunglasses to gaze up at the broad latticed windows. 'It's every artist's dream.'

I used to dream of exhibiting in galleries across the globe, back when I was a fresher, immersed in colour and hope. But I wished she'd stop calling me an 'artist'. I'd already told her I hadn't painted in years. Not since university. Not since I'd finished the painting that now hung on her wall, or Sam's wall, *whatever.* Before I could object, she had already stepped inside. I followed her into a lobby I had only seen in the pages of magazines and gazed up at the domed ceiling above us. One of three receptionists smiled at Jamie before disappearing to fetch Tim. Above the reception desk was a blank white wall, demanding to be filled.

'Jamie! I know we said coffee, but I need a *drink*,' said a man I could only assume was Tim, as he cast a hand to his lined forehead, desperation in his eyes, before proceeding to stroke his other through his long grey hair down to his well-kept beard. I looked down at my black jeans and white shirt, comparing them with his leather trousers, asymmetrical ripped T-shirt and thick-rimmed glasses. He was so much to look at.

'Well that's what we're here for,' Jamie said as she turned to me. 'This is Jess.' She ushered me to take a step forward but Tim was already striding with purpose towards the door from which he had entered. We followed into a people-free gallery space, with colourful abstract shapes hanging from ceiling to skirting board. Their beauty caught in my throat as we passed them, turning the corner towards a small meeting room in the back. Mismatched furniture filled the room, each piece a work of art in itself. I pulled out a white iron chair, its delicate patterns reminiscent of lace. Tim went to the tall wooden cabinet, gorgeous in its archaism, bending down to retrieve a bottle of bubbles that looked almost as old.

'Oh, Tim, you don't need to do that.' Jamie raised a hand in polite objection. 'We'll be fine with a coffee, won't we, Jess?'

I nodded, mute.

'No, *I* need this,' Tim said dramatically. He filled three flutes, two mid-way, the last one right to the top. Jamie and I accepted the glasses that were half full.

'Bad day?' Jamie asked.

'You have no idea.' Tim took a gulp, shaking the question away but clearly longing to go on.

'Have you heard from him?' Jamie took a cautious sip, seemingly reluctant to lose control. I looked between them, assuming that *him* must be Carlo, Tim's ex-partner.

'Have I, fuck.' Tim rolled his eyes, taking another swig. 'Probably sunning himself in the tropics, laughing into his Long Island about leaving me in the lurch.'

Jamie shifted in her seat as she tried to maintain her smile, clearly not comfortable with conflict. I guess even her brief disagreements with Sam, simmering under her surface, had told me that.

'Could you not just have cancelled the contracts this time, called off the exhibition?' Jamie tried to reason, as I studied the bubbles rising in my glass. Now didn't seem like a great time to ask for a favour. But what choice did I have? Jobs wouldn't be coming up until summer. Sydney was on lock-down. Sam had said so. And both of them *wanted* me to offer; at least I could solve someone's problem whilst trying to solve my own. I guess getting a place like CreateSpace on my CV wouldn't hurt either.

'What? And let Leo Todd, CreateSpace and the Australian public down?' He flung a large hand to his forehead with a flourish. *And let Carlo think I can't do this alone?* I could read between Tim's worry lines, partially because I knew the impress-my-ex routine too well. And did he just say Leo Todd? I searched my mind to place the name before recalling the artist who had started his career as my peer – applying to the same damn competition – before rocketing past my wildest dreams. I looked at Tim, desperately not wanting to work here, but feeling pretty desperate myself.

'The Australian public?' Jamie repeated. 'I know Leo's work is great and all, but I think *the public* will have lots of other things to worry themselves about.' Spoken like a true doctor. I knew those lines well.

'I think Leo's work is great,' I said over the rim of my glass, although no one had asked me. I looked at Tim and held my breath, hoping he wouldn't ask me why or what my favourite piece of Leo's was. Other than his application piece way back when, my jealousy had limited my knowledge of him to the fact that he was a British artist with an *international* flair. Thankfully for me, he had chosen to keep his identity private so I'd never had to see his silly smug face. No doubt wanting 'the public' to give him a backstory better than the truth: he was born posh, privileged and with a London postcode. I'd naively tried to avoid his type even at *Art Today*. Now I wanted to bloody mount his masterpieces. I couldn't think of anything worse – other than, perhaps, Sam finding out what a screw-up I'd lied my way out of being.

'I just need a spare pair of hands, someone to oversee the installation of the pieces, to hold my flipping clipboard, for Christ's sake,' Tim went on, choosing to completely ignore Jamie's suggestions and my attempts to impress him. I sat on one hand, the other shaking as I lifted my glass to my lips, looking for an out, any other way. 'Jesus, I'd even take a day, two, pay cash in hand, offer free booze.'

Jamie looked at me, her wide eyes willing me to bite.

'I could do it,' I said, the words spilling out before I could stop them. What was I doing?

'Could you?' Tim asked, both hands now resting on his beard-framed lips, rimmed eyes widening with glee.

'Oh, Jess, that would be amazing!' Jamie added, beaming from ear to ear.

'Just for a couple of weeks,' I added.

'That's when Jess starts her new job,' Jamie said, obviously thrilled to be helping Tim out. *Please stop*, my eyes willed her to steer clear of the details. But why would she? She had no reason to doubt them. I looked to Tim, taking another gulp of his champagne. Maybe he wouldn't even ask. 'At *Art Today*,' Jamie added, with excitement. Oh crap. I forced myself to smile and nod.

'You're at *Art Today*?' Tim gasped. I remained silent, reluctant to incriminate myself further than I already had. I *was*, I *had* been. For years. If Tim checked with the magazine, I could just laugh away the crossed wires, save my standing in a world I didn't even want to be a part of any more. 'I'll take you for as long as you've got,' he continued, clearly impressed by my magnified credentials. He was so desperate, I'm sure he wouldn't even have cared if he did know the truth. 'Just to tide me over, any time you have to give, really.'

I could say exactly the same. Just for a week or so. Just to tide me over. Then I'd get a real job – 'an offer I couldn't refuse' – and slowly wriggle free of the bind I'd got myself in.

'Great!' Jamie said, a problem-solver just like Sam; at least they had one thing in common.

'Great,' I said with caution.

'Can you start tomorrow?' he asked, although it didn't sound like a question. I mirrored his smile as best I could, nodding. 'Thank you, Jamie-boo,' he near enough sang, rising to his feet to kiss her on both cheeks before turning to leave the room. 'Who needs Carlo?' he muttered as he started to lead us back through the gallery, a spring in his step.

'Thank you,' Jamie said to me, as we followed Tim. She paused by one of the canvases. It was narrow but stretched from floor to ceiling, covered in orange sweeps of every shade broken by jagged black lines stroking every which way: a burning beanstalk beckoning us somewhere magical. 'It's so good of you to use your two weeks off to help Tim out.'

'It's the least I could do,' I said. Despite my better judgement, I felt a little accomplished at having somehow got myself two weeks' worth of work at CreateSpace. My twenty-year-old self would be buzzing. Now, my late-twenties self was just trying to keep up.

'No seriously,' she said. 'It's so good of you to give up your precious time off.' Turned out time wasn't that precious when you had little to fill it with. I studied her profile, testing her tone for hints of sweetness or sarcasm.

'No, no,' I objected, genuine relief at my short-term solution making it harder and harder to hide my gratitude. I might actually be able to sort this all out before Sam found out after all. 'Helping out CreateSpace – it's an honour.' Only a half-truth. 'Thank you for suggesting it.'

'You're so welcome.' She turned away from the painting to me. 'As I said, any friend of Sam's…'

She sure seemed to like Sam, even though they were on the rocks. If we were going through a rough patch *everyone* would know about it. And Sam would be living a nightmare until he bought me flowers, made me dinner and kissed me on the neck and…

'Well, I really appreciate it.' I smiled in return, going to look at the next painting, which was just under a metre wide and a metre high. I studied the fine brushstrokes of the geometric shapes – orange, yellow, red and gold in squares and shards and jagged marks. 'All of it.' I smiled again. She had been so cool about everything, even having me stay in the spare bedroom, in spite of it all. I took a step forward until the painting was all I could see, savouring the unfamiliar safety of immersion, a feeling like a memory I couldn't quite recall. I actually had a job. Temporary, yes. Clipboard-holding, absolutely. But a job in CreateSpace nonetheless. The turn of events made me dizzy. 'It kind of feels like fate bumping into Sam yesterday,' I mused out loud before stopping myself, turning to face Jamie, forgetting for a second she wasn't my friend. For a moment there, it kind of felt like she was. 'Not like romantic fate, just fate, fate,' I backtracked as she looked at me with the same bemused expression Sam had worn the day before.

'I don't really believe in fate,' Jamie said, shaking her ponytail ever so slightly.

'Of course you do.' I shook my own head to less effervescent effect. 'Everybody believes in something.'

'I didn't say I don't believe in anything,' she said, her eyes wide with wonder.

'What do you believe in then?' I asked, my voice echoing around the spacious studio.

'I'm a Christian.' She smiled proudly.

Oh, crap. She even had God on her side.

'You're a what?' I asked, taken aback by the thought. The only practising Christians *I* knew were called Mavis and Doris and had a combined age of one hundred and fifty.

'A Christian,' she repeated, looking equal parts amused and confused. 'Sam didn't tell you?'

I shook my head. Maybe that's why they broke up? Their inability to see eye to eye on the man in the sky? Sam always had to know he was right, making little room for doubt, no space between his facts and figures for something as 'flimsy' as faith.

'No… it didn't come up.'

'I thought he must have when you didn't question why we'd decided to sleep in separate beds.' She laughed. 'That usually leads to *lots* of questions!' It did; it had. But not those sorts of questions. I guessed they weren't having sex – any more. But never in a million years did I think they would be choosing not to. That *Sam* would be choosing not to. Sam, who I had lost my virginity to. Sam, who definitely, *definitely* didn't lose his virginity to me. Sam, whose friends carelessly joked that he was going to 'shag his way around his swim club' after our break-up. That Sam? That Sam couldn't be living with a girl and not sleeping with her – especially not a girl who looked like Jamie.

'I, erm… I thought…' I stuttered, losing the ability to form a sentence once again. My mind had just about made sense of their arrangement, their relatively recent separation, her moving out, my undeniable moving in…

'You thought we were just friends?' Jamie asked, turning from the painting she was now fixed on to study me, her expression open and kind. My heartbeat started to rage in my chest as I felt panic wash over me anew. They weren't breaking up? They were saving sex for marriage? *Sam* was saving sex for marriage? Sam was happily dating a girl who believed in everything his own medic mind had refused to understand?

'Yeah… maybe,' I said, cautiously.

'Oh honey.' She smiled, looking down at me and putting a light hand on my shoulder. 'We're more than just friends.' She smiled again. 'We're engaged.'

*

26 September 2013 – Nottingham, England

'You're engaged?' I could hear Austin's voice bellow from the end of Sam's phone even though it was glued to his face. His accent could be loud at the best of times but when Austin was drunk it was like he was trying to shout across the Atlantic. I looked across from the laptop, perched on the broken coffee table before us, next to the half-eaten Domino's. I watched Sam laugh openly, shaking his head and replying, 'No, dude. I said, "We're otherwise engaged." You know, as in busy.'

'Oh, right,' I heard Austin say, before adding, 'You might as well be. Dude, you're *whipped*. It's a Thursday night. Come out.' Sam rolled his eyes, holding the phone away from his ear as we heard his best friend rant on. 'You're flipping *married*, bro.' I looked at my slippers, resting on the armchair across from the stained sofa. It wasn't normal behaviour for two students, I'd give him that, but between Sam's shifts and sports commitments it was becoming harder and harder to spend time just the two of us.

'Not yet.' Sam laughed. 'Mate, we might come out later.' Sam shook his head in my direction, leaning even further into the sofa. 'I'm just going to spend a bit of time with Jess.'

'Fine dude, *fine*,' Austin said in a way that suggested it was clearly not fine before hanging up. Sam leaned forwards to put his phone face down on the coffee table and took another slice of pizza, putting his other arm back around me.

'You're sure you don't want to go out? I'm happy to, you know,' I said, already half asleep but still not wanting to be the reason Sam's friends would give him shit.

'Seriously, Jess, there's no place I'd rather be.' He leaned in to kiss my shoulder tenderly.

'What a *line*.' I laughed, pulling away.

Sam grabbed me back, engulfing me in a hug. I feigned a struggle but we both knew he'd already won. 'You love it. Anyway, you cancelled your painting class for me; the least I can do is say no to that fool.' He laughed at the thought of whatever Austin would be getting up to now. I didn't want to know. 'I still feel bad you had to cancel. It's just hard because I have swimming and shifts…' Sam's sentence trailed off as he kissed my shoulder again.

'It's okay,' I said. More than. 'I haven't seen you properly all week.'

'Yeah, I know.' Sam looked apologetic. 'They said this year would be a step up, but I never thought it would be this hard.' I looked across at him, his familiar face a little more worn than the fresh-faced fresher I'd met the year before. 'Is the class the same time every week?'

'Yeah.' I nodded. 'But I think I'm going to stop,' I continued before he could interrupt. 'It's been hard enough finding time to see each other as it is. Something's got to give, right?'

'But didn't that *Art Today* contact sort them out?' Sam shook his head. 'I'd give up swimming for the team but…' He looked down, tracing his thumb as it stroked my hand.

'You've just got captain. I know, you can't.' I squeezed his hand a little tighter. 'It's okay; I'll leave the painting for now, maybe next year.' I smiled, confident and content.

'Are you sure?' he asked, his face falling at the thought of me going without. 'To be fair, I've seen your art. I think you'd be teaching the teacher a thing or two.' He sat up a little straighter, reclaiming his hands to run his fingers through his already messed-up hair.

'Yeah, if it's the right thing, the opportunity will come round again. Things always do.'

Sam smiled, rolling his eyes at the words we both knew I was thinking: *it's fate.*

I savoured the rare silence of Sam's student house, before the boys blustered back in. Sam liked to pretend he enjoyed their antics as much as the next 'lad' but I could see his inner overachiever starting to strain. 'How long until everyone gets back?'

'Long enough.' Sam grinned, only two words needed to shift us from friendly to flirtatious.

'Three minutes?' I opened my mouth mockingly. Sam laughed, reaching under my top. I could feel each kiss stealing my words, silencing my thoughts but before drifting into him completely, I had to ask. 'Not yet?'

'Huh?' Sam replied, breathing a deep sigh of lust or surrender.

'You said "not yet". Earlier on, when Austin said we were married, you said "not yet".' I looked into his increasingly hazy eyes, unable to guess his response.

'Well yeah,' he replied, pushing himself up on his forearms – surrender, not lust. When I wanted to talk there were few things that could stop me. 'Obviously, we're going to get married one day, aren't we?' he continued, entirely unfazed.

I pushed myself back to sitting to look across at my boyfriend, frozen and perplexed. I studied his expression, not a hint of sarcasm or irony about it. 'Don't get me wrong,' Sam continued, sitting up, increasingly baffled by my comatose response. 'I'm not proposing. We're in uni for Christ's sake, but you know… one day… I thought, that maybe…'

I propelled myself forward to kiss him full on the mouth. He laughed through the kiss.

'Well, one day, when you ask, I'll say yes,' I promised, talk of swimming and shifts and painting classes all but forgotten. 'But no best man's speech,' I said, raising an eyebrow at the thought of Austin spinning a yarn in front of all four sets of our grandparents.

'And no kids,' he replied, shaking his head. 'Too messy and they always stop half of the wedding breakfast from being able to drink.'

'And no slow dances,' I chipped in, torn between Biffy Clyro and Jason Derulo.

'And no church,' Sam added. 'Just me and you. On a beach somewhere far, far away.' He smiled, his fingers finding their way to the flesh of my sides once again.

'Like Sydney?' I asked, relaxing into his touch.

'Yeah.' He smiled, softly moving his hands up my bare back. 'Just like Sydney.'

Chapter Ten

2 August 2020 – Sydney, Australia

A hopeless waiter made hopeless moves on Jamie.

'You look like that model,' he swooned, topping her wine glass up to dangerously generous proportions.

She turned to me with an apologetic shrug. 'I get that a lot.' Oh, please.

She put the drink to her pristine lips, her fourth finger bare as the day she was born. Engaged people were meant to wear rings. It was a sign, a warning. And after waiting so long for mine, I'm afraid her 'I was taking it on and off so many times for work that I just bring it out for special occasions' line wasn't going to cut it. Not for me, at least.

I looked around the restaurant. Under a canopy, fairy lights illuminated every corner of the outdoor terrace. I'd love to say it was too much but it was perfect; no doubt a favourite haunt for the soon-to-be newlyweds. I looked around for Sam. Where the hell was he? My stomach felt sick at the thought. I forced my attention back to Jamie, torn between avoiding the punch of her flawless profile and desperately wanting to work out which model she looked like.

After our chat in the gallery, neither one of us had mentioned her divine revelation but talk of the wedding now flowed as freely as the waiter's overly generous, you're-never-getting-in-her-pants-mate wine. I had nodded and smiled and smiled and nodded whilst Jamie had explained in excruciating detail how Sam had led her to the top of a hill, got down on one knee and finally asked for her hand in marriage. 'What about the rest of you?' I had joked like the weird uncle at a family gathering, just trying far too hard to break the ice. But the ice, like my heart, was cracked. Jamie had forced a laugh before carrying on, informing me that they had been dating for two years and were getting married in two months. *Two months.* As in eight weeks. As in fifty-six short days.

'That's all a bit… quick,' I said, barely loud enough for her to hear me, reluctant to open my mouth too wide for fear that I may throw up on her orange patent heels, which I was pretty sure cost more than my monthly London rent. She smiled, a stupidly attractive smile, sparkles lighting up her eyes. Of course, it didn't feel quick. They'd decided to wait until the wedding to have sex. Sam must have had the two slowest years of his life. Meanwhile I had had the three slowest years of mine. Three years. *Three.* I knew I should be over him by now. I'd thought I *was.* But we were together for five. He was the love of my life. I thought I was the love of his. I looked across at Jamie and tried not to draw comparisons. We had had it all planned out, our whole future, both our names scribbled on every single page. Ours wasn't how love stories ended so I guess I refused to believe we had.

And then it had started again, the universe bringing us back together, until…

'Over here, honey.' Jamie ascended to her modelesque height, whilst the waiter stared on agog. Sam smiled broadly, canines and all, as he walked across the restaurant toward us, turning the heads of one or two of his own admirers as he did. Overwhelmed and at a loss for words, I rose out of my seat to give him a brief hug, one of those awkward near-embraces where you don't know if the other person is going in for a hug, one kiss or two. It was easier when we just kissed – *oh, just like that*, I thought, as Sam planted one on his perfect girlfriend's mouth. Sorry, *fiancée*; his perfect fiancée's mouth. I slumped back into my seat and tried not to think about how he used to do that to me.

'How was CreateSpace?' Sam took a seat, a sip, and looked over at me eagerly, figuring our conversation would flow on seamlessly from lunch. When was he planning to tell me?

'Good,' I said shortly, looking him dead in the eye. Sam sat up a little straighter in his seat.

'It was great, thanks, Bub,' Jamie said over the background noise, reaching a hand out to rest on his tanned forearm for all – and especially me – to see. 'Jess is going to use her time before *Art Today* to help Tim out with exhibition.' Sam sent a quick glance my way. And *he* thought he was the productive one out of the two of us. Here I was using my fake spare time before my fake new job to help out my fake new friend, Jamie.

'That's amazing, Jess,' Sam said, trying to read my deadpan expression. 'Thank you.'

He looked at me again and I refused to meet his eye. They still thought I was trying to do them a favour, like my free time would have just been spent mooching around the city.

'Wanted to use my time well,' I muttered, insinuating that any time spent hanging around his apartment wouldn't be, a little dig that I'm sure didn't even scratch the surface.

'Well, that's great!' Sam recovered after a long silence, his words characteristically a little too late, reaching his hand out to rest on mine. I looked down at it for a moment, hating it for being on mine after all his omissions but not knowing if I wanted it to move.

'CreateSpace is a pretty big deal in your world, right?' he added. My world. I guess it was, until I'd let my world become him. 'And it'll definitely help Tim out.' I hoped to God it would help me out too. I needed to get some money and get out of Sam's stupid flat. 'He's pretty useless without Carlo.' *And I'm pretty useless without you.* 'New jobs, new cities, man, I can't keep up!' Sam joked. That made two of us. 'I guess we need some bubbles to celebrate?' he continued, removing his hand from mine to return it to Jamie.

'I think we do,' I said flatly, resting bitch face now very much active. Jamie no sooner looked around the room before the waiter was on her like a rash, pouring champagne into three narrow flutes.

'To new jobs.' Sam raised his glass in the air.

'To new friends,' Jamie joined in, reaching her delicate fingers high. *Friends.*

'To new engagements,' I said, a smile on my face. I turned to look at Sam, whose own face was a picture: stunned and scared. He should have been the one to tell me and his expression told me he knew that too. He should have told me the second he'd seen me, the second he'd brought me back to his place. He'd had so many opportunities to tell me the truth. Yes, I had lied too, but never about him, never about us. Jamie took a sip and placed her glass down, as Sam did the same. I took a big fat gulp and placed my glass down with a thump that said: *don't pretend you don't know why I'm pissed, Sam.*

'I'm just going to pop to the bathroom,' Jamie said and rose to her feet to give both me and Sam another look at her toned thighs. 'If the waiter comes' – unlikely without her there – 'I'll have the usual.'

*

15 December 2012 – London, England

'The usual?' I muttered the question under my breath. Sam placed his strong hands to rest on my hips on and smiled. 'At Soho House. He has a *usual?*' I demanded as best I could through a whisper. He shrugged, hands still on my hips. The 'meet the parents' charade was nerve-racking at best, never mind when it turned out your boyfriend's parents were stinking flipping rich. I looked around the gilded room, at the plush velvet sofas that lined it and the ornate picture frames hosting paintings I could barely even dream of owning, never mind painting. And this was just the corridor. 'I mean, I guessed you didn't grow up in squalor.' I looked my boyfriend up and down again, his hair pushed back and his face closely shaved. He had told me his parents were both doctors, but had neglected to mention that his dad was an important oncology consultant who made regular visits to the city – so regular that Soho House considered him a close personal friend. Not to mention (and Sam certainly didn't) that his mum was a visiting lecturer at University College London in her spare time – like doctors had all that much time to spare. 'You could have told me to wear something nice,' I went on. Sam's firm grip never wavered. He held my gaze just as steady; I could tell he was trying hard not to laugh. 'I wanted to make a good impression!' Was I being dramatic? Maybe I was being dramatic.

'Who cares if you impress them or not? You impress me, okay? If anything, they should be trying to impress *you*, soon-to-be award-winning artist.' Sam tilted my chin up to kiss him, all annoyance melting at the mention of my favourite accolade: I still couldn't believe that they had actually liked my portfolio. 'And my mum's already invited you to Christmas carols; that's a pretty big deal in their world.' He laughed.

'Are we going?' I wrinkled my nose, not sure I could stand singing carols next to Sam in church and still keep a straight face.

'Hell, no!' He laughed again, pulling me tighter still. 'But they invited you, which means they like you. You're in.' Sam leaned in closer to whisper into my ear, as if I'd somehow made my way into their secret society. I hoped it included membership to Soho House. 'We should go back to the table,' Sam sighed, pulling away. 'Or they'll think we're up to something.' I took his hand as he guided me through the dimly lit restaurant, fairy lights illuminating hidden corners, with merry businesspeople filling every space, toasting the festive season. Weaving left and right through the restaurant's many rooms, Sam stalled at a bauble-covered tree, his dad's voice bellowing from our table behind it. 'A fine art degree, what's she going to do with that? My money was on Sam meeting another doctor…'

Sam gripped my hand tighter and tried to pull me forward, longing to stop the overheard conversation in its tracks. I halted, a cocktail of embarrassment, curiosity and stubbornness fixing me to the spot. Sam glanced at me, panicked, his own face fixed with confusion, like he had only just realised I wasn't a doctor too.

'She could do a lot of things, John.' Sam's mum spoke up from the other side of the tree. Its happy lights mocked me, no longer as jolly as they had first seemed. 'Art therapy, art journalism… She's clearly a very bright girl, she can do a lot more than just paint.' Sam's eyes were still glued on me, his hand willing me forward. I didn't want to move, not sure if I should feel insulted or affirmed by Molly's latest comment.

'You're right, Molly. You're right,' I heard John sigh as I imagined him placing a hand on Molly's arm, in the same way Sam did when he surrendered to me. 'And they've only been together for what, three months? It's not like he's in love with the girl.'

Sam squeezed my hand harder as we emerged, both his parents looking up, mouths zipped, smiles painted on; the moment was over, poise resumed. Sam slid into the booth first and I followed, forcing a smile onto my own face as I tried my best not to cry. I wanted them to like me. Sam loved them; I *needed* them to like me.

'Food shouldn't be long now, sweetheart.' Molly placed a hand on Sam's arm, which he quickly shrugged away. Molly stiffened in surprise, using the same hand to push her grey-blonde bob behind her ears and reveal a set of large emerald teardrops dangling there. 'Great choice with the chicken, Jess. You'll want two!' I knew she was trying to be nice but now it felt like a comment on my assumed stomach capacity. I forced another smile, weak and worrisome.

'I am,' Sam blurted out. He looked from me to his mum and dad in turn, a quiver of anger tightening his lips.

'You are what, darling?' Molly asked in confusion.

'We heard you, just then, saying I'm "not in love with the girl yet" but I am; I really am.' Sam turned to me, the same look of apology on his face. I was too; I knew I was. I was just waiting for the right time, waiting for the right place – which I never thought would be across from John and Molly after they'd just made it clear that I wasn't the girlfriend they'd hoped for their son.

Sam looked deep into my eyes. 'I'm in love with you, Jess.' He smiled. 'I am.'

'I'm in love with you too,' I whispered back, despite being mere inches away from his parents. Out of the corner of my eye I could see both of them stir, but my focus remained on him. He leaned in to give me a parent-appropriate peck on the lips. The moment stretched on before it was finally broken by a throat-clearing cough from John and an apologetic flurry of, 'I guess we need some bubbles to celebrate?'

Chapter Eleven

2 August 2020 – Sydney, Australia

'Jess… I…' Sam began to stutter, taking another sip of champagne. I took another gulp.

'How dare you?' I hissed under my breath. 'How dare you invite me into your home with *her* and let me use your room and pretend everything is so totally completely normal only to have Jamie tell me – not you, *Jamie* – that the two of you are *engaged*?'

'Jess, I…' Sam repeated again; he always *did* forget his lines. 'I tried to tell you but then…'

'You said you were home alone most of the time—'

'I told you there were two of us,' he argued back, knowing he hadn't said enough.

'You should have told me more. You should have told me everything,' I whispered furiously, knowing I had already said too much.

'I tried to tell you, last night, I tried, but then—'

'You should have tried to tell me again.' I knew Sam would do anything to keep the peace, to please anyone, everyone – but for a smart guy he didn't seem to realise you couldn't do that without tying yourself in knots. 'Just tell the truth, for once.' The irony of the comment wasn't lost on me, but right then I felt I was less guilty than him.

'Jess, I think you are overreacting.' Sam looked shiftily across the courtyard.

I knew I was overreacting. And yet, I didn't care. I didn't give a shit. I took another gulp.

'Overreacting? How would you feel?' I said, leaning in further still. 'You bump into me, looking great…' Sam grinned for a moment before my glare took the expression straight off his face. Now wasn't the time for all his misplaced flirtation, if it had ever been there in the first place. 'And you tell me not to worry, I can come back to yours and drink wine – and then you offer me the spare room but neglect to tell me you have a live-in fucking fiancée.' I winced at my final words. I couldn't help it; tears were starting to prick in my eyes.

'Jess, it's been years. I know we ended badly but I didn't think it would affect you so much.'

'Then why didn't you tell me?' I asked. 'If it was such a non-thing, if *we* were such a non-thing, then why didn't you tell me about Jamie the second you invited me back to yours?'

'Because…' Sam stuttered, eyes darting around the room for his fiancée to return.

'Because what, Sam?' I snapped. 'Tell me why I've had to fake my "I'm so happy" face whilst I feel this small.' I gestured, pinching my finger and thumb together, my hand shaking. 'I wish you'd just told me, so I could have avoided this situation entirely.'

Overreacting was now an understatement, but between the anger and the champagne bubbling in my stomach I was finding it impossible to stop.

'That's the point,' Sam said. 'I didn't *want* you to avoid my place. Jess, I've missed—'

'Jamie!' I exclaimed, seeing her three feet away from the table.

'We ordered?' She looked from me to Sam. *Say something, Sam, say something. And not that you miss me. Not as we are toasting your engagement.* Why was I here, in this impossible situation? It had been years. And yet, it still meant something to me. And looking over to Sam, all panic and confusion, it looked like it still meant something to him too. But what did that matter now?

'No, baby,' Sam said, looking from Jamie to me, his lady to his tramp. I bit back angry tears, trying not to cry. I wouldn't give him the pleasure, *never ever again.*

'No worries,' Jamie replied. She looked around the room and two seconds later our orders were taken. Five minutes later our food had arrived – I suspect stolen from some less attractive diners who would now have to wait another forty minutes for theirs. Two salads and a burger and fries. If I was going to sit through a dinner with my ex-boyfriend and his fiancée, I sure as hell wasn't going to do it eating a salad. I took a gulp of my wine. And another, and another, just enough to turn their chatter into white noise.

'So tomorrow, nine a.m.,' Jamie's voice interrupted my thoughts. I looked into her perfect face, now slightly blurred. Another gulp.

'Huh?' I asked, as I slapped away the waiter's ever-attentive hands; there were five fries left on my plate. You could take my boyfriend, Sydney, but you'd never take my fries.

'Your first day at CreateSpace? You'll arrive at nine a.m.? Sam and you can carpool.' Jamie smiled, entirely unaware that anything or anyone around her was anything but perfect.

'Oh no, I've put you out too much already.' I shook my fuzzy head. 'I'll make my own way there.' *And once I've earned just a little bit of money I'll be out of your stupid hospitable apartment and stupid hospitable lives for good.* Less than one week to sort it out and *get* out.

'Jess, did you not just hear me say?' Sam asked. Evidently not, Sam. 'My surgery is pretty much next door to CreateSpace, in Woolloomooloo.' Was I the only one who couldn't say it?

'No seriously, it's okay.' I fixed my stare on Sam, eyes telling him to back off in the subtlest of ways; I knew he could feel it but was pushing for me to accept the lift, to pretend – for his sake or Jamie's – that nothing was wrong.

'I'll be driving that way anyway, I can show you the area, make sure you're on time…' Sam said, his eyes begging me to let him make everything okay again. Something told me he wouldn't let it go, that all of this was signalling, screaming: he couldn't let *us* go. But what did that matter now? He was getting *married.*

'Jess?' Sam asked again, pleading for me not to make a scene.

'Yes, yes, fine,' I said, a little too abruptly. 'Me and Sam. Carpool. Woolloo— tomorrow.' They smiled knowingly. Me and Sam. In a confined space. Alone. Where he could finally explain himself, and finish that sentence. I've missed… I've missed…

Chapter Twelve

3 August 2020 – Sydney, Australia

I've missed my alarm.

'Jess? Jess?' I could hear Sam on the other side of the door. 'Can I come in?'

'No!' I shout-whispered, clambering out of bed and accidentally knocking Jamie's photo off the bedside table as I did. *Shit*.

'What was that?' Sam hissed.

'Nothing, nothing,' I assured him as I collected the shards of glass that had broken in the frame. Rushing to the mirror, I smoothed down my hair. Unlike yesterday morning, today was not a good make-up-less day. Today was a hungover, far from Clinique-d, slightly green-looking make-up-less day. How much had I drunk? The fact I couldn't remember told me all I needed to know. I didn't have time for this.

'You almost ready?' Sam asked in a whisper, despite the fact that my recent photo-smashing incident had probably already woken Jamie – and the neighbours as well.

I looked at myself in the mirror again. If I was going for the homeless-meets-scarecrow look then yes, yes I was ready. Emotionally, on the other hand, I couldn't think of anything worse than another day spent tangled up in Sam's new life whilst trying to untangle my own.

'Almost,' I lied. Just a couple of shifts at CreateSpace and I'd have some money to move, not that I hadn't outstayed my welcome already. If my comatose response to Jamie's church-going confession didn't do it then my anger at Sam's omissions certainly would.

'Great, I'll start the car,' I heard Sam call, before his muffled footsteps faded into the distance on the other side of the door. *Shit.*

Quicker than a Katy-Perry-at-the-VMAs costume change, but much less glamourous, I slipped on a pair of ripped black jeans, my favourite bra (and the only one I could find) and an oversized sheer white blouse and headed for the door. Sam sat in the driver's seat, door open, shirt collar undone, sunglasses on, a silly grin dancing across his face. Oh God, did he have to look like that? All this time and I still wasn't immune to Sam in a suit. I smiled back. Thank God he didn't have to wear a tux to work. A tux. Just like the one he would wear in two months. Eight weeks. Fifty-six days. And my smile was gone. How the hell had Sam convinced me to stay without telling me he planned to stay with Jamie forever?

'Taken the laid-back look for your first day?' Sam joked. How dared he? If he assumed we could just forget about yesterday's humiliation and move on, he didn't know me that well.

'Hey,' I began, hand on hip, hating every inch of that smile I had once loved. 'I'll have you know artists love the no-make-up look.'

'Yeah, it was more the no shoes look that I had in mind.'

I looked down at my feet. *Oh crap.*

'Be right back.' I turned on my naked heels as I heard Sam, against all his better judgement, burst into laughter behind me.

Kitten heels on, I strutted towards the car, sliding into the passenger seat. Sam closed his door and turned to me, the same smile circling around his silly, pretty mouth.

'Yes?' I asked, all attitude, eyebrow raised. 'What are you waiting for?'

Apart from your crazy ex-girlfriend to prove she can dress herself in the mornings.

'Where to?' he asked, grin holding fast. *How dare he?* Was he actually joking? Trying to make light of the fact that he'd lied me back into his life – well, kind of.

'Across the city,' I replied, turning to close the door behind me.

'But where?' Sam's smile broadened. He was going to make me say it. Woolloo…?

'CreateSpace,' I replied defiantly.

'I'm going to need you to say it,' he said, 'just one more time.'

'You're a wanker, you know that, right?' I smiled oh-so-sweetly in reply, never meaning words more. 'Just drive.'

Sam laughed again as he turned the key in the ignition – clearly this, *us*, was a joke to him. Or maybe it was the lightness and laughter he missed? His mornings must be so much less entertaining now that he wasn't landed with a crazy woman for a girlfriend. In fact, I *knew* his mornings would be less entertaining; Sam always loved to wake up and… shut up, shut up, *shut up*. I turned the radio up to drown out my thoughts. A couple of tuneless tracks later, he reached to turn the volume back down.

'Thank God,' I half-joked, rolling my eyes. Sam's taste in music was as bad as his taste in movies.

'J,' Sam began earnestly, not taking his eyes off the long, commuter-filled road before us. 'About last night.'

I inhaled silently, heart beating faster. Why did it still do that? Didn't it know that it wasn't supposed to do that around him any more? He was engaged. *Engaged.* But as much as he should have been the one to tell me, the fact that this broke my heart was *my* shit to deal with, not his. He had welcomed me into his home after a shock neither one of us could have ever expected. After spending our early twenties thinking we had everything mapped out, we were now in uncharted territory. Plus, if we were going to chart up our recent lies and omissions, I wasn't sure I had any legs – or shoes – to stand on.

'I overreacted,' I said.

'Yeah.' Sam nodded, still not taking his eyes off the road. I thumped his arm. '*Ow!*'

'That's not your line!' I moaned, turning to face his stubbled, strong profile.

'Well, you did.' He didn't back down. 'But I owe you an apology all the same.'

'I think so.'

'Jess, would you shut up for *one* moment?' Sam asked. 'I'm trying to *apologise.*' He elongated the word. 'I'm sorry I didn't tell you I was living with Jamie when we met, and I'm sorry you had to find out about our engagement from her. That wasn't fair – at all. It's the last way I would have wanted you to find out and I guess the truth is, I knew you'd be bothered. Because… well… the truth is, I'd be bothered too. Really bothered. We spent university together, we thought we were in love.'

Thought? I was. Hopelessly, uncontrollably. Impossibly.

'We were each other's first…' he continued. I raised an eyebrow. We both knew I was far from his *first*. '…real relationship, each other's first real love.'

Or so we *thought*, Sam.

'I know we talked about our own wedding.'

Mix-tapes as favours and 'Gettin' Jiggy Wit It' for the first dance.

'And I know it was all tongue in cheek…'

There was *nothing* tongue in cheek about Will Smith.

'But I knew that when one of us got engaged for real, it would hurt and, well… I didn't want to hurt you. I was going to tell you, *obviously* I was going to tell you, but I just knew that if I did you'd never come back to ours and I was so excited to see you, and I've missed you and… I'm sorry.'

Silence filled the inside of the car and for the first time in my life I longed for Sam's music.

'I…' I began, looking out at the rolling coastline. 'I've never heard you say so many words in one go.'

Sam took his eyes from the road to flash me a mock-evil stare, a hint of his playful grin dissolving the tension between us.

'Okay, I'm sorry too. I overreacted. It's just you – here now, on the other side of the world, with me again – and Jamie – she just caught me off guard.'

'Yeah me too,' Sam agreed, his grin unfolding like the cat who got the cream. 'This whole thing, you being here...' He shook his head at the road, the sentence dissolving. 'I'm so sorry, Jess. Honestly.' His sincerity softened my hurt. I hadn't been perfect either and neither one of us had seen this, any of this, coming. He sighed again, genuinely gutted at the mess he'd got us into. 'Do you think we can start over? You know, as friends?'

I sighed too. We had never been just friends. From the first night of Freshers' Week to a whole year after graduation, we'd become best friends, sure, but we'd never been *just* friends. And here I was lapping up every kind scrap about our relationship Sam cast my way. I didn't want to be just friends. But he was happy now. And I wanted him to be happy – kind of. And then there was the small detail that his offer of free accommodation and this temporary job was the quickest way I could think of to get a deposit for my own place without telling anyone back home what a royal screw-up I'd made of this whole new start. Without telling Sam that all my moves and lies had always led back to him. Just a few days, a week, tops – of long shifts, of cash in hand – just to keep me going until the summer set in.

'Yes. Sure, let's start over,' I said.

'Great. How about lunch? There's somewhere I'd like to show you.' He smiled, his green eyes still knowing just how to convince me.

'Lunch. Just the two of us. Just friends?'

'Just friends,' Sam said, relieved somehow that everything was out in the open – for him at least. 'Now out you get, you ripped-jeaned, shoe-wearing artist, you.' Sam pulled to a halt outside CreateSpace. 'Go, hold Tim's clipboard like a pro.'

*

I was holding the clipboard. I was holding the clipboard like a pro.

'Jessica, could you just come here and hold this?' Tim ushered me over, beckoning me to grab hold of the corner of a large, paint-splattered canvas. I walked across the exhibition room, the blank white of its walls just waiting for the pieces to be hung. The magnitude of the gallery sank in, and I was ashamed for once thinking that painting professionally was something just anybody could do. I took hold of the canvas and cocked my head to work out which way up it was supposed to go. The dense horizontal brush strokes, rising with warmth and intensity, told me which corners to grab. After brushing up on my Leo Todd knowledge, it didn't look like one of his, but I knew by now that Tim was drawing in a whole host of local artists into the same show. This abstract painting, heavy with texture, rugged then smooth, was breath-taking. It reminded me of the kind of pieces that I had passed on to Devon, in the hope that she'd take note. I sighed; it wasn't like I was here for the art, but I was holding the canvas like a pro. This job would be easy. Not that it was forever, or even for long – the thought made my stomach sink. I had one week to get out of Sam's. Less than one week. I'd have to ask Tim to pay me early to give me even a hope of not handing my first paycheque directly to the hostel staff. I looked at the painting as panic started to set in. At least it was CreateSpace – that name on my CV might even be enough to entice Hannah Sommers to give me a minute of her time.

Tim tutted at how long I was taking. I looked at his hipster attire, long grey T-shirt further highlighting his long grey hair. He was a true artist. In fact, everyone he'd roped in seemed to be, in some form or another. That, in many ways, was the problem. Throw a bunch of artists into a room and ask them to orchestrate a travelling exhibition and for all your creative 'big picture' thinking and passionate temperaments, you're lacking some serious administrative details. Plus, the exhibition had been assigned two large gallery spaces to fill, so there was twice as much scope for things to go wrong. It was chaos. I'd been here almost five hours and already voices had been raised, four paintings had been misplaced, ticket enquiries went unanswered, we had had two IT meltdowns and one (suspected) broken finger. And that was just Tim. He was a genius, sure – I'd googled his work just moments after I'd met him – but it also didn't take a genius to work out that this Carlo guy had handled all of the practicalities. Tim needed help. And that was why I was here.

'Jessica. Where's my clipboard?'

I put it down when you asked me to pick this bloody great canvas up. 'Just a second!' I said, running obediently across the room to place the clipboard back in my hand.

'What's the time?' he demanded.

'Five to two,' I read off the clock (that we could both clearly see, but hey, I was here to help).

'Great, we can still get the Room B paintings unpacked before lunch,' Tim said, pushing his thick-rimmed glasses further up the bridge of his nose.

'Well, actually I…' I began, as Tim began to walk away, clearly losing interest. 'I… was going to meet someone for lunch.'

'Someone?' Tim stopped and looked at me intensely. With just white space behind him, his one-tone outfit made his long limbs look even more imposing. It took all my strength to hold his gaze.

'A friend,' I said, awaiting his reply with trepidation. I'd forgotten that first days were almost as nerve-racking as first dates.

'Jessica, you can cancel on friends. Lord knows you'll have to in this job, even more so at *Art Today*.' Tim dismissed my personal life in the way only someone without one could. 'Now, the canvases are in the van parked out—'

'My ex-boyfriend,' I blurted out, surprised as the words filled the air.

'Well,' Tim began again, looking from the clock (I *knew* he could see it) to me. 'Why didn't you say so, Jessica?' He let his glasses fall a little further to the end of his nose as his expression softened. 'Lunches with ex-boyfriends can be few and far between.' He didn't need to know that mine was a little closer to home, that I was currently living with the said ex-boyfriend and that this particular ex was actually his friend, engaged to be married to his other friend. Tim sauntered over to gaze out of the large open window. I hoped he couldn't spot Sam waiting outside. I tried to maintain the same expression while questioning whether Tim was the type to enjoy the drama of a love triangle regardless of whether his friends were involved.

'Go. And show him what he's missing,' Tim said with flair. I thanked him, smiled and turned to walk out of his studio before he could ask any more questions. 'And Jessica?'

'Yes?' I turned back to look at my new boss.

'For the love of God, put some mascara on.'

Chapter Thirteen

I could finally breathe. My heart rate slowed with every step I took away from the gallery and into the open air, feeling caught between needing a job and wanting to run away. I had left this world behind – badly, but still. I couldn't keep pretending to be an artist forever.

I loathed *Art Today* for reasons I struggled to articulate, for want of words and want of time, but at least handling Devon's emails and personal fancies was a safe distance away from the rare few artists that had actually made a living out of art. It had taken my whole time at uni to grow up from that dream. No one wanted to be that time-waster with a guitar still trying to land a record deal. I wondered how many musicians had made their way from centre stage to helping to make the media, like my own journey from paintbrush to actually being paid.

I saw Sam leaning against a brick wall on the other side of the paved square that backed onto the gallery. Top buttons still undone, sunglasses still covering his eyes, he effortlessly emitted Shoreditch-meets-Sydney chic – something I had been trying and failing to master ever since I had arrived. And I'd spent way more time in London than him.

'Hey, trouble,' he called over, even though I had clocked him the second I had walked out. I strutted across the palm tree-dotted paving, careful not to trip in my kitten heels – heels that I wouldn't even be wearing were it not for Sam. Boyfriends really were useful. Not that he was my boyfriend. We were just friends. Going somewhere he wanted to show me as just friends. Missing me as *just friends.*

Together, we strolled away from CreateSpace and I quickly glanced back to see whether Tim's statuesque figure was watching from the windows. I tried to savour being alongside Sam but Jamie's presence was palpable despite her not being there. Turning a corner, we came to the harbour and both of us sighed upon seeing a hint of the sea. At least that still thrilled me every time I saw it. It reminded me that I was actually in Sydney. Yes, in the box room of my engaged ex-boyfriend, but in Sydney nonetheless. As we walked, Sam and I tried to chat like the 'just friends' we were pretending to be now – him asking about my morning, telling me about his. Winding our way up a cobbled side street, Sam abruptly stopped, turning to face me, a big grin spreading across his flushed face. I stopped to look up at him, heart caught in my throat, pace quickening.

'Jess?' he asked softly, taking a step towards me.

'Yes?' I mimicked his tone, taking a step closer in return.

'Guess what?' He gazed down at me, taking off his sunglasses to reveal a sparkle in his eye.

'What?' I looked up at him, hope filling my own. We were just friends. *Just* friends. Sam took another step closer, placing a strong hand to my side, steadying me.

'I think you'll be pleased to know…' His voice hushed to a whisper. Pleased to know what? I couldn't take any more surprises and yet there was one I knew part of me wanted to hear.

'We're here!' he said, stepping back again and putting the same hand out to indicate the dubious-looking café we were about to enter. Oh, for fuck's sake. I followed him inside. Just friends, we were just friends.

'This is the best brunch spot in Sydney,' Sam boasted as he thrust a menu in my face.

'But it's not brunch time,' I objected, checking my watch. I had an hour for my lunch break, but putting on a lick of mascara had bizarrely bought me an extra five minutes.

'Oh, J.' Sam smiled, shaking his head and ordering us two banana smoothies. 'You have so much to learn.' He leaned further across the table. 'Here in Sydney, it's always brunch time.'

I laughed. Okay, I could make my peace with that. I studied his features, open and warm. I hated that I could never hate him – believe me, I had tried. All his looks, his touches; were they all just the actions of a friend missing a friend?

'So, what's good?' I asked, telling myself again that I was happy to be here with him in his very special brunch spot. The yellow walls needed a lick of paint, the tiled floor could do with replacing, but something about the laidback staff and acoustic music playing made it feel like home.

'Well, Jamie always gets the Big V,' Sam explained whilst I tried not to spray my first sip of smoothie in his face. 'V stands for vegan, Jess, vegan.' He smiled and shook his head at me again. Of course Jamie would be a vegan. Typical.

'And what do you get?' I asked, moving swiftly on, eyes staring at the menu without taking in any of the words.

'I get The Best,' he said. It felt like a dig. Then Sam pointed his finger to indicate the item on my own menu. Oh, 'The Best Breakfast'.

'Two of The Best it is.' I looked at Sam, flashing him my best smile and fluttering my eyelashes just a little more than usual (thank you, Tim). Even though I couldn't have him, I still wanted him to want me. It confused me how much I thought he already did.

Five minutes later our plates arrived – in fact, I thought they did, but I couldn't actually see my plate for the sheer amount of food piled on it. Sam smiled, raising an eyebrow as if to say: *I bet you can't eat it all.* I raised my own: *game on, Sam, game on.*

Together we devoured the food and devoured each other – conversationally at least. He wanted to know everything. How I'd been over the past few years, how I found my job at *Art Today*. How did CreateSpace compare? (Well, one's a magazine and one's a gallery, Sam, but allow me to humour you.) How long did I plan to stay in Sydney? Was I *sure* I didn't leave a special someone behind? I answered him honestly – for the most part – leaving aside anything about housemates, tequila and the fact that I wasn't really an editor.

'It's crazy that you're here.' Sam looked at me and forced a laugh as the waiter cleared our plates. I finished mine, Sam struggled; not half the man he used to be. 'I remember…' he began, but stopped himself. 'Do you need to get back to the gallery?' he asked instead. Well, I did. But not until he had finished what he had started to say.

'You remember what?' I asked. Sam shook his head at me for the trillionth time. He knew I wasn't the type to let things go.

'I remember sitting here and writing you a postcard once,' he explained, playing with the cuffs of his crisp white shirt.

'A postcard?' I asked. 'I never received a postcard.'

'That's because I never sent it,' Sam said with a weak smile, shuffling a little in his seat. I wasn't used to seeing him this uncomfortable.

'It was when I first arrived in Sydney. I was sitting here, thinking about you and how we ended, and how I had never told you I was leaving the UK, and I wanted you to know that I was okay, and I wanted to know that you were okay and, well…' He looked down into his empty smoothie jar, all of a sudden at a loss for words.

'Why didn't you send it?' I asked, laying a hand on top of his. To anyone else we would have looked like a couple; I guess we didn't know how not to. *But he has a fiancée.*

'I just thought, what's the point? I was here and you were in London.' He shrugged and raised his eyebrows, locking his eyes back on mine. A petite waitress returned to our table to ask whether we had finished. Sam asked for the bill, a shyness coming over him, as I wondered whether he preferred coming here with Jamie or me. For all the excruciating moments I had shared with them both since blundering into their box room, I hadn't seen him laugh much, not really. Sure, her Sydney-Sam was more relaxed about work, but somehow he seemed more on guard about almost everything else. My Sam had a silly side, a flirtatious, frivolous side, a side somehow finding itself sitting right across from me, all over again.

'I think I would have liked to have got it,' I admitted, lowering my voice just enough for him to have to lean into me a little further.

'I met Jamie the very next week,' he said. 'Funny how these things happen, eh?'

'Yeah, hilarious,' I muttered.

'Well it's nice to tell you all about it now,' he said. Three years too late.

'Yeah, now that you're engaged.' Bitterness escaped my clipped response, before I salvaged the sentence with an upward inflection. 'I can't believe you're getting married!'

'Yeah.' Sam's smile looked a little forced. 'Me neither. And I can't believe you're here now,' he continued. Something told me he could say it a thousand times and it still wouldn't make sense to him, to either of us. 'Great timing, Jess.' His face softened, eyes still weary. Sadness filled my stomach. 'We're late.' Sam resumed his chipper tone, taking in the time from his expensively hedged wrist. It was all a little too late.

Sam paid for lunch and wouldn't let me argue. I mean, it was probably for his benefit; the sooner I could save my wages and get out of his and Jamie's place, the better. Not that it would be his problem after this week.

Retracing our steps, we walked a little closer together. It was strange to walk side by side without holding hands, our lunch making it feel stranger still.

'Oh, before I forget,' Sam began, turning to face me. 'Jamie and I are having some of our friends round from church tonight.' Oh. We hadn't even talked about the whole church thing. 'You're welcome to join us if you like.' Happy families and the live-in riffraff. I'd rather go for that run.

'Oh thanks, I actually…' I scrambled for another lie, scared by how easily they were surfacing. 'I actually have plans with the people from work tonight. I'll just let myself in later. If that's okay with you?' Sam looked satisfied and discontented all at the same time; something told me I wasn't the only one caught in the push and pull of our past and present.

'Look at you, J!' Sam patted my shoulder as I tried my best not to feel patronised. 'Making friends already!'

'Yeah.' I offered him a smile, one that didn't reach my eyes. Maybe I could see if Tim or the guys on reception wanted to go out. I'd need to find something to fill the time.

'Well I guess we'll see you later, then?' Sam smiled again, a confused expression darting across his brow. 'Or if it's a late one, I'll see you in the morning.'

He turned to walk in the direction of his surgery. 'Oh, and J.' He looked back over his shoulder. I met his gaze, hungry for his words, hoping they'd make everything feel right again. 'Try to remember shoes this time.'

Back in the studio, I found Tim a few degrees away from a meltdown. He and Olivia, a member of his team he'd clearly got custody of in the break-up, had begun to unpack the second set of pieces from the van, which were now scattered haphazardly around the room. The paintings were propped up against the wall, their unprotected edges rubbing against the dirty studio floor. Had no one ever heard of a dust sheet? My heart sank at the mistreatment of these abstract works of all shapes and sizes, exploding with colour, many boasting a similar texture to the canvas I'd been carrying earlier that day. Their colours and contours demanded my gaze like long-lost friends before Tim's voice grabbed my attention.

'It'll never fit, it'll never fit,' I heard him mutter as I approached, clipboard duly in hand.

'There are worse problems to have,' I joked, a sarcasm-fuelled comment met with we-wish-looks-could-kill stares. Now wasn't the time. 'What's the problem?' I asked pragmatically, pretty sure I wouldn't have the solution. Tim began to explain in a flurry of broken sentences. The pieces. Too big for the space. Too many. Not in line with Paris and Milan. Not what the attendees would expect. I looked at Tim, his authority fading before my eyes.

'Slow down, slow down.' I found myself soothing him like a child, not entirely sure what I was going to say next. It wasn't like I knew anything about curating an exhibition.

'What's the problem?' I asked the same question again, slower this time, my eyes pleading with Tim for a clearer response.

'That bastard promised Leo Todd's team we had space for the entire collection.' Tim shook his head. I didn't need to guess who 'the bastard' was. 'Exactly how they were displayed in Paris and Milan.' *Leo Todd has been shown in Paris and Milan. You didn't even get through that competition.* 'Then promised *me* my idea to get the local artists involved was a good one...'

'It was a great idea,' Olivia piped up, brown-nosing before Tim could shoot her down.

'But now we don't have enough space for everything,' Tim flurried on in hysterics.

'Can't you cut out some of the local artists?' I asked and both Tim and Olivia looked at me like I was from another planet.

'No,' Tim objected and I had to commend his loyalty. 'Plus, I'm not letting Carlo think my ideas have to pander to his.' So not about loyalty at all then. 'Leo Todd has a specific way of doing things, a specific order, a specific... Oh God.' He held his head in his hands as I tried to work out whether Tim was enduring a break-up or a breakdown. Not that the two were mutually exclusive. I should know.

'What does the contract say about the layout?' I asked.

'The contract?' Tim asked, confused. 'Olivia, have we got a paper copy of the contract or did that bastard take that too?' Tim turned to Olivia, who looked on the verge of tears, like a child fed up of her two work-dads fighting. She tottered across the room in her six-inch stilettos (I really must upgrade the kitten heels) grabbed the contract from the next room and tottered back towards us, stumbling as she did (maybe I'd stick with the kittens after all). I thanked her and fastened it to my clipboard – wow, these things really did come in handy. I scanned the contract, something I'd got annoyingly used to doing during my time at *Art Today*. You'd be surprised how many embargoes and libel claims got thrown around the more-money-than-sense art world. Sadly, in my case, the senselessness had come without the cash.

'And?' Tim demanded. I looked up from the contract; was he really asking for my opinion? Devon never had.

'It's fine,' I replied as Tim and Olivia looked from me to the mess of paintings around us. I'd admit it didn't look fine. 'Look, here.' I pointed to a clause in the contract and the two of them looked at the clipboard. Neither one of them attempted to read it. I looked up for Tim's permission to continue; I couldn't tell if he was confused or simply not listening. 'It says here that we are contractually obliged to use eighty per cent of Leo's pieces in the exhibition, so we can leave' – I looked around the room, quickly counting the paintings – 'six of the pieces out. And it says here that we have the artistic freedom to arrange the pieces how we wish provided we can explain our rationale and seek approval from Leo's agent. Who is Leo represented by again?' I felt like I should know.

'Lucy James,' Tim replied, voice still wavering.

'Great, well it would be good to let her know.' I nodded, whilst both of them nodded back. Was I in *control*? 'And send a courtesy email to the artist. What's Leo like?'

'Never met her,' Tim said. *Her.* I'd always thought Leo Todd was a *he.* Clearly, her anonymity was working. 'Still based in Britain.' He looked at me, like I already knew; like perhaps we were neighbours on our picturesque isle. 'Somewhere in the North, I think?' he continued, as if that was narrowing it down. So Leo wasn't London born and bred or a man. Leo was a woman, a Northern woman – a little like me. I looked around at her colourful pieces, comparison and jealousy swimming in my chest. I pushed it back into place, breathing deeply, forcing my attention back to the contract. She was nothing like me. 'Before she moved to Sydney, of course,' Tim pressed on, as I looked to the sands and skies washing colour around the room.

'She's living in Sydney?' I asked. Okay, so she moved to be in Sydney too. But still, she was *nothing like me.* I doubt she fibbed her way into CreateSpace too.

'You do know Lucy James is *Australian*?' Tim asked, as if everyone ought to.

'Of course I know Lucy James is Australian,' I echoed; just one more fib. 'In any case,' I continued, Tim and Olivia still nodding along, even though I knew I may as well have been speaking Japanese. 'That means that even though Paris and Milan set the pieces chronologically…' I tried to hide the brief Google-search I had swiped to behind my clipboard barrier. I really needed to get me one of these. 'We could place them thematically.' Tim and Olivia continued to look at me blankly. 'Basically, we can use the pieces in a way that makes sense in our space, local artists included.' The penny dropped. Tim smiled broadly even though Olivia still appeared light years behind.

'Jessica, you're a genius!' he exclaimed, grabbing the clipboard from my hand and proceeding to look at (and yet still not read) the contract before him. 'We've needed your calibre of expertise for quite some time.' Olivia became increasingly interested in the shine of her shoes as I was hit with a wave of guilt, desperate to dispel any misplaced pride. 'Quite some time' clearly meant since Carlo left a hole that Olivia had failed to fill. 'Now hold this.' He thrust the clipboard back into my hand. 'We've got work to do.'

*

4 September 2016 – London, England

'You have so much *crap*.' I heard his exacerbated tone ring out behind me, as I looked at the same yellow and blue splattered canvas that Sam had first set eyes on in my old uni room.

'Well, if that's what you want to call it,' I snapped as I placed the canvas on top of my bed and began to unwind the bubble wrap protecting it – like it was worth being protected at all.

'I didn't mean your paintings are crap.' I felt his arms wrap around my body from behind.

I guess I knew that, but somehow a day of lugging them from Nottingham to London had made them feel like baggage.

'Are you okay, J? I know it's a big move.' He held me tighter as I softened into his arms. 'One more year and then I'll be applying for placements.' Damn me for dating a doctor. My heart sank at the thought of all the days we'd have to spend apart between now and then. 'Then I'll be down to London and moving my boxes into this room quicker than you can say…' His phone buzzed to life in his pocket; I didn't need him to tell me it was from the hospital. I looked down at my own to see a missed call from Zoe. I'd call her later; right now I needed to make the most of Sam, before he went back to our old home. Zoe would understand. This was mine and Sam's first long-distance stint. I knew we'd make it but it didn't mean I had to like it.

'Sorry about that, J.' He stashed the offending phone back in his pocket. 'Right, what's next?' He bent down to open another box as I busied myself doing the same. 'Jess?' Sam's voice called from behind me, my face inches deep in the next box. 'I know this moving thing is crap, but I find sometimes you just need to…' I looked up to see Sam now wearing one of my old Nike running shirts, the 'Just Do It' slogan stretched across his muscular torso, his belly button and lower abs displayed for the messy room to see. 'Just do it.' Sam pointed to the shirt, smile broad, far too proud of himself. Despite my mess of emotions threatening to surface, I couldn't help but laugh. I clambered over the boxes of marked-up junk I had moved from city to city.

'Sam, you look ridiculous.' I placed my cold hands onto his bare stomach, making him flinch, enjoying the feeling of the smooth skin on my hands. He bent down to snuggle his face into my hair.

'I'm going to miss you, J.'

'Have you finished yet?' my dad called from outside the door. Oh God, I hoped he meant unpacking. Sam pulled his arms away from me and tugged at his shirt, unsure what my dad would find worse, him in my T-shirt or him topless in my room. He decided on the former. 'Jessie J!' my dad exclaimed on seeing the work left to be done. I loved his name for me, even more so because he thought I was the only Jessie J in the world. He wasn't to know the name had been usurped by someone more famous; popular culture wasn't his thing. 'But looking good, Sam!' Nor, for that matter, was fashion.

'I was just helping Jess throw out some stuff, Dave.' Sam shrugged off the shirt and replaced it with his plain white T, my mum appearing just in time for the show. Throwing our meal deals onto my unmade bed, I tried not to draw comparisons with Sam's family. One day we'd start our own and our differences wouldn't mean a thing.

'I'd like to propose a toast.' My dad reached into the Tesco bag to pull out a Coke and raised it. 'To Jess and her new job. Nottingham's loss is *Art Today*'s gain – and one day both of you' – he gestured to Sam, as his permanently tanned cheeks began to blush – 'are going to *own* this city.' I was pretty sure he'd picked up the phrase from Sam and was trying it out for the first time. 'Sam and Jess take London town.' He spread his free hand across the air like a headline. 'London won't know what's hit it!'

Chapter Fourteen

3 August 2020 – Sydney, Australia

I breathed in the cool evening air, letting my shoulders soften as I looked across the illuminated square surrounding the gallery. Fairy lights climbed up each of the palm trees, the lunchtime busyness replaced by meandering locals and lovers with all the time in the world.

It was nearly seven p.m., I was exhausted and my kitten heels were staring to rub; still I smiled. It had been the first day in Sydney that I had actually almost enjoyed. The gallery life wasn't for me, I knew that; it would take more than one day to change that, but at least I'd felt useful. The fact that this sensation felt so foreign only further cemented how many years I'd wasted feeling wasted. After my genius revelation (Tim said it, not me), we had spent the afternoon brainstorming and making a case for the many ways we could play with the layout of the exhibition. After swinging between hysteria and sheer delight (again, Tim, not me) we finally settled on strong and evocative tonal groupings. Leo's work had clear and distinctive palettes, much like Picasso had his Blue and Rose Periods but without all the angst and shit-scary clowns. I had to admit *her* work was stunning, though I'd still make some alterations myself – a little more tension to her generously applied blocks of colour, some well-placed interruptions, the hint of figures hidden under the abstract sweeps of skies and space. If I was still painting.

I meandered away from the harbour and towards the bus stop. I'd forgotten how good it felt to add value. I had only officially been made redundant a few weeks ago, but my role and even our magazine had felt redundant many months before. It was hard to remain motivated while the rest of your team felt like they were on a sinking ship and had clearly chosen you to be the first overboard. Somewhere along the line I'd mentally surrendered to treading water before my boss had finally put me out of my misery. Today reminded me of how good it felt to care about what you did. I passed a couple wrapped around each other on the other side of the road. Brunch with Sam had been nice too.

I wandered the last stretch towards the bus stop, just in time to watch the right bus pull up. With aching legs, I clambered on board. Taking a window seat, I let my body soften and my heartbeat settle for what felt like the first time all week. Gazing outside at the sun-kissed sky spinning by and inside at the group of friends chatting on the bus beside me, I thought of the one person other than Sam I'd want to share this fleeting feeling of success with. I looked down at my phone; Zoe's messages were still demanding to be read. I flicked them from first to last:

How's it going?

Hey J, how's it going?

Jessica, don't play hard to get

Jess?

I shouldn't have left it this long. I'd been so busy drawing a caricature of Zoe as too busy at work, too busy with Ben, that I'd convinced myself she was too busy for me. But she was my best friend, of course she'd be worried about me. I calculated the time difference – it was around eight in the morning in the UK. Zoe would be at work by now, but there was still a chance she would answer. At least the whole 'I was waiting for a good time to call' line might soften the blow.

'Zoe speaking. Oh, hello there!' She sounded overly formal. Before I could answer, I heard her rest a hand lightly on the mouthpiece, turn to a colleague and say, 'I have to take this outside.' A pause and then, 'Jess?' Her voiced sounded louder, sharper, colder, clearly now out of eavesdropping range. 'Are you okay?'

'Of course I'm okay.' I laughed off her concern. 'Why wouldn't I be?' After my shift and brunch, I'd almost convinced myself I was.

'Oh, I don't know,' Zoe began after a three-second delay; I could still hear her sarcasm loud and clear. 'Maybe because the last I heard from you was this time last week and you've been incommunicado ever since? And you're staying in a hostel. People *die* in hostels, Jess.'

'I'm sorry.' I cleared my throat and prepared my line. 'I've been waiting for a good time to call.'

Cue another three-second delay; this time it had nothing to do with the distance. I could tell Zoe was biting her tongue, weighing up whether to tell me she'd been worried sick or whether to let it go. I heard her sigh. 'That's okay,' she said. 'I can grab five minutes; they think I'm speaking to a client.'

'I know, I heard. Bravo. Oscar-worthy,' I joked, and as she laughed, I could feel the ice melting between us.

'So, how's it going down under? Still loving it?'

Still. I never was. It's been horrible Zoe. It's been…

'Yeah, it's going great, thanks!' I replied. Bravo. Oscar-worthy myself. 'I've got a job at CreateSpace.'

'Where?' Zoe replied. I had told her about it once, but I guess we hadn't really talked about my painting or the art world much lately – except maybe to slag off Devon.

'That cool contemporary place I told you about.' I tried to jog her memory of a time we used to sit up in bed, late into the evening, drunk and dreaming.

'Oh wow, not heard you talk about that in years. Jess, that's amazing!'

Amazingly temporary.

'And have you found somewhere to live?' she continued. I wanted to tell her the truth, but I didn't want her to worry more than she was already. She was on the other side of the world; it wasn't like she could come to my rescue.

'Yeah, I found an apartment.' The words caught in my throat. I could just leave it at that; she didn't need to know the details.

'Awesome. Give me the deets.' *Shit.* 'I want to send you something.'

The bus lurched around a corner as my heart raced. A wedding invitation. Surely not. Surely not yet. I couldn't handle any more milestones whilst I felt like I was struggling to even get my foundations in place. First Sam, now Zoe. 'Just a little house-warming gift,' Zoe continued. I really needed to sort this housing thing out. 'What's the address? I've got a pen and paper now.'

'It's not actually ready yet, I'll get it to you next week or something,' I replied, glad she couldn't see the shame written on my face. I could almost feel the confusion etched on hers.

'Ready? So where are you staying now?'

Oh *crap*.

'I've been…' I searched for the words. 'Staying at a… friend's.' I settled on elusive.

'But we don't have any friends in Sydney,' she said as I cursed the fact we knew all the same people. Well, she knew all of my people.

'Not a friend exactly,' I began. God, I wanted to tell her. Just tell one person. About the improbability of it all, about the fact he was engaged, about the fact I was pretty sure part of him didn't want to be, the part of him that was really glad I was here. 'I'm staying with Sam,' I finally admitted and our three-second delay stretched into ten.

'Sam-Sam?' Zoe finally interjected. 'As in ex-boyfriend, love of your life, took you ages to get over Sam? *That* Sam?'

'That's the one,' I said, bracing for the onslaught.

'What the…' Her words trailed off into the ether. My heart hammered in my chest. I'd always wondered whether she'd kept our pact, whether she'd severed her ties with him as she'd forced me to block him on every one of my social media accounts. But she'd never have suggested coming to Sydney if she'd thought for one second that he'd be here.

'Sam is in Sydney? Why?' Zoe asked, proving my point. Before I could even begin to answer, Zoe added, 'What the *hell*? And you're staying with him?' I could almost see her pressing her hand to her forehead. 'Jess, this is a bad idea. It's taken you long enough to get to…' My heart hammered harder. Why did I think Zoe would find this anything other than frustrating? She'd never understood that our story had never ended.

'Zoe?' I heard someone's voice echo in the stairwell where I knew Zoe would be sitting on the top step, phone pressed to her ear, knees pulled to her chest. She'd taken many calls there on my behalf. 'Zoe, Ben's on the line. Something about a fridge-freezer delivery.'

'Oh right, I…' I could almost hear her mind whirling, trying to weigh up the urgency of our calls. 'One minute,' she said.

'That's okay, I can wait,' I replied, both scared and eager to hear what Zoe would say next. I imagined a lot. Frustrated she may be, but the Sam story had her hooked.

'No, Jess, I'm sorry, I have to take this. Look, I'll try and call you back soon, okay? I want to hear *everything*.'

Just not right now.

'In the meantime, just be careful, Jess.' Her voice was full of concern. 'I'd get out of there and into your apartment as soon as you can,' she urged, as if I was in danger.

That's the plan.

'Speak soon, I promise,' she said, her steps echoing as she went back towards the office, towards her call from Ben. 'I miss you.'

'I miss you more,' I whispered into the dead line.

Like, really miss you. And who we used to be.

*

23 May 2013 – Nottingham, England

Morning light sparkled across my bedspread, undulating over his breathing body. I could have watched him sleep forever, his new shifts contantly shifting the sleeping patterns between us. He looked like a painting, peaceful but with hidden depths never fully discovered. I'd happily spend a lifetime trying to figure them out. Three sharp knocks broke the silence but before either of us could scramble for pyjamas, the door was flung open and Zoe drifted in, not the hurricane she so often was, but lighter, less present. Something was wrong. Sam grasped the bed sheets as Zoe sat at the foot of the bed.

'That's fine, Zoe, come right in.' Sam pushed himself up to sitting, his words heavy with sarcasm. 'Not like we were sleeping or anything.' I pressed his leg under the duvet, forcing him to sense the tone. Sam was so used to seeing her boisterous and carefree that I was pretty sure he wouldn't recognise her any other way, wouldn't realise anything was wrong. But I could.

'Sam, can you just… give us a sec?' I turned to him, eyes wide with meaning.

'Are you kidding me?' he asked, looking from the sheets wrapped around him to me. I shook my head, sorry to kick him out but knowing in this moment that Zoe needed me more.

'Alright.' Sam's tone softened, a look of genuine concern spreading across his features as he finally twigged. I loved him for that. 'Zo, close your eyes.' He smiled and she did, snuggling a little further into the sheets. Sam dressed, mouthing 'hope she's okay' before leaving the room.

'I'm so sorry.' Zoe looked up from her spot, lying across the foot of our bed. She looked younger without make-up on, but there were red marks circling her eyes.

'Don't be.' I moved to sit beside her, bed sheets still pulled close, stroking her hair the way I had when her wildness had taken her too far. Like everyone else, Sam had egged her on at first, but now that we were getting more serious, it kind of felt like Zoe should be doing the same, like maybe it was time for us all to start growing up, preparing for what was next.

'What's the matter?' I asked, pretty sure I already knew the answer.

'My dad got in touch.' She confirmed my thoughts with tear-stung eyes.

'Thought so.' I nodded, stroking her again. Zoe's dad had left their family just months before we'd started university. It was messy and so was processing it. That was why I had never questioned her partying or never wanting to settle down; life could be unpredictable. I knew I was lucky mine was so stable, my future with Sam so clear.

'What did he say?' I asked, quietly, conscious Sam was waiting outside, but knowing I'd move mountains to give Zoe all the time in the world.

'Not a lot.' She shrugged, tears falling freely. 'Not enough.'

I held her tighter as she sobbed.

'I'm sorry.' She wiped her tears with the back of her hand. 'I'm so sorry, I didn't mean to interrupt your morning… I didn't mean to…'

'Zoe.' I held her hand in mine. 'We're best friends.' I smiled down at her, wanting to fix everything but knowing I couldn't. But for every promise her dad couldn't keep, I knew I could at least make one. 'Crack of dawn to the middle of the night and every bloody minute in between.' I squeezed her hand tightly in mine. 'You'll always be my priority.' New tears brimmed in her eyes as a smile spread across her wet cheeks.

'And,' she whispered weakly, before salvaging some strength, 'you'll always be mine.'

Chapter Fifteen

3 August 2020 – Sydney, Australia

I dragged myself off the bus and stepped into the evening in Coogee. The streets were alive with groups of friends, joggers and commuters happy to be on this side of work. I leaned against the back of the wooden bus shelter and looked out across the sea. My eyes traced the burnt horizon as I tried to recapture the feeling I'd left work with: useful, wanted. Zoe was busy, she was at work. And she was still worried about me, she still cared. Not that she needed to be worried. I'd had a good day, seen Sam, I'd even made my way back from Woolloomooloo alone. I had a job – kind of. I'd be out of his apartment by the end of the week, for sure. Everything was going to work out. It had to. Walking on the pavement, tracing its way along the beach, I looked upwards at the endless ascent before me. Jamie would just take a cab, too gorgeous to break a sweat anywhere but her early morning runs. But then I wasn't Jamie. I wasn't a doctor with legs for days. I had to walk – or rather climb – step by step. At least this time, Sam wasn't around to see it.

'Jess?'

Shit. I turned to find the tall, slender figure of Jamie's friend beside me, the one who seemed to share her ability to eat pancakes without gaining an ounce of weight.

'Alice?' I asked, as I put one leg in front of the other and tried not to cry from the blisters. Alice's long limbs stretched out beside me, making the climb look effortless. 'Good day?' I asked, accentuating the question mark to differentiate from the fact I wasn't just saying hello again. I would fit in here if it killed me, which, judging by this mountain, it might. She smiled as I willed the redness of my cheeks away.

'Busy but good.' Alice gave a brief nod; but of course, it was going to be busy if you worked as a doctor and still insisted on going for early morning runs. 'How about you?'

'It was, actually,' I said, trying not to sound too surprised or give too much away; I knew anything I said about lunch would get back to Jamie quicker than you could say 'Big V'.

'You're helping with the Leo Todd thing, right?' Alice asked. News sure did travel fast – was there anyone in their circle who wasn't also in the loop?

'Yeah.' I grinned, trying to catch my breath. 'Just for a bit. You into art?' I asked, keen to keep the conversation on safe ground, nowhere near Jamie, even further from Sam.

'A little,' she said, not bothered or breathless. 'Anything that gets me out of the hospital.' She shrugged. 'Maybe we can go for a culture-binge sometime?' I glanced down to her pin-legs; evidently culture was the only binge Alice would be having anytime soon. I shrugged away the offer, cursing myself for how much I wanted to be her friend, *anyone's* friend here.

'So, you work in a hospital?' I asked in an attempt at small talk. Thankfully, she took the bait, chatting about her day in a blur of patients, drugs, sickness and health, as I put one wrecked foot in front of the other until the turn-off to Oberon was blissfully in sight.

'This is me.' I slowed to a halt where the street met the main road. Alice looked back at me, her long brown hair pulled to one side.

'Me too.' She smiled. Oh, they were neighbours; I guess that made their decision to run together at dawn make a little more sense. I continued down the drive towards Sam and Jamie's with Alice's footsteps behind me. 'I'm not stalking you,' she laughed. 'I'm having dinner round yours tonight.' Alice smiled, narrowing her all-knowing eyes, but what could she know? In any case, it was kind of her to refer to it as mine when it was clearly anything but. As I turned my key in the door to let us both in, the sound of chatter and music coming from the kitchen-living room filled the corridor before me. *Shit, shit, shit.* That was why Alice was here. Jamie's church friends were round. And I'd told Sam I would be out, suggested I had my own friends to hang out with now. I froze, the door still open behind us, as I tried to work out if I could turn around and escape. It wasn't that I had anything against the said church friends, or even against church in general. It just wasn't really for me. Apart from the odd Carols by Candlelight, the last time I had stepped foot in one, I had ended up being kicked out of a Remembrance Day memorial service with the Brownies (apparently turning the collection bag into a hand puppet was *not* a funny joke) and I hadn't really given it a chance since. But I'd given it a hell of a lot more of a chance than Sam. Where me and church seemed to have come to an agreement that we were better off as long-distance, see-them-once-a-year-at-Christmas friends, Sam had actively had a problem with it – a reluctance to entertain any mystery he couldn't understand. Just seeing him nodding along with Jamie, getting passionate about her perspective in a way he never could with me made me want to run in the other direction, blisters be damned. I hadn't even taken my shoes off; if I could just turn around and sneak back out maybe they'd never know I was here. Before I could act, Alice shouted, 'We're here!' just as another familiar face poked his head around the arch into the hallway, his floppy surfer's fringe falling effortlessly to one side.

'Alice!' Joshua greeted her, before turning to me. His eyes darted to my ripped jeans, more relaxed than yesterday's outfit, up to my oversized blouse. 'We've saved you both some food.' He looked from Alice back to me. Oh crap. I bent down to prise off my shoes.

'Oh, you can leave them on,' Joshua said.

You'd have to pay me, Joshua.

Ouch, ouch, ouch. Shoes now off and now my true five-foot three, I walked meekly into the busy kitchenette. Sam clocked my arrival immediately, leaving Jamie's side to greet me.

'You're here.' He handed me a glass of wine – my favourite again. 'I'm glad you are,' he added. At the dinner? In Sydney? I unglued my eyes from Sam's intensity just long enough to see Jamie nodding her welcome from a distance.

'Want some food with that?' Sam asked. He'd changed out of his suit and was now the picture of comfort in his statement white T and blue jeans. I took a sip of wine, savouring the smell, swirling it around my mouth, my eyes closing just a little. Sam's laugh broke its spell. 'You never did look at me the way you looked at wine.' He laughed again. We both knew that was a lie. My eyes darted towards Jamie, behind her to Joshua. Sam needed to keep his voice down if he didn't want me kicked out in two seconds flat. Ex-girlfriends in box rooms was surely not the done thing in these circles. In any circles really.

'Food, Jess?' Sam asked again.

'I'm still stuffed from brunch,' I said.

'Great, wasn't it?' The food or the company?

'It really was,' I whispered into my wine.

Jamie appeared by Sam's side, bringing me back to reality. 'Hey.' She beamed, hooking her arm under Sam's. He smiled across at her, her hair now loose, her spray-on jeans replaced by a bohemian sundress, midnight blue. 'How was CreateSpace?'

'It was good actually,' I said, revelling in the truth for as long as I could.

'Great!' She smiled again, stroking his arm back and forth, back and forth. 'I can't thank you enough for using your spare time like that,' Jamie went on as my stomach sank; spare time, spare bedrooms, always the spare something. 'Let me introduce you to some people, Jess,' she offered, unhooking herself from Sam to place a cold hand on my shoulder. Clutching my wine, I followed Jamie over to the sofas. There were about seven or eight people gathered there, some sitting on dining chairs pulled over from the table and others sitting on the floor with their backs against the legs of those lucky enough to get a seat on the couch.

'Guys, this is Jess,' Jamie addressed the room. 'Sam's friend from the UK.' I felt all eyes on me, as if my status as an ex was about to be outed. In quick succession, I was introduced to the smiling faces around the room.

'Mark.' A tall, dark-haired guy extended a hand out towards me before offering me his seat on the sofa. 'And this is my partner, Andrew,' he said, before nudging Andrew to surrender his place.

'Oh no, you really shouldn't,' I began, before Andrew obediently followed Mark to sit on the floor.

'I do as I'm told.' Andrew rolled his eyes as everyone laughed. Joshua and Alice filled their spaces.

'Hey!' Mark laughed at them, pretending to be annoyed. 'That was for our guest!' I know he was trying to be nice, but calling me a guest only made me feel more like an outsider.

'On your feet, lose your seat,' Alice laughed, winking in my direction; was she trying to be my *friend*?

'Hey, there's still room for a little one!' Joshua objected, nodding to the too-small space between him and the arm of the sofa. He forced himself even further towards Alice until their tanned arms blended into one. I wasn't sure I believed in God, but it was fair to say these creatures were blessed.

'Joshua,' he joked, leaning back slightly to offer a hand in my direction even though he could barely extend his arm. His face was inches from my own; I was practically sitting on top of him.

'Jess,' I said in response, laughing.

'You look nice.' He nodded down at my almost sheer blouse whilst I tried to cover my bra. I glanced over to where Alice was busy chatting to Jamie. *Not in comparison to them, I don't.* Turning back to Joshua, I took a good look at him in return. Hipster beard drawing attention to sky-blue eyes, floppy hair pushed to one side.

'Thanks.' I shrugged, looking around the room. Sam was still in the kitchen, but his eyes kept glancing in our direction, caught between a look of confusion and admiration. I could swear I saw a hint of envy mixed in his expression.

'How are you feeling about the apartment?' Joshua asked. 'Can't be nice to feel so unsettled.' Unsettled. *Settled.* That damn word again.

'Yeah, just excited to get in now,' I lied.

'I bet.' He raised one eyebrow before looking down at his rough hands. You could tell he was the kind to throw himself around on a surfboard. A little like Sam. He looked at me again, opening his mouth to speak but hesitating for just a moment before saying, 'Bit weird about your landlord and the renovations, eh?' My eyes couldn't help but widen, feeling the burn of Joshua's blues ones, like a spotlight in an interrogation room. I looked around the room for sight of Sam, longing for him to save me before I could incriminate myself further.

I was sure Joshua could see right through me. Perhaps years of reading defensive youths had prepared him for detecting my lies. I wanted to move but his gaze held me still.

'Yeah.' I held his eye contact a moment longer, taking another sip of wine. 'Weird.'

'And did you get everything sorted at the magazine?' he pressed on, as I caught my breath.

'Huh?' I couldn't help but spill the sound, trying my best not to spill my wine.

'They wanted to check something yesterday?'

'Oh right, yeah.' I sighed, struggling to keep up with my own secrets around him. 'Just confirming a few things for when I start.'

'In two weeks' time?'

'Yes,' I said, cementing my lies. 'In two weeks' time.'

'Must be pretty stressful.' Joshua cast a brief look to Sam, still shooting glances over at us – at me – from the other side of the room.

'What?' I asked again, distracted. Seriously, Joshua was going to start thinking there was something wrong with me – if he didn't think that already.

'Like, do you have someone to talk to about it? Not being able to get into your house, temping at the gallery until you're able to start your real job…'

I gulped; right now there was nothing real about it.

'Hard to be in a state of flux at the best of times, never mind so far from home,' Joshua said, casting another look towards Sam, so brief that had I blinked, I would have missed it. There was nothing to talk about. Nothing at all. And if there was, why did Joshua think I'd be talking with Sam? Had Sam told him about us, about how close we were, how we used to share a home, how once upon a time he *was* my home?

'Not really, but it's fine, honestly,' I said, stuck between Alice and a hard chest. I mean, *place*. A hard place.

'Oh.' Joshua looked taken aback, bringing his full attention back to me. 'Well, if you need someone to talk to, I'm never too far away…' He smiled, a smile so warm and full it seemed to deserve the kind of honesty I couldn't give. I had to sort this on my own, do *something* on my own.

'That's okay, I'm sure you're really busy with your young people,' I said.

'No, seriously, Jess.' His hand seemed to move closer, which was pretty improbable given our proximity. 'If you need to chat, I'd make it a priority.'

My stomach flipped as my mind went to Zoe, now prioritising her fridge-freezer. But something told me telling Joshua a little would lead to telling him a lot. I let out a nervous laugh as I observed the group around us. Jamie and Alice chatted, Sam was topping up Mark and Andrew's wine glasses, the perfect host. He looked over to me as I checked my watch – half past eight. Surely too early to go to bed? Joshua moved beside me, reclining further, his shoulders resting against the back of the sofa, one arm around Alice, one arm around me. He grinned again, like he was about to ask me another question.

'Right, guys.' Sam's authoritative tone drew the attention of the room as he came to sit on the floor, completing the circle of people. The happy chatter died down as all eyes turned to him. What was he doing? 'Thanks for coming tonight. So, the agenda is pretty simple for this evening.' Agenda? There was an agenda for tonight? Was this the part where Sam started to explain his twenty-point argument on why the dinosaurs undermined the existence of a deity? What was going on? 'As you know, it can be pretty hard to get to know people properly in just a few hours on a Sunday.' I hung onto each of his words as I tried to make sense of them. What was happening on Sunday? Everyone around me smiled and nodded, clearly getting something I didn't. 'And so that's why we try and meet midweek to eat together and be together and you know, just build community.' They continued to nod. I'd never seen Sam look so confident; I'd practised his medical presentations with him time and again at university; he had fluffed and fumbled every line. I mean, I had thought he looked cute doing it and he had always pulled it together in the end but public speaking just wasn't his forte.

And yet, here he was, stringing sentences together with charisma and clarity. My wine started to tremble in my hand. 'Some of you may just be trying this Home Group out – and that's okay. Some of you will want to come every week – and that's great, but whatever your decision we hope it will bring you closer to God and closer to the church.'

Heads nodded, and smiles beamed around the room. I was too distracted by this new confidence to concentrate on his words. Something about God, something about church? But I thought Jamie was the Christian? Sam certainly wasn't. He wouldn't even go to church with his parents at Christmas. And he had hated all my fate malarkey. He thought horoscopes were shit. I'd only heard him invoke God's name in one situation and it wasn't one he'd want repeated in church.

'If it's okay with you guys' – he cast a fleeting look my way – 'I'd just like to start by saying a little prayer.'

Holy shit.

Heads bowed around me as my eyes stayed glued on him before glancing to Jamie, who was doing the same, eyes fixed on her fiancé, encouraging him on.

Sam hadn't just changed. He was changing for her.

Chapter Sixteen

4 August 2020 – Sydney, Australia

I headed towards the car; this time I was up, dressed, wearing shoes and mascara, and ready to talk. All night my mind had been running a mile a minute, trying to make sense of the fact that my adamantly atheist ex-boyfriend now seemed to be hosting some sort of church in his living room. Like I said, I had nothing against Christianity. I had nothing against any religion. It was the twenty-first century for Christ's sake, people could believe what they wanted. I just knew my ex-boyfriend wasn't one. He might think he'd found God after seeing his smoking hot girlfriend in a bikini, but one Charlie's Angel did not a Christian make. Clearly it was a phase for him; and that was okay – people went through phases. But marriage is not a phase; in fact, it's meant to be one of the most permanent things this side of heav— wherever. And then there was the doubt in his eyes every time he talked about it, every time he looked at her and then at me. I just didn't want to see him trapped into something, trapped into some*one* he was going to regret.

'You managed shoes today!' Sam called out from his open-door driver's seat. 'It's a miracle!'

I cringed. Was he trying to say these things on purpose? Did he say them before, when religion was just a man-made construct to him? I forced a weak smile as I got into the car. I caught Sam looking me up and down as I did: the same ripped jeans as yesterday but this time with a blocky oversized T-shirt, jet black – not a hint of yesterday's inappropriate sheer in sight. Sam turned the key in the ignition and started to drive, the backdrop beautiful even though the sun still refused to shine. I said very little as I searched for an opener. *Sam, I don't think you are a real Christian; are you sure you've not accidentally joined a cult?* No, that didn't seem right. *Sam, I know you think you love God, but you actually love Jamie.* No, that wasn't right either. *Sam, please don't marry her unless you really believe it's right.*

'You're uncharacteristically quiet today, J,' Sam said, briefly taking his eyes from the road to raise an inquisitive eyebrow in my direction. The sound of Sam's music in the background failed to distract either one of us from the tension that filled the car. How could everything feel exactly the same between us when his whole bloody outlook had seemingly changed?

'It's just last night, really,' I said, hoping the next part of my sentence would just flow from there even though my mind was struggling to form coherent thoughts.

'Home Group?' Sam asked. I wasn't down with the lingo but yes, I guess that was what I meant. The question lingered as I searched around for the right words.

'Yeah, Home Group,' I said, the words tasting foreign in my mouth. 'I guess I'm a little confused as to why you are suddenly into all of this stuff. It's just not you.' I looked at him, my words hanging in the air like a bad smell.

'Oh, J,' Sam began, the way he often did. 'You're right.'

I smiled, somewhat surprised that I was.

'It isn't me, well… it wasn't me, the old me. But things change, I'm different now.' He briefly looked my way again to see the smirk fall from my face. 'And I know that may seem sudden to you, but it's been a slow journey for me and, well, all my questioning has led me in one direction,' he explained, eyes now back on the road.

'To Jamie?' I asked.

'To God,' he replied. Well, if that was what he wanted to call her. I swallowed hard.

'Which came first, Jamie or the God stuff?' I asked, slightly awkwardly. Sam sighed. I knew it.

'Jamie,' he replied reluctantly.

'And she, erm…' I went on, knowing I was treading on eggshells, searching for the right words. '…*encouraged* you to convert?'

'No, Jess, Jamie didn't *encourage* me to do anything,' Sam said, shaking his head but not taking his eyes off the road. 'We met in the hospital we were working at together and we started talking and, well, there was just something different about her,' Sam explained, romantic nostalgia in his voice.

'I'll tell you what was different about her, Sam,' I began, desperately trying to act like 'just friends' but knowing 'just friends' shouldn't care this much. So what if Sam said his outlook had changed? I didn't buy it, and I'm pretty sure Sam didn't either, not really. 'She's gorgeous. She's a *doctor*. You took one look at her and knew you'd do or say whatever—'

'Jess, please. That is *not* what happened. I asked her out and we went for dinner and Jamie explained how much her faith meant to her. She was so full of life, so *together*, that I just thought… I thought, I wanted to find out why she was like that…'

'And now you know?' I asked, stung by the 'together' comment as I felt anything but. This was ridiculous. I wasn't saying Sam should be with me – well, not really – but to be with someone who made him completely change who he was surely couldn't be the right thing. She was successful, together. That part made sense at least. Heart-wrenching sense.

'I think I do,' Sam replied, his voice softening.

'But you're not sure?' I asked. See, I knew he had doubts. I knew he wasn't convinced.

'Jess. This stuff's pretty big, right? Sure, I have my doubts. But I've felt enough to make me doubt that God *isn't* real.' Sam hesitated for a moment, sheepish at sharing something so sensitive. 'I've started to have a relationship with him and…'

A relationship with *him*? This was too much. Sam was not a Christian. He was a materialistic sceptic who had never given this stuff a second thought in the whole five years we were together. Brainwashed was a strong word, but he'd been surrounded by friends, colleagues and one persuasively hot girlfriend who believed this thing. It was bound to have an effect. It could have happened to anyone.

'And your relationship with Jamie, getting married and everything.' I stiffened beside him and Sam seemed to follow suit. 'You're pretty sure about that too?'

I shouldn't have said it; I shouldn't have said a lot of things. Not when I wasn't sure I wanted the answer. But then how else could I explain Sam's eagerness to see me, be near me? I needed to know what it all meant.

He sighed deeply again, not taking his eyes off the road as I felt myself going more and more off-piste. 'I mean, do you feel… sure?'

He'd always felt sure with me – until, of course, he didn't.

Changing lanes to avoid the traffic, Sam turned his head, eyes heavy with confusion. Trying to shake away the moment. He looked trapped, manipulated by his own mind. Confused about what he wanted even now. Now I was here. And he'd been the one to welcome me into his home, his home with her. And he'd said he missed me.

Sam's phone started to ring on the dashboard: Jamie – always managing to get in the middle of things. Sam reached for it and turned the screen face down.

'Woah, sounds like a sure thing at the weekend,' Sam said as he turned up the radio to hear Saturday's surfing conditions. So surfing was a sure thing, but what about Jamie? A woman so fundamentally different to me, so different to him, that he'd forgotten who he was in the first place. Sam's change of topic drifted into the background as I tried to order my rising thoughts. He didn't want to be surrounded, he wanted to question, he wanted to doubt; maybe that's why I was here. Maybe it was fate after all. The reason I was here was to remind Sam of who he really was. Like Sam had said: what were the odds of bumping into each other here, after all this distance, after all this time?

Sam reached a hand to the radio dial and changed it back to his so-called music. Even the throbbing bassline of the track couldn't drown out the voice in my head. I needed to save Sam from making the biggest mistake of his life, a lifetime of being someone other than the man I'd always known him to be. And I had less than two months, eight weeks, fifty-six flipping days to do it.

*

20 October 2012 – Brighton, England

His hand moved up my thigh, hungry for more. I grabbed it at the top, escorting it back down. I thought I was the spontaneous one but there was something about our being here that made Sam relax, become more messy, untethered.

'*Piss off.*' I looked up to see the figures of Zoe and Austin in the distance, Austin trying to trip her up whilst Zoe ran along the sand in search of ice cream. It was freezing, but true to form, Sam had had a picture in his mind of what he wanted our first trip to his hometown to look like. And I thought I was the artist.

'To think that they could have ever been together.' Sam laughed, shaking his head at the thought. It was never going to happen, but bless the boy for trying. I pulled Sam's hoodie further around myself, snuggling into his side, our bodies morphing together: the perfect fit.

'So, this is home?'

'Yeah,' he said, gazing out to the horizon. 'See the old pier there? That's where my cousin first took me out on a board.' He grinned, eyes full of nostalgia. 'He held me up on it and I felt like I was flying.'

'Sure you weren't just second-hand high?' I nodded to the circles of youths lighting up under the pier. 'What does it feel like?' I asked, so used to seeing Sam passionate about patients and professionalism, not something so raw and instinctive as riding the waves.

'Getting high?' Sam raised his eyebrows, knowing that was not what I meant. 'When I surf? I guess I feel like all the pressure just fades away.' He was looking out over the water, grey-blue for as far as the eye could see. 'All thoughts of grades and getting jobs and making the right choices and doing the right thing just disappear.'

I had always envied kids who went to private schools and grew up in posh houses until I met Sam. It seemed privilege was synonymous with pressure.

'I leave all of that behind,' he continued. 'And all that's left is the feel of the cold water, the sound of the waves, the taste of salt, and the feeling…' His sentence trailed off, for the first time not knowing precisely where he was going. 'Have you ever felt that way?' he asked. I was feeling that way now, feeling the rest of our surroundings slip away until all that was left was Sam. But I had felt it before, in the smell of paint and the strokes of colour and the feel of my brush on a once-blank canvas.

'I feel it when I paint. Maybe not the same, but similar. That can be your next class…'

'Only when I get you on a board,' he teased. I shook my head, breaking away to look out at the frosty ocean, laughing nervously at my own trepidation. 'Guess we're pretty different, right?'

He was a soon to be doctor with his future planned out. And I… well, wasn't.

'Yeah, I guess.'

He laughed again. 'Good job I've been looking for something different, then, isn't it?'

Chapter Seventeen

I walked into CreateSpace, head still buzzing, adrenaline pumping. Sam couldn't get married. Not to Jamie. They were too different. He was too different. I had to make him remember who he was before that temptress came into his life. Well, *temptress* was a bit strong, but still, Sam couldn't get married to someone who didn't know who he was. The same damn kitten heels from the day before bit at my ankles as I smiled at the receptionists, striding past the gallery's shop purposefully into the exhibition space. *Do not bring personal stuff to work*, I reminded myself. It had been my mantra at *Art Today*. Although, Tim's insistence that I put on mascara before seeing my ex-boyfriend seemed to indicate he knew I had some extracurricular drama afoot. And everyone in Coogee knew about him and Carlo. Clearly, the line between work and pleasure was pretty blurry around these parts.

In the first room I was greeted by the vision we had agreed upon yesterday, my vision, of tones and textures telling a story of time. The blue and yellow hues surrounding me were reminiscent of the Sydney sky between morning and midday, transporting me to an upside-down world where everything was cheerfully simple, just as it was meant to be. I had spoken and, for some reason, they had listened.

One particular painting stopped me in my tracks. It was a large landscape of three messy horizontal lines: blood orange, deep blue, light grey, interlacing intermittently and fading into one another – the sand, the sea and the sky, sometimes so distinct, at other points so soft they slid into one. For just a moment their colours dispelled all anxiety, before my pressing to-do list unfolded in my mind: save wages, find apartment, get a proper job. *Save ex-boyfriend from living a lie.* I looked around the gallery, tasting the irony: it wasn't like being honest had got me here. Tim thought I'd be an editor at *Art Today Australia* by the end of the month.

I dreaded to think how late Tim and Olivia must have stayed while I was busy discovering my ex-boyfriend had not only saved me in Woolies but had been *saved* himself. I couldn't see them, but I could hear the sound of Olivia's heels clicking and the flamboyant exclamations of my born-for-Broadway boss coming from the second room. It wouldn't surprise me if they'd slept here. Sure enough, I walked into Room B to be greeted by Olivia pacing and Tim holding a hand to his perfectly sculpted chin. At least their anxiety was set against a backdrop of dusky pinks and sultry greys, the dusk to darkness colours of the collection, just as we had planned. En masse, the ensemble looked stunning, abstracts so amazing that they invited the mind to imagine more. Tim and Olivia, on the other hand, looked spent. They didn't even notice me walk in. I cleared my throat loudly. Nothing. I turned; maybe I'd be able to grab myself a coffee from the staff room before they even noticed.

'Jessica.' Tim turned to me in disdain. 'Please tell me you're not leaving already after we've been here all night.' Of course he'd look now. I'd thought *he* thought I was doing him a favour. Looking at him now, hand on hip, I should have known better.

'I, erm… This. Looks. Great!' I replied, turning to retrace my steps towards them and throwing my arms wide to admire the space. Olivia looked up, fear in her eyes. I'd said the wrong thing. Why did I always keep saying the wrong thing?

'This looks *great?*' Tim echoed, evidently thinking it looked anything but. '*Great?*'

'Well I… I think it does,' I replied honestly, not sure whether I lacked the artistic skill to see the issue or the artistic temperament to care.

'We stayed up all night,' Tim said, exasperated. 'All night! And still we can't fit in *Tuesday's Slumber.*' He gestured towards a canvas, leaning against the studio wall. Ironic, I thought, given that it was a Tuesday and both had gone without sleep. But I knew now wasn't the time. I looked to the piece, almost a solid block of blue until you stepped closer to see the small, scratchy jagged brush strokes, a fractious sleep painted like the patchwork sky of Van Gogh's *Starry Night*.

'We can't fit them all in. It's impossible. It's either *Tuesday's Slumber* or *Patience*!'

I desperately prayed for the latter. We'd already established that we didn't need to use them all, but judging from how Tim looked at *Tuesday's Slumber* and how Olivia looked at *Patience*, I knew better than to suggest we leave either of them out.

'I think we should go for *Patience*,' Olivia bravely suggested, gesturing to the light grey swirls scrawled across the canvas, so calm and unobtrusive that they could settle into either space.

'And you'd be wrong,' Tim snapped in return. Bloody artists. Olivia bit her quivering lip; she'd need a thicker skin if she was going to survive this level of sass.

'Now,' I began, sounding a bit more authoritative than I'd intended as my voice bounced around the room, 'it's all going to be okay. I have an idea.'

Tim and Olivia took a step closer to me in perfect unison. The meek and the mighty, hanging on my every word. I looked at Tim, glasses perched on the end of his nose, his grey T-shirt tucked loosely into his ripped jeans. I looked at Olivia, delicate in her designer gear. Why were they trusting me with this?

'You're both right,' I said slowly – a win-win answer undoubtedly received as lose-lose. 'Personally, I think *Tuesday's Slumber* is the stronger piece.' Tim drew back his shoulders, broad and boastful. 'But I think Olivia is right too – *Patience* is more cohesive with the rest of the collection.' Tim's face fell and he placed his hand on his hip again as if to say: *and that helps us how?*

'I say we hang *Patience* in here and we place *Tuesday's Slumber* in the foyer, above the reception; that way, the press will have something to get excited about as they make their way in.'

'What press?' Tim asked, confused. 'Leo's agent said she didn't want to do press.' Yes, she wouldn't; 'Privacy Over Publicity' – that was the headline Mary-Anne's latest feature on the artist had gone with. I think she had even referred to Leo as 'him'. Mystery was her publicity. But that didn't mean the *gallery* didn't need it, that we didn't need to actually tell people that the up-and-coming Brit's work had arrived even when she hadn't, and that local artists were welcoming her too. I breathed deeply and stared at *Patience*.

'Yes, but what about general publicity, a press night?' I asked, unsure as to what tantrums or breakdowns my words might unleash. Dramatically, Tim sat on the floor – an act of protest or defeat, I couldn't tell. Olivia remained perched on the tips of her stilettoes. I stood a little too close to her just in case she began to fall.

'Did Carlo—' I began before Tim cut me off.

'Yes, Carlo used to handle the press. He used to handle everything…'

I would have rolled my eyes at him throwing his toys out the pram if I hadn't spent the last three years doing the same; we'd both lost our better halves. I bit my lip; I couldn't fall apart now. For the first time in a long time people were expecting me to be the strong one.

'It's okay,' I said, crouching into an uncomfortable mid-squat next to Tim. 'Some of the details get swallowed up in the big idea.' Tim hugged his ripped knees. Honestly, he was in his fifties – either that or he'd partied *really* hard when he was young. 'It's all going to be okay,' I repeated for what felt like the hundredth time since I had entered CreateSpace, expectant to meet the self-confident artists working inside. 'I have a plan.'

Fifty going on fifteen, Tim lifted his head from his lap.

'I'll write a press release and call in some favours from the contacts I worked with – *work* with – at *Art Today*,' I corrected, before Tim could object. 'I'm sure the other PAs will know who the best person to contact at each—'

'Other PAs?' Tim looked inquisitive. 'I thought you were an editor.' Damn it. Most people did. Largely because I tried to make them think I was. The truth was that archiving the print issues in alphabetical order was the closest I had got to the content. I had known twice as much about art than any of the editors there but without those stupid evening classes, more qualifications or a heftier portfolio, I was stuck covering for Lady Devon Atwood every time she came to work with a hangover from 'networking' too hard or walked into a meeting with no preparation. But you couldn't maintain a long-term, long-distance relationship without a little bit of sacrifice. Life was just too busy to do it all.

I could just tell him the truth. I'd actually done a good job in the couple of days I'd been helping them out here and he'd said it himself: he was pretty useless without Carlos. He needed me. And I needed him: I needed a job, rent money and my temporary living situation was, well, complicated. Surely Tim would understand. But then he might tell Jamie, and Jamie would tell Sam and Sam needed to trust me right now, needed me to be me right now, just a slightly more together me.

'I am,' I replied, just milliseconds before Tim began forming his next question, the next chink in the flabby armour I was trying so desperately to work around me. 'An editor.' I nodded, trying the word on for size for the millionth time. 'I just started out as a PA, worked my way up,' I explained. That was always the plan after all, until I got myself stuck. 'Don't worry,' I continued, a record of reassurance stuck on repeat, for whose benefit I wasn't quite sure. 'I'm still in touch with the PAs and although editors are well connected' – I nodded, as if imparting this editorial nugget – 'PAs know *everyone*.' I rallied some more enthusiasm as I finally felt the tremor of the truth fade away. 'I'll write up the press release and get to work. Trust me, our opening night will be filled to the brim with media bods and art editors. And better still, *Tuesday's Slumber* will meet them at the door.' Tim jumped to his feet and Olivia looked like she was trying hard to jump up and down but couldn't lift her red-soled heels from the floor.

'Jessica, you're a genius!' Tim exclaimed, engulfing me in an over the top embrace. I sighed. They were exhausting. But then I smiled. Tim thought I was a genius, *again*. Maybe now was the time to ask for my early pay packet? I only had four days left to get myself an apartment, leaving Sam with Jamie – a place I was growing less sure he wanted to be.

'And Hannah Sommers will be a shoo-in?' Tim interrupted my less-than-formed thoughts.

Why? My eyes betrayed a flash of fear, mind racing from deposits to divas.

'She's your new boss, right?' Tim pushed his glasses further up his crinkled nose.

'Right.' I matched his smile, careful not to send us back over the edge. 'She'll be there.'

'Do you think I should send out personal invitations?' Tim asked, still seeking answers.

'No!' I objected without a beat. 'No.' My voice softened. 'Leave the publicity to me. You have to keep the mystery. "The Mystery

Artist with the Mysterious Curator".' I painted the headline to Tim's silent applause. He could leave Hannah to me, no need to get involved, no need to risk a mix-up. And once I'd got her alone, once her edges had been softened by a couple of champagnes, I could finally have a second chance at getting her to convince *Art Today* to give me the same.

Chapter Eighteen

Having spent the rest of the day immersed in the room of slumber hues, hunched over Tim's beloved clipboard and brainstorming copy for the press release, it was good to be outside. I hadn't had a moment to think about deposits or apartments, but at least getting my five minutes with Sommers was looking more likely. She was bound to accept the invitation – CreateSpace was to Sydney what The White Cube was to London – undeniably one to watch. My chances of her accepting my CV were slimmer. But not impossible. Improbable but definitely not *impossible.* I held on to that glimmer of hope. Resting against the wall Sam had leaned upon the day before, I waited for him to arrive. My stomach sank. I had been so busy writing the press release and reaching out to PAs that I had barely given Sam a second thought. But then reality reared its ugly head. Above the worries about finding a flat and a job, Sam was engaged to be married to a woman who had changed him completely. And I was here now, out of all of the people he could possibly have bumped into. If the reason I was here was to stop him marrying into the biggest mistake of his life, I had little time to do it in.

'Jess?' I turned around to see him standing there, his suit slightly crumpled and his tie stowed away in his pocket. 'Sorry I couldn't meet you for lunch,' he apologised. He needn't have; he'd never had time for lunch when we were together anyway. At least this time I was rushed off my feet too, not sitting at home waiting for his call. 'Good day?'

'Crazy day,' I said, but then smiled. 'Good crazy.' And I meant it.

'Got to love a bit of good crazy.' Sam laughed warmly as he began to lead the way to the car. Wait, was he talking about me? I picked up pace to walk alongside him and he put his arm around my shoulder and gave it a little squeeze, a familiar glint of cheekiness in his eyes. He was. In the past, I would have shrugged him off and jabbed his ribs in mock aggravation, knowing he'd just hold me tighter. This time his familiar embrace felt fragile, like if I moved I might never get it back.

'Ready to go home then?' Sam nodded towards the car. Home. To Jamie. If I was ever going to remind Sam of what he really wanted I'd need to spend some time with him alone, away from the influences that had surrounded him all day, every day, since his own new start.

'Sure, although it's still pretty light out. Fancy walking to the beach?' I turned to him with what I hoped was an enticing smile. I knew he couldn't resist the ocean. Surfing to Sam was like Malbec to me: hopelessly irresistible. It was just a shame that one of us got fit whilst the other got pissed.

'Jamie's home already,' Sam replied, a hint of disappointment in his voice. 'And she'll worry. She just texted actually, she's made us dinner – says you're welcome to join us.' Sam rested a hand on the top of the car, hesitant to open the door and get in. 'In fact, I think she'll like it, she loves being a host.' *Yes, I know*; she'd made that part abundantly clear.

'That's nice of her,' I said through gritted teeth. When was she not nice? And more to the point, when was she not *home*? I thought doctors were supposed to be workaholics. Jamie just seemed to lounge around in leggings. I bet she wasn't even a doctor. I needed to get Sam by himself. Just a bit of time for us to have some fun and hang out for longer than sixty minutes (sixty-five if I piled on the mascara). I knew the one thing he couldn't resist. Well… that could be Plan B. But his *second* favourite thing could work for sure.

'Hey, Sam?' I asked, as we got into the car. 'I've been thinking.'

'Don't hurt yourself,' he quipped and promptly received his overdue rib-jab.

'I *think*' – I accentuated the word in mock defiance – 'I'd like to learn how to surf.' I smiled, trying to look wistful as I gazed out of the window, oceanwards.

'You're kidding me?' Sam shook his head. 'I tried to get you to surf with me *so* many times when we were together.' He turned the key in the ignition and started to drive. He had tried to get me to do a lot of things when we were together – read the newspaper, exercise on the weekends – surfing was one compromise I wasn't willing to make. *We* knew there was a limit to the kind of changes people in love should make.

'I just thought you wanted to see me in a wetsuit.' I raised an eyebrow in his direction.

'Well there was that.' Sam grinned. Was he flirting with me? Surely a *happily* engaged man shouldn't be flirting with his ex – not to mention inviting her to stay with him? 'But honestly, I used to beg you to go surfing. Why the change of heart?'

As if he needed to ask.

'That was Brighton, Sam. It was freezing.' I looked out of the window again. The sun was still refusing to appear – but surely it had to be warmer than bloody Brighton. 'You reckon you could arrange a lesson for me?' I asked, my blood pumping at the thought of Sam's body behind me as he corrected my stance. Sam grinned for a moment, as if imagining the same.

'Absolutely!' He said, placing a warm hand on my thigh, before quickly removing it; old habits die hard. But right now, it didn't seem like a habit he wanted to kick.

'I know you probably go with Jamie all the time…' I forced her name into the conversation, if only to test the water. He seemed more content to be here with me.

'Sometimes. She goes out with Joshua more though,' he sighed, disappointed at the thought. My mind jolted at the mention of Joshua, but forced itself back to Sam. For once I knew this was the right next step. 'How about this Saturday – Coogee Beach – ten o'clock?' Sam continued, his eyes lingering on my collarbone before searching for my smile. 'The waves are gnarly that time of day.'

'Sam, don't try and pull off "gnarly". It didn't work then; it doesn't work now.'

'Pipe down, J.' He shot me a glare before turning back to the road. 'You up for the challenge?'

'Hell, yeah,' I replied. He had no idea how up for it I was.

*

31 May 2016 – Nottingham, England

'Are you sure you want to do this, Jess?' Zoe gestured to the offer letter held in my hands; why were they *shaking*? This was what I wanted. I looked across at her, our memories captured in Polaroids pinned to the thin wall behind her.

'Yeah.' I looked down at the *Art Today* logo, heading a letter so different from the praises and promises of the one they'd sent me years ago telling me I'd been shortlisted. At least an admin position would get me down to London. 'It's the next step, isn't it?'

'To what?' Zoe looked up from her own position sitting cross-legged on my bed, adding another layer of polish to her chewed-down nails.

'You know, *forward*…' I waved the paper in her direction, '… into adulthood.' I perched on the edge of the bed.

'I don't think that's a destination, Jess.'

I looked down at her bright yellow nails. If it was, she wouldn't be arriving any time soon. She was set to go travelling, to postpone the 'next step' as long as humanly possible, before following Sam and me down to London.

'You know Sam's been planning the London move for *ages*.' I forced a smile, willing her to give me one in return. The pace of the hospitals was different there. In a city of almost nine million, how could it not be? I was excited for our pace too. Moving down, moving in; starting a new chapter in our own love story.

'I know, I know.' She raised a hand up to blow on her nails. 'It's just I thought *your* plan was to go pitch up shop in Cornwall, buy a little gallery…'

'And live off what?' I laughed, flinging my legs fully onto the bed, sending it bouncing.

'Beans on toast?' Zoe quipped.

'We're not freshers any more,' I said, as our minds recalled a time when everything was on toast, everything so simple. 'I need a bit more than beans.'

'But I didn't think you were bothered about journalism?' Zoe pressed on. Why wouldn't she stop? Why couldn't she just be happy for me? I batted away her words, not letting them hit me; journalism would be fine, better than fine.

'I think I'm starting to be,' I replied, far from convinced. I was graduating soon and one by one friends were lining up internships, securing jobs, planning moves, taking steps. Part of me envied Zoe for having the freedom to do whatever she wanted, wherever she wanted, to forge her own path. But I got to forge one with Sam and I couldn't really imagine it any other way. 'It's a good way to use my degree,' I pointed out. 'And it'll get me down to London. Maybe I could try and pick up those evening classes again?'

'You trying to convince me or yourself?' Zoe smiled, her eyes a little sad.

'Maybe a bit of both.' I shrugged, genuinely not sure. At least I was sure of him.

Chapter Nineteen

5 August 2020 – Sydney, Australia

'Are you sure you're okay, baby?' I heard Jamie's voice in a low whisper, stopping me in my tracks before entering the living room. 'You don't seem yourself,' she continued.

'I'm fine,' I could hear Sam say, his steps getting nearer.

'Are you sure? Sure you don't need some *space*? Some *quality time*?' Quality time; once again Jamie and I were after the same thing.

'I'm sure.' I heard him cut her off, as Jamie let out a sigh. I remembered that sigh. I also remembered tickling away his seriousness until he finally manned up and talked. Clearly, Jamie didn't know that secret. I wondered what else she didn't know about him?

'I know when you're hiding something,' she whispered back. 'Is it J—'

'Seriously, I'm *fine*,' Sam said, tone clipped, not raising his voice. 'I'm enjoying having…'

I listened intently, skin tingling at the mention of my name, nose tingling with… oh crap, I was going to sneeze. *Hold it in, Jess, just hold it in. Shit.* I lifted my finger and thumb to hold my sneeze from escaping into the silence, powerless against it, unable to stop it…

'Jess?' Sam called around the corner as I emerged slowly, feigning nonchalance.

'Morning.' I smiled at them both, Jamie's weary concern clashing against the energy Sam was exerting to pretend I belonged there. 'Am I interrupting something?' I asked, sure that I was. Jamie looked at Sam.

'No, not at all,' Sam objected, standing up and pulling out a chair beside him. 'We were just talking about dinner, weren't we?' He looked at Jamie, pleading with her to agree.

'Yes, we, er…' She could do with a few lying lessons herself. 'Want to join us tonight? I can cook.' I wasn't sure if she was offering me her food or her credentials. I studied her smile, striving for perfection even though she was clearly pissed off.

'Thanks.' I smiled back, still genuinely appreciative they were making space for me, even more so for the fact Jamie's aggression was still passive. Just three more days. I looked at Sam, a sadness escaping through his smile. *Three more days to let you know that you don't have to do this. Not if you don't want to. Not if you're confused.* I was almost convinced that my own 'are you sure you're okay?' would be met by a more honest response – at least he knew I wasn't perfect. He knew he didn't have to be anything other than himself around me. 'I'm actually checking out the apartment after work,' I said. Drama be damned, I needed that deposit from Tim today. I'd have to see what happened with Sam and Jamie from a distance – hopefully the distance from Randwick to Coogee. Jamie softened; the end was in sight.

'Cool,' Sam said, walking across to the living room to gather his gym stuff from the airer stretched wide and covering the room's initial cosmopolitan sheen with an unmistakable air of domesticity. 'Want some company?'

Jamie's modelesque frame stiffened all over again.

'No, it's okay. It'll be boring.' I shrugged, though my heart started to thud harder. It was okay, they had dinner plans anyway. 'Just admin.'

'You sure? Sure you don't want a lift?' he continued, overcompensating for not being able to give me one this morning. 'To Randwick?'

I smiled, shaking my head. One hundred per cent. Not until I knew my own address.

'I'll be okay.' I said. 'Thank you.' I turned to Jamie, who matched my tired smile as she gathered the breakfast bowls from the table, clearing the mess away.

'See you at home after?' Sam asked. I nodded. Home after. *After* I'd found a home.

A buzz interrupted the click-clack of my heels. I stalled on the steps leading into the gallery to retrieve my phone from the worn pocket of the only jeans I'd, naively, packed for Sydney. I froze as I saw the sender's name: H. Sommers. I swiped open the body of the message, heart in my mouth, subject line dancing: *Re: The Mystery of Morning – Leo Todd And Friends Launch New Exhibition at CreateSpace.* My hungry eyes devoured the words: *Dear CreateSpace.* I'd erred on the side of caution and kept my own identity anonymous too, content to hide behind CreateSpace's email account. *I'd like to accept your invitation to the opening night of your new Leo Todd exhibition. An opportunity I couldn't possibly refuse.* I hoped she'd feel the same about my working with her. I swiped across to my personal account, trying desperately to not mix work and what I wished was pleasure: turned out a handful of acceptances and rejections for a bunch of studio flat viewings in and around Randwick wasn't all that pleasurable. Not when a big part of me wanted to stay close to Sam. At least Sommers' reply might buy me some grace when I asked Tim for this week's wages. He'd made it very clear on my first day that he was going to pay me more for my *Art Today Australia* expertise – an offer I wasn't sure would stand up if he discovered that I'd only ever been Devon Atwood's PA. I imagined even less so if he exposed me as unemployed. I didn't have time to negotiate; I had to move forward with this today.

Pushing open the door, I found Tim and Olivia in situ. Tim was dressed in black dungarees, a flesh-coloured polo underneath that made me do a double-take. His hair and beard looked like they hadn't been trimmed in weeks. Devon would have never let her beauty regime slide. Once again, I blamed her skewed priorities for my redundancy – it was all about keeping up appearances for her. Olivia looked as pristine as ever, tapping manicured fingers on the laptop resting on one of the two flat-pack desks we'd erected as our makeshift office in the corner of the room. I sat at the second desk, quietly so as to not set off any more mood swings. They both nodded to me, but a comfortable silence fell between the three of us: my problem-solving had earned their trust.

'Jessica.' Tim's voice sounded anxious. 'How are the RSVPs coming?' He furrowed his brow. Yesterday he didn't care that the press weren't even coming, so I struggled to see how he could now look so concerned by the numbers. He made a gesture that seemed to say *hurry up* with one hand, unwilling to wait for my response.

'Good,' I said, drawing my loose hair to hang to one side. Sam used to know that was a sign I had something awkward to ask. Thankfully, Tim was unaware of this. 'Hannah Sommers just added her name to the list.' I beamed like it was an achievement, but Tim accepted this as a given: *she's your future boss, after all.*

'And what did you say back?' His hand encouraged me on. Nothing. It was just an RSVP. Tim noticed my blank stare. 'I actually have a question to ask her,' he said.

'I have a question to ask you too,' I interrupted, keen to ask about my wages in this brief moment of calm. As if on cue, Tim's phone vibrated on the desk. I tried to make sense of the clipped ends of his conversation. He didn't sound happy. I just couldn't work out whether it was a 'your ASOS order isn't coming today' or a 'we need to call it all off' not happy. Either way I needed that money before going to see the flats in Randwick tonight. It felt like a year raced by while Olivia and I waited with bated breath for Tim to hang up the call.

'It's bad; it's very bad.' Tim shook his head, removing his specs for dramatic effect. I waited for him to go on. Given the other outbursts I'd seen this week it still could have been the ASOS thing. 'That was the website developers,' he went on, beginning to pace. 'The ticket price has been listed wrongly this whole time. We'll be losing money on every sale.' His face looked as grey as his beard, his eyes searching mine for answers. I'd solved the layout issue, the lack of space for *Patience* and the press debacle but clearly Tim's bar was set higher than a hat-trick. 'Jess? We can't change the price now, can we?'

I was meant to be doing Tim a favour, not running the show. But my God, I *was* running the show. I looked into his questioning eyes: *can we?* It would look bad, sure. But we had to. We couldn't keep selling them at that price, not given how much Tim and Carlo had promised CreateSpace the exhibition would bring in. I'd always begrudged the pompous prices that seemed to follow the art world around, but the fat figures detailed in the contract had sent my mind into a spin. 'Spin.' My whisper escaped into the space between us. We just had to spin this. Lord knows I'd had to spin a yarn and turn a tale or two at *Art Today.*

'Okay, here's what we'll do,' I said. 'Get the developers to design a flash saying visitors have twenty-four hours left to buy tickets at the Early Bird rate; we'll then push up our original price a little to cover the projected loss – the publicity should enable the exhibition to carry a higher price.'

'Great – I was just about to say that,' Olivia chipped in, grasping for a little of the limelight. Turned out not everyone was qualified in bullshitting – you needed years as a PA for that.

'You think that will work?' Tim asked, peering over his glasses.

'Yes?' I replied, not meaning to send my inflection soaring in the process.

'Then great, we'll do that.' Tim nodded, smiling again. 'What would we do without you?' He cocked his head to study me closer. Olivia sat up a little straighter.

'You'd be fine.' I looked from Tim to Olivia, not meaning my voice to waver.

'No, seriously.' Tim's smile vanished, worry drawing lines across his face. 'We *can't* do this without you.' That seemed a bit rich seeing as I'd been with them for less than a week, but I couldn't help that feeling from filling my stomach afresh, telling me again: you're useful, *wanted.*

'Tim, I—'

'Jessica, I—' His question interrupted my own. I nodded to him to continue; he was my boss, after all. 'How do you think Ms Sommers would feel…' He had always called her Hannah before. He must really want something. 'If you were to stay with us a little longer, postpone your start date with the magazine a little – just until we have the opening night out of the way?' He stood a little straighter, overcompensating for the vulnerability scrawled across his face. He really needed me. And I needed him. I needed the job, the money. Most of all I needed to stop myself from leaping into his arms at the offer of a whole month of work.

'I… erm,' I stuttered, unsure how to play my response, how to make the doubt sound sincere. 'I think she'd be okay with it actually.' More than okay. I'm pretty positive she'd be alright.

'Are you sure?' He raised his bushy brows high, pushing his glasses further up his nose. 'Do you want to ask her now?' He motioned to my phone, already clutched in my hand.

'Oh, er – yeah – sure.' I pulled up her email and tilted the phone away from him, typing as quickly as I could: *Dear Ms Sommers, Great news. Can't wait to welcome you then.* When I could guide her around the gallery, until we were in a quiet space and I could ask the questions that would finally make my Sydney make-believe life real again. 'I'm sure she'll be okay with it. It's CreateSpace, after all,' I assured Tim, as he puffed up his shoulders, the compliment overshadowing the uneasiness of the moment. I couldn't help but match his smile; I'd finally loaned myself some time. But now to loan myself an apartment.

'Tim, could I…' I looked at Olivia, not wanting to force her out but needing to get myself *in*, into a ruddy apartment. 'Could I just have a quick word?'

Tim looked confused, like a *quick word* was what we were just having, but obliged all the same.

'Tim, I was wondering, what with me staying to *help out* a bit longer…' I emphasised the words, reminding him of the ones he had just said: *what would we do without you?* 'Do you think I could I get my first week of wages a little early?' It felt good to finally ask. I needed this. Just like he'd said he needed me. 'It's just, you know, kind of a little *tight* moving countries and everything. Hard to navigate…' Especially when you tie your new life in knots.

Tim looked at me, neither nodding nor shaking his head.

'I think, maybe, *you know*…' I kept saying those two little words as if any part of Tim could possibly identify with where I was at. 'When I start earning in the dollar, it might be easier spending in the dollar so if I could just get—'

'How early?' Tim finally interrupted, bringing my rambling to an end. I'd just pushed back my fake start date for him, the least he could do was be grateful.

'Today early?' I asked, wishing I'd sounded a little *more* entitled.

'Well, I wouldn't usually…' Tim glanced briefly at Olivia on the other side of the room.

'I understand…' I began, preparing myself for the let-down.

'But you've been so good to us,' he said. 'Flexibility begets flexibility.' He didn't need to know that everything about my life right now was flexible.

'I'm sure that'll be okay,' Tim added for good measure. I couldn't help but smile from ear to ear. I was starting to think I'd be okay too.

Chapter Twenty

This one *had* to be okay. Trepidation filled every fibre of my being as the estate agent turned a key in the lifeless white door to the last apartment on my list – at least it didn't have a cockroach crawling up it like the last one, or eight people sharing the same kitchen like the one before that. Standing to one side, the agent gestured towards the sitting area-cum-kitchenette, accentuating the 'flood of natural light' – *translation: at least this one has a window.* The room's features took less than a minute to go through – sofa, cooker, fridge, a *little* TV – it was strange how she used 'little' for that part, like the flat wasn't small all over. Two of the bedroom doors were locked as they were being used by the landlord for storage – making this seemingly the only one-person apartment in the whole city that I could have a hope of renting. As she led me into the available bedroom, I was surprised to find a double bed with clean bright sheets. After the three terrible viewings I'd endured, it looked irresistibly attractive. 'Call me Mimi' paced across the room, the noise of her heels on the stripped wooden floor drawing my attention to the authenticity of its planks – a nice touch. She opened a pine door just like the one we had walked through to reveal a modest en suite, almost new. I liked it. The living space even looked better as we walked back from the bedroom. I could get a few plants, put up a picture or two, add in some photo frames. I mentally started to move my limited stuff in. Thanks to Tim and my willingness to stay on at CreateSpace, a hefty deposit threatened to spill from my back pocket into Mimi's hands.

'You like it?' she asked, almost as desperate as me for the answer to be yes.

'I do.' I nodded.

'And you have your deposit?'

'I do,' I said again. I always thought I'd be saying those words around now standing across the aisle from someone handsome, soon to return to our three-bedroom house – not agreeing to stay in an apartment as small as Zoe's front room. But it was Sydney, a flat in Sydney.

'And your first month's rent?'

'I, er – I'll have it by the end of next week.' I gritted my teeth, eyes pleading.

'You *do* have a job here?' She gritted her own, eyes narrowing.

'I do.' I didn't skip a beat.

'A permanent one?' Her eyebrows accentuated the request. Was I really that easy to read? It sometimes felt like I had 'TEMPORARY' written across my forehead.

'I won't fall behind with payments, I promise.' I evaded the truth, forcing a smile wide enough to fill the room.

'Okay.' Mimi's voice softened. 'There's one other couple looking at the room,' she explained. Of course there bloody was. I circled on the spot to take in the room again – it took all of two seconds.

A couple would be on top of each other in here. Maybe that was the point? I tried to mask my jealousy, from Mimi and myself. This was a step forward.

'Leave your number with me and I'll let you know who the owners decide to go with by tomorrow morning at the latest. Sorry if that's a bit last minute.'

Three days to get my life together, find out where Sam's head was at and move into a new place. Mimi had no idea how last minute my life had become.

*

6 August 2020 – Sydney, Australia

My phone buzzed violently. It was on silent but the racket of its vibrations on the wooden bedside table was anything but. I reached out to rescue it in one ninja-like swipe. It wasn't like I had to 'come round' – I'd been shuffling from one side of the bed to the other all night.

Clearing my throat to answer, I smoothed down my hair as if the caller could see me. All those hours watching *Made in Chelsea* had made me forever on guard, as if anyone would be interested in watching my messed-up reality. About to put the phone to my ear, I looked down to see the alarm icon mocking me, the face of the clock swinging from side to side. 'Call me Mimi' *still* hadn't called. I needed that apartment; I was running out of time.

'Jess?' Sam's voiced called on the other side of the door. I ran to the mirror to check my appearance; although he'd seen me every which way as a girlfriend, my ex-girlfriend status mandated much higher standards. My mind flicked forward to Saturday as I wondered how the hell I'd maintain them on a surf board. Something told me it would be nothing like the movies. But Sam had wanted to get me surfing for such a long time. The thought of his hands guiding my hips onto the board lifted my hopes. 'Do you want a lift?'

'Yes please,' I called. 'Five more minutes.'

Sam's laughter rang through the door. 'If I had a penny for every time you'd said that!' Thoughts of winter mornings wrapped in duvets floated through my mind, soon to be followed by sweaty evenings, bodies pressed together, trying to keep quiet. I erased the thought, applying a quick dash of concealer, a lick of mascara, a crumpled pink blouse and my over-worn jeans.

Opening the door, Sam filled the space between the box room and the landing, one hand leaning on the door frame, the other clutching his gym bag. Did he have to be so fit? His gaze went from my blouse up to meet my eyes.

'An old favourite.' His smile was fleeting and flirtatious. Moving out of the way, I walked with purpose to the car. I was too nervous about the apartment to think about much else. I wanted to get it, to turn my lie into the truth before I got found out. Opening the door, I found Joshua, already in the back seat.

'Sam's giving me a lift.' He smiled, indicating the angry-looking sky and rolling his eyes. I could see that, but for some reason him being here made me all the more on edge. 'Forecast for thunder.' I could see that too. Why couldn't he see that three was always a crowd? Hopping into the passenger seat, I played with my hair, Sam sending a glance my way as he took the wheel.

'How you going, Jess?' Joshua's thick accent rang out from the back seat as Sam started to speak in unison, their sentences lacing together.

'Almost a week at CreateSpace done,' Sam said over Joshua's question, though he continued to keep his eyes on the road. I glanced at Joshua, who grinned, conceding to Sam.

I turned back to Sam, his profile a little darker, his facial hair a little thicker. It suited him. 'Ready for another fresh start the week after next?' He took his eyes from the road for a moment to offer me a little smile. I felt Joshua's gaze from behind me. I wanted nothing more, nothing more than a fresh start, to go back and do it all over again. 'Back into the editing game?' Like I was ever in it. I didn't even make the qualifying round. Not that I was going to tell Sam, Joshua, Tim or anyone else this side of the equator that.

'Actually,' I began nervously, aware that Joshua's bullshit radar was unnervingly on point. 'I'm going to spend a bit more time at CreateSpace. Tim really needs me for the exhibition—' I was brought to a halt as my phone came to life in my pocket. I looked down at the screen: MIMI APARTMENT. This was it. My eyes darted to Sam; he'd already seen the caller ID. Shit.

'Hi, Mimi,' I answered, a slight break in my voice as I caught Joshua looking at me inquisitively in the rear-view mirror. Without moving the phone from my ear, I felt for its buttons and turned the volume down, my free hand reaching to grab a chunk of hair and twirl it around my fingers.

'Hi, Jess.' Mimi mirrored my tone as I took a sharp intake of breath. Sam shuffled beside me, reaching to turn the radio down a little further. Both boys had their eyes fixed on me, their ears pricked for what I might say next. Why did that never happen when I wanted it to? Breathing deeply, I braced myself for Mimi's next words. 'I'm afraid the owner decided to go with the other couple. They're local and, you know, planning to stick around for a bit longer.' That stupid temporary forehead-sign. 'I hope that's not too disappointing,' she apologised, the hint of sincerity in her voice causing an unexpected lump to rise in my throat.

'No, that's okay,' I replied, as chipper as I could, Sam and Joshua both absorbing my every word. I couldn't look too disappointed, or they'd know something was wrong. 'Thanks for calling.' I hung up the line, returning my phone to my empty pocket, my deposit now waiting in an envelope back at Sam's. It'd have to wait for a little longer.

'Everything okay with the apartment?' Sam asked, his forehead crinkling in concern.

'Yeah, fine,' I lied. He didn't need to know. It wasn't his problem. *I* wasn't his problem. In the rear-view mirror, I could see Joshua fiddle with his fingers, awkward all of a sudden, as Sam pulled to a halt a few streets away from CreateSpace. Joshua pushed the door open and got out as Sam signalled to me to hang back.

'Have a good morning buddy,' Sam sang out of my open window towards him.

'Oh, okay.' Joshua looked back at me, still sitting in the passenger seat. I was pretty sure we were meant to be walking the same way. 'Thanks for the lift, dude.' Sam and I watched Joshua's figure fade into the distance, the air between us feeling close.

'Jess.' He turned to me, his voice laced with sincerity. 'How long have we known each other?' A kind smile reached his eyes as my heart hammered in my chest. 'I know when you're not telling the truth.'

I pursed my lips, trying not to react, waiting for what he might say next.

'You're all good for moving in this weekend, right?'

Thank God he wasn't as good a truth-teller as he thought he was.

'Right.' I nodded, reaching for the door handle and pushing it open. Sam's hand reached out, stopping me. I turned back to look at him, trying hard not to cry. I wanted to sort so much out, all of it – but every time I tried to move on…

I looked down at Sam's hand, now holding my hand in his.

'Jess,' he repeated, quieter now. 'If you need to stay a little longer, that's absolutely fine. We've loved having you.' We both knew the 'we' was a stretch.

'No, it's fine,' I assured him, wriggling my hand free to push open the car door again. 'Seriously, Sam. Come Sunday night, I'll be out of your hair. You've got a wedding to plan!' I feigned enthusiasm as Sam looked confused, struggling to do the same.

Chapter Twenty-One

8 August 2020 – Sydney, Australia

Saturday morning and it was still bloody raining. Yesterday at CreateSpace had been nonstop, helping to fit the exhibition, calling in favours, contacting the media, soothing the creatives who were acting like children. I had used my brain more times in one week than I had in the past few years combined. I was exhausted. I hadn't even had a moment to stop and think about my next move. I had every reason to stay in bed. But I had just one reason to get up. Sam was giving me a surfing lesson today; the thought sent waves through my stomach.

Apart from our brunch and trips to and from work, we hadn't had a second just the two of us. Jamie was there all the time. Even when Sam wasn't. Clearly, she had no idea that we had ever been more than friends. She was still trying too hard to be mine. Either that or her passive aggression had shot into overdrive. I didn't know how many excuses one could give for not going on a jog, but I was surely in the running for gold. After Jamie had finally cornered me for 'girl talk', I had avoided the living room like the plague. It wasn't like when she asked me what my 'type' was I could have said 'your fiancé'. And it wasn't like when she told me *her* type was 'indie band boys', I could have quipped 'so nothing like your fiancé then?'

But now Saturday was here. Saturday, when Sam and I could finally spend some time alone, together. He'd looked so worried about me since our last conversation about the apartment, at least now I had the chance to show him I was more than okay, to remind him that *he* was more than okay just as himself, not as the perfect partner Jamie was forcing him to be. Slinking out of bed, trying hard to forget how hospitable she had been, I walked across to stand in front of the mirror. It had been raining for most of the week, but I could have sworn I was getting more tanned – though I'd always been one for wishful thinking. I smoothed down my hair and carefully applied the super waterproof mascara I had bought the day before – turned out Woolies was good for some things. Rummaging in my rucksack, I fished out my bikini for the first time since I'd arrived. Putting it on, I stood back to study my reflection. Every single inch of me was larger than Jamie. Two specific parts included; that had to count for something, right? Throwing on a T-shirt dress and hoodie, I headed out of the bedroom. No one was around, so I guessed Jamie was out and Sam must be meeting me there. He'd given me the time, the location and, thankfully, it was only a stone's throw away – well, one of Sam's stone throws, not mine. Locking the front door behind me, I walked down Oberon and onto Arden Street, taking in the views across the rolling beach and out to the endless ocean. The waves were high, crashing down on the dusk-damp sand. I would have felt scared had I not known Sam would be with me; reading the ocean was second nature to him. As I descended the hill and the gradient softened, I squinted to see if I could spot him. I sat down on the Coogee Beach steps and waited, watching permanently tanned locals pass by. I longed to be one of them. The rain had subsided into a drizzle, but still I wrapped my hoodie further around me in vain; I was about to get a lot wetter than this. Staring straight out into the angry-looking ocean, the waves in my stomach began to rise. I had to go in there. It'd better be worth it.

'Jess!' I heard a voice call from behind me, but this time it sounded suspiciously *not* like my ex-boyfriend. I turned to see a skinny black-jeaned, T-shirt clad figure walking towards me – it was Joshua, again. Please tell me he wasn't coming surfing too. This was meant to be mine and Sam's time, our time; our time *alone.* Why couldn't we just be alone?

'Oh hi.' I gave a little wave, noncommittal, part of me hoping he'd just walk past but knowing he wouldn't. My heartbeat quickened. From the brief moments we'd shared together, I felt sure he already had my number. Moving towards me, Joshua came into focus, his floppy dark hair damp and waving in the wind. As he drew closer, I could see his black jeans and T-shirt were in fact a wetsuit covered by a silly surf-shirt thing, the kind Sam was always banging on about. Shit. He was surfing too. After his regular appearances at Sam's, I wasn't sure why I was still surprised. Meeting me on the steps, he sat down and gave my cheek a kiss, then the other, confident and self-assured.

'Great weather for it, eh?' he asked rhetorically, gazing out across the ocean and beginning to study the waves, stretching out his limbs. I was so confused. Where was Sam? He said he'd be here by now. 'So, Sam says you want to learn how to surf?' Joshua turned to me, his smile breaking through the otherwise dull day.

'Yeah… I…' I began, looking at Joshua but not quite able to make eye contact. 'Sam said he was going to give me a lesson this morning…'

'Did he?' Joshua looked genuinely concerned. 'It's just, Sam messaged me on Tuesday evening, and said you wanted to learn and could I teach you? Saturday, Coogee Beach, ten a.m.?' Joshua started to scramble around for his phone in his backpack. 'Unless maybe I got it wrong?' Joshua's hair flopped in front of his face as he continued to search. He hadn't got it wrong. I had. Sam had never said it would be him teaching me to surf. My heart dropped. My stomach churned. But I couldn't let Joshua know I was disappointed.

'No, no,' I said, trying desperately to pin a smile to my face. 'That's right. Ten a.m., Coogee Beach. Sam – Sam's teaching me another day…' I lied, saving face.

'Oh, thank God,' he said; now I knew he meant it. 'Jamie said she and Sam were going cake-tasting for the wedding today. She would *flip* if he'd forgotten.' Joshua laughed, reaching into his backpack and pulling out a mass of black material. In the week that I had known her, Jamie hadn't struck me as the kind to flip, more bubble under the surface in secret and then try her best to keep the lid on her emotions like the grown-up I'd never really worked out how to be.

'Lesson one.' Joshua smiled. It really was a lovely smile. 'Put on wetsuit,' he said, standing up and throwing the black material into my lap. I held it out at arm's length. It was tiny. 'It's Jamie's old one. She said you could borrow it,' Joshua explained. Great, Jamie's hand-me-downs. Jamie, who just so happened to be twice my height and half my width. As if reading my mind, Joshua added, 'They expand when they go in the water.' Cheers, mate.

As I stood to follow Joshua, the waves became bigger with every step I took. 'There's no waves at Coogee, no surf.' Joshua looked out across the horizon. *No waves?* It looked terrifying. 'But I thought we'd go through some technique before we take the boards down to Bondi.' I looked back to the ocean. Was I really going in there? Without the incentive of Sam's hands holding my waist as I jumped onto the board, the cold August sea and rising swell no longer carried the same appeal.

'Joshua?' I asked.

He turned to look at me, his backpack flung on the beach and his bare feet sinking into wet sand. He stood, toned legs wide, smiling like a kid in a cake shop. I could see why he and Sam were friends. Best friends, friends who seemed to pop up when you were least expecting them. Not that I was one to talk.

'I'm not sure I want to go in.'

Joshua's smile faded as he took a couple of steps towards me.

'Jess,' he began, using the same tone I had employed to navigate Tim and Olivia's mood swings all week. 'I thought you wanted to learn how to surf?'

'I did,' I replied, trying hard to ignore the sound of the *apparently* non-waves, once so mesmerising, now so menacing. 'I wanted to…' Well, I did when I thought Sam would be taking me. Joshua's kind eyes narrowed as he took another step towards me and placed a hand on my shoulder. Tilting his head slightly to study my fearful expression, he laughed.

'I'm afraid, to surf, you're going to have to go in the water. Maybe that should have been lesson one?' Slowly, Joshua took the wetsuit out of my hand. Maybe he was going to let me off the hook. Then he bent down, holding the suit apart so that I could easily step in. *Trust me, Joshua, there is going to be nothing easy about this.* Pulling off my dress, feeling more comedy act than superstar, I stepped one foot into the leg hole, then the other. I looked down at Joshua, still crouched down by my wetsuit-covered ankles, stunned into immobilisation by the sheer awkwardness of our situation. Joshua looked up past my legs, through my boobs and smiled; I wanted to die. I was never going to fit into Jamie's kid-size wetsuit. I yanked the suit further up my thighs and managed to fit my arms into the armholes and prise the top up. Thank God.

'Could you…' I turned to Joshua awkwardly. He was still grinning, having just witnessed the strangest reverse striptease you would never pay to see. 'Could you do me up?'

'Sure,' he replied, no doubt eager to get in the water. He stood behind me and I breathed in as I felt his breath on my neck, yanking the zip higher and higher. The suit squeezed me in until my boobs were under my chin. He pulled harder; I breathed in more. It wasn't going to work.

'Erm…' I heard Joshua's voice behind me, right on cue. 'I think you're maybe a bit bigger than Jamie on the, the… shoulders,' he saved himself. He sure seemed to know Jamie's body well. Although, religious or not, who wouldn't check out Jamie's physique? 'It's okay, I have an idea.' Joshua tapped his hands on my shoulders even though he already had my attention. I turned to him to see him pull off his silly surf top, his outstretched arm highlighting the muscles rippling below his wetsuit – not so skinny indie boy after all.

'You can have my rash vest.' *Rash* vest. I knew it had a name. 'Right. Ready to get the boards?' He smiled towards Sam's car parked on the road, the boards strapped on top. I knew better now than to think he'd be inside, knowing he'd be by Jamie's side whether through desire, obligation or fear. He'd just let Joshua borrow it; Sam was good like that. I looked to the car, the distance from beach to boards stretching between us. I felt more comfortable with his oversized vest on, but I still wasn't sure I could move without ripping the wetsuit. *It expands in the water.* Maybe if we went in for a quick swim first I wouldn't chafe my tan off before it had even begun. Gazing out to the churning grey sea, I swallowed my fear and suggested we go for a quick dip to warm up.

'Yes! Love it!' Joshua said, pushing his floppy hair out of his face and taking a tie from his wrist, to scrunch it into a manbun. It looked kinda hot. 'I find it's better just to run in.'

Running or walking being the very thing I was trying to avoid. Joshua took my hand and began to run, dragging me along with him as our feet crashed into the water. *Shit, that is cold!* This was meant to be Sydney. It was freezing. I held my breath as Joshua, now waist deep, let go of my hand and dived into a crashing wave. In a split second, I knew I had to do the same, that or face the wave – literally. Bloody hell, I was going under. A rush of heart-stopping water pressed against my body as I pushed through the wave. Rising to the surface, I turned, disoriented, to find Joshua cheering just metres away. Christ, the water was cold. And if these waves weren't big enough to surf on, I wasn't in a rush to get to Bondi. Joshua gestured towards the horizon as another one approached. I pushed myself under the surface and through the wave once again. *Arghh*. Resurfacing, I swallowed sea water. Somewhere Sam and Jamie would be swallowing cake. I dived under water again. Suddenly Joshua was beside me, beckoning me out of the water to get the boards. As I struggled to stand, he grabbed my waist and pulled me to my feet.

'Don't you just feel alive?' he buzzed, reminding me of Sam and all the times I had refused to surf. I looked back into the angry ocean, my mouth hanging wide, breathless in disbelief. I couldn't believe I had just been in there. I looked back to Joshua, his inquisitive face still waiting for my response. I felt cold, I felt messy, I felt scared. But deep down – very deep down – I felt a little exhilarated. And, deep down – *very* deep down – I guess I felt a little more alive.

I collapsed on the Coogee Beach steps as Joshua strode away in search of coffee – a search that in a suburb where there was a 1:3 coffee-shop-to-person ratio took him all of three minutes. I looked across the ocean, trying to slow the rapid pace of my heart. A heart recently and repeatedly submerged in the Tasman Sea.

Along the beach I could spy Joshua returning, both hands clutching steaming cups of coffee towards his bare chest. His turned-down wetsuit top trailed behind him, as did three other figures walking with him on either side.

'Look who I found,' he hollered. Through my salt-stung eyes the faces of Alice, Andrew and Mark came into view. Sam and Jamie's church crew. I tried to flatten down my sea-slung hair. Randomly bumping into people on a Saturday? It was the kind of community

I'd naively hoped we'd all have in London. Instead, I'd found myself forty-five minutes from everyone – and made to think that 'wasn't all that bad'.

'I didn't know you were a surfer,' Alice said, a raised eyebrow stretching above her Ray-Bans, cup of coffee clutched in her manicured hand – it wasn't even sunny. Just once, I wished she wasn't seeing me sweaty, wet or out of my depth.

'I'm really not, I'm—' I began, before Joshua cut me off.

'She's great. You should have seen her out there.' He sat down beside me, smiling and handing me my coffee. I let the heat of it warm through my hands and lifted the steam closer to my face. I'd earnt this.

'You should see Mark.' Andrew lifted his own cup to take a sip. 'Words cannot describe—'

'How great I am?' Mark interjected, exchanging smirks with his partner, trying and failing to hold back a laugh.

'Sure,' Andrew agreed, his words dripping with sarcasm, 'that's exactly what I was going to say.' He looked at me, rolling his eyes. 'Just like you're an amazing flower-arranger.' Andrew and Alice laughed in unison as Mark faked disdain.

'Sam kind of… double-booked himself.' Alice turned to me to explain, even more bronzed again a backdrop of beach. I tried my best not to think about what else Sam had been double-booking: he had me and Jamie living in his house, didn't he?

'To taste cake or select centrepieces, that is the quest—' Andrew began.

'A question no one ever asks,' Mark interrupted again, as they all laughed.

'Anyway,' Alice pressed on in spite of them, 'Jamie asked us whether we could fill in for one of their appointments, check out some blooms for their big day.' A familiar sinking feeling filled my belly.

'Jamie must have been so mad.' Joshua shook his head, covering a smile with his coffee cup, another image of Jamie jarring with the 'little Miss Perfect' I'd been shacked up with all week. Did she even get mad? So far, she'd been able to keep her cool with me but something about their nods told me she could blow.

'I said we could take the cake-tasting,' Andrew continued in between sips of coffee.

You could tell the chatty one of the two.

'But we got landed with the flipping flowers. Thank God we had this one.' He squeezed his partner's leg affectionately. 'And his expert eye.' Andrew winked at me again. Clearly it wasn't as expert as Mark liked to think.

'We still didn't get it right,' Mark said, a genuine glimmer of regret in his deep blue eyes. 'We needed you with us, mate.' He smiled at Joshua and the three of them nodded in agreement. I looked into my coffee, unsure what qualified Joshua for the job. Other than being a pretty decent guy. I took another sip, letting the hot liquid warm me from the inside out. I shivered again as Mark and Andrew fell into a heated 'dahlia or delphinium' debate.

'Here, take this.' Joshua pulled a jumper out of the rucksack he had either trustingly or naively left alone on the beach as he had surfed and I had pretended to.

'Thank you.' I smiled as he held my coffee and I pulled the jumper over my still-damp wetsuit. Every inch of me hurt. Joshua looked at his friends, who were getting passionate about peonies, then turned his full attention towards me.

'It gets easier the next time,' he said, boldly assuming there would be a next time. I had only suggested surfing to spend time with Sam. 'We'll get the boards up to North Bondi or South Maroubra where the waves are really gnarly.' Joshua's teeth blinded me in the sunlight. He could actually pull that word off. And that rash vest. He could definitely pull that off again. 'You really did look good out there,' Joshua went on. I raised both eyebrows. Wasn't lying a sin? 'No seriously.' He laughed warmly. 'Jamie didn't even stand up the first time we went out together.'

I looked back at Joshua – for the first time praying my waterproof mascara was punching higher than its five-dollar weight – and smiled; Jamie hadn't even stood up. I felt a glow of pride warm my chest. Somewhere between the disappointment, the awkwardness and the inability to feel my toes, I guess I had felt something of the exhilaration Sam had banged on about all those years we were together.

'She was hilarious,' Joshua said, taking a sip of his coffee and shaking his wet fringe out of his eyes. 'She finally thought she'd cracked it… until she realised the board was beached up on the sand!' He continued to laugh, caught in a precious moment he had shared with a wetsuit-cladded Jamie. He sure seemed fond of her. And he seemed to know her taste in flowers. Sam should watch himself; wasn't 'indie band boys' her 'type'?

'You should have seen her with my youth group.' Joshua mistook my silence for permission to carry on. 'Jamie helps me on our trips out sometimes. At least *I* try and encourage her. But kids can be brutal.' He wiped a tear from his eye; a private joke I wasn't invited in on. They'd been surfing with the youth; they'd been surfing alone; he even knew her chest size.

'You and Jamie sure seem close?' I questioned out loud, whilst the other three continued to chat and sip coffee, perfectly at home on the beach. I just wanted to feel at home *somewhere*, though preferably in an apartment in Randwick.

'Yeah.' He beamed at the thought of her; the Jamie effect. 'I love that girl.' Did she really need to take all the guys? I gave him a weak smile in return. Poor Joshua. It didn't even make sense. Here was a gorgeous, adventurous, church-going man who loved her. And still she wanted Sam. *Jamie and Joshua*; it even sounded right. And Lord knows, Sam and Jess had always sounded right. Clearly fate had got its wires crossed. 'We couldn't be closer,' Joshua reiterated. A glimmer of an idea darted across my mind. We'd see about that.

Chapter Twenty-Two

The photograph of Coogee Backpacker mocked me from my phone, warped at the corners to make the dorm rooms look more spacious than they were. With my early pay packet I could afford to stay there for a bit, but I couldn't help but feel like I was throwing money away. And I needed a semi-permanent address if I had a hope of getting myself a semi-permanent job. I looked again at the misleading pictures: a downgrade from Sam's box room for sure. As painful as it was, I'd almost enjoyed being in such close proximity to him. And I knew he'd enjoyed it too. But could I really take him up on his offer to stay? He thought I was moving into my apartment this weekend. Hearing Sam's key turn in the door, I stashed my phone and shelved the thought, reclining on the sofa. It was gone one o'clock and they'd only just arrived home from church. I'd thought it was an in-and-out situation, especially given Sam's 'a couple of hours on a Sunday' comment during the other night's living room affair. I quickly stood up to check my reflection in the mirror. Hair waved, make-up applied, in a loose-fitting and low-cut black dress enhancing my two USPs,

I looked ten times better than the heroin-without-the-chic mess Sam had rescued just over a week ago; but I guessed that wasn't saying much. I smiled at my reflection. Living arrangements be damned; this was going to be great.

Jamie had near enough squealed when I'd suggested we invite Joshua around for lunch. Smiling broadly and bounding over towards me, she had squeezed my arm and gushed: 'Oh, Jess, I thought you'd never ask.' She laughed as if recalling a private joke she and Joshua clearly shared, before adding wistfully, 'He's *such* a great guy, Jess.'

That he is, Jamie; and absolutely made for you.

'There she is,' Sam exclaimed as he entered the kitchen-living room to see me casually flicking through the pages of whatever magazine I had just picked up from the coffee table. I looked up to see his gleeful expression. 'I love your hair like that,' he added. I knew he did. I mirrored Sam's smile in return. For a moment I felt nineteen again.

'Hey, Jess,' Jamie interrupted, catapulting me back into my twenty-seven-year-old self. Jamie looked great. Of course she did, effortlessly pulling off a loose-fitting jumpsuit, her blonde hair cascading down her back in natural waves; unlike the ones I had spent the last two hours trying to make look natural. 'No sign of Joshua? He set off on his bike before us,' Jamie said, taking stock of the room, concern flashing across her face. Of course Joshua rode a bike; one step up from a skateboard, I guess. Just as Jamie put her too-expensive handbag down on the marble kitchen surface, another key turned in the door and there were heavy footsteps in the corridor. Jamie's face lit up. He had a key? Why the hell would he have a key? I looked at Jamie's grin, seductive and suspicious. Maybe I wasn't the only one with secrets? Sure enough, seconds later, Joshua popped his head around the archway into the room.

'Joshua!' Jamie squealed as she flung both arms around his broad-shouldered frame. He embraced her tightly, hands resting on her upper back, face nestled in her freefalling locks. I glanced towards Sam, whose head was downcast, his hands fiddling with the buttons on his shirt. He looked up at Jamie and Joshua briefly and then turned to me, holding my gaze for a little too long. He was never one for details but even he must have been able to feel the chemistry between them. Slowly letting go of Jamie, Joshua turned to me and gave me the same assured kiss on the cheek; no squeals, no lingering hair sniff. He then put his arms around Sam, giving him a backslapping man-hug. Sam's smile looked strained.

Before I even noticed her knocking together our starters, the wooden table in the centre of the kitchen was set with a colourful display of Mediterranean tapas. Bread, oils, olives, halloumi; it was a doppelgänger for the dinners Sam and I had shared on our graduation getaway. I'd had to hold out after my own graduation for Sam to finish the following year, and I'd had to go with his lot, not mine. And yet, stealing away from his medic friends to grab a moment alone with Sam in Cyprus had been worth the wait.

I sat down at the table and stretched my hand out to the halloumi; Sam did the same, our hands colliding in the middle. 'After you,' Sam said; like he had a choice. He pulled his chair closer to the table, his foot grazing my own in the process, muscle memory bringing our bodies back together.

'This looks amazing, Jamie,' Joshua gushed, placing an affectionate hand on her angular shoulder. 'Thanks so much for having me.' Their eyes met. I looked at Sam, who was looking from Joshua to me. Even I couldn't read his expression.

'Hey, it was Jess's idea,' Jamie deflected. Joshua grinned in my direction. Somewhere in the back of my mind, I could imagine Zoe pacing the floor, gesticulating with her hands, telling me again and again that this was a stupid idea, that I should stop meddling, that I should let Sam move on. That I should do the same. Reaching across the table for another pitta, I silenced the thought. Zoe wasn't here; she hadn't even called me back. And I wasn't meddling. My suggestion had got Joshua sitting opposite the girl of his dreams. And it just so happened that it had also got me sitting in front of the man of mine.

By the time Jamie had served the main dish (lamb tagine and couscous with a fun-free version for her), the table conversation was in full flow. Jamie and Joshua had shared everything but an awkward silence; their connection was undeniable.

'Joshua, that sweater is *such* a good colour on you… Joshua, the work you do with the youth is just amazing… Joshua, it's so good to have you here with us…' I wasn't sure whether Sam noticed the fact that Jamie had complimented Joshua more times in one and a half courses than I'd seen her compliment Sam all week. After all, I had done all in my power to keep his attention on me. And that was working perfectly. Topping up our glasses at twice the rate as Jamie and Joshua, our own conversation flowed as freely as the wine. It was almost like old times. You know, except for the fact his fiancée was sitting beside us.

'Do you remember that time? Austin. The pool?' Sam struggled to say through his laughter. After five years together, we'd developed a few private jokes of our own. I snorted my Sauvignon. I remembered it well. Unbeknownst to Jamie, her medi-spread had prompted no end of medic-holiday memories. Sam was in his element.

'I literally couldn't get the image out of my head for days!' Sam wiped away a tear. I did the same, looking up at him and holding his gaze for less than two seconds before he crumbled into laughter once again. One week, six boys, three girls and a whole lot of alcohol.

'Not the only thing that happened in that pool.' I grinned, my eyebrows raising as Sam shiftily glanced at his fiancée. Jamie was fully occupied, laughing and joking with Joshua but I saw Joshua send a brief glance in my direction. Sam looked at me, a question glimmering in his eyes. I'd have loved to know what was going on in his head. He lowered his voice a little as he said, 'Now that image really will stay with me for a long time.' I looked at Sam, his face bashful yet cheeky; there he was. My Sam. I looked back at Jamie and Joshua, happily chatting away about youth group and the restaurants and shops they knew so well. Joshua was the perfect distraction, his black band shirt complementing Jamie's jumpsuit. They even looked great together.

This was perfect; why couldn't things just stay this way?

'Stay a little longer, Jess.' Sam's voice was low as Jamie and Joshua continued to chatter.

'What?' I looked up from my plate, confused.

'That call, the apartment.' He took another sip of wine, shaking his head. 'I know when you're lying, Jess,' he said, not a speck of doubt darting through his words. Did he? 'If Joshua wasn't there in the car, if we'd had longer just the two of us, you would have told me, right?' He cast a look to him and Jamie. If Jamie wasn't here, he would tell me stuff too. 'The renovations aren't done yet are they?'

'No,' I admitted. That part was true at least.

'Then stay a little longer,' he offered, unsure why I seemed reluctant. Part of me was unsure why he wasn't *more* reluctant.

'You've already had to sleep on that sofa for a week.' I shook my head. The fact that Sam so wanted me to stay was quickly making me forget all my reasons for leaving.

'Don't you know how freaking comfy that couch is?' He laughed. I couldn't imagine it was comfier than a bed. I placed my knife and fork down together in something like surrender.

'We should do this again.' Jamie stood up, beginning to gather our empty plates together. She looked down at me and smiled as Joshua began to clear the condiments off the table.

'Absolutely!' Joshua said, moving across to stand behind her at the sink, wrapping his arms around her waist. I glanced at Sam. What were they doing? I guess this was what I had hoped would happen but not in broad daylight, not in front of Sam. Now that it was, I almost felt sorry for him. Was that why he wanted me to stay: to make her jealous? My eyes flitted between Jamie and Sam, trying and failing to work out their ever-changing dynamic. Jamie turned around to look up at her boy-band counterpart, their faces inches away from each other.

I held my breath.

'Always lovely to spend time with my little sis,' Joshua said, giving her another squeeze.

Sister. Of course she was his sister. He loved her. They couldn't be closer. And here I was, trying to use him as a bloody distraction so I could remind her fiancé of what he was really missing. I guess they'd just assumed Sam had told me and let it fall through the cracks; just like me. Rock bottom was becoming a second home to me.

Zoe was right; this situation was stupid. I had to get out of here. I had to get a new place, move away from him, start again – again. Do it properly this time.

'I've missed this,' Sam said, leaning across the table and drawing my attention back to him. He lifted a hand to rub his chin. 'I haven't thought about that holiday in years. It feels like just yesterday, eh?' It always had to me. Joshua and Jamie had let go of each other and were now doing the washing up, the sound of pots, pans and chatter giving Sam and I yet another moment to ourselves.

'Just seeing you reminds me of it all.' Sam smiled broadly, reaching a hand across the table to rest on mine. 'So you'll stay until your apartment's sorted?'

I looked at Jamie and Joshua and again at Sam, savouring the feeling of his skin on my skin and his eyes on mine. Maybe I could stay just a little longer.

*

11 July 2016 – Nottingham, England

'I can't wait forever,' I heard Zoe shout from outside the changing room door. I swung it open and stood unceremoniously in what could only be described as a long top.

'Jess, you look *amazing*,' she squeaked.

'I look like a call girl,' I objected.

'No.' Zoe shook her head in a way I had grown accustomed to over the past four years. 'You look like an escort – two very different things.'

Not a lot had changed over our time at university but somehow going from call girl to escort felt like a graduation. Thankfully that wasn't the only graduation imminent, but I sure as hell couldn't receive my BA Hons wearing this.

'Well at least buy it for Malta,' Zoe insisted. She looked stunning in the short rainbow dress she was trying on.

'You know I can't come to Malta,' I said and her smile vanished. 'I've promised I'll go to Cyprus after Sam's graduation; I just can't afford both. Don't worry, you guys will have fun without me.'

'I'm not worried about that.'

Ouch. Thanks, Zo.

'Then what are you worried about?' I didn't mean to snap.

'I'm worried that you'll regret missing out,' Zoe began with trepidation. It sounded like the start of a conversation far too serious for someone wearing a dress that short.

'Cyprus will be worth the wait,' I deflected confidently, turning back towards the mirror. Zoe came to stand behind my right shoulder.

'Maybe.' She hesitated. 'But what if Sam's not?' she asked in a voice far quieter than normal, placing her hand on my upper arm. I turned to face her, shrugging it off, defences now fully engaged.

'What do you mean?' I lowered my own voice, not wanting us to be the kind of young women who argued in public, especially ones wearing dresses only just covering their underwear.

'I don't know,' she began, although it was clear she did. 'It's just, a year is a long time. A lot can change. He could change. You could change,' she mused.

'Things won't change,' I snapped a little too quickly, the edge of my words cutting the air.

'I know but,' Zoe began again. 'It's just —'

'It's just what, Zoe?' I asked, her nervous energy rubbing off on my own.

'It's just, I've seen you sacrifice quite a lot for him over the last few years. Nights out, art stuff... I just don't want you to regret any of that in the future.' She gazed at me, her usually effervescent face serious.

'Oh, Zoe.' She didn't understand. She couldn't. She hadn't had a relationship like ours; she didn't know what it was like to be in something long-term. She didn't even want to be. I smiled at her. 'Sam *is* my future.'

PART TWO

Chapter Twenty-Three

4 September 2020 – Sydney, Australia

'For the love of God, Jess, please tell me that's not Sam's stupid surfboard behind you?' Even Zoe's scowl transmitted through Skype. I turned to look at the mounted board and then back to the screen perched precariously on the bed, close to the edge.

'Shhhh, Zoe, don't say that, they'll hear,' I whispered.

'It is!' she exclaimed, and then even louder, 'For Christ's sake!'

I turned the laptop volume down a bar or two. Yes, I was still in the box room. But I could explain. For one, the past month had gone by in a blur; from CreateSpace to surf lessons, the days had galloped by as winter was finally starting to fade. We'd fallen into a pattern: carpools to work, helping each other out around the apartment. It just seemed to be, well – working.

Unlike Sam and Jamie. Her happy-go-lucky façade had started to crack soon after the Sunday lunch that had seen Sam convince me to stay. The closer they drew to the wedding, the further apart they seemed to be. There was just under a month to go and at the rate they were arguing I was almost convinced that it wasn't going to happen. They were just too different. Of course, for Zoe's benefit I'd elected to share the edited explanation.

'I've been so busy with work,' I half-truthed. 'The exhibition opens tonight; once it's over, I'll be finding my own place.' I smiled and nodded, tilting the screen so that Zoe could see the blouse I was going to wear tonight hanging proudly against the outside of the wardrobe.

'Finding your own place?' Zoe's face grew a little bigger in the centre of my screen as she reached forwards to take a closer look. I knew she wasn't looking at the blouse. 'I thought you had one, the one you've been waiting bloody ages to get into?'

'Oh yeah, sorry.' I pushed my hair behind my ears. 'That's what I meant.'

'That's bullshit,' she cut me off. I knew the renovation fib was wearing thin – with her, with Jamie, most definitely with Joshua – but it only needed to hang on a day or two longer. 'You just keep pushing it back, hoping that if you stick around long enough Sam will stick it to her.' She always suspected the worst, but even Zoe couldn't comprehend my fabricated life, that my apartment didn't even exist. 'You never change.' Zoe shook her head.

I knew that. I'd kept up my end of the bargain, if only everybody else could do the same.

'That's not true,' I objected, praying my confidence would convince her. It wasn't, was it? I couldn't help it if Sam kept inviting me for lunches, stealing little moments…

'I say this with love,' Zoe began, her classic precursor to some cold hard truth. 'You really need to move on.'

I looked down at the screen, at my beautiful best friend in her beautiful new living room, happy and settled in Colchester. I had tried to move on, honestly. I had tried to leave my whole flipping life behind and start again in Sydney. And yet, here I was, and here *he* was – why could no one see that had to mean something?

'Look, Zoe,' I said matter-of-factly, gearing to say anything but truth. 'That's not why I'm here. Once the exhibition opening is over I'm out of here.'

Zoe raised her perfectly plucked eyebrow, unconvinced. I sighed, the distance between us feeling greater than ever. Friends always promise they'll remember what it feels like to feel confused, directionless, like life isn't playing fair. But then they start to navigate it all so well that they forget what it's like to be lost in the first place.

'How's the house?' I asked, knowing changing the subject would be easier than changing her mind. It was the perfect bait. She couldn't help herself; talk of shower poles ensued until it was finally time for her to say goodbye, and for me to start my day. *The* day.

Stashing my laptop away, I forced Zoe's words from my mind. I couldn't think about leaving their apartment right now anyway, not with the exhibition opening tonight. I needed to get my head in the game. Reaching down to open one of the drawers of Sam's bedside table, I reached for the brown A4 envelope I had stowed inside, hidden slightly by a handful of Sam's odd socks that hadn't made their way into the master bedroom. Unlike Sam, who would find his way into the master bedroom very soon, *if* the wedding went to plan – but I had to keep my sights on my own plan. I lifted the unsealed fold and pulled out the fresh print-outs displaying my credentials. The smooth opening of our exhibition was one thing; convincing one of our most notorious guests to give me a job without anyone else knowing was something else. I figured I'd only have enough time to cajole her into going for a coffee and a chat some other day. But it wouldn't hurt to have my CV to hand, just in case. Checked, returned and re-stashed, I clambered over the mound of decorative cushions that had mercilessly been thrown towards the side of the room.

I reached down into the shopping bags crumpled in the far corner and pulled out a silk dress, light blue and almost invisible against the colour of the box room's walls. Ignoring the itch of guilt shifting around my body, I proceeded to hang up a new skirt to match my blouse. Technically, my wages should be buying my ticket out of here, stockpiling that rent money until my place in this city was secure. But with Tim and Olivia as colleagues who seemed to be cut from the pages of *Vogue*, I knew I had to up the ante – especially for tonight.

'*Sam*, can you please concentrate?' Raised voices drifted into the room. 'This is important.'

Jamie's insistence that pre-work wedding planning trumped Sam's wake-up surf had no doubt hit him where it hurt. It turned out Jamie didn't spend her days lounging around in Lycra after all; her recent rotation was piling pressure higher than the cushions in my room.

'I thought we sorted this yesterday?' My ears picked up at Sam's reply, as my eyes stayed fixed on the outfit displayed in front of me. I guess it wouldn't hurt to look nice in front of Sam either.

That was, if he was coming this evening. I had mentioned the exhibition plenty of times in passing; after all, Jamie had kindly got me my job at CreateSpace, and as far as she was concerned, it was the reason I was still in their hair. One of the reasons. But Tim had left inviting them to me and I hadn't *technically* done that yet, buying time while I decided if I should. I had tried hard to make the exhibition a success, but I needed to corner Sommers to get a job they already thought I had and I didn't want anything else to distract me; either Sam and Jamie being there, or Sam and Jamie's refusal to be.

'We did.' Jamie's voice reverberated against the thin box room walls, louder with each word. 'But now two people have dropped out, which actually changes the seating plan, because we *planned* for them to be *seated*…' Her words drifted off as she reclaimed her inside voice.

Maybe they wouldn't even notice the exhibition come and go. But then again, they'd probably hear about it from Tim and wonder why I hadn't invited them along – that was, if they hadn't heard from him already. I looked at my watch. It was still early, hours before I had to be at the gallery, but I was up now; I needed coffee.

Stepping out of the bedroom, I prayed Tim hadn't told them about anything else. No mysterious lunches with mysterious men. Jamie and Sam would know for a fact that I wasn't spending time with any men other than…

'Joshua?' I walked into the kitchen-living room to see his familiar face grinning up at me from the end of the kitchen table, a mug of hot coffee clutched in his hand, his hoodie pulled over his messed-up morning hair.

'Coffee?'

He looked cute – a hint of sleep around his eyes, like the coffee hadn't quite kicked in. I nodded and pulled out a chair beside him, accepting the mug with more appreciation than was necessary.

'Sam, you were supposed to check the shared diary first. You can't just keep booking things without asking me.'

Joshua and I both turned our heads in the direction of Jamie's voice as she walked in to join us in the kitchen, Sam trailing behind. Somewhere during the last month filters had fallen by the wayside. Jamie grabbed two mugs from the cupboard and filled them with coffee, passing one to Sam.

'I was trying to use my *initiative*,' Sam said and took a sip, raising his eyebrows at me and Joshua as Jamie reached into another cupboard for the cereals. It was a nod to yesterday's disagreement, the one about Sam's inability to pre-empt anything. Joshua and I exchanged a wink. He resumed his serious face before Jamie turned back around.

'I know, baby, but we keep double-booking ourselves and I don't know if I'm coming or going,' Jamie replied, free hand on her hip. Unlike me, she didn't have a scrap of make-up on and yet she still looked better than me, a little more tired than when we'd first met, perhaps, but still better than me. Maybe now wasn't a good time to remind them about tonight.

'It's okay.' Jamie sighed, softening upon seeing Sam's sorry expression. I had been a sucker for it too. 'Let's have a look at the diary now,' she continued, walking across to the sofa. Obediently, he followed suit. Joshua rolled his eyes and leaned in closer to me.

'You look beautiful,' he said, taking in my silk dress and made-up face. I looked up at him, glimpsing a genuine look of admiration on his face. I savoured it as best I could while still trying to catch clipped ends of conversation from the other side of the room. 'But a bit too… erm…' He searched for the word, as I cast a nervous glance towards my cleavage. Too much? Not enough? 'Bit too polished for surfing. Thought we were going to squeeze in a session before work?'

'Oh *shit*.' Between the exhibition, my chat with Zoe and tracking Sam and Jamie's straining relationship, I had completely forgotten. That, and the fact that the only pre-work activity that had been on offer in recent years was breakfast.

'That's okay, we don't have to.' Joshua took another sip of coffee, failing to mask his disappointment. 'You've got a big day after all.' At least one person had remembered.

'No, no, it's fine,' I objected. He'd biked all the way over; I couldn't just blow him off. 'Let me just get changed.'

Joshua's bearded face broke into a smile, warm and familiar.

'You guys going surfing?' Sam lifted his head from the wedding planner to enquire across the room; all three of us could detect the disappointment in his voice.

'Yeah, well, I get a slightly later start today and…' I trailed off, noting Jamie's intensifying stare and tightening grip around Sam's shoulder. I was distracting him. Again.

'Just a quick one, mate.' Joshua saved me from a look that could kill. 'Jamie said we could borrow your car for the boards, head up to Bondi.'

'Oh, did she?' Sam narrowed his eyes from us to her, pretending to be pissed off even though we all knew the only thing annoying him was that he wouldn't be hitching a ride to the water with us.

'Got a spare half hour?' Joshua asked cheekily; he already knew the answer. Sam glanced at Jamie, sleepy-eyed but every bit as gorgeous as when she was made up.

'Sorry, mate.' Sam shook away his disappointment. 'Wedding stuff before work.'

I nodded in acknowledgement before bowing out of the room to get dressed, silently enjoying knowing that this time he would rather be with me.

Joshua was heading out of the car and into the water before he'd even put the car in park, carrying both boards balanced on his head. I laughed, following suit. I folded Joshua's rash vest over my arm, my own wetsuit tucked underneath; nobody needed to know that I'd replaced Jamie's with one two sizes bigger.

Without thinking, my legs walked our now well-trodden route down to Bondi Beach, my eyes scanning across the horizon to check the swell. It looked good, and I congratulated myself on not feeling scared shitless to get in, even as we pressed our feet into the damp orange sand.

'Feeling good?' Joshua flung the boards onto the shore, his svelte arm muscles straining from the weight of them. He still wouldn't let me carry mine all that way. Standing tall, he turned his gaze towards the waves and breathed deeply, used to giving me more than a moment to reply.

'Yeah, actually,' I responded. He turned back to me in surprise. I usually took a bit of psyching up before we got started. 'It's just good to get out of the house.' The words spilled out before I had time to stop them. If I really wanted to get out of the house, I could just go. It was what Jamie would want, but Sam – I could tell Sam wanted me to stay.

'Yeah, I've noticed the tension,' Joshua said, pulling his trademark band shirt up over his head to reveal his tanned chest. I tried to keep my eyes on his face but his bearded grin told me he'd caught me looking. Damn it. He began to pull his half-folded wetsuit up over his arms. 'Jamie can get a bit stressed at the best of times but I guess planning a wedding and hosting and…'

I busied myself by pulling my own wetsuit up leg by leg, avoiding eye or ab contact. I had seen Jamie getting more on edge, but I didn't want to think it had anything to do with my being there. Sam had said it made *him* more chilled; I guessed that counted for something.

'Stay at a mine for a bit,' Joshua said, making quite a big offer sound like no big deal. 'I mean, my place is tiny, but I don't mind you bunking up with me.' Surely he didn't mean *with* him, with him. 'You know, get a bit of space? While your apartment gets the longest renovation known to man.' His eyes scanned my face as if waiting for me to admit the truth. I finally turned to face him, not quite sure what he had just asked me but knowing for sure that space was not what I needed. Space had never been what I had needed.

'It's fine,' I replied, flashing him a feigned grin of my own. 'I'm comfortable there, and it won't be for long now. After the exhibition opening I'll have the head space to work out what the hell the landlord is doing!' I laughed away the absurdity, knowing no laugh would be loud enough. Joshua lifted a strong arm to run his hand through his hair, something he did when I knew he was holding something back. He sighed deeply.

'Okay then, but you have to let me help you move into your new apartment.' He started to wade into the water until he was pushing his floating board at waist height.

'Promise.' I looked at him, knowing I had nothing tangible to back it up. Thank God I'd managed to keep the specifics of my fantasy apartment so vague, despite Joshua trying and failing to place me on the map, keen to get his hands dirty and help speed up the renovations. Sam, on the other hand, hadn't tried, more content with having me stay.

'It'll be nice to spend a bit more time together, you know? Get out of Jamie's hair?'

I nodded, half listening, distracted by the water. I might be in her hair but Sam still wanted me in his and until he'd made it absolutely clear he was absolutely sure that he wanted to marry into this new life, then I was never going to be too far out of it.

'And if you ever need a change of scenery,' Joshua continued, walking towards the waves, 'you know where I am.'

I followed him into the water, gazing out across the pinks and blues of the morning dawn, stretching as far as the eye could see. I flung my body onto the board, starting to paddle. I was surfing in Sydney, on the morning of opening night, with Sam waiting back home, knowing he'd rather be here with us, with *me* – for the first time in a long time, this kind of scenery was exactly what I wanted to see.

Chapter Twenty-Four

'It looks *fabulous*.' Tim elongated the last word as I walked into CreateSpace. 'Tonight's the night!'

The PAs had rallied and finally we had an opening night guest list to rival an old-school Taylor Swift sleepover. 'So, the plan…' Tim puffed out his shoulders authoritatively, giving me one of the first glimpses of the fifty-something-year-old his ID claimed him to be. 'Olivia, you arrive at six p.m., sharp.' Olivia nodded, though she may as well have saluted. She rocked on her heels and held onto the clipboard a little tighter. Somewhere over the last month or so I had been promoted out of the clipboard-holding role – I still wasn't entirely sure I deserved it.

'Welcome the guests, steer them into this room,' Tim continued, throwing his arms wide against a backdrop of morning sunrises and bright blue skies. 'Offer them champagne.' He gestured to a long wooden table, now placed in the centre of the space. 'Jess, you are to arrive at eight p.m.' Olivia's wrinkle-free face looked like it was trying to frown. The temp-help shouldn't get a later call time than her. 'I want you to make an entrance. Fashionably late – emphasis on the *fashionable*.' I knew he was being nice, but it sounded like a threat. I reached for my phone and pulled up a photo of the outfit I was planning to wear, seeking managerial approval. He gazed at the image, his expression noncommittal. 'You'll handle the interviews as we agreed.' The thought of handling the publicity still sent waves through my stomach, nervousness setting in. It was a long way from my usual position, behind the scenes. But I needed Tim worlds away from Sommers. His commitment to mystery, his Banksy-esque, Leo Todd-inspired anonymity was the only thing that would keep him out of the journalists' paths for sure. My pulse started to race faster, heart caught in my throat as imposter syndrome hung heavy on my shoulders. Could you still blame imposter syndrome when you had knowingly created the imposter in question? 'Unless you don't want to?' Tim must have noticed my hesitation. Showing the press around, being left alone with Hannah Sommers – it was petrifying and perfect at the same time.

'I can do that,' I assured Tim whilst also assuring myself.

'Good.' He nodded, as if I didn't really have a choice. 'I want those journalists to flock to you, for there to be a real buzz.'

My phone vibrated in my hand, just on cue. We both looked at the screen. It was a text from Sam.

lunch?

I swiped the message away. After a few boozy brainstorming sessions, Tim knew drunken scraps of what was going on; that there was an ex-boyfriend on the scene and that he was no longer available. I was pretty sure his artistic imagination had filled in the elaborate affair-fuelled blanks. All bar one: that he actually knew the man and was friends with the reason he couldn't currently be mine.

'Sam?' he asked, although I knew he had just seen it. 'Is he coming tonight?' Tim looked somewhat hopeful. I had figured from the way he gushed about Jamie's fiancé that he may have a soft spot for him too. I shrugged in response; I really didn't know.

'And how about your… man?' Tim lowered his voice so Olivia wouldn't hear. Even though she was next to us she was already miles away. I knew he had spied the mysterious stranger standing against the wall outside on several occasions and suspected he'd also developed a fantasy crush on my fantasy man. Thank God he was too short-sighted to realise he and Sam were one and the same. 'Invite him,' Tim commanded, stealing the guest list clutched in Olivia's hand.

'But what if he… doesn't come alone?' I asked, eyes flitting to Olivia, who was still too busy to be bothered. 'This is important to me. My… *boss* will be there,' I stuttered. 'I… don't want to lose my focus…'

Tim looked at me earnestly, his glasses perching on the end of his nose. He sighed and then smiled. 'Honey, trust me, if you're wearing what you've just shown me' – he nodded to my once outfit-displaying phone – 'the only one losing focus will be him.'

*

11 September 2019 – London, England

'Focus, Jessica, *please*.' Devon stopped her pacing to stare me dead in the eye; thankfully I had just looked up from my phone. I'd have felt half bad if she wasn't regurgitating yesterday's notes verbatim and passing them off as new. I had every intention of emailing over yesterday's and changing the date.

'Are you even listening?' she asked, walking her bright white pant suit over to sit on the other side of her grandiose desk. I could just glimpse her green Jimmy Choos below and willed myself not to become the same colour.

'I am.' I nodded. And I was. And I'd listened the first time she'd told me, yesterday.

She cocked her head with a non-frown, which in her case equated to a smile, and began to pour herself a glass of wine. I watched her hand quiver as she filled the glass.

'Oh.' She started laughing to herself. 'This isn't what it looks like.' It looked like *Art Today*'s editor-in-chief was drinking red wine at ten in the morning, like she had stayed out so late rubbing shoulders with whatever influencer was now in vogue that she needed a bit of hair of the dog to bluff her way through the day. 'You know I have a Skype meeting with Sydney now, don't you? It's nine p.m. there and Hannah suggested wine. International networking, you know,' Devon carried on in a way that made clear that I didn't know, that I couldn't possibly be privy to something as highbrow as *international networking*. 'In fact, Hannah will be ready now. So, *focus*, Jessica.' She pointed a manicured finger at my notepad before opening her laptop screen so that its back faced towards me, making my notetaking invisible to Hannah Sommers. I knew the drill. Devon was to match Hannah wine for wine, whine for whine, as I – sober as a judge fresh out of rehab – was to discreetly record Hannah's boasts of exclusives and trends to enable Devon to play a grown-up game of 'anything you can do, I can do better'.

Before I could even entertain the thought of objecting, the iconic Skype bloop filled the room and Devon's face disappeared behind the monitor. Now safely under my powers of invisibility, I pulled my phone back out to sit on the table, hidden from Devon by the screen. I flicked back to Austin's Instagram. I hadn't seen him since the break-up. We'd all moved on from uni anyway – I got Zoe, Sam got him – and I'd promised her I wouldn't look back but what she didn't know couldn't hurt her. He looked to be doing well though – back in his Texan namesake, drinking, working and, by the looks of things, dating. My fingers hovered over a picture of him in a suit, arm slung around a pretty blonde, her face turned slightly to look up at him, proud of her man. I looked up from his feed to scribble Hannah's last sentence, sung out from the screen before returning to Austin. He looked exactly where he'd always wanted to be. My fingers almost went to check his friends list, seeing if he and Sam had stayed in touch – but I wouldn't, I couldn't.

I flicked away from Instagram and pulled up WhatsApp to contact Zoe:

Hey, want to do something tonight? Bored at work x

I watched as my message went from one tick, to two ticks, to blue ticks. *Typing… Sorry babe, with Ben tonight x*

I flicked away WhatsApp, and returned to Austin's America and Sommers' Sydney. London was meant to be the city of socialising, the city of success.

'Jessica.' Devon's voice shook me from my thoughts. 'We're done. You can leave now.'

Stashing my phone, I rose to leave Devon's office, wishing I could walk further and further away.

Chapter Twenty-Five

4 September 2020 – Sydney, Australia

'Here she comes! The famous curator,' Sam hollered from his normal position against the wall on the other side of the paved courtyard, clapping his hands in exaggerated applause. I laughed as I strolled confidently towards him. What had once felt like a handful of pity-dates, I was pretty sure, had become the highlight of Sam's day. A welcome relief from wedding planning, no doubt.

'Now I know you look all fancy and all,' Sam continued, pushing himself away from the wall and meeting me in the middle. I smiled; he had noticed. 'But the sun is out, and you *need* to take me to the beach.' He smiled broadly, slinging an arm around my shoulders and letting his weight rest on me long enough to signal just how exhausted he was.

I laughed again and looked up at his face, partially hidden behind his sunglasses, shaking my head affectionately. 'You're not a dog, Sam.'

'Can I have that on record, please?' He laughed. Oh shit, I had called him that once. In my defence, he had left me waiting at the table for half an hour while he chatted to his pretty doctor friend at the bar. He deserved it. I shook away the memory.

'I'll deny saying it at all costs.' I turned towards the beach. 'You coming, then?'

'Gosh, it's like I'm destined to be surrounded by bossy women!' He raised an eyebrow as he turned to follow me. Together, we walked towards the beach until it was time to prise off my heels and let my feet sink into the fluffy white sand. I had tried my best to convince myself I was a city girl, but day by day I was falling for the ocean life. I smiled down at my bare feet. I gazed across the horizon and breathed deeply, inhaling the salt-scented air. I turned to look at Sam, who was already looking at me rather than the sea.

'What?' I demanded, delighted to be catching him in the act.

'Nothing,' he said, looking down at his own naked feet. 'It's just, Sydney suits you.'

I smiled. I was beginning to feel like it did. 'I always liked that you were a bit of a free spirit,' he said. Well, he had at the start.

'Shame your parents didn't,' I said to the sand, looking up at Sam's stunned face before my little laugh softened the blow. 'Bet they're chuffed you're marrying a doctor.' I laughed again, but we both knew I wasn't joking.

'Yeah.' Sam forced an awkward laugh, not looking nearly as 'chuffed' as we both knew they were. 'They always liked you though,' he added. They had called me *creative*, *unique* – worlds away from what they knew. Jamie ticked the doctor box, but I wondered what they thought of Sam's new location or new-found faith. But maybe he didn't care quite as much what they thought any more.

'Hmmm,' I said, not entirely convinced; Sam's parents had always been a point of tension.

'So you're not in a rush to see them at the wedding?' Sam said, pressing his feet further into the sand. Oh crap, of course they'd be coming over for the wedding. But it wasn't like I'd be there. Was it? He was joking, right? Sam walked a step ahead of me, leading the way towards the beachfront café as I searched my mind for ways to ask what he really meant. Smiling at the guy behind the kiosk, Sam ordered, 'One bacon and avocado sandwich and…' He turned to me to check he'd got my order right. He had. Of course he had. 'And a crayfish salad, please.' He smiled back at the man. I looked at him in confusion.

'Jamie's got me on this pre-tux diet.' He rolled his eyes. I shrugged and accepted my sandwich, the grease seeping through the brown paper bag it was wrapped in. Sam gazed at it with desire. Walking across to the beach steps, we sat, side by side, both dressed too formally to have our bare feet in the sand.

'I wasn't sure whether you'd be able to make it today.' Sam looked across to me and smiled. 'It's tonight, right? The opening.'

I couldn't believe he had remembered. I knew we were living in the same house, but even when we were sleeping in the same bed, dates and times had never been his forte.

'I was going to come,' he continued. I sensed a 'but'; there was always a 'but'.

'And we'd usually be there to support Tim. But, Jamie is getting more and more stressed about the wedding; she's suggested we stay in and do some wedmin.' He looked down at his crayfish salad and shook his head. 'There was once a time when I didn't even know

the word *wedmin*.' He laughed to himself. 'It was simpler then…'
Simpler with me? 'Anyway,' he said, forcing the conversation
forward. 'We'll see how it goes and maybe we'll be able to make
it later.'

Stepping back into CreateSpace, I marvelled at my footwear. Gone
were the biting kitten heels of the last few weeks. In their place
were a pair of glorious black courts with the kind of designer soles
catfights have been fought over. The guys behind reception greeted
me, looking me down from my dark straight locks to my bright
red bottoms; they didn't need to know they were second- or maybe
third-hand from eBay. And naturally, I had hidden them from Jamie
and Sam, not wanting them to think I was getting too comfortable,
that I wasn't preparing to live alone in one of the most expensive
cities in the world.

Pacing across the entrance hall towards them, I looked up to see
Tuesday's Slumber hung proudly over the reception desk, filling the
gap I had always felt was there. The artist's thick impasto style was
even more eye-catching under the bright reception lights, the dark
blues of the piece dramatic against the white of the walls. Another
colleague popped their head around the open-plan gallery shop and
waved. I had browsed the shop once or twice, the tickle of brushes
in my hand a relic from the past – like feeling the T-shirt you had
once loved, now worn and outgrown.

I turned my attention away from the shop and towards the
first room of the exhibition, catching a glimpse of myself in the
reception's floor-length mirrors. I had obediently brought the Tim-

approved image to life, pairing a plunging yellow-gold silk blouse with a violet A-line, ankle-grazing skirt. The yellow of morning, the violet of evening, making sure I'd look right at home in either room, against either hue, of the exhibition. Sam had looked me up and down as I had headed out of the box room less than an hour before. I could have sworn I'd seen a look of nostalgic desire skim across his face. Jamie characteristically interrupted our moment: 'Oh, Jess, you look fantastic. Doesn't she, Sam?' She dangled me like a carrot in front of her fiancé.

'You look like a pansy,' Sam replied, deflecting any sexual tension that had hummed between us until Jamie had entered the room. 'A pretty one, though,' he added. 'We might see you later.' Jamie looked toward Sam, serious and stern. 'But first, wedmin!' He smiled obediently, but as Jamie turned to face me, Sam let me catch him rolling his eyes.

The mirrors in CreateSpace had always been forgiving. Smoothing down my skirt, I took a deep breath and turned towards the door. Another deep breath and I walked into the open space of Room A, bracing myself for chatter, activity, applause for… no one.

I looked around the empty space. This wasn't right. The happy, bright colours of the collection mocked me as I searched the room for people, for answers. Had no one shown up? Had I told them the wrong date? A sinking feeling filled my silk-covered stomach. I had been so preoccupied by lunches with Sam, surfing with Joshua and making sure I looked the part that it was possible that my too-quickly-sent press release had been littered with mistakes. Or that I'd been so focused on making sure my replies to Sommers were typo-free that I'd neglected to reply to any other requests. I'd taken the exhibition's air of mystery too far. I glanced at my phone, panicked, trying to pull up the press release. This was classic Jess. I couldn't do anything right.

'Jessica?' Tim emerged behind me, a white kaftan draped over his ripped denim, a glass of champagne clutched in his hand.

'Tim.' I turned, panic setting in. 'Where is everyone? Did anyone show?'

'Jessica,' he began. I braced myself for bad news. '*Too many* people showed. We had to move the drinks reception into the bigger room. Come with me.' Tim turned on his heel towards the door into Room B and, smiling broadly, pushed it open.

Hundreds of eyes turned to look at me as I walked, as if in slow motion, into the heaving room. 'Ladies and gentlemen,' Tim said, extending his arms towards me; ever the dramatist. Clearly his anonymity hadn't lasted long, I just hoped I could keep him away from our press contacts, one in particular. 'Introducing, Jessica, my co-curator on this show.' Co-curator? The promotion appeared to have passed me by, but I'd take it. I wondered if it came with a pay rise? I smiled broadly as the room filled with polite chatter. 'Soon to be joining the team at—' Without thinking I grabbed his shoulder, cutting off his sentence. 'What?' he hissed, half of the room's eyes still on us, the other resuming their chatter.

'This is CreateSpace's night, Leo's night, *your* night.' I forced a smile onto my face before lowering my voice further, 'Your chance to show that you don't need Carlo – trust me, my job at *Art Today Australia* shouldn't even get a look-in.'

Tim's face froze for a second, registering the words before he threw back his head and laughed, wrapping one arm around me.

'So bloody modest,' he said to the room, a handful of people joining in with his laughter. He turned his attention back to me. 'Now Jessica, let me get you a drink.' Tim swanned across the room and I finally realised what he had brought to his partnership with Carlo: he was one hell of a host.

As soon as the bubbles touched my lips, I knew we would be in for a good night. It wasn't so much that the champagne was remarkable – even though it was – it was more than that, a flavour I hadn't tasted for a while: the taste of success. This was real. I had actually worked hard on this, *contributed* to this, even made it what it was. And it looked great. A buzz of pride shot through my stomach. I walked forward into the rabble, ready for my first interview. There was little doubt that Tim was the star of the evening. He'd never really stood a chance at blending in – especially at the rate he was knocking back the drink. It really was good, though. I placed down my empty glass on the tray of a waiter passing by and was soon handed another. *Fabulous.*

'Can I have a word with the co-curator?' a male voice said softly behind me. At last, my first interview. My stomach filled with nervous excitement as my glass was re-filled again. I turned, pinning on a smile, trying to keep my cool.

'Joshua!' I still had to look up at him despite the extra inches of my heels. Handsome in his fitted suit and open collar, Joshua embraced me in a hug. I could feel Tim's gaze burning through my back.

'So beautiful.' I heard his words over the chatter of the crowd.

'I know, isn't it?' I said, admiring the sultry hues of the collection surrounding us.

'I meant you.' He smiled down at my pansy outfit; definitely not a wallflower.

'Oh, thank you.' I suddenly felt shy, before a waiter interrupted the moment with another top-up of champagne.

'So, what's your role tonight – no clipboard-holding I hope?' Joshua asked, before I forced a finger to my lips. The fact Tim was still watching us made me nervous in more ways than one. I had told Joshua too much to give him free reign to broadcast my bitching right now.

'No, I actually get to *talk* to people tonight. Tim wants me to handle the press interviews so pretend to look important,' I joked.

Joshua laughed in return. 'You may want to lay off the booze then,' he said, at the exact same moment the waiter came back to top up my glass. *This is how Jamie and Alice must feel every day*, I thought, as I thanked the over-attentive help.

'I'll leave you to it for a bit.' Joshua raised his eyebrow and grinned as the same waiter poured him a poor excuse of a portion. 'But, Jess,' he added sincerely, 'you really should be proud of yourself.'

As I watched Joshua disappear into the crowd, I scanned the room for Sam, who was nowhere to be seen. It was early though. There was still time. There was definitely still time.

*

16 June 2016 – Nottingham, England

I unglued my eyes from my watch to look around the gallery, at the buzz of people filling the room. I could see my mum and dad chatting happily to my old tutor, no doubt waxing lyrical about the fact I had just got an internship at *Art Today*. I couldn't blame them. I still couldn't believe that I had, that I'd be spending four weeks down in London, getting a taste of my new life with Sam. Now that the news had had time to sink in, the thought still thrilled and petrified me in equal measures – at least Zoe would be following me down soon, so she would never be far away.

I could see her mincing around the room with Austin, arm in arm, carrying glasses of champagne, their pinkies raised and every so often saying things like 'spiffing, darrrrrling' and 'it's bloody well marvellous'. Needless to say, it was the first time either had been to an art exhibition. I couldn't believe they were here for me, couldn't believe it when one of the emails I had sent round to galleries with my portfolio finally got a reply. They didn't want every piece in it, but they fell in love with one; sometimes one was enough.

I smiled to myself as Zoe tripped over her floor-length dress and clung to Austin, rescuing her drink at the expense of her dignity.

'Nice trip, darrrrrling?' I overheard Austin ask, failing miserably to don a British accent.

'It was bloody well marvellous,' Zoe oozed, before the two of them fell about laughing again and trotted towards me. 'Jessica darrrrrling,' Zoe began, arms outstretched. 'This gallery is simply *marvellous*, and that painting of yours – *that* painting…' She emphasised the word so forcefully that she made the couple next to her jump in surprise. 'Well, my darrrrrling, it's a *triumph*!' She pushed her non-glass-bearing hand to the ceiling in an over-pompous 'huzzah!'

'Thanks. It's only one painting.' I shrugged, still proud. I looked over to it, the oils on the canvas depicting a large sweeping landscape, loose abstract lines detailing the undulating hills even though the colour palette nodded to a scene more coastal, the browns, sands and golds making the exact location hard to place. At least I knew it lay somewhere between Brighton and the Lake District, somewhere between me and Sam.

'Tosh, Jessica. Tosh. It's ruddy spiffing!' Austin interjected with a flourish. Honestly, you couldn't take them anywhere. And yet, I was so glad they were here.

'No sign of young Sam?' Austin questioned, not tiring of his Windsor-meets-wally persona.

'There's still time.' I smiled weakly, looking towards the ornate clock, comparing it to the dainty hands of my watch. Both faces patronised me: *it's two and a half hours since opening and your boyfriend still isn't here.* I shook away the thought and picked up another glass of fizz. There was still time. He'd be here any second. I reached into my clutch bag and pulled out my phone. Nothing. Sam's shift finished half an hour ago, but they usually overran. He couldn't help it. And anyway, he probably thought it was no big deal. I had painted it so long ago. I began to type but then instantly deleted the words.

'He'll be here, soon,' I said, taking one last look at my phone, as it suddenly jumped to life. I swiped open the message and read:

J, I'm so sorry. Work's mad. See you later, yeah?

And then instantly, another:

Wish you were here x

I stashed my phone in my clutch bag and looked up at my friends. They didn't need to ask.

'Let's go and slag off the other paintings.' Zoe broke the silence, eyes full of mischief.

Austin nodded. 'We can start with this one.' He pointed to the painting hung next to mine, its soft lines suggesting the shape of a female nude. I bit back tears, trying my best not to be exposed. 'It shrinks in comparison to our Jessica's.' His fake accent remained unwavering. I tried my best to play along, but Sam's texts played on loop in my head. *Wish you were here*. For once I wished we could be where I wanted to be instead.

Chapter Twenty-Six

4 September 2020 – Sydney, Australia

I scanned the room again. Tim had cornered Joshua, picking imaginary flecks of fluff off the poor boy's narrowly cut suit jacket. I wondered how long it would be until he realised who Joshua was related to – it had taken me long enough. If I had a sister I'd tell everyone but I guess Zoe had always been like mine. Olivia was slaloming throughout the room, clipboard in hand, checking everyone was happy, checking everybody was in. Sam and Jamie were still nowhere to be seen.

'Jess, this is great!'

I turned around to find Alice, her hair loose and wavy, her make-up dewy and natural. She had a way of looking like she never gave a shit, not in a mean way but because she simply didn't have to.

'Congratulations.' Andrew grinned eagerly beside her, while Mark waited in line for his turn to kiss me on the cheek.

'I can't believe you guys made it.' I smiled, genuinely, careful not to let my voice crack. I couldn't believe they were here for me. Joshua must have told them about it.

'You kidding?' Mark asked. 'Support our friend and get free champagne? Try and stop us.' 'Our friend' seemed a stretch seeing as they had always been Sam and Jamie's friends but I couldn't help feeling accepted; they liked me. And, looking around the room, it seemed people were enjoying the exhibition. The champagne didn't hurt either.

'Well thanks, guys, I really appreciate it. I hope you enjoy the—' Olivia silently appeared to cut me off. She must have finally invested in some stiletto silencers.

'Sorry to interrupt,' she said to Alice, Andrew and Mark, who smiled, nodded and diffused into the crowd. 'Jessica, this is Giorgio Stefani. *Art editor. Vogue Australia.*' She whispered his credentials, but she needn't have bothered; I would recognise his slicked-back hair and chiselled cheekbones anywhere. 'Giorgio would like to ask you a few questions, perhaps if you two would like to head out to the reception and you can talk through the exhibition as we visioneered?'

Visioneered. Like, engineered a vision? You may be able to afford brand new Manolo Blahniks, Olivia, but that does not give you the right to edit the Oxford English Dictionary.

'Sure.' I smiled my most professional-looking smile, extending a hand delicately and silently thanking Tim for booking me into a mandatory manicure only days before. 'Follow me,' I said, picking up two fresh glasses of champagne from a passing waitress and handing one to Mr Stefani. I led him out of the room, head high and legs a little shaky. How many glasses had I had now? Tottering into the reception, I donned my best Olivia impression – sadly, my movements were less slaloming, more dribbling. Mr Stefani followed.

'So, talk me through this one.' Mr Stefani gestured nonchalantly up to *Tuesday's Slumber.*

'Well, Mr Stefani,' I said, nerves turning my sentence into stuttering. *Vogue Australia. Vogue Australia.* I had been allowed to email him an invoice. Once. I hope he didn't twig and wonder why he had been landed with the PA. But I wasn't the PA any more, I was the co-curator. I guess it was time to start acting like one.

I began slowly, describing the impasto style, the short brush strokes, the abstract detail of the deep blue piece. 'The decision to place the piece here was twofold.' Running out of things to say about the painting, I went on to our positioning, sounding a little too similar to the gallery toffs Austin and Zoe had pretended to be all those years ago. 'Firstly, practical – making the best use of our beautiful space.' I cast my arms wide and my eyes to the ornate ceiling as Mr Stefani followed my gaze. 'Secondly, anticipation.' I returned to look at him with a dramatic pause. 'We wanted you to *feel* the exhibition before you even step in.' I certainly sounded like a co-curator.

'Fascinating.' Mr Stefani stretched out the syllables.

I smiled. 'Let me take you to the next room.' Leading the way into the first room, bursting with the colours of sunrise, I began to warm up, explaining each painting with a flourish. I had studied the notes for each since arriving at the gallery, reluctant at first but as I researched more and more, I fell headlong into Leo Todd's vision: what she had hoped to achieve and create. Her piece *Sunrise on the Eighth* was made during her first week in Sydney, and featured real pieces of sand stuck into the yellow and orange stripes, getting thicker and more sweeping as the colours exploded from the centre of the piece. *Broken in Blue* invited viewers into a stark white canvas, thin blue lines etched ever so softly in scars that could only be seen close up. I showed off each piece with a pride and familiarity for her. She was my age. Strong women everywhere would be proud of her, cheering her on, but somehow that realisation made me feel like I was slipping even further behind – until tonight, until I shared in her success, until I used *my* brain. As I spoke, I felt it retrieve facts from the dusty degree in my mind, surprised that their years unused hadn't rendered them forgotten. For years, my knowledge of artists and their paintings had felt as useful as a soup fork. But now, now I felt like it mattered; I felt like I mattered.

Twenty minutes later, we had made it back into the main room and Olivia was replacing our empty glasses. Probably a bad idea. But almost on autopilot I accepted the full glass without question and turned to my interviewer. 'Thank you for your time, Mr Stefani. I hope you enjoy the rest of the exhibition.'

'Please,' he began, resting his free hand on my arm. 'Call me Giorgio.'

Call me Giorgio; I savoured the moment. Somewhere deep inside me the worn-down and worn-out girl at *Art Today* rejoiced: before me was the art editor of *Vogue Australia* telling me to call him Giorgio. If only I could bottle this feeling.

'Jessica.' Olivia nudged my elbow and I glanced up from what must be my seventh glass of champagne. 'Hannah Sommers, editor-in-chief at—'

This one I knew for sure. '*Art Today Australia*.'

'I believe you two have already—'

'Thank you, Olivia.' I interrupted her sentence before she could finish, steering the elegant older woman dripping in jewels before me, away from Olivia and the rest of the crowd. Here she was, finally, in the flesh, I had my chance to convince her to offer me another pocket of her time as soon as her packed-out diary would allow. Gone was her barrier of bourgeois beauties, gone was the faceless voice asking, '*Have you got an appointment?*', and gone was my inability to fight for what I wanted. It was time. Rewinding to the start of my tour, I took Hannah over to *Tuesday's Slumber*.

'I couldn't wait to visit.' Her pompous tone rang through her Australian accent, a universal arrogance translating to either hemisphere. The Sydney-based artists I had come across seemed so genuine and down to earth, but the pomp and prestige of the *Art Today* empire was international. 'Lots of the girls and boys in our offices wanted to join,' she droned on. *Women and men*, I corrected in my mind, grinning and nodding along, never skipping a beat. I needed too much from her – a good review, a job. Just looking at her perfectly lined eyes reminded me of Devon, her final smirk of dismissal still haunting me from across the globe. I bit back the thought. Slagging off her rival may get us a good review, but it wouldn't get me that job. For better or for worse, *Art Today* wanted all of their staff to be married to the job. Outside of the magazine, bitching was banter. From inside, it was betrayal. 'But they're just so busy. You know how it is,' she said as I joined in with her laughter, unsure as to quite how true she knew that statement to be. 'I guess that's what you get for being part of the greatest art brand on earth.' She reeled off the company strapline as I took another sip of my

champagne, forcing my eyes to fix on its bubbles and not roll in
their sockets. On and on she went, listing the accolades of the *Art
Today* empire.

'*Patience* is breath-taking,' she oozed, gazing into its soft greys
and ironically frenzied swirls. 'You should have opened with that.'
She gave me a hard stare over her cat-flick glasses. I got the feeling
that if we had, she would have commented that the piece would
have looked better in the body of the collection. I knew all too well
that *Art Today* editors were impossible to please. God, she didn't
half go on, though. Question after question. Each time I began to
respond, Hannah cut me off to answer them herself. Clearly, I was
the student in this scenario; student or servant – I wasn't sure. Either
way, I couldn't imagine she'd mind me polishing her Pradas. She
filled our silence with chatter as I hurried to work out how the hell
I was going to invite her out for coffee or broach the topic of a job.
Maybe if I just weaved in the fact that I used to work at *Art Today
UK*? Like I said, it wasn't like I got fired; I was made redundant.
Devon had made me so bloody redundant.

'I want to include everything.' She looked at the next painting.
'But as you know, every page of our publication is prime real
estate.' Even chased with gulps of champagne, her ego was hard
to swallow. I glanced down at my too-quickly drained glass, then
around the room for someone to deal with it. This was my 'Call
me Giorgio' moment and she was ruining it. I finally felt good at
something. I wouldn't let someone take it away. A waiter placed a
topped-up glass in my hand, and I studied the bubbles rising as a
thought rose in my mind.

I wouldn't let her take it away.

I didn't want to work at *Art Today*; I had never wanted to. Not really. Not then, not now. I cast my eyes across the room around me, filled with chatter, brimming with success. I had helped make this happen. I looked from Olivia to Tim, weaving through the guests. We were a good team. Surely they would want to keep me around? Carlo was still MIA and it was opening night; our journey with the exhibition had only just begun and given the press I'd managed to get here, who knew where else it might take us? For once, I wanted to be there to find out, to see what opportunities might come along. I looked at Hannah Sommers, so similar to her UK counterpart despite their disdain for one another. But wasn't that always the case? Two women more similar than they cared to think, wrestling for a space life told each one of them they could only occupy alone, like there was a scarcity of happiness or success to go around. Europe, Australia and all the world over, it would always be the same. I couldn't go back there, not now. I had to move forwards, to stop living that past. I looked around the room again, for Joshua, Alice, Mark – anyone who could receive my SOS and come to my rescue. Then I saw the back of a head I would recognise anywhere. As if in slow motion, he turned. Catching my eye from across the room, he raised his glass and nodded his head in my direction.

He was here. Finally, three years too late, but he was here.

'… Rebranding… out with the old… in with the…' Hannah Sommers' arrogant spiel had become monotonous white noise as my attention focused on Sam. Jamie was nowhere to be seen.

'… *Art Today* empire is thriving…'

Sorry, what did she just say?

'And for once the UK office is starting to shape up…'

'Thriving?' I asked, too abruptly, forcing my attention back to her. Hannah looked shocked at someone having the guts to ask a question. Taking a leaf out of her glossy-paged book, I answered it myself. '*Art Today UK* has just made half of their staff redundant. Their print issue is losing money. How can that be *thriving*?'

Maybe it was the champagne, maybe it was Sam – but I didn't need her to make my move to Sydney a success. I could do that on my own.

'Only those who weren't pulling their weight,' Hannah replied coolly, blissfully unaware that she was talking to one of them. But I wasn't weak, not then, and certainly not now; I was a 'Call me Giorgio' co-curator surrounded by people who had turned up to support me. Across the room I could see Sam edging closer towards us.

'… And with Devon at the helm the ship won't sink…' she went on, still keeping up appearances, although I was sure there was sarcasm escaping through her gritted teeth. Were they planning to get rid of her too? At least Hannah and I saw eye to eye on that. 'She's such a visionary…'

'Yeah, of second-hand visions.' I smirked, both shocked and proud as the words came out of my mouth. I could feel myself cracking. I'd kept her incompetence and misplaced priorities a secret for far too long and I knew full well that Hannah would love my gossip. I didn't want to work for her, but I knew how to get us a good review, how to let her know CreateSpace was on her side.

'I beg your pardon?' She looked at me intently. I could have sworn I saw a sneer flit across her face. Of course she wanted to know more. This was their trade. 'What are you insinuating?'

I looked into Hannah's wide eyes, willing me to go on. Maybe I should stop? From her smile it looked like I'd already made my point, that in their race to the top I considered her the winner. And judging from her reaction to our exhibition, perhaps she didn't need warming up to give us a shit-hot review. But then, she was here now, didn't she deserve to know the truth? And what had Lady Devon ever done for me? Apart from belittle me, hold me back, make me lie for her and then make me redundant. From the corner of my eye, I could see Sam moving closer and smiled: one killer review coming our way. 'I have it on good authority' – aka I worked for her for years – 'that she steals all of her best ideas from you.'

Hannah smiled, showing a perfect set of white teeth. If this wasn't going to get us five stars, I wasn't sure what would.

'She wouldn't.' Hannah leaned in closer, a sadistic look in her eyes, her smile spreading wider.

'Oh, she would,' I said. I could feel Sam's presence. I turned to acknowledge him and then moved my attention back to Hannah, who was packing away her iPhone into one of this season's Miu Miu clutches.

'Thank you for the interview, Jessica. It's a fantastic story,' she said, looking around the exhibition space. 'And thanks for the heads-up,' she whispered. 'I didn't think Devon had it in her.'

'Trust me,' I continued, drawing strength from years of staying silent. 'There's nothing that bitch wouldn't do.'

'Hey, Pansy.' Sam looked at my outfit from top to designer bottom and smiled. He looked effortlessly gorgeous in a dark grey suit and white open-collared shirt, showing just a hint of hair on the strong chest I used to sleep against. 'This is so great!' he said, casting his eyes around the bustling exhibition. It was beautiful, and I had played a part in pulling it together. And I felt beautiful too. The surfing sessions with Joshua were clearly starting to do the trick, tightening my arms and relaxing my mind. Maybe Sam was right; maybe Sydney was good for me, too. I was getting excited for what my future could hold here.

'I didn't think you were going to make it.' I smiled; I'd had every reason to believe he wouldn't.

'Jess, I wouldn't miss it for the world.' He placed a hand on my upper arm and squeezed, saying the words I had always longed to hear. 'I'm really proud of you.' I almost felt like he wanted to kiss me. Why wouldn't he kiss me? 'Jamie sends her love as well.' Oh yeah, that was why. But he was here now, and we were finally alone, with the whole evening in front of us. 'She tried to get me to stay to do wedmin for another hour, but I told her I really needed a break.' He looked serious for a moment before covering the look with a laugh. A break from wedmin or a break from Jamie? 'It all just gets a bit too much sometimes, you know? So, going to show me around?'

Repeating the tour again, taking a bit more time than I had with Call me Giorgio and Hannah Ego Sommers, I walked Sam through the themes and highlights of the exhibition. In the slightly quieter 'morning' room, one or two people milled around holding glasses of champagne and taking in the art.

'So, tell me about this one.' Sam mirrored the posture of those more well-versed in gallery etiquette around him. *Nameless* by

Anonymous was a smaller supporting piece. It was hard to top Leo
Todd for mystery, but this unknown local artist had gone and done
it. Compared to the vast canvases nearby, it lacked some of the same
impact. And yet, it caught my eye every time, almost like a memory
I couldn't quite recall. Where had I seen this artist's work before?
I'd asked Tim again and again if we had been given a name for the
plaque, but it was always a no. Knowing him, he'd probably gone
and lost it. That, or Carlo had stolen it to spite him. About half a
metre wide, the canvas was painted in oils that faded from light
blue to dark blue with increasingly intense brushstrokes and texture,
a little like *Tuesday's Slumber*, but softer, kinder, like inviting you
into warm water or a restful dream. I turned to look at Sam, tall
and handsome as he tried to make sense of what stood before him.
Art was outside his area of expertise. He never did used to get it.

'No.' I turned to look at him, as he took a step back, surprised.
'You tell me about it. What do you see? What does it make you feel?'

'I don't know,' Sam said sheepishly; such a perfectionist, never
wanting to get things wrong.

'There's no right or wrong answer, Sam.' I laughed kindly and
turned back to the canvas. 'Ever heard of the phrase "it's an art,
not a science"?'

'Well, I see blue,' Sam began. Good start; at least he was trying.
'Like the sea.' Honestly, he sounded like a child. 'And it gets deeper,
and darker and then there's… like… more going on under the surface
than we see… and it's messy and real and… I like it.' Sam finished
his analysis and looked at me as if to ask if he had got it right.

'Cool,' I said, noncommittal, lust and champagne pulsing around
my body. I had waited years for Sam to give art a chance; he never

did like dealing with things – or people – he didn't understand. I allowed myself to look into the picture again, not wanting to ruin the moment. I studied the use of colour; it was a blend of blues, so deep, so unique, I knew I'd seen it before. It was the colour of the painting I had printed off an image of and pinned up to my desk at work. The last idea I had bothered to suggest to Devon. Now she was miles away, and I felt miles away from that bored and hopeless girl. Without speaking, I tried not to stumble as we went on to the next piece, right outside the door to Room B. It was time to enter the crowds again. Sam followed. Looking up at the yellows and creams of the large canvas that hung before us, I felt Sam close behind me and could almost feel his breath on my exposed shoulder.

'Jess?' Sam asked, gazing up at the piece. I turned around to look at him. 'This is really great.'

'The piece?' I asked, looking up at Leo's work, my pride for her now outweighing any envy.

'Not just the piece.' He shook his head and looked down at his shoes. 'The piece, the exhibition, the art, you.' He looked me in the eye and smiled. 'I'm sorry I didn't say it enough when we were together, but I loved that you were artistic, that you were into all this stuff. I loved that you saw the world differently from the way I do.'

He was telling me things I wanted to hear, and yet one word rang out, drowning out all of the rest. Loved. Past tense. *Loved.* Sam broke off as he saw my face fall.

'What's wrong?' He put a hand on my arm, his skin melting into my own.

I'd drunk too much. I shouldn't say it. But he was here, and Jamie was not. And he'd said he wouldn't miss it for the world. I looked into his eyes, his face inching towards me with every bated breath occupying the space between us.

'Loved. As in the past,' I said quietly, trying desperately to stifle memories of all the times he had told me in the present tense; before love turned to loved.

Slowly, Sam placed both hands on my shoulders and pulled me into a big bear hug. My safe space. Encased by strangers and surrounded by brushstrokes, his head nuzzled into my hair and I heard him breathe, 'You know I'll always love you, J.'

*

15 July 2017 – London, England

Sam sat across from me in silence, the sunshine dancing on the Thames behind us. Large speakers blared out; it was London Bridge's Summer of Love. This was meant to be fun.

'Are you okay?' I asked, stroking his arm, trying to rescue him from his thoughts.

'Yeah, just thinking.' He smiled, leaning his head onto my sun-kissed shoulder.

'Don't hurt yourself,' I quipped, kissing his fluffed-up hair. He tickled my ribs, lifting his head back up to take a sip of his beer. I watched him cast his eyes back out across the water. Armies of tourists lined the riverbank, arms extended for the perfect selfie. Couples cuddled each other as families licked ice creams. I had watched them all week, waiting for Sam to visit. And now he was here. Less happy than in my imagination.

'About?' I asked. Sam's stressed-out hospital weeks were sending him further into himself.

'It's just, sometimes, I can't imagine living here any more.' Sam must have felt me stiffen as he quickly added, 'but then, I'm not the imaginative one.' He smiled, the warmth of his grin reflecting onto my own. I was desperate for him to move down to London; that was always the plan. That was what he'd said he wanted. That was the reason I was here, surrounded by people but so often feeling alone. Holding him closer, I nestled in the crook of his neck, placing a light kiss on his clavicle.

'That's okay,' I whispered against him. 'You'll love it when you get here.'

'You think?' He tilted his lips towards my forehead. I could hear his heart beating in my ear.

'I know,' I assured him. 'And until then, I'll imagine for the both of us.' I grinned, savouring the sky as it turned from blue and white to orange and pink, a painting of our future so close we could almost touch it.

Chapter Twenty-Seven

5 September 2020 – Sydney, Australia

'You can let go now,' I said into the warmth of his shoulder, nervous that my make-up might make a mess of his white kaftan. Tim pulled away, sincerity written on every inch of his face.

'You've done a great job, Jessica, incredible, even,' he said, as I let his words warm me from the inside out. 'We couldn't have done it without you.' For a moment he looked worried at the thought of doing just that, his Carlo still nowhere to be seen even though my Sam had shown. But soon I'd tell him that he didn't have to. That I wasn't going to take my job at *Art Today Australia* after all. That I was ready for something different, something new.

'Need a cab?' Tim looked over my shoulder in the direction of the voice that had spoken, grinning from ear to ear. I turned to see Joshua standing there, his casual shirt now a little more undone. 'Sorry for interrupting,' he added to Tim, who was already pushing me out of the door and in his direction. I'd had no idea Joshua was still here; had he been waiting for me? I scanned the room in search of Sam even though I knew he was long gone, back home to Jamie though his words were left with me: *you know I'll always love you.*

*

Following Joshua into the taxi, my feet felt like they were floating across the ground. The champagne was only partially responsible.

'You did amazingly, Jess,' Joshua said as I gazed out of the window, watching the late hour of the night turn into the early hours of morning, just like the exhibition we had left behind. 'Want to do anything to celebrate?' Joshua's words faded into the distance as the coastline was slowly illuminated by the promise of sunrise. Like the colours of the sky, morphing before me now, I wanted this night to stretch into the morning, for the warmth of this success to stretch on for days. There was only one thing I wanted to do now.

'Are you sure?' Joshua replied, obviously not sure it was a great idea, given how much I'd drunk. But before he could object I was waving him off and winding my weary feet onto the Bondi to Coogee coastal path, content to savour the slow walk home.

Heels now in hand, I put one bare foot in front of the other as I watched the sun start to show, scattering glitter across the great expanse of ocean before me. I watched as the burnt orange of the sun started to emerge from the vast mystery of the sea, bringing the work of Leo Todd and the other artists of our collection to life right before my eyes. I had helped make tonight happen. I'd impressed Sam, Tim – I'd impressed *myself.* I embraced the early sunrise, holding Sam's sentences closer still. This was the Sydney, the new start I'd been chasing. A new day had finally arrived.

*

My mind woke up, but my body remained dead. I reached for the bottle of water on my bedside table, right where the photograph of Sam and Jamie used to sit. I took a sip and sighed; it had been a great night. In quick succession, I ran through the highlights: the turnout, the friends, the interviews, that moment with Sam, the sunrise. This was one of those rare times where the hangover was probably worth it; last night was a blast.

Forcing my feet to the floor, I stood up, pulled on a hoodie and threw the now drained water bottle into the bin. Turning the door handle to exit the room, for once I hoped Sam wasn't waiting for me with pancakes in the kitchen. I wasn't in a fit state to see anyone. I wasn't in a fit state to eat pancakes. I'd speak to Tim next week about staying on with the exhibition; my steady wages would finally get me in a place nearby. And I'd be around to see how things worked out – or didn't – with Sam and Jamie. I was already starting to see the real Sam revealing himself, the old Sam coming back to me. Finally, it felt like everything was how it was meant to be. Walking down the corridor, I heard the familiar sound of feet pacing and knew I wasn't alone.

'Jess, can you get through to Sam?' a frantic-looking Jamie asked as I entered the kitchen-living room. *Believe me, Jamie, I've been trying to.* I thought back to last night again, Sam's words still ringing in my ears, champagne pounding in my head. Had he even come home? For a moment I felt bad; Sam was almost a married man. The looks, the touch, that sense, that sentence, it all ran on repeat in my mind. But didn't Jamie deserve to know the real Sam too? No one could wear a mask forever. I was just encouraging it off a little sooner. One day she might even thank me. I looked at her, perfect in her skin-tight black jeans and black tank top. Just look at her. Even with worry sketched across her forehead she was the kind of girl who would always be okay. And I was starting to think I'd be okay too, more than okay.

'Um,' I replied, guilt shooting through my body. I tried to bury it as quickly as it came. 'I haven't tried, want me to give him a call?' Jamie nodded, panicked. Sam had headed home before me last night but I couldn't remember seeing him on the sofa when I finally returned home. Come to think of it, I couldn't remember much after my magical moment at all. 'I'll try now,' I assured her, hitting Sam's number, half hoping he wouldn't pick up on the first ring. It would be too brutal for Jamie to take right now. Within moments, Sam's answerphone clicked in. I looked to Jamie and shook my head.

'Damn, his phone must be dead,' she said, placing a glass of fresh orange juice in front of me.

'Thanks.' I smiled. A pang of empathy crossed my chest as Jamie paced the kitchen floor. I'd been met with Sam's answerphone a thousand times before when he was lost in the depths of Nottingham's A&E. 'I'm sure nothing's the matter.'

'It's not that, J.' Jamie had adopted Sam's nickname for me by proxy. Each time she said it, it made me feel just a little bit worse. 'He's surfing but we're supposed to be meeting our sommelier for the wedding later. He was going to go straight there and I've just got called into work. He never checks his phone.'

I nodded in sympathy. She was right. He didn't. I'd had no end of evenings waiting with two place settings and a cold dinner while Sam worked. But what could either of us say? I know I didn't want a doctor boyfriend who left someone dying because he was dying to see me. I would have thought Jamie of all people would understand. Sam used to say I would too if I had his job. Jamie placed her left hand to her forehead, blinding me with her rock. I could see why she didn't wear it all the time; she'd have one arm muscle bigger than the other.

'J?' She paused, as if weighing up whether this was a good idea or not. She opened her mouth to speak and then closed it again. Maybe I wasn't the only one keeping secrets? I looked down at my drink, preparing myself for whatever she was going to say next.

'You don't think you could… go instead, do you?'

I looked up from my orange juice. Huh? Go where, with who?

'You wouldn't have to go for long, I just don't want him to wait and worry when I don't turn up.' She began to pace again. 'God, if only he'd charged his phone for once. They're called mobiles for a reason!'

I looked at Jamie, worry lines etched around her eyes. Had they always been there? I forced my blurry eyes to look a little closer, trying to work out whether I was the cause of them or whether my jealousy of her had clouded any imperfections that had already been there when we'd first met. Right now I didn't want to think about it. All I wanted was to bask in that sunrise, to prolong the moment of knowing I was exactly where I needed to be.

'You want me to go meet Sam and this sommelier?' I had heard the term before but couldn't conjure a picture in my mind. Jamie stopped pacing to look down at her phone.

'Yeah but only for a bit. You don't have to try all the wines, if you don't wan—'

'Wine?' I interrupted; I couldn't hack pancakes, but hair of the dog was the oldest hangover cure in the book – that much I'd learnt from Devon. And a post-surf Sam had always been refreshing. And for some bizarre reason I felt like I was doing Jamie a favour. I had no idea how long this high was going to last but after all the lows of the last few years, I was sure as hell going to ride it.

'I've got the day off today, it's no bother,' I said, wondering for the umpteenth time why being around her made me say things like 'no bother' and 'quite the day'. Jamie didn't seem to notice, too occupied with staring down at her blank screen. 'I'll go and meet him, tell him you've been called into work and maybe try a few wines for you. I've had… some experience in that department.' It was true; of all of the things I was good at, wine was up there. 'It would be my pleasure.' I hoped she didn't know how true that was. The truth was, she had had me at 'Sam'. I had to find out what last night meant, what all of this meant, what would happen next.

'Thanks.' Jamie smiled, her stance softening as she moved across the room to embrace me before half running towards the doorway to get her scrubs on. Before she disappeared, she turned. 'You're a real saviour, Jess.'

Walking into The Argyle to meet Sam felt like a dream, perhaps because of all the residual champagne in my system, but most probably because of its iconic building: an 1820s style warehouse, all exposed brick and cobbled floors, nestled into the heart of The Rocks. Donning my shades, I navigated my way across the sandstone courtyard, through the impressive high archways and across the timber floor, all in last night's designer heels. With little time to get ready, I had thrown on the same sky-blue dress as yesterday morning, managing to look a lot better than I felt, which, right now, wasn't saying a lot.

After last night, the thought of adding more alcohol to the mix between Sam and I felt dangerous and desirable all at the same time – but this week was about taking risks. A handful of hipsters looked up from their drinks as I tottered by, finally feeling the part. Others sauntered up one of two wooden staircases that disappeared out of sight. Jamie had told me to stay on the ground floor. Coming to stand by one of the restaurant's many bars, I pulled up a high stool and looked up to the beamed ceiling and smiled; it was so romantic. All I had to do was wait. It was something I'd got pretty used to doing, but somehow it felt like the end was now in sight.

'Can I get you a drink?' An impeccably well-dressed woman behind the bar asked, as I peered back through my sunglasses.

'No, that's okay, I'm waiting for my boy—' I paused. 'Friend.'

'No worries.' She smiled. And there weren't any. Sam thought he was coming to meet a stressed-out Jamie and instead he had me. Just like how last night's admin had made way to Sam joining me at the gallery. This was another perfect opportunity to show him how carefree, fun-loving and undeniably perfect for him I could be, and the universe was now doling them out for free. My long overdue payback. Even though I was still struggling to remember scraps of last night, I knew I'd finally become the kind of ambitious professional he'd always hoped I'd be. Someone with their shit together, someone like...

'Filling in for Jamie?'

Not again. Sure enough, I turned to see the bearded face of Joshua beam out from behind his own set of Wayfarers. I'm not sure how I was still surprised by these run-ins.

'Filling in for Sam?' I asked, not wanting to know the answer.

'Yeah, his phone died but he needed to go and meet someone from church. He asked me to come and tell Jamie.'

He wasn't coming. Again. I wondered if he had known it was me who was waiting for him, whether the result would have been any different.

'Oh well, no harm done,' I said. 'Should we get back then?' I felt silly and overdressed and ready to just go home. My headache was really starting to kick in, stale wine now swirling in my stomach. Maybe I could continue to ride my exhibition high after a really, really long sleep? Joshua looked my sundress up and down, the same way he had over the breakfast table yesterday, and smiled.

'Looking like that?' He pulled out a stool beside mine and sat down. 'Hell, no.'

'But I…' I began, looking around the room for a reason to excuse myself.

'Excuse me?' Joshua took off his Ray-Bans and gestured to the barmaid. 'Myself and my fiancée are here for our wine-tasting.' He looked over to me and smiled. 'Sam.' He extended a hand, which the woman behind the bar simply ignored. 'And this is my fiancée, Jamie.'

I smiled nervously; even the thought of pretending to be her made me feel out of place, like mutton dressed as lamb. Not that vegan Jamie would consider dressing like either.

'Come this way.' Together we followed the woman into a discreet side room with a table in the centre laid out with a dozen glasses and wine bottles to match. 'Take a seat.' She gestured towards the sturdy wooden chairs. Joshua pulled one out for me and held a supportive hand out as I sat down. The lady looked at me – with irritation or envy, I couldn't tell.

'Here at The Argyle,' she began, 'we like to offer an intimate tasting free from our own opinions.' Her tone was wooden, her shift far from over. 'This brochure will tell you everything you need to know about the wines and I'll be just on the other side of the door should you have any questions.' She said the final sentence with a slightly raised eyebrow as if to say: *so no funny business.* She wasn't to know that Joshua was my ex-boyfriend's fiancée's older brother and that 'funny business' was not on the menu today. I nodded eagerly in agreement and watched as she left the room, closing the door behind her. We were finally alone. Except, sadly, the wrong 'we'. Not that Joshua was going to know I cared.

'So, future Mrs Sam,' Joshua began; my heart sank. 'White or red?'

'White?' I suggested; no one wanted to look like they'd been face deep in blueberry pie on a date. Not that this was a date. Joshua poured wine into two glasses, one more generous than the other. Just like the waves on our first surfing lesson that had once seemed so large, I wasn't sure the wine looked as inviting without Sam by my side.

'Trying to get me drunk, Sam?' It was a sentence I'd said a thousand times before. If we kept this role play up, I'd need a bigger glass.

'I'm on my bike,' Joshua explained, shedding his role as my ex-boyfriend as I finally caught my breath. 'I'll have to watch what I drink.'

'Look, I know those cycling proficiency test things tell you not to drink but if you just go slow on the cycle path…'

Joshua raised his eyebrows at me. 'You think I ride a pushbike, don't you?'

'I… don't you?'

'Jess, I ride a motorbike,' he said matter-of-factly. 'I've told you that.' Had he? I scrambled around in my mind for this hidden information. It was unfortunate that most of the time we'd spent together I was trying to save myself from drowning, or trying to find out more about Sam and Jamie. 'Sometimes I think you don't listen to me.' He smiled and shook his head.

'I listen to you.' My objection was laced with laughter, trying to keep things light. Just maybe not very closely when Sam and Jamie were around. 'I love to listen to you.'

Joshua reached a hand to mine. 'I'll give you a lift home tonight.'

'I don't want to drink all this if you're not drinking,' I argued, actually telling the truth; my stomach churned.

'That's okay, just have a sip if you like…' Joshua began, but I was too busy gulping down glass number one. Hair of the dog; it was worth a shot, right?

'Wow, this is…' I pointed to the glass as Joshua opened bottle number two. 'The one.'

Chapter Twenty-Eight

'Ding, ding, ding, ladies and gentlemen – we have a new winner!'

Joshua laughed out loud. Was I drinking too much? I was drinking too much. Again. At least this morning's hangover was nowhere to be seen.

'You said that about the last one.' He laughed; he was wearing his Ray-Bans again after I had told him for the thousandth time he looked good in them. We had dissolved into laugher as the woman who had welcomed us had popped her head around the door to check on us to find us on our third bottle of red and wearing our sunglasses inside, an arm each slung over one another like the Blues Brothers we weren't.

'The last one set the bar,' I replied. 'This one just smashed it!'

After her last check-in, our host had finally left us to our own devices. Poor Joshua. Through his sunglasses, I couldn't tell if he wanted to go home.

'Bet you wish Jamie was here?' I put my hand on his in a drunken slur.

'I don't actually.' He grinned, his eyes searching across my face, hoping to find something. 'As much as I love her, I—'

'When we first met, I actually thought you did love her,' I interrupted through unwarranted laughter. 'Before I knew she was your sister, obviously.'

'I *do* love her.' He shook his head, confused but smiling, sunglasses now removed, his blue eyes piercing mine. It was that look of confused endearment again. I had no idea why that kept happening around me.

'No, like, actually *love*-her love her,' I slurred. It worried me how sober he seemed and how *not* sober I was beginning to feel. Why was I telling him this?

'Jess!' He laughed, putting his glass-free hands to his eyes as if the mental image of the two of them had hit him square between them. 'She's my *sister*.' He laughed again.

'I didn't know that at the time!' My laughter joined his, as I pulled my hand to my blueberry-stained lips; sometimes it was just too hard to say no. 'Just like you guys don't know…' I stopped myself. My filter wasn't great at the best of times, never mind when we were three bottles in, and I dreaded to think what proportion of those Joshua had actually had drunk.

'Don't know what?' He smiled coyly, moving in a little closer. His eyes looked so kind and trusting, I almost wanted to tell him everything. Plus, he was one of my only friends this side of the equator. One of my only *just friends* at least. I imagined confessing everything: I never had an apartment, I never had a job. I was winging it this whole time and now it was finally paying off. Oh, and I started loving your sister's fiancé at the age of eighteen and never really worked out how to stop.

'Jess, anything you tell me will stay with me,' he encouraged, leaning closer still, placing a hand on my upper thigh, his touch as light and welcome as the summer breeze we were all waiting for. 'Sometimes you just have to stop worrying about what other people will think.'

'I don't know…' I began as he leaned a little closer. Even in my familiar drunken haze, I knew this wasn't a good idea.

'Seriously, Jess.' He grinned again, happy and hopeful. 'You can tell me. It'll be our secret until you're ready to tell other people.'

'How I feel about him,' I whispered over the rim of my glass, gazing up to gauge Joshua's reaction.

'Him?' Joshua's face fell as he pulled back, retrieving his hand, leaving the space where he'd touched me, cold. 'Who?' I couldn't make out his expression.

'Sam,' I admitted. 'Who did you think I meant?'

'It doesn't matter.' Joshua shook his head and poured himself another splash of red. 'I thought you guys broke up years ago?'

God, it was only three years ago. We were together for five. We were in love. We had our whole lives planned out. Why was that so hard for people to understand? Why did— wait…

'You know about Sam and me?' I slurred; he had just said that he did, but it still felt like a confession of his own. I thought that they thought we were just friends, had always been just friends. That's why I'd never said anything about our relationship, why we'd both been so careful not to.

'Well, yes.' Joshua looked bemused, disappointed and a little bit angry all at the same time.

'So, Jamie knows about Sam and me?' There was no way. Why on earth would she let me stay? Even I could admit live-in ex-girlfriends and wedding planning were not a good mix. The proof was in the painting, hung up in Jamie's bedroom, soon to be theirs, but with a big dose of me messed up in the mix.

'Well, yes,' he said again, stuck on repeat, his tone soberer by the second.

'But she's not said anything?' I took another large gulp of wine. She'd never said anything, not once. Not when Sam invited me to stay in the first place and not since.

'Why would she?' Joshua looked from me to his empty glass of wine. He really needed to hold off if he was going to drive us home. Not that I could say anything; I was hardly proving myself to be the queen of quantity control.

'I don't know.' I shrugged, suspending the fact that Joshua was Jamie's brother for a second and speaking to him as a friend, the friend he thought I was – that *everyone* thought I was. 'I reckon I'd have a thing or two to say if my fiancé brought home his ex-girlfriend to stay in our flat. In fact, she'd be out of the door quicker than you could say—' I flung my glass-holding hand in the direction of the door, sloshing red specks onto the carpet, making a mess.

'Jamie doesn't feel that way.' Joshua smiled weakly, no doubt growing tired of my increasingly drunken outpour. 'I'm pretty sure she's secure enough in her relationship to not be threatened by an old girlfriend from uni.' Joshua looked at me. Through blurry eyes, I couldn't tell whether he was trying to be mean or just achieving it regardless.

So that's what Jamie thought we were, that's what she thought I was. Just an old girlfriend from uni, Sam and I two people too young to have experienced anything real. I was staying in their box room, her fiancé was sleeping on her sofa, we went for lunch and laughed like more than old friends, and still she wasn't threatened.

I looked down at my sky-blue dress, dotted with damp specks from where I'd been drinking. Was I really that pathetic? My mind darted to Zoe's words to me just yesterday morning, tired of telling me to move on. To my parents, nervous to let me travel to the other side of the world for fear that I'd cock everything up.

I looked down into my wine glass; maybe she was right not to be bothered by me. I was just an old girlfriend, it was all I was, and she was a goddess. A goddess with the guy. A goddess who had won. I looked up at Joshua, watching me like a glass about to break. But I wasn't just an old girlfriend. We'd been in love, we'd said we'd get married, with our bare feet pressed into the Sydney sand. And now we were here, fate finally fusing our stories back together. And Sam and I had been getting closer. He'd loved having me around. He'd said he missed me, and then he said he loved me. I knew he still loved me. I could feel it. I gazed down into my empty wine glass, blood-red stains circling the rim. I held the glass stem a little tighter. I was not *just* an old girlfriend; I was so much more than that. If Jamie knew about me, if Jamie knew *everything*, it was about time she knew that too.

As I stumbled to Joshua's bike, he turned to help me put my helmet on in silence. He hadn't said much since our conversation, a conversation that never should have happened. Of course he wouldn't have responded like a friend. Sam was his sister's fiancé, for Christ's sakes. As I sat on the back of the bike, Joshua turned to me and said, more forcefully than I'd ever heard him: 'Don't let go.' Despite my drunkenness I knew he was talking about the bike, but still my brain hurtled on, speeding a mile a minute. I was not just an old girlfriend. We were in love. He was everything. Joshua was wrong. Jamie was wrong. Three bottles deep, I could see everything clearly. Jamie wasn't the woman Sam wanted her to be. Sam wasn't the saint Jamie thought he was. And then there was me. Here, when I had every reason not to be. Here, when Sam could have kicked me out weeks ago or never invited me back in the first place. Something was making me stay. And Sam didn't want me to leave. Was I the only one who could call a spade a flipping spade? They weren't a perfect match; they weren't built to last. I held on tighter as scenes of inner-city life shot by. This city suited me, Sam had said. And Sam's words from last night were planted firmly in my head like seeds in bloom. Expanding and expanding, until they filled my mind with nothing but his words: *you know I'll always love you, J, you know I'll always love you.*

Pulling up to 341, Joshua helped me off the bike and unclipped my helmet. I looked up at him through bleary eyes to see his own blue ones staring back, wide and sad. Had I really just told him I was still in love with his sister's fiancé? I silenced the thought again. There was no going back now. He'd tell her in the morning and I'd have my bags packed and out by the afternoon. Joshua leaned down to peck me on the cheek, the same sadness etched into his face. Another friendship ruined for sure, each of them fading away through my inability to shut up or keep up. He held my arm and helped me to the door. I fumbled for my keys, forcing them into the lock. The door swung open and I turned around to say goodbye. Joshua had already started to walk away.

Stumbling into the corridor, I closed the door behind me as quietly as I could. Letting the darkness surround me, I breathed.

I was exhausted.

I was angry.

I was – *hammered.*

Walking further down the corridor, I tried to keep quiet. The walls were spinning; I clung to the sides in failed attempts to steady myself. Kicking one heel off, and then the other, I felt my way along the corridor. Tumbling into the dark kitchen, I tripped across the floor. I needed to lie down; I was going to be sick if I didn't lie down. I headed towards the sofa, heart starting to race, temperature beginning to rise. On autopilot, I pulled off my dress. The stupid blue dress I had bought just for Sam. I flung it on the floor. I stared into the darkness, the thick swell of alcohol washing over me, making it impossible to think. Box room. I should go to the box room.

I felt my way along the corridor walls, trying to find my way back. To where Jamie wanted me to be. Close enough to watch me. Far enough away from Sam. *Just an old girlfriend*; the words danced around my head, taunting me as I stumbled in the darkness. *Just an old girlfriend. Just an old girlfriend*; the words played over again and again. Four silly words, interrupted only by seven more: *You know I'll always love you, J.* Head spinning, mind moving back to the box room, but feet, in reality, moving me to the wooden kitchen floor. I needed to lie down.

Scrambling to take off my bra, I headed towards the sofa. I felt my way to lie down. I felt the sofa. I felt the cushions. I felt Sam. Of course, he was there. Sleeping on the sofa. For me. Making that sacrifice, for me. Because he would always love me. His words and all that alcohol span round in double time. *I'll always love you, J.* Box room. I should go to the box room. But I was already lying down, stretching out, falling into sleep. Without thinking, I lined my body up against Sam's back. He stirred. Without waking, he pushed his back further into me, fitting the shape of my body naturally. Muscle memory, reminding us of what we had been. What we were. I placed my arm around him, my mind somewhere else entirely. Still half asleep, Sam felt for my hand and pulled it up to his lips, giving it a kiss: soft but firm. Warm and safe. I was drunk and drifting. Drunk and drifting. Drifting. Drifting until finally we were gone and only silence remained.

*

5 September 2014 – Nottingham, England

Silence filled the room, apart from the soft snore of Sam's steady inhale and exhale, his breathing always heavier when he'd been drinking. His body, his hands grabbed my arms and pushed down softly, encouraging my body to turn to face him.

'Morning, gorgeous.' His eyes were wide now, his hands guiding my leg over his and pulling me to sit on top of him.

'It's not morning yet.'

'Yes it is,' Sam objected. It was morning when he had let himself into my room, morning when he had squeezed himself into my single bed.

'Well, technically yes.' I smiled through a whisper, careful not to wake my neighbour on the other side of the thin walls. 'But it's not time to get up yet.'

'You're unbelievable,' he whispered into my hair, pulling me closer still. 'I want you.'

'I can tell.'

'I love you.' He looked into my eyes, both of us calmed by the words, like the ocean that so often roared between us was, in that moment, still.

'I can tell.' I leaned in to kiss him again, letting him run his fingers through my hair. I pulled away, struggling to hide my smile.

'Go back to sleep now,' I whispered, the magic words reminding him of the time and making his eyes fall heavier by the second. 'But when we wake up,' I whispered, pulling myself off him to snuggle back into his side, 'you can tell me again and again and again.'

Chapter Twenty-Nine

6 September 2020 – Sydney, Australia

'Fuck. *Fuck.*' Somewhere in the distance I could hear Sam's voice. Somewhere on my skin I could feel him move. I stirred myself awake, but still felt like I was dreaming.

'Jess, what are you doing?' I felt Sam's breath on mine, his face now inches away from my own. I looked into my ex-boyfriend's eyes, full of fear. I looked down at my body, naked apart from my lacy French knickers: once so sexy, now so sinful. *Shit, shit, shit.* We couldn't have? We wouldn't have?

'I erm… did we?' I asked. This was what I wanted. But it didn't feel good. I didn't feel right. I sat up, pulling the bed sheet around me, hiding the parts of me Sam had seen countless times before, suddenly ashamed. I looked around the open-plan living room – too white and too bright; I closed my eyes again. My head began to spin. I leaned over as if I might be sick. I actually might be sick.

'No, we didn't.' Sam shot to his feet, naked apart from his white boxers, brighter against the bronze of his skin. 'Get your clothes on. *Now.*' His face was white as snow, his tone as cold as ice. *Get your clothes on*; the harshness of his words hurtled around my mind. I wanted to. I really wanted to. But I couldn't move; I sat there motionless, slightly hunched over, trying not to be sick. Sam pulled on his jeans, flung on a T-shirt and left the room in double time. My mind had slowed to a halt; this couldn't be happening.

He returned moments later, face like thunder.

'Sam… I… I can explain,' I began, even though I couldn't.

I stared back at him, not moving an inch, not saying a word. *Please smile, please laugh this off like old times.*

'Jamie's gone,' he croaked, on the verge of tears.

'She's… gone?' I asked, still drunk and dumbfounded. I looked around the room, not knowing who or what I wanted to appear. Sam was always the one to save me.

'Gone,' Sam said bluntly before starting to pace the floor. 'She must have seen you there, seen us there and thought… oh God… what must she think?' He stopped to look at me, and then, unable to bear it, began to pace again.

'Maybe she's just gone to work?' I asked, clutching at straws whilst clutching my stomach.

'No, Jess, she's gone. She's taken some of her things, she's… oh God…' Sam continued pacing as tears started to brim in my own eyes. 'What the fuck did you think you were doing?' he demanded.

I flinched. This was a far cry from the prayers he'd filled this room with weeks ago. This was the old Sam, feisty and unfiltered. That is what I wanted, right? The Sam I could get a rise from, the Sam I could always calm down. Except his stony face told me that was no longer the case.

'I… was drunk,' I stuttered, pulling the bed sheets further around my nakedness. 'And I just thought… I thought—'

'You thought what, Jess? Give me one good reason…' Sam cut me off. One good reason. I looked down to the sheets, pulled around me in shame. I must have one good reason.

'I thought this is what you wanted.' I lifted my head to look up at him, eyes full and wet.

'What I wanted?' Sam yelled louder than I had ever heard him yell before. 'What I *wanted*? Jess, I'm engaged. To be married. To a woman I love. Who's now gone. What on earth made you think that this is what I wanted?'

The tears started to fall. I tried to bite them back, but it was impossible.

'The look you gave me the day we bumped into each other. You invited me to stay with you. You didn't tell me about Jamie. All the lunches, all the moaning about the wedding. And then… and then you said you'd always love me…' I said through sobs, begging him to agree. All of that had happened; all of that was true.

'As a friend, Jess.' Sam stopped pacing and looked at me intently. 'As my friend.'

'But we were never just friends,' I said meekly, knowing no words could help now.

Sam looked at me with an unfamiliar expression. I couldn't make it out, but I knew it wasn't good. I'd thought this was what he wanted.

'Jess, we're not even just friends any more.' Sam shook his head and bit his quivering lip.

'What?' I asked, barely audible through my tears.

'You need to leave.' Sam's words hit me with force: calm, distant, decisive. 'Now. Get your stuff and go.'

'But where will I go?' I asked, naked and vulnerable. I needed my problem-solving Sam. Surely he could fix this.

'To your apartment, Jess. The one they've been bloody renovating for over a month.' He shook his head, looking at me with an expression I'd never seen before. It was like he was seeing me for the first time. 'No.' Sam looked me in the eye. 'No,' he repeated. 'Jess, tell me there *is* an apartment?'

Stripped naked; there was nowhere left to hide.

'You're unbelievable,' he whispered under his breath, too angry to keep his eyes on me. 'And to think Jamie's been so hospitable, tried so hard to make you feel at home.' He shook his head. 'And you never even had one.' He let out a hollow laugh; there was nothing funny about it.

'I'm not kidding, Jess.' He forced himself to look at me one last time. 'You need to leave.'

'Where will I go?' I repeated, crying out for him to save us from the mess I'd made.

'I don't know, Jess.' He exhaled deeply. 'But I know where I'm going. To find my fiancée – if I still have one – and make things right. When I come back, when *we* come back, I want you gone.' Sam turned his back and headed away. This time, I knew not to follow.

Shit, shit, shit. Tears streaming down my face, I headed to the box room. What had I done? I pushed the thought from my mind. I needed to get my things. Fast. Scrap by scrap I forced the semblance of my messy life back into my rucksack. Sam had made it look so easy to lug around. Now I had to carry it alone. Hoisting it onto my back, I made for the door. I couldn't bear to look at the sorry reflection that taunted me from the floor-length mirror. Sam's pretty pansy was gone.

I placed my hand on the door handle and looked back across the room. It was just how I found it; like I was never here, except… I reached down into the bedside table and pulled out the broken photo frame I had stashed in the drawer. I placed it back on the table top. Sam and Jamie, the perfect couple, broken and cracked. Because of me. I took one last look at the photograph, one final look at Sam's surfboard, and then turned to leave the box room for good.

Chapter Thirty

I looked down at my rucksack on the pavement, quite literally kicked to the kerb, as I heard the bus pull away behind me. I bent my knees and prepared to lift it. I already had the weight of the world on my shoulders, now I had to lug this bloody great thing around too.

This couldn't be happening. Sam had missed me; he'd said he loved me. But as a friend. I replayed our time together, unable to marry my version to his. Friend; I could really do with one of them right now. At least I had a job, I thought as I walked across the road to CreateSpace trying hard not to compare my rucksack-clad, puffy-eyed self to the designer-draped co-curator from two days ago.

It was time to tell Tim that I had decided to stay on, to see the exhibition through to the end and to explore how we could work together in the future. At least I'd be making one person happy. The exhibition would be opening to the public tomorrow and if the press event was anything to go by it should be a sell-out, keeping all three of us busy all hours of the day.

I breathed slowly, trying to salvage the scraps of my Sydney life. Maybe things would be okay. I didn't need Sam and Jamie and their box room to make something of myself here. If there even was a

Sam and Jamie any more. The thought made my stomach churn. I had been so happy, knocking back drink after drink with Joshua. And now I'd hurt his sister. And him – someone who had only ever looked out for me. I tried desperately not to question what he must think of me now, his disappointed eyes piercing through the foggy missed memories of last night. Something told me our Saturday surfing sessions had seen their last.

As I walked into the reception, the guys at the desk barely lifted their heads. Friday's compliments and smiles were gone. Had Jamie told Tim what had happened already? My sickness reared. I wouldn't have made anything of myself here without Jamie and her connections. I stashed my rucksack behind the desk. Neither one of the receptionists questioned it – maybe the answers were too obvious. Slowly, and with shaking hands, I opened the door into the first room. The morning colours, once so joyful, now glared garishly down at me, causing a new wave of nausea to rush through my body. Tim stood, looking into *Nameless*, the same small blue painting that Sam and I had studied only days before. My heart ached at the memory. I swallowed the thought and hopelessly gathered the sparse shards of strength and sobriety I had left.

'Great piece, isn't it?'

Tim didn't respond. He didn't even turn to look at me. He knew. I had hurt his precious Jamie, after she had been so generous and hospitable and perfect. And I hadn't exactly been a great friend to him either; all of those extended lunchbreaks with my mystery man and not once did I tell him he was pushing me further into the gap between his two friends, that he was an accessory to my ex-boyfriend-seducing crime. I probably wasn't the worst person in the world, but I couldn't think of anyone more deserving of the title right now.

'Tim?' I asked again. 'I have something to tell you.' I knew he was angry. But I couldn't stand here in silence all day; the volunteers would be here soon – at least now he'd know his understaffed days were behind him.

'Jessica.' Tim turned to me slowly, long grey T-shirt skimming his tartan-covered thighs. He pushed his glasses further up the bridge of his nose and sighed deeply, his tone indicating that now wasn't the moment for good news. I'd ask him tomorrow. For the meantime, I had to stay and face whatever it was Jamie had told him, to apologise for being so dishonest when I felt like I was the *only* one being honest with my feelings. Tim's tired eyes took me in. Part of me wanted to run away; I couldn't handle another person being mad at me today. I wished that Tim would scoop me up in his big bear arms and let me tell him everything and say that Sam was an idiot and he had led me on and he'd never liked Jamie anyway and that everything would be okay. Everything had to be okay.

'Jessica,' Tim said again, looking down at his feet. 'I have to let you go.'

Let me what? Another wave of sickness hit me and I could feel the tears coming. This couldn't be happening. Not because of one silly drunken mistake.

'Tim,' I began, ready to drop to my knees. 'I'm so sorry.' Tears started to fall from my eyes. 'I was so drunk I could hardly speak and I… I've decided I don't want to work for *Art Today* any more. This gallery, the work, you – you've inspired me so much… I want to stay on, for as long as you'll have me—'

'Jessica,' Tim interrupted, shaking his head and putting a hand to his brow. 'It was a press event; you were meant to represent us. It was your idea to invite them in the first place. I figured you'd had a bit to drink, but so much you could barely speak…' He let the end of his sentence fade into the expanse between us.

I looked at him through tear-filled eyes. Lost, in every sense of the word.

'The press night? I wasn't too drunk at the press night…' I stammered, unable to hide my confusion.

'But you just said—'

'I thought you were talking about…' I stopped myself. Maybe he didn't know about the Sam thing after all. And if he was angry about something at the press night I didn't want to hand him even more material to paint a picture of me as the absolute fuck-up I was clearly proving to be. I racked my brain for press night hiccups, literal or metaphorical, but drew a blank. It had been a success, *we* had been a success. Tim had even said so. Without a word, Tim reached into his pocket and placed a piece of paper in my hand. It was a print-out of an email. Shaking, I read the subject line and the sender's name:

SUBJECT: PA – THETIC ATTEMPTS AT CREATESPACE
FROM: H. A. SOMMERS

I glanced up to look at Tim, who was studying my expression with an intensity that made every one of my hairs stand on end. Hannah Sommers. My mind quickly shot back to our interview, recalling blurry words against the same colourful backdrops that surrounded us now. Had she found out? I hadn't mentioned jobs,

hadn't asked her for anything. And Tim hadn't spoken a word
to her either. Nor had Olivia, other than our introduction – too
fearful of putting her foot in it. I'd made sure of it. I'd kept them
apart. I'd watched Hannah leave. All I'd expected from Sommers
was a stunning review, but looking from Tim's distraught face to
the message in my hand, I knew this wasn't it. I read on:

Dearest Timothy,

*It makes for a catchy headline, doesn't it? I am sincerely hoping
that oour readers at* Art Today *think the same. If I am perfectly
honest – a quality for which I am known industry-wide – I had rather
high hopes for your latest exhibition, hopes that were realised as
I was welcomed by your wonderful receptionists and the glory
of* Tuesday's Slumber.

*However, as the evening unfolded, my reverence for the collection
was somewhat clouded by the slur of defamatory comments and the
smell of bitter champagne emanating from your so-called co-curator.
Disinterested and distracted for the duration of our time together, it
wasn't until your co-curator's bold and misplaced assurances that
my sister is incompetent and deceitful – qualities unseen by the
rest of the industry in which you no doubt are aware she plays a
central role – that I suddenly saw the significant error of your ways
in the employment of this latest exhibition under your surveillance.*

*Needless to say, it didn't take me long to realise that said co-
curator is a previous personal assistant of my dear sister and one
that it was decided she should let go. Clearly, her defamatory slur
was motivated by a personal vendetta, bitter resentment and an*

entirely unprofessional persona. I feel quite strongly that in an industry
where many young people would kill for the chances your co-curator
has been afforded, we cannot allow such an individual to rise. It is
therefore with regret that I advise you to terminate your co-curator's
employment forthwith or you will leave me no choice but to publish a
deeply negative review of her latest work, your exhibition, therefore
preventing this individual from being afforded any more standing in
this regard. I think you will agree it is the best thing for CreateSpace.
I have long admired your work and would hate to see it undermined
by the personal agenda of one misled individual.

Yours faithfully,
Hannah A. Sommers
Editor-in-Chief, Art Today Australia

I looked up at Tim, hands still shaking, this time with anger added into the mix of mounting emotions that were becoming impossible to control.

They were sisters? But I knew the art world. Surely I would have picked up on that? Plus, I had spent years overhearing Devon slagging her off, seething about her success, stealing her ideas. How was I supposed to know they were sisters? How was I supposed to know their relationship was a lie?

'I… I… didn't know…' I stuttered, unable to string my sentence together. 'They're sisters?'

'In law,' Tim said, stony-faced. How didn't I know this? 'Sommers only got the job through family connections and so they keep it out of the media. Plus, it means they can set an international trend or showcase new talent just by picking up the phone to each other. It's the best kept secret in the industry; people on the inside are in the know.' Tim said this last bit in a way that reminded me I was not one of them. I knew Devon was always after Hannah's ideas but she had never given the impression that Hannah may be willing to *share* them.

'But that's collusion,' I argued. 'And this.' I waved the piece of paper in the air. 'This is blackmail. It's immoral. They can't get away with it.' Raw tears of rage fell down my cheeks. 'They're profiting off, well… a lie.'

'Says the woman who lied about her employment history.' Tim looked at me straight on, all warmth there ever was between us evaporating. We locked eyes, his willing mine to deny the truth. Technically it wasn't my history that was in doubt, it was my future. I'd had three bloody years of doubting my future.

'Tim, I'm…' I said, stunned at how rock bottom had turned out to be a trap door. There was no coming back from this.

'I rang her up,' Tim said. 'After the email, to see whether she'd be open to reason, to work out whether she had her facts right. I was so confused that she didn't seem to *know* you, I figured there must have been a mix-up.'

It took all my strength not to look away.

'Turns out I was the one who didn't have my facts right, wasn't it, Jessica?' His sentence was intended to patronise me, to treat me like the child I was proving myself to be. I was a twenty-seven-year-old woman, and I'd been fibbing like a child this whole time. Lying to Tim, to Sam. Lying to myself.

'I'm so sorry,' I whispered, barely audible. It was all too little too late. 'I can explain. Give me five minutes and I can tell you everything, explain it all.' My rage at Devon and Sommers tasted bitter and ironic. People in glass houses shouldn't throw stones. I held Tim's stony gaze; we both knew my house had come crashing down.

'Jessica, I don't have time for this.' Tim looked away from my tear-stained face to the clock on the wall. I thought back to my first day when he had asked me to read it for him, nostalgic for being needed, even in the most miniscule of ways.

'But it's blackmail,' I cried, pleading with Tim to listen. 'If I can just show *this* to the media…'

'And say what?' Tim shrugged, his face deadpan. 'Hannah has a recording of your whole conversation. Let's just say you didn't sound sober.' He shook his head. 'And let's face it,' he went on, 'who are the media going to believe?' He looked at me; a drunk bitter girl who had lied her way across Sydney, or an editor-in-chief known industry-wide for her so-called *honesty.* 'The volunteers are arriving in five. Jessica, honestly, I have to let you go.' He gestured towards the door, characteristically dramatic but lacking some of the gusto of days past. He was tired of being let down; I knew the feeling.

I turned away, walking through yet another door, desperately trying not to question why everything I wanted, wanted to push me away instead. Why everything I had built was founded on a lie.

*

18 January 2017 – London, England

'How's work been?' I asked, trying to bridge the distance between us, physically and metaphorically. I resented the question, so normal and yet it was the kind of 'catching up' statement I thought we'd never need to say. Lives that were in sync shouldn't need to catch up or slow down. I walked into Tesco, begrudging my meal for one, begrudging Sam for not being here yet, for having another year in Nottingham.

'Would you like a bag?' the cashier asked as I shook my head and gathered the meal deal with my free hand. 'Could I grab a ticket for the Euromillions?' I added as an afterthought. Couple of mill wouldn't go amiss right now.

'Did you just buy a lottery ticket, J?' Sam's voice said down the line as I walked out onto the pavement of Vauxhall Bridge Road.

'Yeah, why?'

'I just,' he continued, voice strained, 'didn't know you played it.'

'From time to time.' I shrugged as much as my juggling hands would allow. 'Problem?'

'No, it's just… it doesn't matter.' I could imagine how Sam was shaking his head down the line. I didn't need a visual to know when something was on his mind.

'No, tell me,' I demanded, all of a sudden on the back foot.

'It's not like… a problem,' he said, 'it's just…' He sighed as I walked past couples and friends drinking outside the pubs lining the way to Victoria.

'We're just really different, aren't we?' He said the words slowly. 'I'd never play the lottery.'

I laughed away his comment, stunned by its absurdity. 'It's just a lottery ticket.'

'It's just a bit… It's a bit…'

'What, Sam?' I snapped, feeling the strain of London and my hour-long commutes closing in around me.

'It doesn't matter. I'll tell you next time I see you.'

'Tell me now,' I demanded, not sure I wanted his answer but unwilling to let it wait.

'It's just a bit… well, my parents would say it's a bit… working class,' Sam admitted. 'But I don't think that, really, and there's nothing wrong with being working class anyway – obviously – it just surprised me because I didn't know you played and I never would and you know, we're just different, aren't we?'

'Working class, different?' I asked, anger filling my blood. I didn't realise being a snob was hereditary. Was that what his parents thought of me? Surely society had evolved past that.

'No, that's why I didn't want to say, I don't mean it… I just… we're different, is all.'

'Yeah we are. You're a man and I'm a woman; you're a medic and I'm a creative; you're a judgmental nob and I'm…' Red buses, red phone boxes. Red was all I could see.

'Jess, please, can we just forget about it?' Sam reasoned, like I'd been the one to bring it up in the first place. It was just a lottery ticket.

'I thought you liked that we were different?' I asked, unwilling to back down.

'I did, I do,' Sam said.

'I'd hate to date the male version of me.'

'Yeah me too, well, the female version,' Sam agreed as I remained far from convinced. 'Can we just forget about it? I'm sorry. I shouldn't have said anything. If you want to play the lottery, you play the lottery. You know I love you, every lottery-playing bit of you.' Sam was overcompensating, trying to recover from acting out or acting more honestly than he had done in weeks, I couldn't tell. And I really, really didn't want to find out.

Chapter Thirty-One

6 September 2020 – Sydney, Australia

My mascara-stained reflection mocked me from the toilet mirrors as I tried to tell myself this wasn't as bad as I thought, that this would all blow over, that everything would be okay.

Holding my phone in my shaking hand, I scrolled to Zoe's number and hovered my finger above the dial button. It was the middle of the night back home. And anyway, what was she going to say? It wasn't like she'd been in touch to ask how the exhibition went. And I wasn't ready to hear *I told you so*. Sam had always been the one to rescue me, but I was pretty sure all his efforts were going in one direction right now, no thanks to me. Once again, my mind sifted through people I could call. I could only think of one other person who might be kind enough to hear me out. Scrolling to Joshua's number, I forced my breathing to normalise as I pressed my phone to my ear. I held my breath as the dial tone rang out, then his voice on his answerphone message, telling me Joshua 'can't come to the phone right now'. *Can't or won't?* I knew he was Jamie's brother but hadn't we become friends, too? And he'd said if I needed anything, he was always there. I called again, and again. The dial tone rang on until I heard a quick click and a deep exhale and the pained voice of Joshua: 'Please stop calling, Jess. This isn't a good time.'

Darting from the toilets, through reception, I picked up my bag and didn't look back, striding purposefully across the paved square, past the palm trees and the wall that Sam had leaned against when he came to meet me for lunch. I had nowhere to go, nothing to do, but I wouldn't let the guys on reception know that. I knew I didn't deserve the dignity. I felt their eyes burn into the back of my head as they watched my walk of shame: CreateSpace to empty space. I wasn't a co-curator any more; I wasn't even a clipboard-holder. I wasn't a girlfriend, a friend, I wasn't even a tenant of my ex-boyfriend's box room. I was a joke. A jobless, homeless, hopeless joke.

With nowhere better to go, I found myself on the path to the beach but without Sam and a sandwich or Joshua and a surfboard it felt pointless. *This isn't what was supposed to happen*; the thought circulated around my head, deafening any comforting reassurances I had once been able to tell myself: *Sam will come back; this isn't the end; just wait, your happily-ever-after will come; you can make it; you can fabricate it.* Maybe Zoe was right. I was naive at best, deluded at worse. Sam and I were never getting back together. My future was never going to be what I imagined.

Scrambling to take my shoes off, fumbling under the weight of my rucksack, I let my feet sink into the sand. This time it didn't feel cool, refreshing or nostalgic. It felt like a lie, a promise unfulfilled. Sydney was meant to be the answer. A fresh start. A chance to forget about Sam, to forget about the future I had invested every scrap of time, energy and delayed gratification in. Call it fate, call it the universe, call it God – whatever or *whoever* was up there wasn't looking out for me, they were looking down on me – laughing sadistically. My life was a *Saturday Night Live* sketch for the deity.

Flinging my rucksack to one side, I crumpled down onto the sand. Looking down at my bare feet, I let my mind escape, transporting me to my fifteen-year-old self. Fun-loving, vivacious, ambitious, and with such big dreams for such a small girl. She had never wanted to be an editor, or an art therapist, or just somebody's girlfriend. She had wanted to paint, to be a barefooted, free-spirited artist, with massive dreams; not heels, champagne and flipping *Art Today*. I missed that girl.

I picked up a stone from the sand and flung it out to the ocean. *That's for you, Lady Devon Atwood. Thanks for screwing up my career before it even began.* I was twenty-seven, I shouldn't just be starting out. I was nearing thirty and yet had little to show for my twenties. Zoe had her house. Jamie had her fiancé. Joshua had his youth group. Sam had, well, everything. And I had nothing. I picked up another stone and threw it into the sea, too weak to make a ripple. *That's for you, fucking fate.* My phone jabbed into my back pocket as my arse sank further into the sand. I pulled it out and looked at the screen. No calls. Not one. I scrolled down the list of contacts again and again: Sam, Jamie, Joshua, Tim – it was a who's who of people's lives I had made worse just by being here. Why had I even pretended, even for a moment, that I had things made?

I reached for another stone, and with all the strength I had left, launched it into the ocean. *And that's for you, Jess. You screwed everything up. You always do.* Angry tears started to sting and fall as the stone sank heavy into the water and a thought started to rise: *I have no one to blame but myself.*

*

21 October 2017 – Nottingham, England

'I don't blame you, Jess. I just need space, I just need some time.'

Sam's words filled the room and yet still I couldn't hear them. He stopped his pacing and came to sit down on the bed beside me. I couldn't turn to look at him. I didn't need to. I knew his profile better than my own – strong jawline, but with more stubble than there had been five years ago; deepening laughter lines, so many of which I had been responsible for. The extra etches of worry on his forehead; I guess I'd had my fair share to do with those too.

'I just need space,' he repeated. I had no idea where this was coming from. He'd been happy. I'd been happy. Well, not in work, and not when we went days without seeing each other, but we'd been happy together. We *were* happy together.

I turned to look at him. He looked like a boy, reluctant to extend a comforting arm in my direction for fear that I might shake it off. I desperately wanted him to reach out. I didn't understand, I couldn't. Sam sat rigid, my best friend turning into a stranger right before my eyes. I looked around Sam's bedroom, every inch of it holding its own memory of our time together.

'Space?' The only word I managed to utter sounded foreign in my mouth. *No. Why?* It didn't matter, I'd probably got the wrong end of the stick anyway; Sam was always saying I jumped to conclusions too fast. I looked down and pulled the sleeves of my jumper further over my hands.

'Jess?' Sam gently rested a hand on my shoulder. I saw tears welling in his tired eyes. Sam never cried. My stomach turned in fear. 'You know I love you…' I savoured each precious word, desperately trying to ignore the 'but' I knew was coming.

'I love you too,' I whispered softly, but Sam had already begun speaking over me.

'…amazing times together… five years… best friend…'

My heart ran a mile a minute as I tried to make sense of the words coming out of my boyfriend's mouth.

'…too much… concentrate on work… need time… something different…'

I absorbed his lines in broken shards, trying to process them in a way that led to a different conclusion than the one I couldn't bring myself to think, never mind hear. Sam reached out and took my hand. His was shaking. Mine was still.

'I think we need to be on our own for a bit,' Sam said, tears now falling down the familiar face I had seen mature before me over the last five years. 'You know, find out who we are without each other, who we are outside "Sam and Jess"?'

This was all wrong. It couldn't be happening. I studied his tear-stained face, my eyes tracing his jawline, clenched and sure. How could he even comprehend a future without me? We had it all planned out. Everything we'd be, everything we'd do. I searched for the words. Words that would make him want me. Words that would make him want us.

'But I like "Sam and Jess",' I whispered, so quietly I wasn't sure I'd even said it out loud.

'So did I,' Sam responded, wiping the tears from his cheeks.

Did.

'Sam, please.' I wasn't above begging for what I knew was right. 'I know it's been hard since I finished uni. I know I haven't been perfect, but we're great together, we've always been great together, things will get easier when I get a new job…' Sam placed his free hand on top of my own and squeezed, shaking his head.

'It's not you, Jess,' he said, a cliché I never thought we'd become. 'I'm just not ready…'

'Ready for what?' We could diagnose the problem; we could find the cure. He always did. He'd promised he always would. 'Moving in? Marriage? What, Sam?' We could save this. We needed to save this. 'We can take our time with all of that; we don't need to do anything we aren't ready for.'

'I'm just not ready for what we are, J.' Sam's words cut through my chest. I couldn't lose him. I couldn't. He was my future. I was his. I wouldn't cry. Because it wasn't over. I held his hands tighter, looking down at mine intertwined with his. To have and to hold.

I wouldn't let go.

'Maybe one day I will be.' He reached a hand up to my cheek and delicately tilted my chin to face him. 'Maybe one day.'

I shook my head. This couldn't be happening. It wasn't over. It couldn't be. I leaned my face in closer to his, my lips lightly grazing his nose, then tracing their way to kiss the freckle just above his lips. He breathed deeply, drawing me in, kissing me, firm and strong. Maybe one day. He pulled away and time slowed down. Fractions of moments, like the parts of our past coming undone. Sam offering me a lift to the station. Me refusing. Sam opening the door. Me leaving. Sam closing the door. Me looking back. Then realisation, then fear, then falling, tears falling. Tears and tears and tears and tears until there were no tears left to fall.

But hope, a tiny hope.

Maybe one day.

Maybe.

One day.

*

6 September 2020 – Sydney, Australia

Three words I'd held onto for three years. And for what? A chance rendezvous on the other side of the planet where Sam could dole out scraps of hope – a box room here, a job there, a lunch, a graze, a gaze – and then take everything back like a twenty-eight-day return policy. Keep the receipt. That was probably what Sam had thought about me. And Tim. Take her, use her, be amused by her. And then take it all back. I'd given Sam my truth, every bit of me – it had never been enough. Why would my lies be any different?

I looked out over the ocean, the stones I had thrown lost forever. It was my fault. All of this was my own fault. I wasn't a twenty-eight-day return policy; I was damaged goods, faulty and broken.

I looked at my rucksack, bursting with baggage. I glanced at my watch, thin and cheap. An hour had passed since I had first sat down. But where the hell was I meant to go next? Sam had always been my true north. I pushed my feet even further into the sand. Fucking Sydney. Maybe it was time to go home.

Home; the thought of it caught in my throat. I cast my mind back to London, conjuring images of red buses, red phone boxes and red-faced commuters. It had never really felt like home. Nottingham had always been my home – but that was when we were all there: Zoe, Austin, Sam. I looked up at the waves crashing, churning as realisation rose to the surface. For a long time, home had been where Sam was. Home didn't exist any more. It was like all the tears I had held back since arriving in Sydney were finally coming to the fore. Sydney had been one big disappointment. The past three years had been one big disappointment – but at least they had had the hope of 'maybe one day'.

I tried to imagine the next three years without it, without that shard of hope that the life I had imagined might actually become a reality. Tears continued to fall, uncontrollable and messy. Not content to ruin my own life, I'd had to go and ruin Sam's future too. He'd been happy. I had wanted him to be happy. I sobbed harder, sick to my stomach. I needed to stop doing this, screwing up, leaving a trail of destruction in my wake. I closed my eyes. I needed hope. I needed a miracle. Fuck it. *God, if you're real and you actually give a shit. I need help, I need a plan, I need a job, rent money and somewhere to stay until I get all of the above figured—*

'Jess?' I heard a woman's voice interrupt from behind me. 'Jess, are you okay?'

Chapter Thirty-Two

'Jess, is that you?' the voice rang out behind me. A small part of me prayed for it to be Zoe – stranger things had happened – before I realised she had a thick Australian accent. *Please don't be Jamie.* Please *don't be Jamie.*

'Are you okay?'

I brushed the tears from my face but knew the redness and puffy eyes would take hours to fade. Hopeless. In slow motion, I turned. At least it wasn't Jamie.

'It's Alice?'

My blank stare prompted her to reintroduce herself even though we'd met several times. I nodded in acknowledgement but said nothing.

'Can I sit down?' Alice asked, as if I wasn't down and out but just having a quick sit down. Surely she didn't want to put that crisp outfit on the ground, never mind inches next to me? I was a mess. I shrugged. It was a free country. She sat down beside me, taking no care to stop her clearly expensive knit from catching underfoot. I dreaded to think how much she knew, how much she could tell.

I tried to smile, weak and apologetic. She smiled back. I opened my mouth, but no words came out. Instead, tears began to fall again

– it surprised me that there were any left. Alice didn't say anything but placed an arm around me, no words necessary. I wished I knew how to say so much with so little. She turned her striking profile towards the sea and looked out across it like she had all the time in the world. I let her arm rest there and cried into her cashmere. I savoured the human contact, knowing that the second she knew what I'd done I'd lose her too, an almost-friend who'd never had the displeasure of knowing me better. Moments passed, but still Alice didn't move. I caught her giving a fleeting glance at my rucksack.

'You fancy a coffee?' she asked cautiously, as if knowing I was volatile. 'We could head back to mine?'

I began to well up again. Sam had extended his charity to me the moment he saw me. Now Alice. I couldn't. She wouldn't want me to. Not if she knew the things that I had done, how I'd hurt Sam and Jamie, how I'd ruined everything with Tim, how I'd even managed to anger the kindest man in Sydney. But I had nowhere else to go.

Again.

'Thanks,' I began through sobs, 'but I can't. Alice, I've screwed everything up. With Sam and Jamie, with work – I don't want you to get caught up in—'

'Jess,' Alice interjected, 'it's a *coffee*.' She shook her head and smiled again. She was being so nice and, better still, was making it feel like it was no big deal. That it was no big deal that I'd just fucked up her friends' lives. Unless she didn't know?

'I've done something terrible,' I confessed, struggling to meet her eye through my tears, through my shame.

Alice looked back at me, her hair long and straight, skin brown, eyes wide. She was a doctor, who looked like a model. A church-goer. A good girl. Her head probably couldn't even comprehend drunkenly pursuing your engaged ex-boyfriend whilst living beneath his fiancée's roof, or fibbing your life into shape because it was anything but.

'Unless it's worse than shagging your cousin's boyfriend, you're in good company.'

Alice? She couldn't have. She smiled and shrugged, neither proud nor apologetic as my broken heart shed a piece for her too; I'd thought she was perfect, writing page after page of her story on a pristine white slate.

'Coffee?' she repeated, pushing herself up. Dumbfounded, I stood, lifting my bag onto my shoulders, and followed. Too tired to argue, I shadowed her every step away from the beach, towards somewhere or something I hoped was better than here.

*

4 November 2017 – London, England

'What have I got keeping me here?' I looked across at my mum. Twenty-four and I still needed my mummy to have the answers. 'I'll start again, somewhere new, like…' I searched my mind for solutions. 'Manchester?' I didn't mean it to sound like a question. Mum pushed the menu across the red and white chequered tablecloth. Break-up carbs; it had been two weeks since Sam and I had gone our separate ways and I still wasn't ready for them.

If I was going to be sad, I may as well be skinny too.

'Your friends?' My mum pointed to the carbonara on the menu, my favourite when I was a little girl.

'All in relationships,' I said, as if it discounted them.

'Zoe?'

Even Zoe. Even the relationship-adverse and perpetually single had overtaken me in the race of life. I took a gulp of red: the only thing I could stomach.

'Work?' she asked as I scoffed at the question.

'I'm wasting away there,' I replied, loathing my dramatics but addicted to them all the same.

'Well, you'll be wasting away here if you don't order some food.' She beckoned a waiter over to take our order at the exact same moment I broke into tears. 'We need a bit more time,' I heard her mutter in the distance. She had travelled almost three hours to London for a dinner with her delightful daughter. Sadly, said daughter hadn't shown.

'You should do some painting; you always found that soothed you,' she went on.

'Soothed me?' I scoffed. 'I'm not a baby.' I was acting like one, though. 'I'm done with messing around with that; I need to take life seriously.' I knew that's what Sam had wanted. 'And I need to leave.'

She looked around the room, desperate to make me stay, make me *eat*. 'Oh, Jess,' she said, pulling her chair closer to me. We were causing a scene, but she didn't seem to care. 'You don't know anyone in Manchester. I know it's hard, I know you have memories of Sam here…'

'It's not all about Sam,' I sobbed, forcing away my mum's offer of a napkin. I was a mess and I didn't care who knew. 'It's all of it. I was meant to be the successful one, the settled one, the one who had it all sorted. Do I look sorted to you? Do I?' A passing staff member looked at us, answering my question with one pitying expression.

'You're just having a wobble, love,' my mum soothed. 'It'll pass. It always does.'

'Not without Sam it won't.' Back to it all being about Sam, again.

'Give it a few more weeks. Lay low, don't make any sudden changes,' Mum said. 'And if you're still unhappy here, maybe you can move home for a while? Recalibrate?'

'I don't want to recalibrate,' I whispered, 'I want to calibrate.' I wasn't even sure what that meant. 'I want everything to go back to normal. And I want to go to Manchester.'

Mum sighed. I wasn't making sense. She knew it, I knew it, but she also knew better than to reason with me. I was a walking contradiction: wanting to go back, wanting to move forward, just wanting to be anywhere but here.

'Jess, I know it hurts.' She sighed. But how did she know? She was bloody sorted by my age. 'But you can't keep looking back and you can't keep running away.'

'Then where can I go?' I whispered, sulking like a child pulled off the playground.

'I guess you have to stay in the present and kind of…' Mum struggled for the right words, both of us unsure as to whether they even existed. 'Muddle through?'

*

6 September 2020 – Sydney, Australia

Alice switched on the lights, stepping into the apartment and flinging her cashmere cardigan onto the brown leather couch.

'You take milk?' she asked, walking into the open-plan kitchen space, opening cupboards and pulling out two large mugs. I stood just inside the entrance, rucksack still on, taking in the space. The two large sofas looked every bit as chic as their owner against a backdrop of exposed brick and polished floorboards.

'Make yourself at home,' she said.

With slight trepidation, I peeled off my rucksack and walked cautiously into the room. I was sure Alice would report back to Jamie as soon as I left. Moving a large cream cushion with precision, I sat down on the edge of the sofa. Her kindness felt like a trap. But if her cousin-boyfriend comment wasn't just a ploy to get me into her home then maybe she wasn't as clean-cut as she seemed.

'So, do you want to talk about it?' Alice came over holding two full mugs of coffee in her hands. Did she *want* me to talk about it? Maybe Jamie had her wearing a wire. I dreaded to think how much she must hate me. I looked around the room nervously.

'Not really,' I told my coffee, praying it wasn't poisoned. Alice watched me, suspicion or malice seemingly absent. I caught her thick-lashed eye. Maybe she had the right to know she was harbouring a fugitive.

'I did something terrible, to Jamie – to Jamie and Sam.' And that was just the start of it.

Alice nodded, not really bothered, taking another sip and saying simply, 'I know.'

She knew? And she'd invited me back to her place? Even I could taste the disloyalty in the coffee. Unless, maybe it was poison after all.

'Look, Sam told me what went on. He's trying to sort it out.' She said the words with care, before I could cut her off. My stomach turned, my mind oscillating between wanting Sam and Jamie to be okay and wanting to be okay myself.

'Oh God, he must hate me.' I placed my coffee down on the table and hung my head in my hands. Out of the corner of my eye I spied Alice lifting my mug and slipping a coaster underneath it. She could dress as edgy as she liked but show homes didn't stay show homes by themselves.

'He doesn't… *hate* you,' Alice said tactfully. 'I think he just needs some time.'

I couldn't look at her. I felt sick.

'Stay here for a few days. You can have the spare—'

My look must have cut her off. The so-called spare bedroom. That's what got me into all this mess in the first place. But had their kindness been genuine? Maybe having me around was the instant ego boost everyone was after; nothing like a 'someone has it worse' moment to feel pretty content with your lot, right? I looked at Alice; she didn't seem like a manipulative mastermind. With a warm smile she reiterated, 'I'd be okay with you staying for a bit until you work out your next steps.'

'But why?' My words sliced through her sentence. I'd ruined everything.

'It's a pretty big apartment.' She shrugged. I'd be pretty sure she was boasting if she didn't look so sad about it. 'And because we all make mistakes,' she continued. 'And just because you've done some bad things, made one or two bad moves, doesn't mean you're a bad person.' Based on the cousin, she was speaking from experience. 'And when he asked me to look out for you I knew it was the right thing to do.' She nodded, eyes wide with kindness. Someone was looking out for me.

'Jesus?' I asked, eyebrow raised.

'No, you dickhead.' Alice's laugh was open and warm. 'Joshua.'

Joshua. *Joshua?* He knew what I'd done, *who* I'd tried to do. And must, by now, know everything that wasn't real about me. Even worse, everything that I was. And he'd said he couldn't talk to me, that now wasn't a good time. He was right about that.

I tossed and turned in Alice's spare bed, mortified. It had been hours since we had arrived back at hers. Coffee had turned to wine and sooner or later I had been talked into staying, at least for a couple of days. *That's what you said the last time*, I heard Zoe's voice say in my mind. But still, one thought dominated the rest. He knew what I'd done.

I groaned and turned to look up at the blank white ceiling. But why should I care? He was just some guy I'd been surfing with a few times. The punch to my gut told me that wasn't true. He was more than that; he was my friend. Maybe he could have been more, not that it mattered now. I had been too caught up in my own *maybe one day* to even contemplate a future with anyone else. And now both men needed to get as far away from me as possible. The thought rolled round and round my mind but then, another thought, barely audible above the onslaught of self-loathing, said:

Joshua knew everything, and though he wouldn't speak to me, he was still looking out for me. He was still one step ahead of me, trying to make sure I'd be okay. I tried to cling to that one scrap of goodness as my mind replayed the shitstorm of today. Like a horror movie I cut from scene to sorry scene. Hangover. Nakedness. Sam. Homelessness. CreateSpace. Tim. Joblessness. But then Alice and Joshua. *Kindness.*

Chapter Thirty-Three

7 September 2020 – Sydney, Australia

All I could see was ceiling. Bright and white. For a moment, I was back in the box room. Sam cooking breakfast outside. Jamie bizarrely there too. She had never been in my daydreams before. But Sam and Jamie were over, I remembered, as a wave of sickness washed over me. I'd broken it. Everything. And more than anything, more than ever, I just wanted things to be fixed. I guess I always wanted what I couldn't have. The guilt felt unshakable, but the grief of losing him stretched on. I guess I didn't know *what* I wanted.

Groaning, I turned onto my side and reached for my phone. No messages. No missed calls. Nothing. I swiped to outbound. Seven messages. Five calls. Three WhatsApps. All to one person. Sam had answered none of them. 'Just give them space.' I recalled Alice's advice from the night before. I looked at my outbox again. At this rate, space wouldn't be all Sam would be after; he'd be getting a restraining order. I swiped through to one:

I'm so sorry. Please call me. I'm sorry. I love you. Call…

I exited the screen. I couldn't bear to look at my desperation. Sam no doubt felt the same. But he was my best friend. Or he had been. Before I ruined his life. I needed him to forgive me. I needed things to be fixed.

Forcing myself out of bed, I padded barefoot around the unfamiliar apartment and into the living room. The empty glasses and pile of tissues from the day before had been cleared away, but with a headache now accompanying my heartache, I didn't need reminding that I had had too much to drink last night. I never knew when to stop.

Walking across the open-plan space and towards the kitchen felt like a marathon. Every inch of me ached. I switched on the coffee maker, desperate for caffeine. Scanning the work surface for the abandoned mugs of yesterday, I noticed an open notebook and picked it up to read:

~~Gone for a run, be back soon.~~
Gone to work, be back later.

I had no idea what time it was. The fact that Alice had been for a run, showered and gone off to work told me I must have slept for hours. So why did I feel so exhausted? I poured the coffee, black, and went back to the sofa. I hugged my knees in towards my chest and lifted the hot mug to my lips. Damn hangover, stupid Sydney. Screw-up, me.

Desperate for a distraction, I looked around Alice's pristine apartment for something to do. No TV. No messy stack of Disney DVDs. No corner-torn *Cosmopolitan*s telling me how to supercharge my sex life or bag a ballsy pay rise. This was a grown-up's apartment. I hugged my legs tighter to my chest, trying not to be patronised by Alice's perfect place. At least this apartment wasn't scattered with mirrors like Sam and Jamie's. Instead a large landscape hung above the ornate mantelpiece. A beachscape of Coogee, perfect and promising. It took all my strength not to throw my coffee at it, making it muddy and stained. It felt two-dimensional and predictable, a literal interpretation of the landscape, failing to be a photo but missing all the potential a painting had to add. It failed to capture anything real. It didn't need to have people in it to show the depth of what that view must have seen – falling in love, falling out of it, lives moving on, lives staying stuck. I forced my eyes away from its perfection. I didn't care any more; it wasn't my picture to paint.

Scattered across the mantelpiece were framed photographs of Alice. Alice and her colleagues. Alice and the church group. Alice with Joshua and Jamie. A hall of friendship reminding me of all the bridges I'd burnt in such a short space of time. Finishing the dregs of my coffee but feeling none of the effects, I placed it on the table and pressed myself further into the sofa. Tears rising again, I closed my eyes to stop them falling and let exhaustion engulf me once again.

The creak of the latch and sound of the apartment door opening woke me. Stirring, I glanced down at my pyjama top and scrambled to hide the mess of wet tissues surrounding me on all sides. It was too late. Alice was already strolling across to the kitchen, clicking on the kettle and offering me a drink. She'd woken up, gone for a run, completed an eight-hour shift and returned home; I hadn't put on a bra.

Alice handed me a mug and sat down beside me. Choosing to ignore the bombsite I'd created around me, she asked me about my day. She was sitting right next to me, but her voice sounded distant. My mind was elsewhere. Sam. The thought of him being with Jamie had made me sick. But now, to think he wasn't made me feel a thousand times worse. I'd had my best friend back. And I'd ruined everything. Why couldn't I have just told him the truth? I looked at Alice, trying and failing to hold back tears. Things were going to get better soon. Things had to get better soon, right?

'Oh, Jess.' Alice reached her hand over to give me a little stroke. 'Things will get better soon,' she said, as though she could read my mind. Maybe it was the scrubs she still had on or maybe it was our conversation last night, but the Alice before me looked a lot more human than the one who had called my name on the beach the day before. I looked into her eyes, empathetic and sincere. She understood.

'Give them space. They'll sort themselves out,' she said. 'You concentrate on getting yourself back on track.'

'That's the problem,' I said, through fresh sobs, 'I'm not sure what "on track" looks like without Sam. He was part of my future for such a long time.' There were few secrets between us now.

'Jess, believe me. I've been there.' I believed her, she had. 'For the next few days it will hurt like hell, then one day it will hurt a little less.'

I watched as she looked wistfully towards the painting. I marvelled at her kindness – not to mention her flawless profile – for the thousandth time. More fool the person who let her go.

'Then one day it will hurt a little less than that.' She turned to face me again, and though her voice cracked at the memory she smiled. 'Then maybe one day it might not hurt at all.' Maybe one day.

'Is that what happened for you?'

'Yeah.' She nodded. 'I realised that people screw up, we're human. People lie. They cheat.' Her voice caught on the last word; we both knew that was true for her. 'But my God, we have to have grace for ourselves, or we'd never get out of bed in the morning. For what it's worth, I also realised I didn't need a guy for my happy ending.' She looked at me. 'I could make my own.' She laughed. 'Man, I sound like a greetings card!' She did. But it was a card I wanted to receive.

I began to cry again. Bloody hell, I needed to stop. 'You'll get there,' Alice said again. Would I? Right now, it felt like I was getting nowhere. 'I promise, you'll get there,' she repeated and though everything in me wanted to argue, to ask her where *there* was, if it even existed – I searched her words, like the beam from a lighthouse, hoping they'd guide me to wherever was next.

Chapter Thirty-Four

9 September 2020 – Sydney, Australia

The sun was actually shining for once, though I'd never been a fan of irony. I descended the hill down Coogee Bay Road. But, equally ironically, handing out CVs was proving an uphill struggle. I knew it was time to start again; the only thing worse than staying was going home defeated and proving everyone who had waved me off, sceptical of my fresh start. I had to give it one more go. I had to. But this time, I had to do it properly.

Two girls giggled as they passed me, their red-tinged shoulders telling me they were travelling and had just arrived in Sydney. They were around eighteen, clutching A4 pages of their own, without a care in the world; I was carrying enough for all three of us. I'd set off with ten CVs. Two hours later, I still had nine in my hand and now the shops were starting to shut. I had been told summer jobs didn't kick in until November more times than I could count. 'Summer job?' The words tasted nasty each time I asked them, tacky and temporary. Just like my time here. I paced further up Coogee Bay Road, familiar locals smiling at me but my head somewhere else altogether.

Shit.

I saw Jamie approaching on the other side of the road, jogging in the distance. Without thinking, I turned to walk into the nearest shop I could find.

'Sorry, mate, we're just closing up.' A tall, rosy manager beamed at me, his happiness at going home vastly outweighing his regret at not being able to let me in.

'I just want a coffee to go,' I pleaded, like an addict trying to score coke. He shook his head. 'Can I just use the toilet, please?' I asked.

He raised his eyebrows at me and I turned away. My stomach turned at the thought of what she might do, what she might say if she saw me. I didn't want to find out.

Deciding the hill was probably the best place to hide, I began to ascend. I walked slowly, clutching my papers closer to my chest. Out of the corner of my eye I caught Jamie's svelte figure running straight past me on the other side of the road. I breathed a sigh of relief. Then she crossed the road, still jogging, and turned to loop back on herself. She was running directly towards me, her hair bouncing in the early evening sunlight. There was nowhere to hide. I had a split second to decide whether to smile or stop or duck. Then she shot straight past me, clearly seeing me but choosing not to. Reminding me of what I already felt – inconvenient, insignificant, invisible – and yet, somehow, still managing to get in the way.

*

9 April 2020 – Essex, England

I reached a hand up to the big brass door knocker before drawing it back again. I looked at the duck-egg blue of my best friend's new home, clashing against the green of my jealousy. Zoe was a homeowner; she shared a mortgage with Ben. They were building a life together. I should be happy for them, and yet somehow it felt like she'd stolen a moment that was meant to me mine first. This was stupid. I had a job; I lived in the best city in the world. And being single was better than being with the wrong person, I knew that. I reached my hand towards the door again as it swung open.

'You got me a plant?' Zoe said as I thrust the peace lily towards her.

'Isn't that what you're supposed to do?' I joked, leaning forward to give her an awkward kiss on the cheek. I felt like we were playing grown-ups, but Zoe had taken to her role well.

'I'd prefer wine.' She grinned as she stood back and beckoned me into the front room, walking across the large living space to place the plant on the glass coffee table in the centre. 'Beer?' she asked, already pushing the door into the kitchen.

'Shit, Zo.' I followed her into the kitchen. 'This is an adult house.'

I knew we were in our late twenties, that she was on a decent salary, that Ben was on one too, and yet somehow it took me by surprise. Zoe grinned, eyes wide in pride, as Ben came in from the open patio doors to join us, opening his arms wide to embrace me. If I didn't love Zoe so much I was sure I'd hate him for being so great.

'Burgers are ready.' He smiled, nodding to the spacious patio outside, April's lukewarm temperatures unable to quell his excitement.

'Awesome.' I grinned, grabbing my beer from Zoe and following them onto the decking. The large wooden table was set for three and Zoe and I each pulled out a chair.

'Thanks for having me, guys.' The words felt strange to say, seeing as for most of the time we'd known each other, Zoe's house was usually mine. I looked across at her and Ben, both with identical sauce smudges stuck to their smiles. This was a big step, and I was happy for them, I really was. I stole a glance to the empty seat beside me, trying desperately to ignore the niggle of selfishness rising within me – but I wanted to be happy for me too. I just wasn't sure I could do that here any more, whether I needed to go and find that happiness somewhere else, somewhere new.

*

10 September 2020 – Sydney, Australia

I heard the door slam shut. Alice had a nightshift; she'd be out until morning. Lifting the covers I had been pretending to sleep under, I stood, already dressed in jeans and a T-shirt. I'd felt heavy all week, but now I felt lighter, less tangible somehow. I felt like I was drifting, like I wasn't really here. And very soon I wouldn't be.

It didn't take me long after my failed attempt to find even the most mediocre of jobs to come to the decision that Sydney wasn't for me. It didn't suit me. It never had. I'd tried to fake it until I made it. Now I'd been exposed and there was nothing left to hide. Dragging myself to the mirrored wardrobe, I ignored my reflection as I slid the doors open. Bending down, I picked up my rucksack and began to stuff my clothes into it: the bikini I had hoped to live in here, the blue sundress I had bought to impress Sam, the heels that had made me look the part at CreateSpace. I held them in my hands, turning them over. The red soles were starting to rub off, and with another scratch a large piece of paint flaked off completely; they were fakes. I should have known they weren't authentic, that even though they looked real for a time, they were just a lie. Like everything else in my life, never quite the real thing.

Maybe some people just weren't meant to make it? I would almost believe it if I didn't seem to be the one person royally screwing up their life.

Walking out of the spare room and into Alice's *Homes and Gardens* apartment, I bit back the tears. *Doctor, gorgeous, entirely in control...* I listed her accolades as I slumped down onto her sofa. *Nice, hospitable* – I added countless gifts to her list. I'd been all misery and still she pretended she was fine having me around. Maybe she was fine with it? Maybe she liked the company? But I couldn't rely on other people for the rest of my life, could I?

I looked at my phone: still no calls. No call from Mum and Dad – they probably thought I was having the time of my life here. No call from Zoe – too busy playing house with Ben. *You can't keep looking back.* I heard my mum's comments ring out in my head, the words she had said when Sam had told me he needed space all those years ago. I couldn't keep looking back. Before I could change my mind, I grabbed the rucksack, lifted it onto my back and, with knees buckling, walked out of Alice's apartment, down the stairwell and onto the dusk-lit streets of Coogee, on the road once again.

The fresh sea breeze hit me straight away. The suburb's evenings were becoming more and more beautiful the closer it drew to summer. Tonight, the palm trees were silhouetted against the orange sky. I wished I could enjoy them. I remembered feeling the same way in London, looking at Tower Bridge illuminated against a summer sky, crowds of tourists laughing and taking photos by the Thames. I was the one who lived there, and yet I never quite fitted in. I longed to call my mum, to tell her how I'd screwed up, to ask her if I could come home. But the Lake Distinct wasn't my home either. I had managed to outgrow it without putting my roots down anywhere else. I couldn't keep running back to my parents every time I felt down anyway. I was a grown-up, for goodness' sake.

I forced myself to walk the three blocks across to where the road met the coast. For once the sea looked calm. Could I really leave this place? I longed to jump in, to feel myself duck under the cold water, submerged in its peace. Friends, career, love; I couldn't think of one reason to stay. I had to leave. I had to go back, or go somewhere else. Just go, just escape.

Locals glanced at my backpack and smiled as I walked past, eyes kind as if to say: *enjoy your time here*, mentally grouping me with the eighteen-year-old girls I had seen yesterday. Young and full of promise. Fuck them. Fuck those promises. I was almost twenty-eight and none of them had been fulfilled, not one. My school yearbook spoke of someone 'Most Likely To Be Famous'. Our university friends had already walked Sam and me down the aisle. My dad had told us we'd thrive in London. None of it had come true. None of it.

Stepping one foot in front of the other, I tried not to fall in love with the scenery all over again. Without even realising it, tears were streaming down my face and the expressions of passers-by turned from hope to concern. I was back at square one. But not the square one of a hopeful eighteen-year-old with the whole world at her feet. The square one of a soon-to-be thirty-year-old who never thought she'd end up here. As the Coogee hills started plateauing, I stuck my hand out to call down an oncoming cab.

'Where to, mate?' The cabby leaned out of the open window. I bit my bottom lip. I hadn't even thought. I just wanted to get out. *You can't keep looking back*; I heard my mum's words play around my head again. I reached out for the warm metal door handle. *But you can't keep running away.* I wasn't running away. I just didn't belong here. I had no reason to stay. I wasn't…

'Bloody tourists!' the cabby scoffed as the lights turned green and he pulled away, just another person impatient for me to get it together. 'Jessica?' *Shit. Shit. Shit.* 'Where the hell do you think you're going?'

'Olivia?' I turned to see her tottering towards me on her heels. All Sydney women seemed to share the ability to make me feel like a fat, broken blob.

'Please tell me you're off to Manly for the weekend?' She eyed my backpack with suspicion. I had never seen her so forceful.

Without speaking, I shook my head, the same fat tears rolling down my cheeks.

'I should tell you now,' she said, 'I'm not very good at this *emotional* stuff.' She reached out a hand to indicate that I was the said 'emotional stuff' she was referring to. Ironic, given that I'd pretty much had to pick her and Tim off the floor of CreateSpace more than once. Like a porcelain doll, she reached up both arms in unison and awkwardly positioned them around my body. 'I'm taking you for a drink,' she said, equally woodenly, reaching into her Mulberry bag and placing a pristine tissue in my hand.

'I don't want to talk about CreateSpace,' I said, through child-like sobs.

'It's nine p.m. on a Thursday evening and I've only just left the gallery.' Olivia looked me dead in my tear-flooded eyes. 'Do you really think *I* want to talk about CreateSpace?'

Olivia led me and my backpack into the beer garden of the Coogee Bay Hotel, a backpackers' knees-up type place that I could never picture her enjoying. I sat at the wooden bench table, conscious of bumping into anyone else I wouldn't want to in this state. Jamie, Sam, Joshua, Tim – the sheer volume of people to avoid was testament to my cock-ups. Olivia went to the bar and came back with two large glasses in her left hand, a bottle of white in her right.

'Now, drink up,' she said, placing the glasses down and filling mine to the brim. I took one reluctantly; this past couple of weeks was enough to put me off drinking for good. 'And tell me why the hell you're leaving?'

I looked at her pretty, pale profile. She must be the only person I'd met in Sydney who didn't look like they lived at the beach; maybe because she was always with Tim at CreateSpace.

'What?' She looked at me, her slightly smudged eyebrows raised – imperfections I'd never notice if we weren't close up.

'Nothing, it's just…' I began, not knowing how or if to phrase it. 'It's just, you never seemed this feisty at CreateSpace.' I thought back to her obedient clipboard-holding and her reluctance to speak up in front of Tim for fear of being shot down.

'And you never seemed like a coward,' she quipped in return. Ouch.

'I'm not being a coward,' I objected, lifting my glass to take a gulp, but stopping myself, remembering again that this was what had got me in trouble in the first place. Instead, I took a small sip. 'You don't even know what this is about.' I shook my head at her, even though she was too busy looking down at my overfilled backpack, slung mercilessly to one side on the floor.

'I can give it a good guess.' She lifted her eyes away from it, full of disdain. Why had she invited me for a drink if she was just going to lay into me? With nowhere better to be and nothing better to do, I motioned to her to carry on. 'My guess is that you came to Sydney thinking it would be easy to start a new life here, a new career, a new man. And now that it's not, now that you've got caught out, got some push-back from a fifty-year-old prima donna and, I imagine, been swiped left by lunchtime mystery man, you're running off again in search of something easier...' She trailed off.

I really didn't need this right now.

'I don't need this right now,' I voiced out loud, edging my full glass of wine in her direction and standing to go.

'Leaving again?' She raised her eyebrow again in mock surprise. *Bitch.*

'That's not what this is,' I objected, parking myself back down all the same.

'So, it's not about a boy?' Olivia asked and for the first time in a long time I realised it wasn't. It had been – or I thought it had. But it was bigger than that.

'I don't think so. Not entirely.'

'No?' Olivia softened a little, inviting me to carry on.

'I'm just not where I thought I'd be right now, you know, in life. I was the sorted one, the one who was settled before I'd even left uni, and now…' My voice trailed off. 'I just keep hoping that I can work it all out, force my life back on track somehow.' I looked across to her, perfection personified. 'You wouldn't understand; you've got it all together. I just feel like a mess.'

'You think I've got it together?' She let out a little laugh. 'I'm a thirty-three-year-old gallery assistant who still rents in a houseshare twelve miles from the coast so that she can afford to keep up the appearances needed to get ahead in her industry. I don't date; I don't really have a social life because I work so damn hard, but if you think I've got it all together…' She shrugged, taking another sip of her wine.

'I… I had no idea…' I said, taken aback by Olivia's vulnerability, an openness I didn't think she had to give.

'You wouldn't. Because when someone's unhappy they tend to be a bit, well' – she hesitated on the word and I nodded for her to say it anyway – 'self-centred.'

'Self-centred?' I repeated the word, letting it settle, thoughts of Sam and Jamie and Zoe and my parents running through my mind.

'Like Devon Atwood, for example,' Olivia continued. *Devon?* 'Tim told me what happened, and I know it's shady that Sommers was forcing you out before she'd even found out you…' Olivia paused.

'*Lied*,' I said, filling in the blank. They say the truth will set you free, but right now I still felt trapped.

'Yeah well, you didn't lie about Devon being pretty shit at her job from time to time,' she continued, 'that was true, at least.' *All the time*, I almost corrected but had strength enough to stop myself. 'But did you ever think that she might be drowning, ripping off everyone else's ideas because she just couldn't keep up with the pressure to perform, to stay reputable, *relevant* after all this time? That she might need help rather than your hate? You can only see it from your side. It's okay, we all do it – but sometimes, I find it helps to, you know…' She didn't need to finish her sentence to make her point.

'You're right,' I admitted, looking across at her dark hair pulled tightly behind her ears and her hand shaking slightly as she took another sip of her wine. I had never deserved to be promoted over her, even when they thought I was who I said I was, but she'd shut up and supported me all the same. She didn't need to put me down to make herself higher.

'Thank you, Olivia.' I meant it. Neither of us needed to say what for. She shrugged away my kindness. If I'd known she'd been this feisty at CreateSpace we would have been out for drinks ages ago. 'So why do you do it?' I had to ask. 'If work costs you so much, why do you even stick around?'

'Because I love it.' She smiled. 'I love what I do. I know it might sound stupid, but for me, it's worth the cost.' She took another sip of her drink and looked around the courtyard, suddenly nervous about letting herself lose her composure. I guess she figured it would be me doing the talking.

'Olivia, that's great,' I said, putting a hand across the table to rest on hers. She didn't pull away. 'And it doesn't sound stupid.' I shook my head. 'It's amazing that you've found something you're really passionate about. I guess I'm just not sure I have that…'

'Sure you do,' Olivia said, waving away my comment once again. 'You've just forgotten or not found it yet. But, Jess' – it was the first time she'd called me anything but my full name – 'I promise you, if you stop running for long enough, if you stop trying to force things into what you *think* they should be, then you're bound to find out what it is.'

Chapter Thirty-Five

13 September 2020 – Sydney, Australia

'Jess? Are you awake?' Alice knocked softly on the door and I began to stir. I sank further into the sheets I had spent most of the last week tangled within. I still hadn't got a job and Sam still hadn't called. He wouldn't even answer. He probably thought I'd be ringing to beg for him back; why wouldn't he? Every inch of me had been begging for him since I had seen him for the first time in Woolies. All I wanted to beg for now was forgiveness. For screwing things up for him, for never letting him go. Something told me I had lost him for good this time, even as just a friend. Then there was Joshua.

'Jess, are you up?' Alice repeated from the other side of the door. Awake and up were two different things; I certainly wasn't the latter. And I didn't want to see anyone. But I didn't want to be alone either – forever imbedded in contradictions.

'Yes,' I replied, eventually.

The gap in the door got bigger and bigger until I could see Alice in her dressing gown standing between the door and the exposed-wood frame. I pushed myself up to sitting, pulling the sheets around my overflowing pyjama top. I smiled at her. She didn't need to do this, even if Joshua had given her the heads-up that I could do with a friend; no one had said she'd have to house me for this long. Although, given where I'd come from, maybe she should have expected it. Coming across to perch at the end of the bed, Alice smiled in return. I shielded my phone. She didn't need to know that I'd still been pushing the boundary between sorry and stalker. Sam needed space. She had said that. I had heard that. But still, it was a week on and I still hadn't heard from him. I'd gone years without contact, and yet a few weeks had managed to rewind the clock. My sanity depended on his acceptance of my apology. I just really wanted to make it okay, to make sure he was okay.

'Sleep alright?' Alice stroked her hand across the bed sheets. I nodded.

'Have you got work today?' I asked, even though the fact that she was in her fluffy dressing gown past nine a.m. would suggest she didn't.

'No,' she confirmed, and I smiled. Maybe today we could go out and do something, something that didn't involve looking for jobs, homes, or anything else that reminded me what I didn't have. 'But I am about to head out,' she continued. It was a weekend day off; of course she had plans. 'Church this morning, but I might do a bit of shopping in the city after, if you fancy joining?' Alice stood, heading for the door. Church, with Sam? Perhaps I could go, just catch him for a minute. 'Help yourself to breakfast, or anything else…' Alice continued, mistaking my silence for refusal. I couldn't blame her for questioning whether I'd get out of bed today.

'Can I come with you?'

'That's what I just asked.' Alice shook her head, laughing, 'I could meet you about midday.'

'No, to church.' *Where Sam is.* 'Could I come along?'

A little smile spread across Alice's face. She never thought I'd ask. I was just as surprised as she was, but needs must. She nodded, gave me half an hour to get ready, and pulled the door closed behind her just as gently as she had entered. Half an hour. Half an hour to master 'please forgive me' chic. What the hell did you wear to church? My old Brownie uniform probably wouldn't cut it this time. And anyway, it was slim pickings. I approached my rucksack, trying desperately to ignore how it perfectly encapsulated my down and out life. Opening it, my string bikini fell out. Not the one. It might not even get another look-in. I quickly drowned thoughts of surf lessons past. Maybe Joshua would be at church too? But first, Sam. I had to fix things with Sam. I rummaged further into my packed-up life and pulled out the longest black dress I'd brought in case a formal occasion should arise – it was hard to tell what you'd need when you were packing to move to the other side of the world. It even covered my knees. I could just visualise Zoe taking her scissors to it now, forcing my hemlines shorter and my nights out longer. My heart ached for those moments, the start of a friendship I thought would see us through it all. Now with my dress on, hair brushed and a slick of make-up, I headed out of the door to find Alice standing before me. I looked from her flip flops, past her blue jeans, up to her tight white tank top. In return, she noted my kitten heels and formal attire. *Shit.*

'You look gorgeous,' Alice said, in an act of pity or generosity. I looked overdressed. But there was no time to change. I followed bohemian Alice out onto the streets of laid-back Sydney with Sam's words about the city suiting me leaving a bitter taste in my mouth.

I stood outside and looked up at the steeple shining in the morning sunlight. Alice, flip-flopping a couple of strides before me, turned back around. 'Why are you stopping? It's over here.' She pointed to the entrance of a nondescript warehouse, overflowing with hipsters drinking coffee from takeout cups. Crap. I'd look even more out of place in there. Alice steered me into the massive open space of the warehouse. Music was pumping, the lights were low and the people were all on some kind of high. Or at least they seemed it, smiling and waving as I entered the so-called church. Alice embraced person after person as we made our way to our seats. I'd have thought she was some sort of Christian celebrity or something if all the other people around us weren't doing the same. I scanned the room for Sam. I couldn't see him anywhere. *So, this is where God grew them*, I thought, recalling Jamie, Alice and the other miraculous creatures I'd seen mill round Sam and Jamie's 341 Oberon crew.

Thankfully, I couldn't see Jamie anywhere either. If I was her, I'd murder me for showing up here. I was sure they'd frown on that in church. Alice passed me a paper coffee cup and ushered me down one of the rows. I sat obediently, still looking around for sight of Sam. Across the room I saw another familiar figure striding into the warehouse. I tried to turn away, but he had caught my eye – not smiling, not mean, but sensibly keeping his distance. Joshua nodded in our direction. I turned back to Alice, struggling for the right words, but just then the music came to a crescendo and the band took to the illuminated stage.

Alice rose to her feet and I mirrored her cue. Before long, the music had kicked into full blast, young twenty-somethings bouncing on the stage as people around the room swayed in time to the music, some raising their hands to the sky, eyes closed, somewhere else entirely. I wished I was somewhere else too. Between the darkness and spotlights it was almost impossible to search for Sam. On the upside, with everyone's eyes closed at least I didn't have to be subtle. He wasn't here. My heart sank. I'd not only cost him his fiancée, I'd cost him his bloody faith. Old Sam was probably back, shagging his way across Sydney, cynical and certain. I began to close my eyes, hoping the music would drown out my thoughts. But then, I saw them. Across the room, towards the front of the crowd, I saw Sam and Jamie. Both had their eyes closed, one hand each extended to the sky in praise, their other hands held tightly together. I saw their interlaced fingers, steadfast and firm, Jamie's rock of an engagement ring illuminated by the flashing lights. Joshua was right; why would Jamie be threatened by an old uni girlfriend? They had decided to get married, for real, not the naive musings of two love-drunk students. Sam wouldn't 'always love me, J,' not in that way, not now, not ever. And now, not even as a friend. I closed my eyes. I let the darkness cover me, and then I felt a hand slip into mine. Alice, strong but soft beside me. A tear escaped from my mascara-masked eyes and I choked, 'Do you think they'll ever forgive me?'

Alice looked at me, her earnest expression sporadically illuminated by the spotlights. She nodded. 'They're the forgiving type.'

Alice put her hand to my chin lightly and turned it away from Sam and Jamie and towards the stage. 'But for now, don't torture yourself. You've done that enough.'

For a second I wanted to turn my head back round, to stare at the one thing I couldn't have. To stare all my mistakes in the face and just hold on. But I kept on looking forward. I would keep on looking forward. Focused on the stage, my eyes fell to the right-hand side, where I could see a line of people sitting down and facing an array of half-coloured canvases. They were painting. A few seats remained empty, a handful of canvases unspoilt. Alice must have followed my gaze as, unprompted, she said, 'They're for anyone to use, just another response to the music.'

I began to move out of the row and down the aisle towards the front of the crowd. Shaking, I filled the empty seat and looked at the canvas before me. Why was I here? I hadn't painted in years. I reached out to grasp a paintbrush by the side of the canvas, rolling the wood through my fingers. It felt foreign and familiar all at the same time. Looking down at the palette of primary colours laid out before me, I savoured the strength of their hues. Not knowing if I even remembered how to do it, I began to dab red and yellow together, bright orange emerging before my eyes. Covering the tip of the brush, I looked towards the white blank page before me. I began to draw long fluid lines of colour across the canvas, light and neat in a way my life would never be. I painted over the thought. And then again, and again. Each ounce of self-loathing and regret, brushed over. Each lie coloured with something like truth. Tears began to fall down my already messy face. I loved this. *I love this.* The thought reverberated around my mind. *I love that I can do this.*

Thoughts of Sam. Thoughts of CreateSpace. I painted over them. As the song drew to an end, I sat back to look at what I had made. I didn't know what it was, but that didn't matter; I knew what it felt like. Against a backdrop of brokenness, I had remembered a little thing I loved that wasn't who I dated, wasn't what I did, wasn't who I knew. And it felt a bit like hope.

Chapter Thirty-Six

13 September 2020 – Sydney, Australia

'Jess, it was honestly so amazing,' Alice said, sipping her deep glass of red. Sunday afternoons had never tasted so good. 'Why did you ever stop painting?' I looked down into my own glass. Like yesterday, coffee had been the gateway drug to something stronger; thankfully The Coffee Shop provided both. I looked around at the canvas-covered walls and back to Alice, feeling more at home than I had done in months.

'It's a long story,' I replied. 'Uni happened.' I shrugged. 'Sam happened.' I took a sip, searching my mind for the story I'd always told myself, the one where being a painter was a cute hobby, a little bit *alt*. 'He helped me think about the ways I could make a career out of art. Art therapy, art journalism…'

'Artist?' Alice interjected, smiling as she shook her glossy hair behind her.

'You have to be really good to make it.' I shook my own head.

'You are really good, Jess.' She looked from the paintings hung around the bar back to me.

'Few people make a career out of it,' I argued in return.

Somehow, I had begun to sound like the pragmatic one.

'Yes, few people do.' Alice raised a perfectly plucked eyebrow and took another telling sip. I couldn't be the few. 'You could do something great if you had a little faith in yourself, you know?'

I looked around the artisan wine bar, taking in the beachscapes on the walls. They reminded me of the one in Alice's apartment, each of them too flat and emotionless, failing to capture the textures I had seen in the view from Coogee Beach.

'I couldn't even make it in journalism.'

'Where's *it*?' Alice said, a trick question dressed up in sincerity.

'Huh?' I asked. 'CreateSpace? Woolloomooloo?'

'No,' Alice went on. '*It*, like what does "making it" look like for you?'

I sighed; how to even begin to explain? 'Well, a bit like you, maybe?' I said. 'Like, girl-bossing it, at the top of your game?' I didn't mean it to sound like a question but everything I'd learnt about Alice since becoming closer to her had made me see that it hadn't been easy. It hadn't all just been handed to her on her pretty-girl plate.

'I don't feel like I've made it,' Alice scoffed into her wine. 'I'm not sure anyone does.'

'Well, you have.' I wouldn't let her argue; I was doing enough of that for both of us. 'I know you've worked hard for it. I just can't see what my career will look like, I can't—'

'Stop telling yourself you can't do it,' Alice interrupted, with force. 'If you're passionate about journalism, try harder.'

I wasn't, I never had been.

'If you want to be an art therapist, try that.'

I didn't, that was Sam's idea.

'But if you want to be a painter, fucking paint.'

Alice's swearing took me by surprise, but not as much as her words. Had I ever even tried? I wanted to paint. I wanted to fucking paint.

'Alice.' I took another sip. 'I need to go back to CreateSpace.'

I leaned against the wall where Sam had met me for countless lunches before. I gazed across the square and into the large windows of CreateSpace. I hardly looked inconspicuous in my funeral-formal attire. In just over a week the space leading to the gallery had witnessed my pansy-clad professional high and my rucksack-weighted personal low, and now this. I steadied myself. I knew I could go to any art shop. Oils, brushes, canvases, my shopping list was simple. But this wasn't about speed, it was about something more symbolic. Maybe I was an artist after all. Fortune favours the brave. Tim, on the other finger-wagging hand, favoured the sassy. It could have been the wine or maybe it was because I had nowhere left to fall from where I was on rock bottom, but right now, I was feeling sassy. And, I wanted to paint.

Alice looked across to me and smiled. 'We can go somewhere else, you know?'

I looked back over at CreateSpace, to the line of people eager to get in to the exhibition and the posters I had commissioned adorning the wall. Yes, I may have let Tim think I'd been starting a new job at *Art Today* but I'd never lied about working there – I'd worked there for *three* bloody years. And I'd worked tirelessly for him. I'd put my all into the exhibition and pulled off an opening night everyone was talking about. I'd got a lot wrong – sure. But when it came to this, I'd got some things right too.

And he hadn't even given me time to explain, wouldn't even hear me out. I wouldn't let him just dismiss me like that.

'No, I want him to know I'm not scared of him.' I was making a statement. 'I'm so over being scared.'

Alice nodded. Neither one of us mentioned Sam, the scariest thought of all. But Tim? Tim was a fifty-year-old man-child, too scared of Hannah Sommers to stand up to her or to stand up for me. Too self-centred to hear me out for even a moment, after all I'd done. The receptionists looked up as I walked in. It was like they'd seen a ghost. Maybe in the art world I was one. The ghost of promising staff members past. I looked past them to *Tuesday's Slumber*, at the possibility of what I could do. Turning on my heel, I strutted in the opposite direction to the exhibition I had worked so hard to build and yet was now unable to enjoy. I walked purposely into the art shop and grabbed what I needed. No point in loitering around; the receptionists would tell Tim I was here, ballsy and unafraid. I handed over the dollars, which in just a couple of short months had become more familiar to me than pounds, and headed out of the shop, towards the glass entrance doors.

'Jessica?' My heart jolted as I heard Tim's voice behind me. I turned, and saw him standing there in a metallic silver jumpsuit. He had once told me his outfits got more outrageous with every good review. This latest monstrosity was clearly a good sign. That, and the fact that I had read countless articles and features praising Leo Todd and the latest curator to fill CreateSpace.

'Tim,' I said in return, one canvas under each arm and two bags of equipment clutched in each hand; they were heavy, but I wouldn't show it.

'What are you doing here?' he demanded, pushing his thick glasses up the bridge of his nose. I looked down to the bags. Wasn't it obvious? 'Are you here to see the exhibition? Are you here for your post?' He looked to the corners of the room nervously as if Atwood and Sommers had bugged the place. 'You know you can't—'

'I was just buying some stuff,' I said, but the relief in Tim's face as he realised I wasn't about to threaten his career sent my red wine-induced sass into overdrive. He'd done little to protect mine. 'Actually, I'm not here to see the exhibition,' I continued with increasing pace. 'And do you know why? Because I helped make it happen. I know every inch of it. Probably better than you.' I sounded like a schoolgirl. But in for a penny… '*Tuesday's Slumber* – the one the press called "a bold statement" – wouldn't be there if it wasn't for me.' In the absence of free hands I gestured towards it with my chin, probably looking like I'd offered him a Glasgow kiss. 'The palette-led positioning, which *Vogue Australia* called "a triumphantly innovative expression of taste", wouldn't be there if it wasn't for me. And do you know what? The press – they wouldn't have been here without me either. So yes, I screwed up. I lied to my ex-boyfriend because I was so bloody ashamed of being adrift, I lied to you about having a job with Sommers. But I never lied to you about my abilities, about who *I* am. And I'm not ashamed of this.' My chin gestured to the poster on the wall, mirroring the ones outside. If only he'd found me in the shop and not now, hands full, looking like I'd probably robbed the place. 'I'm proud of the work I've done for you, and the least you can do is acknowledge it. If you'd have listened, if you'd have let me say sorry… But hey, you win some, you lose some… and… and you've lost me.'

My teenage tantrum complete, I turned on my heel and strutted out as best I could laden down with canvases. I didn't need to turn back to know Tim would be nailed to the spot, face shocked and his hip popped, but I didn't look back. I wouldn't look back from now on.

I lifted my shades, only to be blinded by the light, before putting them back on again. My gaze darted from my palette of paints, resting on the paved steps beside me, to the bright blank canvas tilted towards my body, resting on my knees. Every inch of me had wanted to paint just an hour ago, to reclaim the magic I had felt in that church or the magic I had felt the first time I had held a brush in my hands. But now I was here, alone. Just me, faced with a canvas of flawless nothingness and the sole power to screw it up.

I looked across Coogee Beach. There was a man draping his arm around a woman and children playing in the sand. *I could paint them, I guess.* But I didn't know what he was thinking, or what she was feeling, or what kind of day those children had enjoyed. I couldn't paint their stories. I only had my own. I looked again from the canvas to the horizon. Deep blue sea, grey-blue sky, damp golden sand. It was the kind of three-stroke setting that a photo could never capture and a painting could only hope to glimpse. In an instant, my mind went from CreateSpace to the large expanses of block colours and weighty textures, to the way Sam had looked at me as he had tried to make sense of someone else's emotion, encapsulated in a frame. It ran to Alice's apartment, to the way her happy-go-lucky landscape had jarred against my mood. That was someone else's Coogee. Too perfect, too precious – it said nothing of the raw, untamed waves, or the loneliness you could feel when surrounded by people, or the joy you could feel when diving into something new.

I pressed my brush into the paint and started to mix, searching for sand. I looked at the canvas, isolated by its perfection, not wanting to screw it up. Without the music or spotlights or Alice by my side, I felt exposed. Out of the corner of my eye I could see a passer-by hovering, waiting for me to make my move. I splashed colour onto the canvas, thick and dark. It didn't need to be perfect. I laid on another stoke. I just needed to feel it. Looking, brushing, I felt it; I felt every mistake I'd made all over again, and I felt release: the freedom to make mistakes, to learn from them. The freedom to forgive myself, to make wrong turns, to embrace where they were leading me. I felt the cold wet track of a tear falling down my cheek and the sense of finding something I thought I'd lost but was within me all along.

PART THREE

Chapter Thirty-Seven

30 September 2020 – Sydney, Australia

I stood back and watched him press the shutter.

'That's the last one.' Andrew turned towards me and smiled.

'It really is a lovely collection, Jess,' Mark added.

Collection. Lovely. I clung to the words, letting them warm me, letting them be mine. It had been over two weeks since I had first picked up a paintbrush again and now I stood looking at eight canvases that I had painted with scenes of my Sydney, resting against the exposed brick walls of Alice's apartment. Not just curated by me, but built, brush by brush, stroke by stoke. It was what an eighteen-year-old me would have dreamed of but never been able to achieve. I looked at the one closest to me, currently unnamed and yet feeling so familiar: a square canvas opening a window to Bondi. Caught between abstraction and realism, the thick layers of impasto became white foam on the cusp of the waves, built up slowly with greys and blues and whites and greens. They clashed against the sand, softer, more sweeping, a darker shade from the bottom right corner, casting a shadow across the speckled ground that hinted of human silhouettes, two, or maybe three.

It turned out Sam was right; painting didn't pay. But the barista shifts I had finally managed to get did and at least Alice and I were drinking coffee for free now. She seemed to still like drinking them together despite us now being de facto flatmates – her spare room beginning to feel more and more my own with each passing day. And maybe one day my paintings might earn me something. Maybe one day. I thought of Sam and Jamie and my heart sank. They'd be getting married any day now. I'd heard from Alice that plans were hurtling forward, that Sam was stronger than ever, stronger without me. After seeing them at church together, I'd given up trying to call. At least I now knew I hadn't ruined *everything*, even if I had ruined my friendship with Sam. I'd just have to make my peace with that.

Mark grinned and shook his head, saying again, 'It *really* is a lovely collection.' At least the paintings paid in compliments. I looked at the canvases scattered around Alice's living room again and glowed. Each one displayed a sprawling landscape, but every one of them was different, all little bits of me. I had created something I loved. No one had paid me to do it, no one had asked me to do it. And yet, glancing at the faces of three people fast becoming genuine friends, I knew they weren't worthless.

'So what's next?' Alice looked to me, her excitement overflowing.

'I have to go to work,' I replied, making for Alice's spare room.

'I meant with the paintings.' Alice walked over to her favourite, a beachscape from the Coogee Bay steps. It was from the perspective of a figure sitting on the very steps I had waited on for Sam when Joshua had shown up instead. The strokes of golden yellow built up to the vibrant blue of water, dashes of thick white caught on the waves and hints of browns and pinks suggested people immersed within them. It was frenzied, adventurous, hopeful.

'That's the last of the photos online!' Andrew exclaimed over the top of his laptop screen. 'All you need to do is press send.' Andrew turned the laptop around to face me. The screen displayed the press release I'd spent hours working on the night before. When Alice had first suggested I tell art editors about my work I had laughed out loud. Who would want to know? Would Hannah Sommers or Tim try and sabotage me before they could even contact me, like damp fingers snuffing out a flame? But after days of coaxing I had finally surrendered. I still had the press list from the exhibition and I was, after all, now on a first-name basis with the art editor at *Vogue Australia*.

And yet, now I was only a click away from sending it, I couldn't bring myself to do it. Who was I trying to fool? I wasn't good enough. Thoughts of Sam, Jamie, CreateSpace and Tim ran through my mind.

'Press it,' Alice demanded, reading my expression.

'I can't,' I said, before Alice leaned over me and pressed the send button, purposeful and defiant. My stomach sank but my heart leapt. Just like the lies I had spun when I had first arrived at Sam's, there was no undoing this now. Only this time, these paintings felt like the most truthful thing I'd done in months.

'I can.' She smiled. 'Now go get ready for your shift, you slacker.' She gave me a playful push towards the door. 'You never know, it could be your last.'

Chapter Thirty-Eight

I greeted the tanned regulars who sat sipping lattes outside, one couple's legs twisting around one another like the legs of the delicate iron tables that lined the front of the store. The Coffee Shop. The coffee-shop-cum-bar Alice and I had been drinking at when I'd first got the idea for my collection. Turned out the second I stopped trying to find a job, one found me. There had to be a lesson in that, but I was too late for my shift to find it right now.

'Jess!' my colleague Yasmine cried as I joined her behind the counter. 'I'm so glad you are here. Kyle has been such a dick, *again*.' Her brown eyes pleaded with me, her curly blonde hair scrunched up in a bun, emphasising the dynamic angles of her young pretty face. Sweet seventeen-year-old boy dramas. If only I could tell her it was easier at twenty-seven.

'Oh, I'm so sorry, I shouldn't be talking about Kyle the week that your Sam is getting married.' She shook her head apologetically. The fact she referred to him as mine showed that I'd shared my own dose of boy-related drama over our couple of weeks together too. I really should introduce her to Alice and show her that women have far better things to dedicate their brain power to than men. 'How many days is it now?' she asked.

It was four. Four short days. Alice, Andrew and Mark had done a good job at walking the line between Sam, Jamie and I, keeping mentions of them to a minimum when they were with me. But the date of their big day was impossible to forget, ever since Jamie had told me, less than two months, eight weeks, fifty-six days ago.

'Is he still not picking up your calls?' Yasmine asked, reminding me of a young Zoe – a Zoe who actually knew every inch of what was going on in my life. I hadn't heard from her since the morning of the exhibition opening; I guess my staying in his spare bedroom was one Sam-drama too far for her; part of me was beginning to understand why.

'No,' I sighed. Alice had said he wasn't mad any more but had told me just to leave it. Three years since our break-up and I was still here talking about him; clearly 'leaving it' wasn't my forte. 'Anyway, Kyle?' The magic word. Yasmine set off on a long tirade, interrupted only by customers. '… cheat… ex-girlfriend… Americano?… sex with… here's your change, sir… never again…'

The hours passed as I made coffees, cleared tables, juiced fruit, wiped down the bar. My fine art degree raged unused within me, but I ignored it. The Coffee Shop customers had made me feel lighter than I had done in days. Sure, it wasn't CreateSpace. Sure, it wasn't painting. But it was people, familiar faces, friendly conversations and in some strange way I knew it was slowly soothing whatever it was that broke within me when my 'maybe one day' crashed and burned. Plus, it was one of the only things in Sydney I'd sorted out for myself.

I looked out over the small coffee shop, across the smiling faces and chatter of conversations and out the long glass storefront to the sea and— *shit.*

'*Shit.*' I crouched down under the counter. Yasmine, busy clearing a table, instantly appeared by my side. Following my gaze to where it had been only moments before, she saw who I had been looking at. I couldn't let him see me working in a coffee shop, not after the last time we had spoken.

'Is that *him*? Is it Sam? Do you want me to—'

'Yasmine,' I interrupted, 'he's fifty and he's wearing a kimono, of course that's not Sam! That's Tim, my boss from CreateSpace.'

'The one who fired you and then you went back and yelled at?'

Couldn't remember a three-drink order, but she could recall all the dirty details of my demise.

'That's the one.' I smiled ironically.

'I'll cover for you… G'day, sir!' Yasmine jumped up to standing as Tim materialised at the counter. 'What can I get for you, latte, Americano, espresso, skinny cappuccino, matcha macchiato?'

'I'd like to speak with Jessica,' Tim declared grandly. Shit. 'I heard she was working here now?'

I studied his sequin-studded Converse through the five-inch gap between the counter and the floor. I looked up at Yasmine, pleadingly.

'Sorry, sir,' Yasmine began, wooden and rehearsed. 'I'm afraid we don't have anyone working here by that na—'

'I can see her under the counter,' Tim interrupted, deadpan. Oh *crap.* 'Jessica, I'd like to speak with you.'

With shaking legs and a face full of shame, I stood from where I was hiding and brushed dust from the floor off my apron as I absorbed the full extent of Tim's flamboyant attire. I racked my brain for reasons he could be here, none of them good.

'Jessica.' Tim looked down at me through his thick black frames. 'I wonder whether I could coax you onto your break? I'd love to chat.'

Think of an excuse, Jess. Think of an excuse.

'I can hold the fort,' Yasmine said before I could filter through my thoughts of dogs and homework. I had no choice but to say '*Thanks*, Yasmine,' through gritted teeth. 'Could you make Tim an iced green tea, please?' I knew his order well.

'Anything for you?' she asked, an excited look on her face.

Wine? Gin? Valium?

'Just a filter, please,' I responded.

'So, how are you? How's the exhibition? How's Olivia?' Nervous chatter spilled out as I led Tim over to a table. Somewhere between hiding behind the counter and being caught dusty-handed and red-faced, my mind had decided we should go on the offensive. He couldn't get angry without getting a word in edgeways. 'I read the review in *Vogue*, such a—'

'We need to talk.' Four words I had dreaded for much of my adult life. Though I never thought I'd hear them from a fifty-something man wearing adult-sized children's Converse. This was about my appearance at CreateSpace. This was about Atwood and Sommers. This was about that lie. This was about the coffee stain I got on the back of *Patience* that Tim never found out about. I silenced my thoughts and tried to concentrate on his.

'This is about your collection.'

My collection. I had wanted to be credited for my contribution but even I thought calling it 'my collection' was going a bit far.

'Olivia received your press release and passed it on to me.' Oh, my *collection*. My eight paintings. *The Alice's Living Room Sessions*; very much a working title.

'They're very good,' Tim said and very almost smiled as I questioned his use of Botox for the umpteenth time. I accepted the compliment with unease, sure he was lulling me into a false sense of security. Surely he hadn't come here to compliment me.

'Jessica,' he repeated, taking a sip of his tea and glancing over to Yasmine. God forbid it wasn't ice cold. 'Do you know why I wanted to go into the art industry?'

'The free alcohol?' I quipped, regretting it instantly.

'I looked at every other industry and saw order,' Tim continued like he hadn't even heard me. 'Clocking in, holding up a hierarchy, fearful of falling out of line.' He reached for the pot of sugar sachets on our table and started to lay them before him top to tail, to illustrate his point – even his explanations were artistic. His fingers were flecked with a familiar shade of deep blue paint that he'd failed to completely scrub away.

'Artists seemed fearless. They either broke the rules or made their own.'

I nodded along, pretending that I knew where he was going with this.

'I see that same spirit in your work.' He raised an eyebrow in a way that made me question whether 'my work' consisted of my painting, my telling Sommers that Atwood was a bitch or my shameless pursuit of a soon-to-be married man.

'Thank you. I just started painting and it was like I—'

'Jessica. Would you just shut up for a moment? I'm trying to tell you something.' *Well, spit it out then.*

'When I saw your pieces, I was reminded of why I got into art in the first place. To break the rules, to foster new talent, not to be bossed around by an archaic woman with more money than sense…' He trailed off, while I looked on, unsure whether it was my turn to speak or not. I studied his beard, simultaneously well-kept and out of control. I looked through his thick-rimmed glasses to the eyes behind, eyes that were becoming softer with every second. I took a breath, ready to apologise again, to say I never meant to lie to him, never meant for it to get out of hand.

'And do you know *how* I got into the industry?' he asked.

I shook my head, this time knowing to stay schtum.

'I lied,' he said, letting the words hang there. For a moment he looked a little ashamed, then it was replaced with something like pride.

'You did?' I asked, unable to comprehend why he would have to, as if somehow he'd been born a successful gallery curator.

'Well,' he said, as his eyes narrowed in mischief. '*Highly* embellished the truth. It was a group interview and I knew this bitch was beating me—'

'Tim,' I said, interrupting before he could properly get going.

'Jess, what I'm trying to say,' Tim said, 'is that I'm sorry. I shouldn't have written you off like that – not when you'd been such an asset, such a, well…'

I could have sworn I saw his eyes begin to well up. But given the dramatist that he was, I doubted their sincerity. His apology, however, I believed. I smiled across at him, only then realising that when I'd lost my job, I'd lost a friend too.

'Now,' continued Tim, with his customary swagger restored. Apology over, now time for business. 'As a member of my team I won't be able to pitch your work to CreateSpace but together we can get you some bookings elsewhere.'

Hang on. Member of his team?

'We can usually sort something out.' Tim waved his hand as if to illustrate the point. The blue on them reminded me of the painting Sam and I had talked about: *Nameless* by Anonymous. Surely he couldn't be the painter behind it? I smiled at the thought; the symmetry of mystery and the randomness of a world that just sometimes all made sense. But CreateSpace would never let him hang his own work in an exhibition he had curated – he had just said that. Maybe Tim was more of a rule-breaker than he'd even care to admit.

'You will come back to work for me, right?'

I took another sip of my coffee, not that I needed the caffeine right now. He was offering me my job back. I looked around The Coffee Shop, at Yasmine not-so-subtly over-polishing the table besides us. I was a twenty-seven-year-old barista sitting before a crazily talented curator offering me a professional lifeline. The answer was obvious.

'No.'

'No?' Tim questioned. I was as confused as he was. What was I doing? I caught Yasmine looking gleeful behind him.

'Is this because I fired you? Jessica, I'm sorry about that, I finally felt like I was getting somewhere and I had to protect my—'

'No.' I was a broken record, after a life of being a 'yes' person. I was finally putting my foot down, even if I hadn't quite worked out why. 'No, it's not that, it's just, I think I've spent a long time skirting around what I want to do but never really doing it. *Art Today*, CreateSpace, helping to put on exhibitions, it's all *about* painting, but it's not painting. And I've remembered how much I love it, Tim, how it makes me feel, and I'm not ready to give that up right now. I don't want to distract myself with an almost-dream.'

'Jessica.' How many ways could he say my name? 'You are talented but not many people have a future in painting professionally.' He smiled kindly but his furrowed brow exposed his concern.

'Tim.' I imitated his persistent interruptions. 'Take it from someone who's spent most of the past decade investing in a future that didn't exist, I'm okay just enjoying today.' And I was. I had spent so long trying to shoehorn my dreams to make them fit in with someone else's. I didn't want to compromise now.

'Well, I hope you get some funding for your own exhibition one day,' Tim sighed, defeated. 'It really is a great collection. What's it called?' The press release hadn't given it a name. I racked my brain. *Life's A Beach.* Too cliché. *Eight Pieces of Heartbreak.* Too tragic.

'*Starting Over*,' I replied, quiet and confident. And I was.

'To *Starting Over*.' Tim raised his iced tea. I met it with my filter coffee and smiled.

'Oh, and you'll never guess who got in touch to say I'd done a great job, that *we'd* done a great job with the exhibition?' I could only think of one person. 'Carlo.' Tim had finally found him again. 'Bit of a surprise.' He grinned. Maybe he wouldn't miss me at all, the original formation back together again. 'But do you know what surprised me more?' Tim went on. 'I didn't even care. Turns out I didn't need to prove anything to anyone but me.' He polished off his tea, stood, and without turning, thanked Yasmine. She looked sheepish, realising he'd known she'd been loitering there all along. Tim walked towards the glass doors of The Coffee Shop in his sparkly shoes, turning some heads as he did. Then he turned. 'And Jessica.' Oh crap, had I forgotten to wear mascara? 'If you ever change your mind, I still need someone to hold my clipboard.' He winked and left.

Yasmine instantly came up beside me. 'Man, he's intense. Think you've made the right decision?'

'I have no bloody idea,' I replied, honestly.

But for the first time in a long time I was excited to find out.

Chapter Thirty-Nine

I took off my apron and wiped the loose coffee grounds off my black jeans. Sydney was in the high twenties and I was still in my skinnies; maybe I was becoming a local after all. Coogee was changing too, beginning to burst with sunburnt tourists from far and wide. Inside, The Coffee Shop was no exception. At least our hipster six-table capacity meant I only had to deal with a couple of them at a time. Shift complete, Yasmine long gone, I headed for the door as the evening staff were arriving to swap mugs for glasses and cake for canapés as The Coffee Shop morphed into its wine-bar counterpart.

As I walked out onto Coogee Bay Road, towards the beach, I replayed my day as friends, travellers and couples meandered up the street towards their evening reservations. Tim's visit had taken me by surprise, but not as much as my rejection of his job offer. Why wouldn't I take that job? The question reverberated around my brain even though a few hours before I had been excited by the prospect of the unknown.

Maybe if I'd taken the job I'd be able to get my own place sooner. Alice had been so kind in letting me stay at hers. Over the last few weeks she'd really become a proper friend. But I couldn't help but be reminded that she was Sam and Jamie's friend first. And Joshua had asked her to look out for me like one of his teenage mentees. Sure, Alice, Mark and Andrew seemed to enjoy my company, but come Saturday, they'd all be celebrating the marriage I thought one day I'd have for myself. And I'd be alone, in a flat that wasn't mine, waiting for friends that weren't really mine to come home.

I glanced out across the dark sea, the reflections of the street lights dancing on the waves. Sam was getting married on Saturday. I had lived with the thought for almost two months but it still made my heart ache. The thoughts of what could have been had not completely stopped playing on a loop in my brain, but they'd become increasingly drowned out by the laughter of Alice's apartment and become blurrier with every stroke of my paintbrush.

My eyes followed the sound of a giggle across the beach towards a couple of teenagers trying to trip one another over as they walked along the sand. I smiled to myself, remembering how Sam and I had watched Zoe and Austin do the same in Brighton, stumbling over the pebbles underfoot. It was beginning to feel like another lifetime ago. But it wasn't another life, it was a chapter of mine, and a good one. Now I was beginning to allow the pages to turn on. Despite the odd wobble, I was starting to come to terms with the fact that Sam's wedding wouldn't be *my* wedding, but I was struggling to imagine that I wouldn't be at his wedding at all. He'd been my best friend for five years, a friendship that had still seemed to be there despite three years apart. I reached for my phone, illuminating the screen in my palm. Zoe still hadn't called. Nor had Joshua, not that I expected him to. Nor had Sam; I expected that even less. No matter how many times Alice had told me that Sam and Jamie didn't hate me, that they'd forgiven me, that they'd moved on, I still couldn't buy it. How could they? They had shown me nothing but kindness, gone above and beyond, and I had ruined it. I flicked to Sam's number. I wouldn't believe it until I'd heard it from him. I wanted to tell him about Tim, tell him about my paintings, but mostly I wanted to tell him I was sorry. So impossibly, unforgettably sorry. I looked across the beach to the young couple now sitting on the sand, embraced in each other's arms and looking out to the horizon as one. Glancing down to my phone, I swiped to Sam's number and prayed, *please don't hate me, please don't hate me.* I went to dial but just as I did, my phone sprang to life.

'Alice? Hello?'

'Jess, come home now. You *have* to see this.'

I banged on the door of Alice's apartment, regretting that I hadn't accepted her offer to get my own key cut. *Joke's on you, Jess.* I knocked harder, hoping to God she was okay. Had something happened to her? Had something happened with the wedding? The door flung open to reveal Alice, a smile on her face.

'Jess! You're home!'

Yes, because you told me to be.

'Come here, come and look at this!' She certainly didn't look like a woman in crisis. Pyjamas on, her hospital scrubs slung over the back of the leather couch, she beckoned me over to her laptop resting on the dining table and opened the website we'd hosted my paintings on. 'Look what they are saying!' She grinned and pointed. Surely she wouldn't be smiling like that if it was bad. Then again, trolls could be hilarious. I breathed in and out dramatically, like a woman in labour, and sat down at the table, tilting the laptop towards me. She held my hand as I scanned down the comments:

'stunning'
'skilful'
'a real find'
'really speaks to me'

My eyes welled with tears but I held them back so I could read on.

'Where can I buy this???'
'Do you do prints?'

People liked them. People actually really liked them. Years of being under-appreciated at *Art Today* had definitely not prepared me for this.

'This one' – Alice pointed to my favourite beachscape – 'has gone viral!'

It had been shared six hundred times on social media. For a second I wondered whether I should explain to Alice that 'going viral' usually referred to six-digit figures but thought better of it. Six hundred was still pretty cool.

'Check your emails. Anything from the press releases?' Alice asked, excited enough for both of us. I was sure I would be excited too, once I'd finally been able to accept that this was happening.

Unable to speak, I logged on to my emails and watched the loading bar with bated breath, sincerely wishing that I hadn't sent the press release to the 'Atwood' sisters by accident. Four replies. Far from viral but I'd take four over nothing any day. I clicked on the first. It was from a local newspaper asking whether they could include one of the images in a feature. They'd pay me a hundred dollars. I was sure if I had an agent they'd haggle the fee up to two hundred, but having just worked an eight-hour shift at twelve bucks an hour, it took me all of two seconds to accept.

I opened the second. It was from an agent called Tina Conrad. Where had I heard that name before? I scrolled down the email to the footer: Conrad & James – Leo Todd's agency. There was no way; a lump rose in my throat as butterflies flew round in my stomach. She wanted to take me for coffee. I looked across to Alice, reading the email over my shoulder – it appeared the right to privacy was treated with a light touch in Australia. Tina Conrad wanted to take me for coffee. She squeezed my arm. A thrill of excitement filled my chest; surely I must be dreaming. I hovered the cursor over the third unopened email and froze at sight of the sender. G. Stefani. 'Call me Giorgio.' *Vogue Australia.* Alice gasped behind me, holding her breath as I opened the body and read:

Jessica, great exhibition and wonderful collection. You should be proud of yourself. G.

No offer of coffee, no contract on the table. But a demand to be proud of myself, and one I actually felt I could live up to. I felt strength rise up inside me. The feeling I'd had on opening night was nothing compared to this. I'd made something happen by myself.

Last but not least, I looked at the name of the sender of the fourth email and paused.

'Joshua,' I said.

Alice smiled knowingly, proceeding to grab two champagne flutes from the back of the cupboard. *Stop it. There is nothing to smile knowingly at.* Alice returned to the dining table, two flutes in her hands, brimming with bubbles. With trepidation, I clicked, the text of the email for both of us to read:

Hi J. Mark showed me your collection. It's awesome. You've really captured Coogee. Anyway, I just wanted to let you know. Don't be a stranger. Joshua.

Chapter Forty

Comments are like crack. I sat upright in bed, laptop balanced on my knees, scrolling through the posts underneath my paintings until I reached the final one and then started again from the beginning. Somewhere between Giorgio's 'you should be proud of yourself,' Joshua's 'don't be a stranger' and the promise of coffees with people outside the four walls of The Coffee Shop, I had forgotten about calling Sam. It was probably for the best, anyway. But either way you cut it, my best friend of over five years would be taking a monumental step on Saturday while still thinking I was a monumental nob. And now that I could accept I had been, and seeing each new encouraging comment coming up on my screen, I felt an unfamiliar feeling wash over me: the slow release of forgiveness. Not from Sam but from myself. So what if I'd screwed up? I couldn't wallow in it forever. *Note it, learn from it, move on.* Which was why I was sitting here in borrowed shorts about to go running with Alice.

'Jess, are you ready?' I heard Alice shout from the other side of the door. 'Let's stretch before we go, I'm so out of shape.'

I stashed the laptop away and swung open the door to find a tanned, toned, six-foot Alice. If this was out of shape I did not want to see her in it.

'Ready?' she asked again, seeing my oversized T-shirt and shorts, broken at the waistband. I looked like I'd forgotten my PE kit. I nodded. Ready as I'd ever be. I followed Alice's pert bottom out of the apartment, down the steps and onto the street, the pavements already hot from the sunshine beating down.

Alice turned the corner into the park, high enough on Coogee's iconic hills to look out over the beach. She started to stretch in ways I could only dream of. I tried to touch my toes unsuccessfully. Something told me this was not going to end well.

'Ready?'

I wished she'd stop asking that. Either oblivious to my trepidation or choosing to ignore it, she began to run. 'You set the pace.' She turned back to me in a way that told me our ideas of pace were miles apart.

Two boys, both tragically good-looking, passed me on the path. They were walking. Come on, this was Sydney. I was a Sydney-sider now. Running should be part of my adopted DNA. I began to pick up pace.

'There we go!' Alice affirmed, not breaking a sweat. I was breaking enough for both of us. Oh crap. I couldn't keep this up. Alice continued to chat to me as I concentrated on staying alive. Something about how nice it was not being alone in the apartment. If she were saying it over a wine I might have believed her, but the fact that she had taken me on this run was speaking volumes; clearly, she was trying to kill me.

'Look who it is!' Alice turned back to me, struggling to maintain my snail pace. Shit. Please don't be Jamie, *please don't be Jamie*. I squinted through the sweat burning my eyes. Oh *crap*.

'Joshua!' Alice slowed as a topless Joshua jogged towards us.

'Alice.' He leaned in to kiss her cheek, her make-up still perfectly intact. *Please don't kiss me*, I thought for the first time ever when faced with a half-naked good-looking guy who was still managing to pull off a headband.

'Jess!' His kiss sizzled on my red-hot cheek. 'Great to see you,' he lied. 'Great day for it, isn't it?' he said, turning to gaze out across the horizon before us. Light blue sky blended into deep blue water as far as the eye could see. I studied Joshua's profile as I watched him look out across the ocean. I had missed seeing him do that. Between CreateSpace, the box room and lunches with Sam, I had failed to appreciate how much fun our surfing lessons together had been, until it was all a little too late.

He turned to look at me.

'So how are things going over at Team Bride?' Alice chirped, before sending an apologetic glance my way.

'Things seem to have calmed down a bit.' No doubt because of one noticeable absence. 'Thankfully, the closer it gets the more the stress seems to be taken over by excitement.'

Alice and Joshua locked eyes again, shifty and suspicious.

'Guys.' I needed to say something. Both of them turned to me. 'It's okay, you can talk about the wedding. Yes, Sam was a big part of my life; yes, part of me wants to be there but yes, you can talk about it and I won't cry.'

Though I might cry if you make me run one more metre.

'Part of you wants to be there?' Joshua asked, perplexed. I tried to keep my eyes on his face. He was even more tanned than the last time I saw him. It looked good on him.

'Jess?' *Oh crap, concentrate.*

'Yeah of course,' I said. 'You can't be someone's girlfriend for five years without becoming their friend as well.' Alice and Joshua nodded.

'That's what Sam thought as well,' Joshua said and cocked an eyebrow.

'Yes I know. I really wasn't in a good place when we met, and I've said sorry a thousa—'

'No,' Joshua interrupted, 'that's genuinely what Sam *thinks*. That's why he invited you to the wedding. We just assumed when you didn't reply that you didn't want to come.'

Hold up. Sam invited me? If I wasn't going to pass out from the run, this would do it. I needed to sit down.

'Sam and Jamie sent you an invitation,' Joshua said again, confused. I looked to Alice, who was nodding in agreement. Why hadn't she mentioned it? 'After the dust had settled, you know…' *After I woke up with my naked breasts pressed against Sam's back, yes, I think I remember, Joshua.*

'Sam explained to all of us how excited he'd been to have you back in his life. How he'd always felt terrible about how you guys left things, and how maybe in trying to make things right, he'd given you the wrong impression, kind of led you on a bit… Anyway, he said he realised when he saw you how much he'd missed you,' Joshua continued. He did say he'd missed me. 'And that he'd got his friend back, and even if you didn't feel comfortable coming to the wedding he'd still like you to think you were invited.'

I'd had no idea that Sam had felt that way. Like he'd actually led me on. Like he'd let me hang on to the chance of us getting back together. Like he'd only gone and done it again. And all this time, I was the one who was feeling sorry. Maybe it hadn't all been my fault after all; maybe I hadn't got it all wrong.

'I'm assuming from your face that you didn't get the invite?' Joshua gritted his teeth in painstaking realisation. Observant *and* good-looking. 'We sent it to CreateSpace.'

'Oh *shit.*' Alice brought her hand to her forehead. 'You told me not to tell about, *you know,*' she mouthed the words.

'Losing my job?' I looked at Joshua. He looked genuinely sorry.

'So, I didn't and I just assumed they'd sent it to my place and you'd picked it up when I was out and just decided not to say anything; you were working so hard on your painting, so I didn't want to bring it up, bring you down…' If exercise didn't colour Alice's cheeks, embarrassment certainly did. 'I guess that's why Sam and Jamie haven't tried to get in touch, they thought you needed more space…'

'So, let me get this straight,' I said. 'Sam and Jamie have forgiven me for what happened?'

Joshua and Alice nodded their heads.

'And Sam even feels a bit bad about it?'

They nodded again. It wasn't all me; I knew it.

'And they've invited me to the wedding?'

They nodded again.

'And that's everything?'

Joshua shot a glance at Alice, her eyes widening with memory or realisation. What had I missed? Apart from well, everything.

'Oh man, I just remembered I've left my straighteners on!' Alice said loudly, but rather woodenly. Model? Sure. Model/actress? Definitely not. Her hair was scrunched up in a bun. Before I could stop her, she was gone, running back in the direction we had come from. I turned to Joshua, who had taken a little step closer. He really should put his top back on. You'd never get this kind of temptation in England.

'That's not everything,' Joshua said quietly.

Shit. What else could there be?

'The invite wasn't just to the wedding.' I drew the line at going on my ex-boyfriend's honeymoon. 'It was to come to the wedding as my date.'

What?

'I know it might be a bit strange, but then this whole thing has been a bit strange, right? You, sleeping in your ex-boyfriend's spare bedroom. Jamie trying to set us up this whole time…'

Jamie had been trying to do what? Everything suddenly fell into place: Jamie's excitement at having Joshua round for lunch; the one-on-one surf lessons; the wine-tasting, orchestrated for two. Shit. Jamie had been trying to set us up. I looked at Joshua, confused, flattered and knackered all at the same time. I needed to lie down.

'Can I have a think about it?' It was a question I'd neglected to ask myself countless times in my twenty-seven years on the planet and yet, somehow, agreeing to be my ex-boyfriend's fiancée's brother's date to the said ex-boyfriend's wedding seemed to warrant some thought.

'Sure, I'll be going either way.' Brutal; he didn't even care. 'You know, brother of the bride and all.' Oh yeah, of course. This was *too* strange. 'It's good to see you,' Joshua added for good measure. I looked Joshua up and down from his dimpled, chiselled face to his equally chiselled torso. I had to admit, it was good to see him too. 'Just so you know, Alice will be waiting around the next corner, if you want to run along and kill her for arranging this.' He grinned, adjusting his headband in preparation to run on.

'Just so you know' – I looked into his blue eyes earnestly – 'if I have to "run along" anywhere, I'll bloody well kill myself.'

Chapter Forty-One

'So?' Alice emerged from her hiding place. She was around the next corner just like Joshua had said. I stared at her; her face was bright red. It had nothing to do with the exercise. She smiled back in return, eyes all aglow, her embarrassment outweighed by the relief of all secrets finally being out.

'I think you know,' I said, deadpan.

'And? What did you say?' See, she knew exactly what Joshua was going to ask. How long had she waited to ask about this, sounding me out around the apartment with tangential questions to see what I thought about the invitation, even *Joshua's* invitation?

'I can't.' I looked up at Alice, who was trying to read my expression. I couldn't, could I? She shrugged her slender arms as if to say: *why not?*

'Take Sam's fiancée's brother to his wedding?'

Alice wandered towards the edge of the cliff and looked out over Coogee Beach, to the ocean I had first learnt to surf in. I walked across to stand beside her.

'Stranger things have happened, Jess.' She shrugged again. 'I thought you wanted to see Sam get married, you know, as a friend?'

'I did but…' My tired legs finally surrendered and I sat down. Alice folded her impeccably long limbs to do the same. 'What about Jamie? She must hate me.'

'Yeah.' Alice laughed. 'She wasn't your biggest fan at first.' Couldn't blame her. And I couldn't imagine her opinion had changed much since then. Well, maybe for the worse.

Alice shifted from side to side.

'What?' I demanded, giving her a playful poke. I could forgive her for the invite thing but she owed me for abandoning me with a sticky, hot Joshua. He was tanned and topless, anything could have happened.

'Well, you can't repeat this…' Alice said.

I nodded; I wasn't sure if I couldn't take any more surprises today.

'…but she's actually really glad you stumbled into their lives. Kinda thankful for you.'

Now it was my turn to raise an eyebrow in disbelief.

'In a God loves everyone, *all creatures great and small* kind of way?' I asked, thrusting my hands together in prayer.

'No, you idiot.' Alice laughed out loud. 'Now, you can't say anything, but Jamie's faith is really important to her,' Alice went on. 'And, well, for her personally, she can't really imagine not sharing that with someone. Well, when Sam first started coming along to church Jamie thought it was just to get in her pants.'

'So did I!' I was right. I was right. I was – but Alice's look made me zip it.

'Anyway,' Alice continued, 'obviously as time passed Jamie became convinced that Sam's faith was genuine, but there's always been that little doubt that one day he'd change his mind somewhere down the line and then you turned up on her doorstep. Sam's past. Everything he was before. Everything she's not.' Jamie was beautiful, intelligent, kind. I tried not to draw any damning conclusions. 'She trusted him, obviously.' Obviously. 'But I guess, if anything was going to make him change his mind, if anything was going to make him want his life before…'

'It was me,' I whispered in realisation. 'But it didn't.' I said the words matter-of-factly. For the first time in a long time that thought didn't hurt like hell.

'No, it didn't.' Alice looked at me with kindness. 'But you see, now she knows. He's not going to go back to what he was before, what he wanted before.'

I nodded. Now I knew it too.

'And so, even though it sounds crazy, she thanks you.' Alice smiled again, slinging a slender arm around my shoulder. We turned to look out over the ocean. What was even crazier was that one day I thought I might thank her too.

Alice had gone out for her nightshift; let the normal routine commence. Cupboard, Pringles. Laptop, sofa. Sketchbook, open. I used to hate the monotony of my old everyday, all Underground travel and deadlines and umbrellas at dawn. I opened another email from Tina Conrad, my maybe-agent, and put two Pringles in my mouth at once. My Coogee routine was easier to swallow. Our meeting was set for the following Monday. She had suggested CreateSpace. I had suggested otherwise. After Tim's visit to see me at The Coffee Shop, I had received no end of niceties via text, email and WhatsApp. I never had him down as an emoji man. Regardless, I didn't want the scent of Tim – albeit fabulous – lingering around my conversations with Tina Conrad.

I flicked through my sketchbook, full of ideas and possibilities for the future. I turned to a blank page at the end and began to draw, drowning out the *will she, won't she* third-person monologue playing on in my mind. Tomorrow was Friday. Friday came before Saturday. On Saturday, Sam was getting married. Practically overnight, it seemed, two months had turned into less than two days. As I moved my pencil back and forth my mind did the same. I could go and see my best friend of five years get married and show the happy couple that I was okay, that I was moving on. Or, I could stay at home, bury myself face-deep in Pringles and show them just how not over everything I was. *Crunch.* The Pringles made a persuasive point. Then there were his parents. Not that I had anything to prove to them. Then there was Joshua. Who still seemed to like me despite every mess I'd made. Immature delinquents were clearly his thing. But no one likes to take work home with them. What the hell should I do? I continued to draw. I needed a sign.

Then my phone rang. Who would be calling at this time of night? Alice was on her shift and I'd told Tim his breakdowns were no longer mine to fix. Of course, many monkey emojis had followed that. I looked down at the screen. Zoe. I hadn't heard from her since we'd Skyped at Sam's almost a month ago. If she wanted me to fill her in, we'd need more than a twenty-minute pre-work catch up. I'd been pissed off she'd not called in the whole time it had taken me to have an A-class breakdown, but it wasn't until I saw her name dancing across my screen that I realised the full extent of my anger.

'Hello?' I swiped to answer.

'Jess! How are you?' Despite my self-willed frostiness her familiar voice cut through the ice.

'I'm, you know…' I began, before looking down at my laptop screen and correcting myself. 'I'm good.' I was. Or getting there, at least. 'How are you?'

'I'm sorry I've been so busy, and then when I'm not, the time difference is a bitch, but I just wanted to call to check you are okay before Sam's wedding. It's this Saturday, right?' Right. She remembered. She always remembered the important things. I found myself softening. 'Are you invited? I still can't get my head round the fact he invited you to stay with them in the first place.'

'So, I am invited,' I said, searching for the words to explain everything that had happened. 'And I'm not living with them any more.'

'You finally moved out! Well done, Jess, I'm proud of you.'

I squirmed. Technically, I was thrown out. And fifty dollars said she would *not* be proud of why.

'I *knew* you would.' Did she? I hadn't. 'I can't believe you actually live in Sydney,' she went on wistfully, a hint of envy in her voice that I hadn't been able to hear before. I had been so absorbed with my own problems that it had never crossed my mind that she could be envious of me, of my misadventures, of my freedom to go anywhere, do anything, with anyone. I'd forgotten that even the most loving of commitments still came at a cost.

'So, you going to go to the wedding?' It was such a long story. I looked down at my sketchbook: all swirls and shade but not a sign in sight.

'Would you?' I asked, against my better judgement. Zoe and I had been friends for years but I had rarely taken her advice. Maybe if I had, I wouldn't have put my life on hold for Sam in the first place. Zoe had been right; he hadn't been worth the wait – through no real fault of his own, but through all I'd demanded of him, of *us*.

'Go to my ex-boyfriend's wedding?' Zoe reiterated. 'Hell no!' No surprises there then. I swore I could hear her sass-snapping on the other end of the line. Then I heard her sigh and say, 'But then I was never best friends with a long-term ex-boyfriend. I didn't grow up with him, become grown-up with him, well… almost.'

'Hey!' I said, but she had a point.

'A friendship like that means something,' Zoe continued. 'It's the reason Sam's parents have probably insisted on inviting every bloody friend they've not talked to for the past three years to their son's wedding; they might not share the everyday but the important ones? You'd better hope they'll be there.'

She was right. Good friends would be there. And she always had been. Freshers' Week, exams, graduation, first jobs, first exhibitions, break-ups. Sam wasn't the only one who had helped to make each of those memories. Zoe was there too. And though she may no longer be in my everyday, she remembered the important days, the ones that counted.

'You're right,' I said.

'I am?' Zoe asked, surprised.

'Yeah, thanks, Zoe.' I meant it.

'So, what are you going to do?'

Chapter Forty-Two

3 October 2020 – Sydney, Australia

Shit. Ouch. I burnt my neck with my curling iron as a loud knock startled me mid-curl. Stumbling over my empty rucksack, I covered up the red mark at speed. The last thing I needed today was a wannabe love bite. Pulling on my best heels one by one, I ignored the light mark of a blister left over from the exhibition opening. I hoped I wasn't preparing myself for yet another fall from grace. I checked myself in the mirror for the trillionth time that morning. I looked exactly like I had thirty seconds ago. And thirty seconds before that. Well, apart from my new burnt red neck to match my burnt orange dress. At least Tim would approve of my outfit even if he didn't condone my decision, I thought to myself as I heard another loud bang on the door.

Decision; the word felt a bit strong. My RSVP has oscillated between a yes, a no, a *hell no* and an *I wouldn't miss it for the world* ever since I'd hung up from my call with Zoe less than forty-eight hours ago. Tottering out of the bedroom, I headed across the living room towards the knocking. There was no turning back now. I opened the door to reveal the very person I was expecting, but his combed-back hair and clean-shaven face still took me by surprise; a surprise that must have shown because after a lengthy pause Joshua explained, 'My wedding present to Jamie. She's been telling me to shave it off for years.' I had always loved Joshua's surf-bum beard but, paired with his black tux, his fresh face looked good enough to...

'Jess, you look amazing.' He pulled me into a hug. It was so good to be on good terms again. I had missed this. It had taken a while to see it but he wasn't I-wish-you-were-Sam any more; he was just Joshua. 'Are you sure you're okay with this?'

'I think I am.' I forced a smile.

'You know, if you need anything, anything at all, just ask, okay?' Joshua pressed on, grinning from ear to ear. I didn't need to ask to know he'd missed this too.

'I know that,' I said. 'Thank you.'

'Joshua!' Spinning around, I saw Alice emerge from her room, a vision in floor-length canary yellow. Few girls could pull that dress off. Almost every guy would want to.

Alice grabbed my shoulders with her yellow-painted fingernails and exclaimed, 'Jess, you look stunning! And Joshua! Your chin! It's... there!'

'Good to see you too,' said Joshua. 'A date with a canary, aren't I a lucky man?' Joshua turned to smile at me. I flinched, more awkward than I intended to be. I looked at him, one arm now slung around Alice. 'Well, ladies. Our chariot awaits.' He extended a hand in the direction of the door. My mind instantly filled with visions of me and Alice straddling Joshua's bike, silk and chiffon blowing in the wind. 'I've got my dad's car,' Joshua reassured us. He made for the door and Alice followed. She turned around to grab my hand

and squeezed, mouthing the words, 'You sure?' No, Alice, not in the slightest and becoming less and less so each and every time someone asked. And yet, I nodded. I breathed in, I breathed out and descended the steps of Alice's apartment, putting one foot in front of the other until we were on the streets of Coogee. I'd come a long way since I had traipsed through these streets in the rain, jobless, friendless, homeless, hopeless. Joshua opened the back door to his dad's car and smiled. I lifted my dress and stepped inside.

'To the wedding!' Alice thrust her hand forwards, demanding our dapper driver move on. To Sam and Jamie's wedding. Joshua nodded obediently, not about to argue with a six-foot supermodel. Turning the key in the ignition, he drove on, and we descended the hills I had learnt to love, the whole of Coogee sprawling out before us. Summer was getting more and more into swing, the sun sparkling across the sea as bronzed locals and tourists paddled, swam and surfed along the waves. It was the perfect day for it. Twenty minutes of driving felt like five and Joshua and Alice's chatter faded into nothingness as the breathtaking scenes absorbed us all. Eventually, Joshua began to slow as he pulled the car up to the kerb.

'Ready?' Alice turned around from the passenger seat, smiling broadly, nervous energy bouncing between us.

'As I'll ever be,' I said, putting my hand on the door handle. 'Enjoy the wedding!' I shouted to them both as I closed the door behind me. And, turning to ascend the restaurant stairs before me, I realised I actually meant it.

Chapter Forty-Three

2 October 2020 – Sydney, Australia

The Day Before

Should I stay? From the moment Zoe had asked me what I was going to do, that stupid Clash song had played round and round my head. *Should I go?* I walked down Coogee Bay Road, humming to the beat. Not that it was making my decision any easier. Sam wanted me to go to his wedding. Our journey had to count for something, right? You wanted the important people there on the important days. Zoe was right, although I'd never tell her twice.

Without thinking, I walked into Woolworths. Ice cream wasn't going to solve my problems, but it couldn't hurt, right? I meandered down the first aisle, seeking answers in the freezer. And then there was the small matter of Joshua. That man had seen me practically scrape myself off the floor and still seemed to want to spend time with me. Some of these churchgoers were too forgiving for their own good. I turned down the next aisle, resisting the wine. Whatever my tomorrow held, a hangover wasn't going to help.

I tried to imagine Jamie floating down an aisle of her own, barefoot on the sand, dressed in white, flowers in her hair. Sam at the end, broad, barefoot and grinning from ear to ear. I tried to imagine the guests watching on, wiping away a tear, but even my subconscious couldn't decide whether I should be among them or not. Come on, brain. I had to decide. But right now, another decision seemed more pressing. Cookie Dough or Phish Food?

I turned into another aisle, putting items into my basket. Looking up from my collection of chips, pasta sauce, apple juice and aubergine, I saw him. It was a figure I'd recognise anywhere, the same height as he had been the day I'd met him. My heart beat faster as I studied his form for the thousandth time. Though his face had aged like a fine wine, his body hadn't changed an inch. I watched him reach a hand out to the shelves, the last time that fourth finger would be without a band. Watching as he grabbed a tube of original Pringles, I smiled. Old habits die hard. He disappeared down the next aisle. I remained frozen to the spot. I could just let him leave, buy myself some time to properly make a decision. But how much time could I really barter for? The wedding was tomorrow. *Tomorrow*. If speaking to him wasn't going to make up my mind, then nothing would. I turned the corner. He was there, again. What were the odds? Maybe it was fate after all.

'Sam?'

He stopped still, his familiar back now inches from my face. Slowly, he turned to face me, looking down with a grin.

'Jess!' He looked genuinely pleased to see me, just like the last time we had shared a moment in a supermarket aisle, though perhaps a little less surprised to find me in his city. Basket full, he leaned in for an awkward embrace. Just two ex-lovers standing in Woolies, one about to be married, the other about to make the strangest pasta bake known to man. Sam looked down at my basket and smiled.

'Still a great cook then?' Nothing changes. Except, it totally had. I wasn't the mess I had been when Sam left me. I wasn't the mess I had been when he found me here less than two months ago.

'I'm a-mazing,' I joked, spare hand on my hip.

'I've heard.' Sam raised a single eyebrow, clearly meaning more than just my culinary skills. He must know about my paintings, about my meeting with the agent. Either that or he was a massive The Coffee Shop fan. I looked from Sam's bright green eyes to his basket: sun cream, deodorant, toothpaste.

'Honeymoon ingredients.' Sam grinned, apologetically. He had nothing to apologise for. He looked down at his shoes, suddenly sheepish. 'Jess, I'm sorry about the way I…'

'Reacted to me pressing my naked body against you?' I supplied the words he was unable to say. 'Yeah, you should feel really awful about that,' I joked. This was ridiculous. He was getting married tomorrow; he shouldn't be stuck in Woolies apologising to an ex-girlfriend. He should be moving on. I should be moving on too.

'No,' Sam said. 'I'm sorry if I, erm… led you on in any way…' Sam shiftily looked behind me to a lingering woman who didn't need to be taking so long to place some Doritos in her basket. Nothing like the word 'naked' to warrant some unwanted attention.

'Erm… are you in a rush?' Sam nodded towards the doors. 'I've got half an hour or so before Jamie's picking me up to do one final check of the venue.'

For a moment, I looked wistfully towards the freezer section lining the back of the aisle.

'Sure,' I replied, a little less than sure. 'I've got a few minutes.'

Paying up and walking out onto the high street, we strolled in silence in the only direction I knew was right: towards the sea. Single man or married, Sam was like a moth to a flame and if my time in Sydney had taught me anything, I now knew why. Looking across the golden sand coming into view, picked up and pushed around by the waves, I felt my heart starting to settle. I waited patiently for Sam to speak before remembering that I'd already waited for him for far too long.

'I'm sorry too, Sam,' I said, not taking my eyes off the blue expanse before us. *For that night, for not telling you the truth, for trying to mess things up with you and Jamie, for making you my everything.* Stopping to sit on the Coogee Bay steps, he looked at me, that familiar face I had written on every page of my future. How could he possibly live up to everything I had hoped for us? I had set us both up for a fall.

'It's okay, Jess.' Sam gave me a little smile. 'You were bladdered; I know you didn't mean to.'

'It's not just that,' I said. 'I put so much pressure on you. I was so sure you were the one, so sure *the one* even existed.' I knew I should probably be holding back the words, but after so long I had nothing to lose. 'After you left I just didn't believe it was the end. I'd believed in us so much that when I saw you here, I just thought maybe… and I got it all wrong… and I'm sorry. I'm sorry for everything.'

'You didn't get it *all* wrong,' Sam said.

I turned to look at him.

'Jess, when I saw you again,' he went on, clearly struggling to find the right words, 'I was so excited. It was you, *Jess*, after all this time.' He smiled like the man I had loved. 'Honestly, after we broke up there was so much I wanted to tell you, so much I wanted to share. But I couldn't. I knew it wasn't fair. I knew you needed to move on. But when I saw you it was like the years of bottling all that up came flooding out and I… I… It was like I'd got my best friend back.' Sam wasn't one for emotions, but I could have sworn I saw his eyes become a little bit fuller, a little bit wetter.

'So, I invited you back and I just wanted to spend time with you but then you were just the same and I…' I was just the same. And he had changed, grown so much. 'And I remembered what it was like to be with you, to be us. To feel so young.' He was right. We were both so young. 'And I freaked. I'm getting married, for goodness' sake.' He looked out across the ocean and breathed deeply. 'You screwed with my mind, Jessica.' He turned back to me and smiled, not a hint of malice in his words. 'It was like my past and my future were colliding – I even started to think maybe God was trying to tell me something.' He laughed. 'And then there was the thing with Joshua, and I found myself getting jealous—'

'Joshua?' I interjected, confused. 'There was no thing with Joshua,' I corrected. Not really, anyway. Not yet. I couldn't believe he'd been jealous too. After all the time I had been cursing flawless Jamie.

'There could be,' Sam said. 'If you wanted to… he invited you to the wedding, didn't he?' Sam raised an eyebrow, all-telling. I smiled and shrugged, taking a tiny bit of pride in watching my ex-boyfriend squirm. Joshua was lovely, sure. But he would always be Jamie's brother, and *she* would always be my ex-boyfriend's wife.

'I guess we both screwed up.' I sighed, turning to look out across the ocean. I smiled. I felt tired, but the tired you feel when you've accomplished something, like you've come to end of a really long run, or a really hard surf.

'Yeah, got a bit caught up in the past, I guess. A bit stuck.' He looked down to trace a finger through the sand.

'And now?' I asked, as his eyes returned to me. 'How do you feel now?'

'Excited. And you?'

I grinned from ear to ear. *Excited.* After all this time, Sam and I felt exactly the same, finally on the same page again. A laugh escaped as I tried to get my head around how different that page was from the one I had been trying to write. But I had never been a writer, or a journalist. I was a messy artist, living outside the lines. I was pretty sure I'd never believe what Sam believed, but I knew for a fact this moment, our being here, our chance encounter, it had all happened for a reason.

'So, are you going to come?' he asked. He just wanted his friend back. But things had changed now. He had changed. I had changed. Maybe I wasn't the only one who was struggling to let go of the past. Maybe we both needed to finally move on.

'I think you'll do fine without me.' I put an arm around him and gave him a little squeeze and he pulled me into his warm embrace.

'I think you'll do fine without me too,' Sam muttered into my hair quietly. Looking out across the ocean, I knew for sure that I would.

*

The minutes stretched on, until Sam's phone buzzed and he got to his feet.

'Jamie's just pulling up.' He cocked his head to look down at me and smiled. 'Want us to drop you off at home?' It was nice that he'd called it my home, though we both knew it wasn't.

'Nah.' I looked up at his wide green eyes. 'I think I'm just going to chill out for a bit.' I looked down at my bare feet, pressing them further into the sand. He nodded and grinned again, and without speaking, turned to walk away. For once, there was nothing left to say. I turned my head to watch him take the few short strides across the pavement towards the edge of the road. Sam's car pulled into view, Jamie behind the wheel. Sam opened the door to the passenger seat and got in. Through the gap in the open door, Jamie's eyes locked on mine, her perfect smile warm and kind. Turning the key in the ignition, she leaned forward to look over Sam's body and lifted her hand to give me a little wave – the wave of a white flag.

Chapter Forty-Four

Right foot, left foot. My heels ascended the sandstone stairs towards the restaurant and away from the wedding guests behind me. In less than two hours' time Sam would be married and I would have had my first meeting with a real-life agent. A meeting about my work. Not Lady Devon Atwood's, not CreateSpace's, but *mine*. Of course, she'd made no promises as to whether she'd represent me but the fact she'd managed to bring our meeting forward at such short notice surely had to be a good sign. If I'd have paid any attention in the response to my press release, I would have realised that she wasn't based in Sydney. Thank God she happened to be in town for the weekend before heading home to…

'Melbourne,' Tina Conrad said authoritatively, sitting before me. 'It's really where you need to be if you want to have a shot at becoming a professional artist. You're not married to Sydney, are you?'

I took a large sip of wine. I shook my head and smiled. 'I'm actually ready for a change.'

When I left Sam behind yesterday it had dawned on me that saying no to the wedding or to Joshua wasn't enough. Everything I had built for myself in this city still involved him. My housemate, my friends, Tim; you didn't have to scratch far beyond the surface to trace the links back to him. They had helped grow me and shape me like good friends do, but our moments didn't need to last forever to mean something. I had never had anything of my own when Sam and I were together; I sure as hell wasn't going to let that happen now that it was just me. And he was getting married, starting a new chapter. We both needed a fresh page.

'You'll have to work really hard,' Tina continued, pushing her hair behind her ears and pausing to order from the waiter. I followed suit, silently hoping that agents were the ones to foot the bill.

'I will,' I said, nodding furiously, knowing it was the truth. I was prepared to fight for what I believed in, regardless of where it might lead.

'In that case,' Tina said, closing my portfolio and passing it back to me with care. 'I'd love to represent you and see what we can do.' She raised her drink as a toast and I lifted mine to meet it, the chime of the glasses not waking me up from this daydream. This was real; I had an agent, and I was moving to a new city. I knew it wasn't as big a transition as moving from London to Sydney, but somehow it felt like an even fresher start.

I looked out of the windows to a stretch of beach I hadn't seen before, imagining myself walking along the streets of Melbourne. New beaches, new streets, new sights. For once it didn't feel like running away. As if reading my mind, Tina said, 'You'll love it. The art, the food, the music, the dating.' She grinned tellingly before pausing. 'You don't have a partner, do you?'

I thought of Joshua, and smiled, thankful for a well-timed reminder that I could develop some kind of feelings for someone other than Sam. Maybe one day our paths would cross again. But it wasn't a 'maybe one day' I would hold onto too tightly. It was a 'maybe one day' that I'd blow like a dandelion into the wind on a wing and a prayer, letting it go and embracing the day, *today.*

'No, it's just me.' I smiled.

Just me. I savoured the way the words tasted. I knew some days they'd be harder to swallow than others; that some days would feel like a struggle. But today, I felt like a boss, like I'd got it all made. Why would I let the weight of the past or the fragility of the future take that away?

Somewhere, right this second, Sam was putting a ring on Jamie's finger, a ring that I'd thought one day would be meant for me. Their new adventure was about to begin. And now I had my own. It wasn't what I had imagined, not what I had planned. But it was real, and it was mine. Just me: free to explore, and grow, and learn and change. Just me – and I was enough.

A Letter from Elizabeth

Dear Reader,

Thank you so much for reading *The Spare Bedroom*. Writing to you (and for you) is literally a dream come true… I hope you enjoyed reading it as much as I enjoyed writing it.

If you did enjoy it, and want to keep up to date with all my latest releases, just sign up at the following link. Your email address will never be shared and you can unsubscribe at any time.

www.bookouture.com/elizabeth-neep

Not only have I loved telling stories since I was a little girl, but the idea for Jess's journey was sparked by an actual dream I had – and then dissected with one of my best friends. In it, I moved back to Sydney, a city I had lived and studied in for a year. Imagining what it would look like to go back, we laughed about how I'd probably bump into my (now married) ex and be so overcompensatingly* friendly that I'd end up shacking up with him and his new wife. 'That would be a good idea for a book,' I said. It was a sentence I'd said a thousand times before, but this time – it kind of stuck.

Little did I know then that I was about to feel pretty stuck myself. As I began writing it, I soon slipped into what felt like the hardest year of my life to date. Outwardly, there was nothing majorly wrong. I had a job I enjoyed, friends I loved, a roof over my head (and a central London roof at that). Inwardly, I was sinking. Everywhere I looked people were moving forwards: promotions, engagements, marriages and babies surrounding me on all sides. Everyone was setting sail somewhere new and – forget missing the boat, I felt like I hadn't even been invited onboard. I tried so hard to fight it, but jealousy, discontentment and immobilising indecision took root until I became anxious about nothing and everything all at the same time.

Into that place, Jess's voice started to speak. Of opportunities missed, sacrifices made, and a whole life lived in the waiting room, just longing for that life she had planned for herself way back when to finally fall into place.

Since then, I have spent over two years working on her story with some incredible women; I have not got engaged, married, bought a house or had a baby but I am learning every day to rest in my messy middle, embracing the gift life is and realising maybe it's not all about me.

This book is for everyone who feels like they are trying (and failing!) to force their life back into the 'plan' or waiting for something to qualify them: a new job, a new partner, a milestone just out of reach. It is for those who feel like life isn't working out how they imagined but don't know how to fix it or even begin to let go of our so-called control.

I do not have the answers (nor, for that matter, does Jess) but I'm starting to have fun trying to figure them out and I really hope you have enjoyed reading Jess's journey of doing the same.

Like Jess, I hope you know you are enough – but not in an 'I am an island, I don't need anyone' kind of way. I fully believe we were all built for community, for relationships – but that perhaps along the way we have defined 'in a relationship' far too narrowly. Being single does not mean you are not 'in a relationship'. Jess ends this journey single but not alone: hers is a story of letting old friends help her, new friends lift her, community build her and the universe (or God or something or someone) make her feel that wonderful weight of the size of the world and the littleness but significance of her life within it – all at the same time.

Thank you so much for giving the book in your hands a read. It really does mean so much to me.

I hope you loved *The Spare Bedroom* and if you did I would be very grateful if you could write a review. I'd love to hear what you think, and it makes such a difference helping new readers to discover one of my books for the first time.

I'd love to connect with as many of you as I can so do find me on Instagram, Twitter or on my website.

All my love,
Elizabeth x

*not a word – had to check it though, ha…

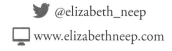

@elizabeth_neep
www.elizabethneep.com

Acknowledgements

This book was born out of crazy hour: an overtired time where my first 'work wife' and I would decompress from a day of pretending to be grown-ups. Thanks, Bex Nelson, for being that crazy one – and for countless reasons beside. It was then shaped by those who shaped my twenties, of which there are far too many to name. If I've laughed with you, cried with you or drunk great wine with you over the past decade, thank you. A special mention must be made to Grace Beecroft – I wouldn't be me without you. To Lindsey Armstrong and Hannah Chambers, for bringing all the love and laughter of Sydney back to London. To the cheerleaders who read along, chapter by chapter, as I wrote them: Audrey Schneider and the incredible Nick Stevenson-Steels. To my second (and current) 'work wife', Juliet Trickey – you inspire me every day. To Grace Carter for being my first editor – and teaching me how to use track changes. And to Steve Mitchell, my mentor, my sponsor and my friend.

You would not have this story in your hands were it not for Sallyanne Sweeney of MMB Creative. Thank you for taking a chance on three unfinished chapters of Jess's story and shaping them with your encouragement, sensitivity and smarts. You have made and continue to make this journey a joy. Thanks to my wonderful editor, Cara Chimirri, for your wise insights and unwavering enthusiasm and to the entire team at Bookouture – from the designers to the sales reps to the administrative angels behind the scenes. Publishing doesn't happen unless everyone plays their part and you all play yours beautifully – thank you.

First and (second to) last thanks are always to the Neeple People – whether by name or nurture, marriage or madness. And finally, 'to him who is able to do immeasurably more than all we ask or imagine', thank-you for smashing my dreams with the sheer size of yours.

Printed in Poland
by Amazon Fulfillment
Poland Sp. z o.o., Wrocław